Bulls Island

Also by Dorothea Benton Frank

Folly Beach
Lowcountry Summer
Return to Sullivans Island
The Christmas Pearl
The Land of Mango Sunsets
Full of Grace
Pawleys Island
Shem Creek
Isle of Palms
Plantation
Sullivans Island

DOROTHEA BENTON
FRANK

Bulls Island

𝒲𝓂
WILLIAM MORROW
An Imprint of HarperCollins*Publishers*

HarperCollins books may be purchased for educational, business, or sales promotional use. For information please write: Special Markets Department, HarperCollins Publishers, 10 East 53rd Street, New York, NY 10022.

A hardcover edition of this book was published in May 2008 by William Morrow and a mass market edition in June 2009 by Avon Books, both imprints of HarperCollins Publishers.

FIRST WILLIAM MORROW PAPERBACK EDITION PUBLISHED 2011.

Library of Congress Cataloging-in-Publication Data has been applied for.

ISBN 978-0-06-207322-8

11 12 13 14 15 ID/RRD 10 9 8 7 6 5 4 3 2 1

For Peter

Toward the Sea

The wind is an empty place. You enter
expecting something softened by the sea.
A piece of cedar shaped into a body
you once loved. Perhaps the hand that held you
from a distance or the face that simply
held you here. Still moving in and out of time
during the hour when night meets day,
you try to find your bearings.
You pick up objects. You want to remember.
Jagged edged rocks in the palm of your hand.
You hold them up in the moonlight.
They are earthbound, filling with sky.
You walk on further, pause to scoop tiny iridescent
shells, the colors of cream and roses.
Little by little the air brightens into hours,
which are either empty or full of all the things
you love and remember, depending
on which direction the wind is coming from.

—Marjory Heath Wentworth,
South Carolina Poet Laureate

Acknowledgments

Special thanks to my dear friend Marjory Heath Wentworth, South Carolina Poet Laureate, whose spectacular words enrich mine. We are all so proud of you, Marjory, and I am particularly honored to offer one vehicle to share your glorious talent, that of a *living American woman poet*, with readers everywhere. Bravo! Also huge thanks to my dear friend, Dana Beach, founder and executive director of the South Carolina Coastal Conservation League, for so many fabulous plot possibilities and details for this story. This would be just another Beaufort Boil without you! And to my childhood friend Anthony Stith, fire chief of the Sullivans Island Fire and Rescue Department, for his explosive ideas!

To my New Jersey literary friends, the geniuses: Pamela Redmond Satran, Deborah Davis, Debbie Galant, Benilde Little, Christina Baker Kline, Mary Jane Clark, and Liza Dawson. Huge thanks for your support and your friendship which I value more than you could know. And my love to all the members of MEWS, which is run by the indefatigable Pamela Redmond Satran, who keeps the five hundred plus writers who live in the Montclair area informed on all issues pertinent to the fun and games of a writing life.

To my South Carolina literary friends, who constantly inspire with their endless wit and the choir of their authentic southern voices: Josephine Humphreys, Walter Edgar, Anne Rivers Siddons, Sue Monk Kidd, Nathalie DuPree, Jack Bass, Tom Blagden, Barbara Hagerty, Robert Rosen, Mary Alice Monroe, William Baldwin, Roger Pinckney, and especially to the sainted one, Cassandra King, whom most of you know is the long-suffering wife of my favorite old grizzly bear, Pat Conroy, who gave me the courage to write and continues to explain the publishing world to me, one drop of ink at a time. To Jack Alterman, for my youthful author photo and for his photographic genius in general.

To the other real people who appear in this book—Jessamyn "Jessie" Jacobs, Ed O'Farrell, Paul McGrath, and David Pinkham—huge thanks and folks, if their characters act out of character for them, it's my fault not theirs. And as always, to the out-of-state belles, Rhonda Rich, Mary Kay Andrews, Patti Callahan Henry, and Annabelle Robertson—love y'all madly!

Again thanks to my agent, Larry Krishbaum, for his excellent guidance and grand humor, and his team of wise warriors, for their support, especially Aubrey Lynch who has the most sympathetic ears in New York.

To the William Morrow dream team, beginning with my fearless and brilliant editor, Carrie Feron, whose truly stellar thoughts and suggestions were invaluable in shaping this entire work—Carrie, darlin', if they like this book, make sure you take a large chunk of the credit! (If they don't, however, it's your fault.) Thank you for everything! And to Jane Friedman, Michael Morrison, Lisa Gallagher, Virginia Stanley, Carla Parker, Michael Morris, Michael Spradlin, Brian Grogan, Donna Waitkus, Rhonda Rose, and Lord knows, to Tessa Woodward—whew! Thank you over and over! And to the marketing and publicity wizards—Debbie Stier, Ben Bruton, Buzzy Porter, Pamela Spengler Jaffee, Lynn Grady, and Tavia Kowalchuk—huge thanks! I curtsy to Liate Stehlik and Adrienne DiPietro from Avon for hundreds of thousands of reasons, to Rick Harris in the audio division, and to the visionaries, Tom Egner and Richard Aquan, for my gorgeous covers.

To Debbie Zammit—what can I tell ya? We're still alive! Thanks for everything, especially the endless hours of scrutiny and your wonderful friendship, compassion, clarity of vision, and humor that saved many a day. To Ann Del Mastro, Mary Allen, George Zur, and Kevin Sherry—you know how much the Franks love all of you and appreciate keeping our mother ship afloat in so many ways. And to Penn Sicre, my friend of many years, for taking the leap (we hope!) from page to screen with *Plantation*.

And to the booksellers—especially Patti Morrison, Larry Morey, Emily Morrison, Rachel Carnes, and every last soul from Barnes & Noble in Mount Pleasant, South Carolina; Tom Warner and Vicki Crafton of Litchfield Books in Pawleys Island; Jennifer McCurry of Waldenbooks in Charleston; Andy and Carrie Graves of Happy Bookseller in Columbia; Frazer Dobson and Sally Brewster at Park Road Books in Charlotte; and to Omar Dowdy, just for the heck of it.

Special bowing and scraping to my wonderful cousin Charles "Comar" Blanchard Jr., whom we adore for who he is and to whom we owe enormous gratitude for everything he does. And additional bowing and scraping, plus a kiss, to my fabulous brother-in-law, Scott Bagnal, of Edisto Beach, South Carolina, for the inside skinny on how to catch mud minnows and the education on Jon boats. And to Jay Adams for setting me straight on Virginia Gentleman, the best bourbon in the world. Cheers!

Obviously, the bulk of all my thanks I should place at the feet of my wonderful, brilliant, handsome husband, Peter, and our two gorgeous, outrageously funny, and smart, nearly adult children, Victoria and William. We are so proud of you, and I thank you for understanding this crazy career of mine and always rolling with the insanity with such warmth and love. I love you all with all I've got. Seriously, I love you and thanks!

And to my readers? I thank you again and again for all your nice e-mails, for coming out to book signings, and for being so great in every way. Your generous words of support keep me going in the tough moments, and I mean that from the bottom of my heart.

All this, all of this, is no "bull!" Love you all!

CHAPTER ONE

Meet Betts

Trouble. In the charcoal shadows that delivered dawn to day in my Manhattan apartment, trouble lurked like a horrible thief. It would snatch my guilty life out of my pocket. I could sense but not pinpoint the exact location. It did not matter. Trouble would get me anyway. Trouble so practiced and seasoned that I would never know its clammy hand, each fingertip as light as feathers had been there mocking me the whole way to ruination. Except for one telling detail. Before I threw back my bedcovers, before I even glanced at my alarm clock, my left eyelid had begun to twitch in earnest. Always a redoubtable warning of approaching and certain disaster. My heart pounded. Was it a dream?

Moments later, real life began again. My cell phone rang *and* vibrated against the blond wood of my bedside table. It was my secretary, Sandi, calling to say Ben Bruton wanted to see me that morning. Wonderful. I was to begin my day with an audience with the Great and Terrible Oz. Not to mention I had a scheduled meeting later that morning with a gaggle of fast-talking suits from Tokyo.

Swell. No one at my level was called to see Bruton unless

he wanted you dead and out of his life—or your status was to improve vastly. I had no reason to fear for my position and no reason to believe I was in line for anything except to continue what I had been doing for the past four years—evaluating and restructuring the distressed properties in our portfolio. Sounds boring? Anything but. Trust me.

I was late, which was unusual. Normally, I'm up at six. My nerves got in between me and everything I had to do. As I dressed, I pushed my toe through an expensive pair of Wolford panty hose, jabbed my eyeliner into the white of my eye, spilled tea on my shirt, on and on it went until I finally got out the door.

I rushed the nine and one-half blocks from Park and Sixty-first to work dodging traffic, juggling my Tazo chai, my handbag, the *Wall Street Journal,* and my briefcase. *Click, click, click.* The heels of my Prada pumps clicked and echoed in my ears as I hurried across the rose-colored, gold-speckled granite floor of the lobby. In my peripheral vision, I spotted Dennis Baker swinging into action, moving toward me like a PI, knowing he had caught my eye.

Why was he always following me? He made my skin crawl. I slipped into an empty elevator, his arm caught the closing door, and I was trapped.

"You look great today. New dress?" he said, exuding enough testosterone to impregnate every female in the five boroughs of New York City.

Except me.

"Thank you." I avoided eye contact and his question.

He leaned against the opposite wall, put his hands in his pockets, and struggled to look adorable. "So, let me ask you something, McGee."

"What?"

"Why aren't you committed to someone who could, you know, see about all your needs? Too risky to get involved?"

"It's not about money, Dennis," I said, looking directly at him without a shred of warmth. "It's about my survival. And since when is my life your business?"

Disbelieving, Dennis Baker's obnoxious eyes surveyed me as though he could not imagine what I struggled to overcome. In his opinion I had no problems because money was the great cure-all. As if I was rolling in it. Would that it were so.

"I've been watching you. And . . . just curious, I guess." Next, with what I'm sure he deemed considerable insight, he said, "Well then, it must be about power. Why you work so hard and why you're such a loner? A relationship might distract your focus and therefore dilute your power. Am I right?"

"Nooooo," I said, assuring him that I had no interest in chatting with him for the minute it took us to rise from the thirty-eighth-floor lobby to the seventieth floor. Any and all conversation with him was exasperating. I stood rooted to my side of the elevator and stared up at the rapidly changing red digital trailer of weather and news.

I said to myself, no, it *wasn't* about power. It actually *was* all about survival. Was it easy for a woman to make it in this business? No. You had to be twice as right, twice as qualified, and twice as anything else the assignment required.

Relieved when the doors opened, I left him to slither back to his cubicle on the sixty-eighth floor.

"Have a great day," he said.

"See ya." I said. Loser.

Dennis was like a swarm of gnats at dusk, annoying and confident that he would eventually get to you. He was fortunate that I had not reported him to human resources for sexual harassment and that I spoke to him at all.

Dennis Baker was one of a dozen male and female secretaries with a degree in chiropractic medicine, culinary arts, or medieval literature who hunted the halls like a hungry animal, searching for prey, married or single, with a mid-seven-figure income that could give them a life of ease. Married with children didn't bother them one iota. And they seemed unaware of a greater truth, which was this: Why would anyone of actual significance be interested in anyone so pathetically amoral? Even the occasional drunk partner or lonely associate knew the difference between a sporting screw and a relationship that could cost them a marriage and, not to be overlooked, a painful division of assets. Dennis Baker was a stellar bartender and amateur sommelier, hence his longevity at the firm.

But back to the more important issue. I had been summoned to Ben Bruton's office, or rather I should say the real estate he occupied in the penthouse of the five floors we owned on Fifty-second and Fifth. When his gatekeeper, Darlene, spotted me, she smiled and pressed the button to his inner sanctum, whispering the news of my arrival as though we were gathered in an ICU with a priest. I sat in the waiting area and then got up to pace. What did Bruton want? I was nervous.

Bruton wasn't the chairman of our private equity firm, but he was well positioned on the launchpad. Our chairman, Doug Traum, who had been on the aura of his own retirement for at least the last decade but was still in the game "for the thrills," was currently aboard the firm's two-hundred-foot yacht, cruising the coast of Croatia, wooing some unfathomable amount of oil money into one of our funds. There, the perfectly toned arms of well-trained shipmates/nymphets were pouring vintage Cristal into Baccarat flutes as the Croatian investor, stupefied by Traum's style of extravagance, wasted on sun and salt, mesmerized by bountiful female blessings and long tanned legs, was wondering how much could be had for a price. Or was it free? Part of the deal?

I could see him in my mind. Traum was smug, rolling an unlit Cohiba from side to side in his mouth—doctor's orders, no more *fumée*—and another deal was struck. No, the chairman was not in the city. Chairman Traum was otherwise engaged, honing his finest skill by topping off our already bulging coffers. Traum, the antithesis of Bruton, was a great beast of a man with a roaring laugh, a mind-boggling compute speed, and a definite preference for the outdoors.

President Bruton was perfectly comfortable at the stateside helm in his steel-and-glass testimony of success. Bruton was another breed. Heartless and bloodless. But a genius with movie-star looks. Everyone acknowledged that he oozed nuclear power. Even the most self-assured predator in the office dared not sniff around him. He would have annihilated them. Bruton was seriously married to a former supermodel with whom he had two small children and had never once stepped out on his wife. If he had, she would have annihilated him, to give you a sense of the family portrait. Tough bunch.

"Mr. Bruton will see you now," Darlene said.

I swallowed hard and opened the door to his office as she buzzed me in. He kept it locked . . . why? For fear that the boy from La Grenouille who was delivering his poached salmon and haricots verts and a bottle of Badoit on the side might be an Uzi-toting terrorist? Please. My eye twitched again.

There he was. Bruton stood with his back to me as he looked out through the wall of floor-to-ceiling windows, high above Rock Center, like a lord surveying his lands. Although not yet forty, he was one of the most influential men in the world of finance. He knew it but he did not take his reputation for granted. Every detail of every deal was scrutinized and given the nod by him. Bruton controlled the firm's oxygen supply, and to be in his presence was exhilarating as well as terrifying.

"You wanted to see me, sir?"

He swung around to face me and actually smiled, something I had rarely seen him do. "Yes, Betts . . . do you mind if I call you 'Betts'?"

"Not at all."

I was dubbed "Betts"—short for Elizabeth—when I was six years old because I never backed away from a dare. To date, I'd always won. At that precise moment my eye twitched hard and my self-assurance wavered. Something told me, something that made me shiver with dread, that my confidence and nonchalance were packed and leaving for an extended vacation in another solar system.

"Please, sit down." He walked around his desk and indicated with his left hand for me to sit in one of the two green leather chairs in front of him. "Coffee? A cold drink?"

"No, I'm fine. Thank you."

"Okay, well then . . . I asked you here, Betts, because I have been following your progress for some time. I have to tell you, companies that my partners would have dumped, you've revived. And turned a profit."

"Thank you, sir."

"Betts? For the sake of my vanity, do not call me 'sir.' We're almost the same age."

"Okay." Pause. "Mr. Bruton."

"Ben. Please."

"Ben."

"Right, then . . . where were we? Ah, yes. That fixtures company? Brilliant. The taxi company? Great work. Dealing with the TLC isn't for pansies."

"No." Foolishly, I began to relax a little. "The Taxi and Limousine Commission isn't for the faint of heart."

He leaned back in his chair, staring with a quizzical expression, trying to comprehend how someone of my gender, age, and size could take on one of the most difficult agencies in the city of New York and emerge virtually unscathed, and yes, victorious. I got the giggles then and he nearly giggled, too. He caught himself, so I stopped and asked him a question.

"Um, Ben? Having trouble wrapping your mind around how a southern girl like me deals with those big tough guys?"

"Well, now that you bring it up, perhaps I was . . ."

"Thought so. I do my homework. And, a southern female can be disarming, and once the enemy is disarmed . . . you see where I'm going here?"

"Yes, I do. That's why I handpicked you over all the other candidates for what I'm sure is the project you'll hang your career on."

"Oh?"

"You're originally from Charleston, South Carolina, aren't you?"

"Uh, yes. Yes, I am." My eye twitched then so badly that I had to hold it still with my hand. How did he know that? I'd told everyone I was from Atlanta.

"You okay?"

"Yes. Fine." No, I was not fine. I was mortified.

"Okay. Know the area well?"

"As well as anyone who's from there, I guess. What's this about?"

"Well, it seems that the state of South Carolina or some governing body cut a deal with a huge local land developer. They're to put up the most expensive gated community ever built on a place called Bulls Island. Ever hear of it?"

I sat up straight in the chair and my mouth got dry.

"Impossible. That land belongs to the Cape Romain National Wildlife Refuge."

"Not anymore."

This could not be true. "No, seriously. It's got a Class 1 rank and is protected against . . . shoot, you can't even spend the night there, not that anyone would want to . . ."

"Interesting comment. Since we're about to invest a fortune there, triple what we've ever laid down on any other real-estate deal, one should ask, why *wouldn't* one want to spend the night there?"

"Gatorzilla, for starters."

"Gatorzilla." Bruton cleared his throat. "This does not sound like a value-added feature."

"Biggest American alligator on record. Over seventeen feet and growing."

"We should assume he has friends and family?" Bruton smirked as though he wanted to meet them face-to-face. They could floss together.

"Legions. Did I mention the bugs?" I could feel perspiration rolling from the nape of my neck, traveling down to my waist.

"I'm sure. But that can be handled."

"Right. Technology can wipe out anything."

"Well, the ink's dry on the deal and we want you to head it up. Can't send a Yankee down there, can we? We need a bona fide belle. Is that the term? You'll be working with Langley Development and . . ."

Twitch! That was *it*! I didn't hear another word he said after *Langley*. I was going to faint. No! I would not faint then. I would vomit. Later. *Langley!* It was just in the odds. No! I couldn't take on a long-term assignment in Charleston. It was impossible. Not happening. Being in Charleston meant I would have to confront my entire family and, God help me, J. D. Langley. J. D. Langley. His mother, Louisa. The whole lot of them. They despised me. J.D. most of all.

No. I could not and would not under any circumstances go back. Entangle my life with theirs again? No! Every strand of self-defense in my DNA was screaming *Don't do it!*

But this was *exactly* the kind of business opportunity I had been lusting after since I walked in the front door of ARC Partners. I knew what it meant. If the project went well, I would get a huge bonus, shares of stock, a better office, and probably some elevation in title—senior vice president. Maybe partner. It would change my world in every way.

I realized that Bruton had stopped talking and was waiting for me to come out of my fog and return to the conversation. His eyebrows were knitted in annoyance. Small wonder. He could not have known that his proposal caused a virtual landslide of chest-heaving emotion as I relived every terror I had ever known in fast frames.

"Sorry," I said.

"Have you heard anything I've said? You seem very far away."

"No, I heard you . . . Well, actually, I did miss some of what you said. It's just that I have issues with Charleston—I mean, not with *Charleston,* but I haven't been there in almost twenty years . . ."

"Does this mean that you're not interested?"

"No!" I almost leapt from my seat. "Of course I'm interested . . . it's just that I have to figure this out. I mean, I never thought I would go there again and I have to think about it a little to see how I can make this work. It's slightly complicated, that's all."

"Betts, we don't have the luxury of time here. If I need to research the ranks again for another candidate, I need to know. Now."

"Of course, and I appreciate the opportunity, Mr. Bruton. Ben. I do. I accept. I'm thrilled! Seriously!"

He leaned back in his chair and looked at me for what seemed a long time. I could see he was trying to get a read on why anyone would hesitate to grab the priceless gem he was offering me.

"Okay," he said at last. "Good."

His tone said it was less than good. There was a crack in my wall and he could see it. There was nothing Ben Bruton and all the leadership of ARC Partners hated more than weakness of any kind. Bruton now believed there was a chance he might have made a mistake in choosing me. The chance of a misstep was enough to make him skittish about me, my commitment to the firm, to my career. What had I done? I stood and extended my hand. He shook it without conviction.

"I'll work it out, Ben," I said, smiling so fake and so wide that my gums were showing, "and I seriously appreciate the opportunity."

"We'll talk tomorrow," he said, and all expression of camaraderie had drained from his face.

"First thing."

My body temperature must have been over one hundred degrees. Bruton had offered me the opportunity of my whole career and I had blinked.

I took the elevator all the way down to the street and began to walk toward Fifth Avenue. I was shaking with nausea and it was all I could do to keep from being ill. I kept walking, sweating all over, and realized after several blocks that I was heading home. I couldn't work that day. I would be useless if I returned to my office. That was it. I would go home and take the day to sort this out. I pulled out my cell and called my secretary, Sandi.

"Where *are* you?" she said. "You've got a meeting five minutes ago with the Japanese investors—they're in the conference room and . . ."

Crap. Crap. Crap. Wonderful. I had to go back. What was I thinking? Hadn't I set this meeting up? How could I forget just like that? What was the matter with me? Okay, I was slightly traumatized! But if I blew the chance to see their presentation on public transportation in Tokyo after we had flown these guys in to meet with the Metropolitan Transit Authority and two of our senior partners, I would be in serious disgrace.

"I'll be there in five. Tell them I lost a cap and ran to my dentist to cement it back in. Keep serving muffins and juice. Tell Paul McGrath to show them the slides of the Los Angeles project and to be brilliant, which he always is anyway. I'm on my way . . ."

It was going to be a rough day for "the belle."

It was. By the time I got home that night at nine-thirty, after a dinner of steak and lobster large enough to feed the New York Giants and a family of six, I was exhausted. All the conversation across the huge table in the private room at the Gramercy Tavern had been about the future of the cities of Tokyo and Nara. For those few hours I had been able to relegate the Charleston assignment to a separate compartment in my mind. But once I was back home, Charleston and J. D. Langley came whooshing through the walls and windows of every room like poison gas. How on earth would I handle this?

I glanced at my wristwatch. It was almost too late to call Sela. Sela O'Farrell, the closest friend of my entire life, would be finishing up the last dinner seating at her restaurant in Charleston, buying some tourists drinks, and thinking about things on the next day's menu she needed to discuss with her chef. Sela was a night owl, which was partly why the restaurant business was a perfect match for her in every way. Sela would know what to do.

She answered on the fourth ring.

"Hey, you! If you're calling me at this hour, it must be drama. Aren't you usually in bed by now?"

"I hate caller ID," I said. "Takes all the mystery out of life."

"Well, not *all* of it. What's going on?"

"How busy are you? Should I call you tomorrow?"

"No, heck no. I'm in my office just signing a pile of checks . . . spill it!"

A long and mournful groan escaped my throat to set the stage and then I told her the story.

"Whew!" she said when I was finished. "So, what's the plan?"

"I'm thinking that I have to do this or my career at ARC is freaking flattened, no pun intended. So, I'm coming down there, renting a condo in an obscure location, and bringing my smart assistant, Sandi, who can wear a wire and attend all the meetings with J.D. No one will know I was ever there. Ever."

"Yeah, sure. That'll fly."

"No, huh? You don't think I can do this and then slip back into the night?"

"No."

"Crap. So what should I do?"

"Listen, you're not going to like what I'm about to tell you, but it needs to be said."

"Go ahead. I've been waiting years for an honest assessment of my life."

Sela sighed long and hard. "Well, girl, here it is. It's time you came clean. That's it. You don't talk to your daddy and he's as old as Adam's housecat. That's wrong because if Vaughn dies before you two reconcile, you'll have to live with it for the rest of your life. Your sister, Joanie, has completely demonized you and you let her. You need to seriously repossess her high horse, and her little soapbox, too. And, missy? You're still dead in love with J.D. and you always have been. And here's the killer—"

"Not true! Stop! I can't listen to this now!"

"Look, Betts. I love you to death. You're like the sister I never had. But this isn't a bunch of baloney and there are other people here who deserve a fair shake."

I knew she was right. "Oh Lord."

"Are we in prayer?"

"Yes. I am deep in prayer."

"You know, Betts, it's time to pull the boogeymen out from under the bed and deal with them. Just deal with them."

"You're right." I did not believe she was right.

"I'm guessing there will be a whole lot of hell-raising to follow, but I've got ten bucks that says it will be worth it in the end."

"Ten bucks? That much? You've got more confidence than I do, Sela."

"Nah. I just like a good scrap. And since when did you ever walk away from a challenge?"

"When I couldn't predict the win."

"You can't see a victory here?"

"No. This looks like a minefield."

CHAPTER TWO

Meet J.D. and His Tribe of Malcontents

Do we have a ceiling fan in the dining room? No. Why? Because five years ago, when we built this massive house, my wife, Valerie, insisted on buying and installing the largest and most expensive chandelier in the Western world. Was the room air-conditioned? Yes, of course. The whole house was air-conditioned. But it was turned off because Mother believed air-conditioning was unhealthy.

If it wasn't a hundred degrees in the dining room, it was damn sure close to it. The wiry horsehair in the ancient cushions of the chairs coiled its way to freedom to itch and torment the backs of my legs through the thin seersucker cords of my trousers. Not that sweltering or oppressive heat was unusual for any Lowcountry July. But my short list of petty grievances seemed to have conspired to compromise my normally hearty appetite. That was a bothersome thing given the platter of roasted quail sitting right in front of me. These days, a man had so few pleasures left in life. You couldn't smoke cigars, eat rare meat, drink too much whiskey . . . it was a tremendous disappointment. The glistening sliced tomatoes from my garden had the perfume of

Eden, the parsley on the roasted and buttered fingerling potatoes . . . well, there it was. One of my favorite suppers was sitting right there and it was too damn hot to eat.

The weather had been stifling for weeks. An early riser, I woke at first light to a slice of hell combined with humidity so fierce that it steamed and actually burned the green from the grass. Our huge lawn that rolled down to the Wappoo River was pockmarked by large irregular brown patches of scorched earth. Even my old chocolate Labs, Goober and Peanut, usually howling with excitement to see me, were downright sleep-walking, having spent the recent days searching for shady spots and drinking bowl after bowl of water. It was even too hot to fish. If we'd had sidewalks, you could have sunny-sided up a slug of eggs. We did not have sidewalks, but I did have a neck, and you could've grilled a steak on it.

The mercury rose with each hour until around four in the afternoon, when the world would darken like a warning to prepare humanity to meet its Maker. With the first thunder-clap, you would hear a sigh of anticipated relief from every-one around you. It meant that while the approaching storm would split the skies wide open with screaming lightning and pounding rain, it would end as quickly as it began, leav-ing the earth slightly cooler for a while. Just for a *little* while. I mean, I'm not trying to exhaust you with a weather report, I'm just telling you that you may be able to run from the federal government, but there was no running from the Low-country heat.

It was on an evening following a trail of such days that Mother found herself trapped in our home by the threat of a sudden squall. She decided to stay for dinner and took it upon herself to turn off the air-conditioning. Just as I opened the French doors to the portico, raindrops as fat as my fist began to splatter the dusty ground with a slapping sound. A meager breeze swept the room, offering little in the way of relief. Just for the record, should my mother and Valerie decide to reincarnate themselves into my next life, I hoped they would get along better than they did in this one.

"Since you're up, will you pour more iced *watah*, J.D.?"

"Yes, Mother," I said, moving around the table with the silver pitcher to refill her glass. "It *is* hotter than usual today." The frost on the pitcher felt good on my hands and I wiped my forehead with the moisture.

"It's as hot as I can *evah* recall," Mother said, fanning herself dramatically with both hands. "The air is so close! Thank you, dear. So close! *The skies look grimly and threaten present blustahs . . .*"

"The Mariner? *The Winter's Tale?*"

"My smaaart son! Yes!"

Mother loved to quote Shakespeare.

Then Valerie piped up with one of her crazy non sequiturs. "Hmm. Do you all think the rain's gonna hurt the rhubarb?"

Faces blank, Mother and I looked at her, waiting for Valerie to answer her own question.

"Not if they put it up in Mason jars!" Valerie began to laugh hysterically.

"Ah don't believe Ah understand the punch line," Mother said, drawling her annoyance.

"You don't get it?" Valerie said, genuinely puzzled. "J.D.? You get it, don't you?"

I scrutinized Valerie's face, her eyes in particular. She was having some difficulty in focusing on mine. Something was wrong. She seemed to be growing drowsier by the second.

"Sure, Val. I get it. You feeling all right?"

"Nope."

"Poor child!" Mother said, with a tsk-tsk. For very good reason, I doubted the genuineness of her concern.

"I feel a migraine coming on. Behind my eyes. I took a Vicodin. It wasn't doing a thing so I had a li'l bitta vodka."

"Dahlin'?" Mother said. "That's not a good idea, especially when you all are trying to conceive . . ."

The gloom of failure filled the humid room and I knew at once that Valerie's and my latest attempt at in vitro fertilization had been unsuccessful. How many times had we tried? Nearly a dozen. All of them resulting in heart-break.

Valerie began to weep a little, as she always did when the announcement was made that she was not carrying the family's heir. Mother looked up to the ceiling for relief. I'll admit, even I was really weary of it all.

"Why don't you just go on to bed, Val," I said, passing her my handkerchief. "I can bring you something to eat later on."

"It's probably best," Mother said.

Valerie looked back and forth across the table at us, wiping her eyes, uncertain if she was being dismissed in anticipation of poor conduct on her part or if we thought she would actually be better off resting in bed, in a darkened room. The truth was somewhere in between, and I knew how this act would play itself out. If Valerie stayed at the dinner table, Mother would become infuriated by her slurred speech and trancelike behavior, Valerie would feel like a small trapped animal, and I would be completely frustrated by my female bookends of discontent. And once more, I would be embarrassed by my wife.

I stood and went around to the foot of the table to hold her chair so that Valerie, my blond bobble-headed, bubble-witted Barbie, could leave the room with her dignity intact. That gesture also closed the door on what I knew from experience was Mother's brewing criticism.

"It's all right, Val," I said. "It's too hot to eat anyway."

"Thank you, J.D. Mother. I'm sorry . . ."

"Don't think another thought about it," Mother said, and flicked her wrist in dismissal.

I walked Valerie to the door, listened as she climbed the stairs and finally clicked the door of our bedroom closed. My spirits sank. Our marriage was cruising in rocky water. When I turned back to the table I saw that Mother had risen from her place and assumed Valerie's chair, which struck me as slightly Freudian, but then I thought perhaps she wanted to be closer to the doors for the stingy air. The room seemed more stifling than ever.

"I feel sorry for her," I said, plopping back in my chair and picking up a quail from the platter with my fingers. I dropped it onto my plate and gave a moment's consideration to eating it with a fork and knife or dismembering it with my bare hands.

"Well, who doesn't? You know what, son? Maybe I'd prefer a tomato sandwich with a little tumbler of bourbon over ice to all this heavy meat and potatoes."

I yanked a drumstick from the little fellow and the meat fell away as I sucked it from the bone in a single noisy slurp.

"You and your father. You all eat like mountain men!"

"I'll ask Rosie to make you a sandwich." I got up without apology, picked up the platter of tomatoes, and headed for the kitchen. Rosie was our housekeeper and cook; she had been in our family's employ for nearly fifteen years. She was a single parent and lived on our property in one of the share-cropper cottages. Her fifteen-year-old son, Mickey, was one the sweetest kids I had ever known, probably because he had a healthy curiosity about everything and a great disposition. I pushed open the swinging door that separated the dining room from the kitchen.

Rosie was stooped over the sink, scrubbing the roasting pan.

"What can I get you?" she asked. When I told her she said, "Your momma's right. It's even too hot for sinning! Tell Miss Louisa I'll have that sandwich to her in a jiffy."

"Thanks, Rosie. It's easier just to give her what she wants. So, what's Mickey up to tonight?"

"Reading. What else? That child! He always has his nose in a book!"

"That's not a bad thing," I said. "Not a bad thing at all. Maybe I'll have a sandwich, too. We got any basil mayonnaise?"

"We will in two minutes," she said.

I went over to the wet bar on the pantry side of the kitchen and poured Mother a drink. I stared at her tumbler for a moment and then poured a short one for myself.

"The quail is delicious," I said to Rosie on the way back to the dining room, and she smiled at me, giving me the "okay" hand signal over the whir of the pale green mayonnaise in the blender.

I placed Mother's drink before her with a minor clunk and went back to my seat, taking another quail to munch on until the sandwiches arrived.

"Poor thing," Mother said, raising her glass to me and taking a long sip. "Is she *evah* going to give me a grandchild?"

"Doesn't look very promising, does it?"

"Maybe you should take her to someone up in New York."

"Maybe. I mean, it has to be a difficult thing to endure all the procedures she had with no positive results—you know, an assault on the value of her reproductive system or something like that."

Mother sighed hard enough to sway the Spanish moss that hung from every camellia bush and live-oak tree on our three thousand acres.

"And to think I chose her for you! I should have had her examined by a doctor!"

What a thing to say, as though we had been in the market for a broodmare. But it was true. In effect, we had been.

I drained my bourbon in a long swallow, swished the ice around, and drained it again. There and then, I decided I'd had my fill of hopelessness in my life.

"We've been discussing adoption," I said. "Now and then it comes up."

"What?" Mother gasped and put her hand to her heart, or where one's heart would be if one had one, and here came her most southern accent, the one reserved for dramatic presentations. "Ah think, no, Ah am *certain* that Ah heard you incorrectly."

It appeared that perhaps I had shortchanged myself in the cocktail department.

"May I freshen up your glass?"

"You cert'ly may!"

I nearly collided with Rosie and the sandwiches on the way back to the kitchen.

"I'll be right back," I said to her, and she nodded, understanding from my tone that a skirmish was about to ensue.

Rosie was a silent veteran but a witness nonetheless of many family differences of opinion. Sure enough, when our paths crossed again in the next minute or so, she asked to be excused for the night.

"No problem," I said. "Give my best to Mickey. Ask him if he wants to go fishing tomorrow. Early, before it's a thousand degrees."

She smiled at me and once again I realized I had crossed the line, encouraged a personal relationship with her via her son. My early-warning system told me this was dangerous. Not my type, but a nice gal. I ignored my conscience and smiled back at her.

"I will. Thanks. I'll put the rest of dinner in the fridge, and if you could just turn the dishwasher on . . ."

"I can do that! You go on and have a pleasant evening now . . ." She *was* a nice gal. Around Valerie's age.

"Good luck!" she whispered, with the crisp understanding that while my mother was taking polite bites of tomatoes on white bread with basil mayonnaise, she was also poised to sink her talons into my jugular. Rosie never missed a trick.

"All right, Mother. Here we are," I said, putting her drink before her and taking my seat yet again.

"There is something I want to say, so I am just going to say it."

Incoming. I took a huge bite of my sandwich and gave her my most innocent look.

"Go 'head," I said.

"Don't speak with a full mouth, J.D. It's very impolite."

" 'Kay."

"Now see here, J.D., I know that you have concerns about Valerie. I share them. Her inability to conceive is a cause for grave concern. And your father . . ."

"Where *is* Big Jim tonight?"

"Down in Savannah at a business meeting."

"Oh."

We both knew that meant he was visiting the strip joints he owned with an anonymous U.S. senator on the border and very likely on the receiving end of the intimate favors of a pole dancer.

"Listen, son. I understand that you want children, but you must also understand that this land has been in our family's blood since the days of King Charles II. Why, we even own Cavalier King Charles spaniels! It is *our* bloodline that has worked this land, fought to hold on to it, and *our* blood that cares so much about it. You cannot, simply *cannot,* bring in some foreign child born to some drug-addicted prostitute and call that child our blood!"

"Oh." I waited a few seconds and then said, "Why not?" I tried to maintain a placid expression to minimize the scuffle.

"Have you and Valerie both gone completely insane?"

"Mother?" I wiped my mouth, put my napkin on the table, and sat back in my chair. "Plenty of people adopt wonderful children who grow up to do great things! I must say, you surprise me. How can a woman like you continue to be so narrow-minded?"

"Narrow-minded? Me? Not in a million years and you know it!"

"Was not our Lord adopted by Joseph? And what about Moses?"

"Beside the point . . ."

"And Dave Thomas?"

"Who in the world is Dave Thomas?"

"Founder of Wendy's?"

"You mean that fast-food establishment?"

"Yes. That fast-food establishment. And President Gerald Ford? Art Linkletter? Even Eleanor Roosevelt, Mother. I mean, come on!"

"Well, I can see you did some homework, J.D. You did some homework. You're just like your father! Always have to have the last word!"

"Come on now . . . let's be civilized about this."

"I just want you to be careful, that's all."

"I am, Mother. And I always have been."

"Don't you worry about Valerie's headaches, too? Heavenly days, it just seems to me that she has a litany of maladies, J.D. Don't you think she should see—I don't know, a neurologist?"

"Who knows why she gets headaches—probably pollen. Fine. I'll take her to a neurologist."

"Please don't adopt, J.D. Please."

"Let's talk about something else." A long pause in our conversation ensued and I knew it was my job to get things rolling on a better and more courteous track. "Hey, did I tell you that we got the permits for the docks out on the Edisto project?"

"No. How?"

"The same way as always—a sack of fifties."

"Everyone has their price, don't they, son? Your daddy has taught you well." Mother smiled.

"Yes, Mother, they certainly do," I said, needing to change the subject. "How are things on the symphony board?"

"Hmm. The symphony? Well . . ."

Mother rattled on for a while about the fall season and the holiday concerts that were being planned and soon I could see she was growing fatigued. The bourbon and the heat had done their job. It was time to send her home. Frankly, I was whipped, too.

"Come on, I'll walk you to your car."

"Thank you, son."

We stepped outside. The skies had cleared and stars

twinkled everywhere. Only distant rumbles of residual thunder and the occasional flash of heat lightning disturbed the landscape. Lowcountry? Swamp? Marsh? We called our locale every manner of thing, but on nights like this when I was a kid, my dad would laugh and say it was a beautiful night in the jungle. The swell of music from the crickets and other critters was the signal that peace had been restored in the world. And yes, it was a beautiful night in the jungle.

As propriety dictated, I opened the door of Mother's station wagon and she slipped in behind the wheel.

"You sure you want to drive? I can take you home and bring the car back in the morning."

"Go on and hush," she said, kissed her fingertips, and touched my cheek with them. "I could drive home blindfolded."

"All right, then. Call me just to let me know you got there—"

"Who's the parent?" She smiled at me and then said, "I'll call your cell, let it ring once, and hang up."

"Okay. Night."

"Naiiight," she said in an exaggerated drawl, and the Mercedes-Benz engine turned over with a predictable purr. "Love you, dahlin'!"

"Love you, too, Mother." I nearly choked on the words every time I said them.

I watched her pull away and thought about how complicated and unsatisfying my life had become. Nothing had turned out the way I thought it would, except for the constant flow of money. It made me laugh. Money for the Langley clan was sort of like manna. It just seemed to fall from heaven. It was true that the richer we became, the richer we still seemed to become. But were we happy? Had any Langley ever thought about happiness? Except me, that is. We spent generations thinking about how the accumulation of wealth and power begets more wealth and power, but we surely never wasted the turn of a tide clock thinking about a trifling thing like happiness.

"The pursuit of happiness is for the poor people," my maternal grandfather, who we always thought was an atheist, used to say. "They will never be rich, J.D., so they coddle themselves with other matters, like the great mythology of Divine Justice and that they will get their rewards in another world, that their enemies will surely burn in the fires of hell. We do not have the privilege of fantasy. We have to concern ourselves with duty and leadership. Creating jobs. Keeping food on the tables of others."

There was a frowning portrait of him over the fireplace mantel in my living room that Mother had given us as a housewarming present. Nice gift. My mother's white-haired father had been a formidable man, stout, bearded, and gruff. Family legend said that he enjoyed a generous shot of whiskey with his morning coffee and not another drop all day or night. I took every word he said seriously, and to this day I have never known a man who spoke with more emphatic self-assurance. Because he dictated our family's mission and because his manner was enough to turn your *own* hair white, I largely agreed with his philosophy. Besides, to disagree was traitorous.

As a little lad, I was terrified by the whole concept of Satan, devils, and the smoldering brimstone I heard about on Sundays when my father would take me to the small Fundamentalist church we occasionally attended down the road. Like her parents, Mother had little interest in organized religion, so my dad and I went to services together. Big Jim would wet-comb my cowlick and tie my necktie, and Mother would yawn, implying that the entire exercise was a complete waste of time. I liked the choir's music well enough, but the sermons were the cause of some serious night frights. Looking back, I think old Big Jim spent more time reassuring me that the devil wasn't waiting around the corner to grab me than he did trying to explain how wonderful heaven would be if I lived a righteous life. His enthusiasm to indoctrinate me into old-time religion began to wane when I called him from his sleep night after night to look under my bed for the dark thing that wanted to gobble me up.

As a result of my childhood psychosis and my father's boyish desire to fish, our participation in Sunday services dwindled down to Easter and Christmas and a healthy donation for whatever the minister needed—a new roof, organ repair, or rewiring. No Langley seemed to possess the aspects of character required to become zealots about anything except net worth, but we padded the church's bank account just in case.

"You never know," Big Jim said every time he signed a check for them.

My parents were opposites in many ways, but I had to admit this much: Mother had made a good marriage when she married my father. That's how they referred to marriages—made well or marrying down. So Mother had married well, but unfortunately her union with Big Jim had only produced one child. Me. The burden of being that one child, that only promise for future generations, was greatly imperiled by my childless union with Valerie.

There we lived on the opposite side of the family's property from my parents, under the constant and unforgiving surveillance of my mother, Louisa, and the distanced but benign eye of my father, Big Jim. It was one helluva gilded cage.

I went back inside to turn out the lights, feeling a little down. I glanced around our Anglophile's treasure trove of a dining room that was proof of the complete absurdity of my life. All the priceless Georgian silver and bucolic eighteenth-century portraits of hunting dogs in the realm could not lessen the disappointment Mother felt toward Valerie, the hysterics that possessed my poor wife, or the aggravation I suffered with both of them. I had a domineering mother and a wife who was fast-tracking toward becoming an imbecile.

I turned on the dishwasher in the kitchen and took the remaining small bag of garbage outside to the shed. One dependable fact about Lowcountry living—you took out the garbage at night or you had a staggering population of bugs to greet you in the morning. So, after stepping out into the night once more, I stopped to feel the air and to consider my life. I threw the bag in the can, replaced the lid, closed the shed, and flipped the latch. My cell phone rang once and then stopped. Mother had reached her home safely.

In a sentimental moment, I strolled across the yard toward our dock on the Wappoo River. The lights were still on in Rosie's cottage. She was probably online, working toward her degree with whatever online university was taking her money. I had to admire her. Although she worked for Mother, Daddy, Valerie, and me, and was a single parent, she was always trying to better herself. I knew she had a little bit of a shine for me and it was flattering in some marginal way.

It was a good thing she didn't know the real me, the one who had given up on life the day my childhood sweetheart, Elizabeth McGee, walked out. Very few people did. So Mother picked Valerie for me to marry instead. I married Valerie. Big Jim wanted me to run the business, so I ran the business the way he wanted, doing whatever it took to get what we wanted. My life was prescribed like an antibiotic a doctor gives a patient, swearing it will cure what ails him. So far, it had not worked for me, and that was probably never going to change. I barely cared.

The moon shone over the Wappoo, throwing everything into a kind of half-light, and in those dream shadows sometimes I wondered whatever had become of Betts. She had never married, so far as I knew. I knew she worked for some kind of huge company in New York because I had Googled her, and that she had done very well. She lived on Park Avenue, I'd heard. She was still beautiful according to the picture on the company's website. It was best not to think about her too much and I had disciplined myself to do that, but still I couldn't help thinking I might drop by her friend Sela's restaurant and try to weasel some news about her. Sela was pretty tight-lipped about anything that had to do with Betts—which told me she knew *everything*. I needed a Betts fix.

Six o'clock the next evening and I was walking through the door of Sela's restaurant, named O'Farrell's for her husband's family from Dublin. I was to meet Valerie there after her appointment with the head of neurology at the Medical University. Valerie hadn't been happy when I told her we were going to O'Farrell's for dinner.

"It's so casual!" she complained.

"It's delicious," I said.

"It's so noisy!"

"Because it's popular," I said.

I loved O'Farrell's, with its decrepit brick walls, sawdust floors, and endless Irish memorabilia hung from every inch of wall space. Big wooden bowls of pretzels were scattered the length of the bar and the menu was written on a blackboard and rarely changed. Shepherd's Pie. Bangers and Mash. Fish and Chips. The Dublin Burger. When they were in season the menu offered fried shrimp and oysters, and when the weather was cold there were endless stews with dumplings and chicken potpie. It didn't matter to me; all the dishes were pretty mouthwatering. No frigging sprouts, no freaking tofu, no girlie smoothies. Sela was a great regulation cook, and when she'd grown tired of cooking, she trained four people to do her job, which should tell you something else about her.

Anyway, I arrived early and there was Ed O'Farrell, Sela's husband, who also happened to be the chief of police for the city of Charleston. Ed was out of uniform and working behind the bar. The regular guy must've been out or late. He saw me in the enormous mirror behind the rows of bottles of liquor and turned around to greet me.

"Well, well! J. D. Langley in the flesh! As I live and breathe! How are you, my man?"

"Good, Ed. Good. You?"

"Right as rain! What can I get you?"

"Harps? On tap?"

"God love ya, man. Harps is mother's milk!"

He filled the mug and put it before me.

"Thanks! So what's all the news in Charleston?"

"Not much new—same old drug business, crack houses, meth labs, the occasional murder . . . you know how it is."

I chuckled, thinking about this fair-haired, blue-eyed fellow, how unthreatening he seemed as a barkeep and how he had this whole other life as a Jedi keeping Charleston out of the hands of Darth Vader.

"Right. Sela around?"

He winked at me, knowing exactly what I wanted, and said, "I'll tell her you're here. She went to the beauty parlor when she saw your reservation."

"Women," I said.

"You're telling me? Watch the till for me, will ya?"

"You know it."

Ed disappeared behind the door to the office and he and Sela came out at the same time as Valerie came in the front door. Valerie despised Sela and any other detail of life remotely connected to Betts. Ridiculous.

"Hi, J.D.," Valerie said, and gave me an air kiss.

While I'm no fashion expert, I thought Valerie was very overaccessorized for the occasion, especially in the diamond department. She had obviously overdressed for Sela's sake, in the hope of sending a message to Betts about what Valerie assumed Betts likely *didn't* have. Sela scrutinized Valerie with such narrow eyes that I was surprised she didn't pull out a jeweler's loupe.

"Hi, Valerie," Sela said. "It's been a long time."

"Yes, it has," Valerie said, in a singsong voice. "Nothing's changed here! Can I get a double Grey Goose on the rocks with a twist?"

"Sure." Sela turned away to fix her drink.

Now, in Valerie's defense, I don't think she really meant to speak to Sela like she was the help or to imply that the joint was a dump. It just came out that way.

"Here you go," Sela said, and placed the drink on the bar. "Hey, J.D.? Did you hear?"

"What?"

"Hurricane's coming down the coast."

Ed and Sela looked at me to gauge my reaction.

"Really?" I said. "Well, that piddling Anastasia was a sorry excuse for a storm. Is this a big one? We're probably due for one."

"I watched the Weather Channel all day long and didn't see a *thing* about a hurricane," Valerie said, and pounded back her cocktail like it was a mere glass of water. "God in heaven, I am so parched! Can somebody please freshen up my drink?"

Sela cocked her eyebrow in disapproval and took Valerie's glass. "Yep, it's a big one," she said over her shoulder.

Coming *down* the coast. The next one would be a *B*. Could it be? "Hurricane Betts" was what Sela meant. Good. I was ready.

No. I was not ready.

CHAPTER THREE

Back to Betts

Sela might have been right about how things were with my family back in Charleston, but she certainly had a short memory. How horrible it felt to re-live a single minute of the past! Jacob Marley's chains were a lovely charm bracelet in comparison to what I remembered. And as to her insistence about my undying love for J.D.? It was not even remotely acceptable.

I was at home, back in my comfortable apartment. It was late at night. Adrian, my high school senior, was in his room fast asleep. The emotional part of me wanted to yank him from his bed and tell him the whole truth about everything. Just get it over with, I would tell myself in weak moments. The other part, the careful, pragmatic, and intelligent part of me, would never just blurt out the truth. But some nagging little voice inside of me knew that the time would come when I would have to tell him. When I did, his world would un-ravel and our relationship would be sorely tested. How would he ever trust me again? I was sure he would hate me. And life as I knew it, loved it, and for the most part controlled it, would be over. I did everything I could to avoid thinking about this.

I had a stack of magazines and newspapers at my side and my intention had been to flip through them, tear out the articles and essays I thought I should read, and discard the rest. But it was impossible to concentrate on reading material when my mind was fixated on Charleston. I was reliving the night that had ruined so many lives and changed all of us forever.

It was 1989 and J.D. and I were at his parents' home for dinner, waiting for my mother and father to arrive. This was to be the dinner to attempt to mend the divide between our families. I thought we were going to discuss the future . . . you know, that *someday* J.D. and I would get married. *Someday* we would all be in-laws, so *now* would be a good time to make that first step toward friendship. J.D. and I had planned the get-together. With some hesitation, both sides had agreed.

It would be a gross understatement to say there was no love lost between our families. The ill will our families held toward each other dated back to so many generations of turbulence that I didn't think either family knew who started the quarrels.

Pecking order. There was no denying that the Langleys had landed in a very young America and therefore considered themselves to be aristocrats of a sort. Their property was a direct land grant from King Charles II during the seventeenth century. Slothful things that *we* were, we got here late, making landfall right before the American Revolution. First, our French forebears and later our Irish. God save us from our money-handling selves; we were merchants. Maybe you would have to be a Charlestonian to understand the subtle difference, but landowners were gentry. They considered merchants—even successful ones—common ruffians.

Their attitude and all the looking down their long noses they did, sniffing at my family, was ridiculous, of course, but each family claimed to have legitimate reasons to dislike and mistrust the other. Frankly, they were legitimate. My ancestors had given money to their slaves to escape to the North and we were deeply involved in supporting the Underground Railroad. J.D.'s ancestors raised the cost of land to astronomical levels in order to discourage its sale to French/Irish businessmen, and at one point they opened competing businesses. Nonetheless, their slaves departed and my great-great-great-grandparents' chain of small groceries, bakeries, and apothecaries prevailed over theirs and became wildly successful. But the alleged royalty in J.D.'s family still despised the alleged commoner in us.

Just to make it more interesting, in the eight years J.D. and I had been together, the fact that my mother's DNA contained some thin strand of Italian nuclei provoked many absurd references to the Mafia. It was all so stupid. That's just how it was. Except that J.D. and I, young and optimistic, were deeply in love and hoped to somehow bring our families together.

That evening late in July, J.D. and I were on the terrace, waiting for my parents to arrive, when he shocked me with an engagement ring. We were just out of college and twenty-one years old. The whole expanse of the Langley terrace was blooming with a profusion of pink and white roses, in beds bordered with thick deep green Mondo grass. Roses climbed the walls along with ivy and the entire area smelled divine. It was almost seven, and there was still plenty of daylight, humidity, and mosquitoes. Needless to say, despite the hour, the heat was still unrelenting.

We were drinking a pitcher of strong lemonade, made with fresh lemons and lots of sugar, exactly the way we loved it. J.D. was wearing khaki trousers and a pale blue oxford-cloth shirt, which was pretty much what he wore all the time. I was wearing a white eyelet sundress and my shoulder-length hair was pulled back with a tortoiseshell clamp. We were sitting in the shade of the awning that covered the glider, moving back and forth to keep the air circulating around us.

"I want you to be my wife," J.D. said. He said it in such a serious voice that it startled me and actually made me laugh a little.

"I know, J.D., and I want you to be my husband." I smiled at him and squeezed his hand. "Who else would I marry? And who else would marry you?"

"But, Betts, I mean now. Soon. This year."

"What?"

That's when he stood up, reached in his pocket, and pulled out the ring. My jaw dropped and he did as well—to one knee, that is.

"Well? Will you?"

J.D. was smiling and he looked so handsome. And fervent. My heart lurched with all the love I felt for him and I choked up.

"Of course I will!" Up until that moment, no single event in my life had ever been more powerfully emotional or profound. We could hardly see through our tears of excitement, wiping our eyes with the backs of our hands, as he slipped the ring on my finger, sort of bumbling around, getting it over my knuckle. I threw my arms around him. He picked me up off the ground and swung me around.

"Oh my God! I'm going to be Mrs. James David Langley the Fifth!"

"Well, dahlin'? Ah 'magine you are." These words came from his mother's lips. I had not known she was watching us.

J.D. plopped my feet on the terrace and I looked up to the unenthusiastic face of my future mother-in-law, Louisa. She was standing in the doorway, leaning against its side, and did not move a step toward us. J.D. ran to tell her what she already knew, but her chilly pronouncement told me all I would ever *need* to know. What would it be like to be a Langley? A living hell, no doubt, when she was around, I thought, then quickly scolded myself for being so cynical, reminding myself that I was marrying J.D., not his mother. But when our eyes met, I knew differently.

She would always resent me. Her only son was marrying into the enemy camp, but I also saw that it wasn't just me she resented. In Louisa's mind, no one would ever be good enough for J.D. or worthy of becoming a Langley by marriage.

"Would you like to see the ring?" I said.

My question just burst forth, motivated by my heightened sense of insecurity. But wouldn't the ring show her that our intentions were real, that our decision was *ours* to make and not hers? She could join in and celebrate our joy from this moment on, couldn't she? Was I giving her an invitation to be a part of this occasion, or was I, in fact, drawing a line in the sand and staking my claim?

It was a line in the sand. That's just the truth.

Despite my insecurity, I held my hand out for her to see the beautiful round solitaire diamond that flashed and sparkled. It was the most gorgeous ring in the world.

"Well, it's lovely, dear. Simple. Perfect for you."

Was that a barb? "It was such a surprise!" I said. "I mean, I had no idea . . ."

"Of course you didn't, or you would have had a manicure," she said. "Come now and give me a hug. I imagine we will have to figure out how you will address me from now on, won't we?"

Why don't I just call you Huge Bitch? I thought, and hugged her from the greatest distance possible. She patted my back twice, in little pats that wouldn't plump a pillow. Then she stood back, raising her chin to me.

"What if I call you Miss Louisa?" I was not about to call her "Mother" or "Mother Langley," and she certainly was not a mom, momma, or mommy type. She gave me the shivers.

"Lovely," she said, with a sigh of resignation. "That would be lovely. Just fine. Ah 'magine we should have some champagne to celebrate? Y'all want a glass of champagne?"

"Should we wait for my parents to get here?" I said.

"They have arrived, dear. Let's go inside . . ."

I thought I heard a distant thunderclap, and sure enough, over the next few minutes a vicious summer storm descended without warning. Torrential rain began pouring from every direction, so thick and so heavy you could barely make out the silhouettes of the trees across the yard. But as frightening as all the sound effects of a huge storm could be, the smell of its approach was an aphrodisiac.

Freshly mowed grass mixed with black dirt. Air infused with the life found in the Wappoo and all around it. Marsh grass. Twenty species of fish. The mud banks. The ripe smells of decomposing branches and leaves. Birds and fish bones. Maybe this sounds unappealing or unappetizing, but once this smell finds its way to your senses, you're hooked on its crazy opiate effect. These elements were spun with roses into a wave of fragrance so strong it would make you forget every trouble in the world. And that's exactly what I allowed myself to do. Taking a deep breath, I remembered J.D.'s love for me, pushed aside his mother's poor manners, and ran to my own mother's arms. My left hand was extended and waving; splashes of light from the facets of my ring splashed the walls.

"Momma! Look! Look!"

"What? What's this? Let's see!" she said. My beautiful mother stared at my hand and then my face. "Oh, my dear child! Are you surprised, Betts? Happy?"

"Surprised like anything and happier than I've ever been in my whole life," I said.

"Then so am I! So am I!" We hugged each other with all our might and I could feel her begin to cry. "Tears of joy! What did you tell him?"

"I told him yes! I said, oh, yes!"

"Oh! My darling daughter! I am so thrilled for you!"

My mother just blubbered like a woman whose baby had slipped from her hands into dark waters, lost forever.

"Come on, Momma! It's all right!"

She quickly composed herself and smiled. "It's silly of me, I know, but I guess . . . oh, there's a part of me that will always see you as my little girl, running to me for a Band-Aid or with a report card, or missing teeth . . . you'll see someday, Betts. There are just some moments that . . . well, you *should* sort of lose it!"

"I am still that little girl, Momma, inside somewhere, but J.D.? Eight years together? It's time, don't you think?"

She nodded. "I didn't tell you, but J.D. came to us yesterday. We met for lunch and he asked both of us for our permission to marry you. Oh, he's a wonderful young man, Betts. He really is."

Just then I noticed that J.D. and his father, Big Jim, were shaking hands with my father, Vaughn.

"I'm gaining a daughter!" Big Jim said enthusiastically. "A beautiful one! A smart one!"

"And our family will finally have a son! I couldn't be more pleased," my father said.

My mother sighed, as she knew full well what chop my future waters held. Exhibit A: she nudged me and nodded toward Louisa, who was listing back and forth, doing a little wibble-wobble, as she silently poured champagne into the flutes. What in the world? Where were her congratulations? Were those few words on the terrace the best she had to offer? Wait! Had Louisa been drinking before my parents arrived? Young and inexperienced with alcohol as I was, I would not have doubted it at all. She had probably watched J.D. propose to me and gone running for the bottle. In fact, during our brief and antiseptic embrace, I noticed her breath did carry a whiff of gin, a smell I had always associated with something foul. I knew she favored martinis, and maybe because she was always so disagreeable, it was a cocktail I would not have consumed at gunpoint. Did she so despise the idea of me marrying J.D. that she had to drink in order to deal with it? Would I be driven to drink in order to deal with her? Perhaps. I knew with certainty that having her for a mother-in-law was going to be a serious challenge.

By God's grace, we got through the toasting and made it to the dinner table, where someone unleashed the hounds of hell between the cucumber soup and the pork loin with mashed potatoes. If the pork was swimming in gravy, my head was swimming with anxiety.

"Ah 'magine we'll want to have our wedding he-ah," Louisa said, with a slight slur, as though the prospect of this was a burden as well a blessing. "Ah mean, Ah have always dree-ummed of my son's wedding taking place he-ah."

"That is awfully kind of you, Louisa, but *I* have always dreamed of our daughter's wedding taking place at St. Mary's downtown." My mother's voice was polite but resolute.

"Oh, Adrianna, a *Catholic* ceremony. I should have known. Well, there's nothing to be done about being a papist, is there?" Louisa cracked a smile of obvious disappointment and sighed. There was no response from around the table to her rudeness. "De-ah me. Well then, we'll have our re*cep*-shun here, won't we, Elizabeth?"

"Actually," I said, "we have kind of a long tradition in our family of receptions at the Hibernian."

"The *Hibernian*? LAW!"

Louisa gasped as though I had suggested a keg party with plastic cups at the worst dump of a broken-down shack on Folly Beach. Men without shirts and girls in coconut bras hopping around in conga lines, eating corned-beef sandwiches and cannolis. I could see that my intemperate future mother-in-law was hallucinating scene after scene of her own social suicide.

Even at that age I knew she was completely wrong and that her behavior was preposterous, but it would have been a terrible gaff to object at the table. J.D. would have to explain the facts to his mother later. Besides, St. Mary's Church was gorgeous and it was the closest place to heaven in Charleston and maybe on earth, except for the Vatican. And the Hibernian? The Hibernian Society hall was a fabulous, glamorous place for a dinner dance.

I looked to Mother, who was just flabbergasted and filled with disgust. I could read her mind: Louisa Langley was an insufferable snob, she was thinking. Was this to be my life? I would be railroaded into accepting my mother-in-law's choices for everything? I could feel bile rising in my throat. I looked to my mother's narrowed eyes for support, but her jaw was locked as she stared at her plate, clicking her fork against the rim of it and making high-pitched *ting* sounds. She would not make eye contact with me. I knew she thought Louisa and Jim Langley had been informed beforehand that this would be an evening of great importance and that Louisa's demeanor was unbelievably cold. Big Jim was nice enough, but he couldn't make up for Louisa.

Things were not going well. At all. With every thought the McGees had, Louisa Langley had another. Louisa was not satisfied to merely host the rehearsal dinner and provide the flowers for the church, which we knew would be extravagant.

"But that's tradition," Big Jim said, trying to be the voice of reason.

"But, dahlin'! J.D. is mah only child," she said with the pout of a two-year-old child.

Louisa wanted control of everything. She always did. So she became more cantankerous and my mother struggled to remain calm. On and on the verbal sparring and innuendo went, like something molten from hell, rolling across the rug, climbing the walls, ruining the night. The storm outside still raged as if Mother Nature had been hired to provide special effects.

"Will you all be serving spaghetti and meatballs?"

"No," my mother said.

"Well, does the chef at the Hibernian know how to cook Italian food? Or is his specialty corned beef and cabbage? You know, lots of potatoes and starchy things?"

"Only on St. Patrick's Day," my mother said nicely, but I could see she was annoyed.

To the complete mortification of the rest of us, Louisa and my mother, Adrianna, were engaged in a full-blown "sandbox" contest of wills.

Finally, the dinner plates were removed and a slice of warm peach pie was placed before each of us. Three empty wine bottles stood on the buffet like generals over a bloody battlefield. It occurred to me that that was a lot for six people in addition to champagne. J.D. and I each nursed a small glass, as wine was not our drink of choice. Like most young people of college age, we drank beer.

"Dinner was delicious, Mother," J.D. said, attempting to lower the sweltering emotional temperature of the room.

It was no use. The continuing swell of my parents' discomfort had caused my mother to stop eating entirely. My father cleared his throat.

"Tell me this, Elizabeth dear. Will you have the courage to wear white?" Then Louisa Langley actually cackled.

I could feel the heat rising in my body and knew my face was bloodred. I did not answer her terribly inappropriate question.

"Adrianna?" my father said. "I think we have enjoyed the Langleys' hospitality long enough."

"Ahem." Big Jim spoke up. "You probably shouldn't drive in this weather, Vaughn. Why don't we go in my study for a cigar?" He said all this with honest concern. But when Louisa arched her eyebrows at him to encourage my parents' departure if they wished to leave, he slammed his fist on the table and added, "Dammit, Louisa, but I just don't think anyone should be out on the dark roads in this kind of rain. Just look at the trees!"

It was true. The sky, black as pitch, was rent every other minute with crackles and jagged bolts of lightning, piercing the horizon in a dozen places at once. It was all I could do to stay in my chair as the French doors around the room nearly succumbed to the storm. In those terrifying blasts of light you could see branches sweeping the ground, seeming to wail in protest against the wind and rain. No doubt children everywhere were crouched in corners, appliances were unplugged, rosaries were being said, and no one was on the telephone. Only a damn fool was driving unless it was a matter of life and death.

Big Jim was right, but my father was already on his feet, pulling my mother's chair away from the table.

"We'll be fine, thank you," my father said as drily as you

might imagine anyone who'd hung on to a remaining shred of dignity in his situation would.

"Vaughn? Maybe we *should* wait until the storm passes?" my mother said, hesitating, and then took my father's arm when she saw the "good riddance" in Louisa's expression.

"You'll bring Betts home later?" Daddy said to J.D. "When the storm passes, of course."

"Yes, sir." The severity of his disappointment in his mother was all over his face. "Don't worry. I'll be careful."

"Daddy?"

He turned to me as I walked with him and Mother to the door. His eyes seemed so tired. I didn't know what to say to him. He was insulted, as he should have been. Mother was furious and I didn't blame her. The good intentions of the dinner had been doomed from the start and then overrun by Louisa Langley. I was so embarrassed I didn't know quite what to do. I was very nervous about my parents leaving in anger, but it wasn't my place to tell my father not to go.

"Please be careful, Daddy."

"You know I will, sugar."

"Love you, Momma," I said, and hugged her with all the strength I had left in me. The torture session Louisa called a dinner party had worn me out.

Momma took my face in her hands and looked deep into my eyes. She said, "Listen to me, sweetheart. Love can work miracles. It happens every day. Wake me up when you come in so we can have a good look at this ring together, all right?" She winked at me and gave me a kiss on the cheek. "My girl!"

"All right. I will." I hoped she was right about the miracles. "Love you!"

"Love you, too, baby! Vaughn? Give me the keys. I'm driving!"

My father reached into his pocket and gave the car keys to her without argument. Well, that was a relief. At least Momma wasn't going to let Daddy drive with so much booze in him. She was sober or seemed so.

When I went back to the dining room, Louisa—that is, *Miss Louisa,* as I would become accustomed to calling her—had disappeared.

"Where did your mother go?" I asked J.D.

He just shrugged. He never said an unkind word about his mother. Never. Tonight it drove me mad.

"I sent her to bed," Big Jim called from his study. "She's as drunk as forty goats. You two come on in here for a minute."

Oh brother, I thought, here comes a lecture to explain why there's nothing wrong with Mrs. James David Langley IV and how it's going to be so great to be Mrs. James David Langley V. Well, he could try his best to excuse her behavior to us, but Mrs. Beelzebub was a formidable opponent.

We ambled into Big Jim's study, which was small but beautiful. Highly polished dark wood paneled the walls and his bookcases were filled with leather-bound books and stacks of *National Geographic* magazines intermixed with photographs of fish he had caught, vintage Chris-Crafts he had owned, and pictures in brass frames of relatives long gone to glory. He was standing at his wet bar, pouring himself a whiskey from a decanter into a tumbler with no ice. The room smelled like leather and cigars. I loved it.

"I'd offer y'all something stronger than a Coke, but I know *you* still have to drive tonight, son."

"It's okay, Dad. You're right." Then J.D. turned to me. "You want something?"

Yeah, to run away, just for a while, I thought.

"No, I'm fine. Thanks. I'll get it if I change my mind."

"Fine. Well then . . . let's sit together for a moment."

I took a place on the corner of the brown corduroy sofa next to J.D. and Big Jim sat in a club chair, upholstered in a fabric printed with men on horseback dressed for a race to the hounds that I wouldn't buy in a thousand years, but somehow it looked right in that environment. I had a lot to learn about things like decorating, I told myself.

"Son? Betts? Mother did not show well tonight."

Was Louisa Langley a show dog? No, but she was a prize bitch, I thought.

"Boy, you can say that again," J.D. said, in a rare moment of candor. "She was really difficult."

I was silent until Big Jim looked at me.

"We all have bad days," I said. I mean, what was I supposed to say?

"Well, I apologize for that," he said. "She said quite a few things that I thought were unnecessary. Entirely unnecessary."

"Well . . . ," I said, and waited for him to continue, which he promptly did.

"Louisa has certain silly ideas in her head and she always has had them. Now, me? I'm much more pragmatic about life. What's in the past is in the past, and believe me, Betts, I know Louisa's heart."

Oh? She has one? I wanted to ask, but did not.

"She'll come around," Big Jim said, continuing. "She's just used to having her own way all the time and I guess she might not have realized that her baby is a grown man who's ready to settle down."

"Probably not," I said, being generous.

Big Jim harrumphed, knowing that his attempt at an explanation had been insufficient and that all present knew Louisa was going to be a nightmare for me. Forever.

"There are other things that concern me, however. Other things."

"Like what?" J.D. asked. "Dad, Betts and I have been dating since we were practically children! You all expected this, didn't you?"

"Yes, well, *I* did anyway. Any fool can see the love between you all, and I'll tell you, it's a marvelous thing to witness. Y'all light up the room with all that passion . . . well, would you listen to me going on like passion is a thing of my past? Hell, I'm still a virile—"

"Dad!" J.D. said, looking at him and then me in mock horror.

Big Jim's virility was about the last thing on earth I wanted to hear about. He was in his cups, and anyway, the entire Western world knew he had a fondness for, well, girls with a generous nature.

"Yes, well, anyway . . . where was I? Right! What about graduate school? I mean, what if a baby comes along? They do that, you know . . . come along. Babies, that is."

"Well, we've talked about that and J.D. is going to Carolina Law School and I know I'm still going to business school there . . . I mean, there's no reason why we can't do that, right?"

"Of course not!" J.D. said. "There are no plans to start a family this year. I think we can manage, Dad."

"Both of you at Carolina?"

"Yeah, I mean, we're both accepted for the fall semester and there's no reason why we can't go, right?"

"Hmmph," Big Jim said. "How are you two going to plan a wedding and go to school at the same time?"

"Well, J.D. and I haven't talked about that yet, but I think my mother has been planning this since the day I was born," I said.

"That's fine with me," J.D. said. "That's her privilege, isn't it?"

"I wouldn't take it away from her," I replied, implying that, if necessary, I would defend my mother's territory.

"Somehow I can't envision you all living in married students' housing and eating hot dogs. Think you're gonna live on love, do you?"

"Why not?" J.D. said.

"We can work, too," I said. "In fact, I've been offered a part-time job in the business school correcting statistics papers. Working with Professor Klinger. He's a former partner at Merrill Lynch."

For minimum wage or less. I had not even asked what the salary was to be. I knew my prospects for financial independence sounded pitiful, but the most promising thing about going to graduate school was that J.D. and I wouldn't be living around Louisa for a few years. And I knew my parents would help us.

"No matter. You're industrious, Betts, and I respect that, but my son was born with the proverbial silver spoon in his mouth. So were you. Y'all haven't got the first clue about how to be poor and happy."

"Oh, that's not true, Dad! We'll get along just fine."

Big Jim sat back in his chair and smiled at us. "Listen, I want to try to make up for your mother's poor performance with a little engagement gift. Langley Construction and Development is putting up some very nice condos not too far from the campus in Columbia. I've got a nice little three-bedroom unit put aside and I'd like y'all to have it. When you graduate, you can sell it . . . or whatever you want to do. How's that?"

"Oh! How wonderful!"

J.D. got up to shake his father's hand, but his father pulled him into a big bear hug. With a free arm, he pulled me up into the embrace and said, "Just call me Jim, Betts. There will be no standing on ceremony between you and me!"

"Well, okay. That sounds just fine."

We talked longer about all our plans.

Then the telephone rang. Big Jim answered it in a jovial tone that turned somber almost immediately.

"Yes, yes." Pause. "Yes." Another pause. "Oh my God. Oh no. Where?"

I started shaking. I knew something disastrous had happened.

"Okay. Yes, of course. Of course." Big Jim gently replaced the telephone in its cradle and turned to face us. His eyes welled up with tears. "That was the head of the emergency room at the Charleston County Hospital. There's been an accident, Betts. A terrible accident. Your father has been treated and is going to be released from the hospital, but I'm sorry to tell you, sweetheart, your momma didn't make it."

"What do you mean?" What did he say? "My mother is dead?"

"Yes. I'm so sorry."

"Oh my God," J.D. said. "Oh, no! What happened?"

"A truck hydroplaned, swung around, and hit the driver's side of your parents' car. Adrianna died instantly."

"How can this be? No! Please! Tell me no! Tell me it's a mistake!"

I dropped to the sofa, put my head in my hands, covered my eyes, and wept. I wept and wept, sobbing convulsively, and I could not be consoled. Not by J.D. and not by Big Jim. Big Jim rubbed my shoulder and J.D. brought me tissues. Finally I knew I had to get out of there.

"I have to go to my father," I said.

"Yes, of course you do," Big Jim said. "Just tell me what I can do to help, honey. I'm so sorry."

"Tell Mother to go to hell," J.D. said. "This is all her fault."

We knew it was true, and J.D. finally had the courage to say it.

J.D. drove slowly. The storm had blown itself out to sea, but it was still drizzling and the streets were flooded in many places. Limbs were down. Trees were broken. I was broken.

I stared out of the passenger window, trying to get a grip on myself, but my mind couldn't hold a thought. We were silent. J.D. and I knew what this catastrophic night meant for us. We were finished.

Louisa had driven my parents out of the house with her insults and hateful words, her ugly vindictiveness. If she had been a better woman, a kinder woman—yes, any kind of a *lady*—this never would have happened. How could I marry J.D. when his mother had been the cause of my mother's death? We both knew I could not. But we couldn't talk about it then. I was in shock. We both were.

When we arrived at my parents' house on Tradd Street, we found my father in the living room, sitting in Momma's favorite chair, crying like a baby. His arm was in a sling and his head had a bandage that covered a terrible gash that had required over fifty stitches. My sister, Joanie, was at his side, sitting on the floor, weeping uncontrollably. She was only seventeen. She looked up at us.

"Get out!" she screamed when she caught sight of J.D. "And you, too! This is your fault, Betts! Yours and his rotten family! Just get out! Both of you!"

She got up and started toward us, with her hand raised as though she was going to slap J.D.

"Joanie! Please!" I cried, reaching out to stop her. "Don't make things worse than they already are!"

"She was so beautiful," my father said in a whimper. "I loved her so . . ."

I grabbed Joanie's hand in midair and she dissolved into tears again. I did, too, and put my arms around her and held her.

"I'm sorry," she said.

"It's okay," I told her quietly.

J.D. stepped away to the hall and picked up the telephone. Then he dialed some numbers. Who he was calling? His father, I assumed. When the doorbell rang minutes later, I saw that I was wrong. There, in torn-up jeans and an old T-shirt from an Allman Brothers concert, stood my best friend since kindergarten, Sela. Her face was streaked with tears.

CHAPTER FOUR

J.D. Remembers

While I drove home from dinner at Sela's in Charleston, Valerie slept in the passenger seat. In our family we euphemistically referred to these traveling naps as *sleep*, but the truth was, she was passed out cold.

Her present state was a curious thing because why would two short watery vodkas and one small glass of white wine turn a grown woman into a taxidermist's prize? But there she was. Yeah, boy. Perhaps, just maybe, the medication the neurologist gave her was not intended to be chased by a cocktail. Yes, that was a distinct possibility.

Let's see, now. Would my wife err on the side of caution? Hell, no. What kind of side effects could the medication have? Nausea? Blackouts? Could she stop breathing? Now, there's a thought. With my luck, she'd live. Who knew? Oh great, I thought. Was I supposed to sit up all night to see that she had a pulse? I sighed and shook my head, knowing I would be holding a mirror under Valerie's nose until the sun came up. Common decency demanded that much. I mean, after all, I was her husband. I told myself to look up her prescription on the Internet because as sure as anything, she would ignore any warnings about alcohol and I could wind up with a comatose wife for the next twenty years. Great. Nice thought.

But there were brighter aspects to life. Such as Sela. Now, there was a great gal if ever there was one. Yes, she was fiercely loyal to Betts, and she was also my lifeline to her. Sometimes a reluctant lifeline, I'd admit. The reason Sela told me anything, other than the fact that she pitied me, was that years ago I'd bailed her out of a financial hole and solved a small legal problem. I guess she felt she owed me. So Sela would toss me little nuggets about Betts the same way I threw scraps of pot roast to my dogs. And I gobbled them up like Goober and Peanut gobbled up peanut butter on Ritz crackers.

For years I had waited for her to say that Betts was coming home. Yes, that's right. *Home.* That was the curse of all Charlestonians. If you'd been born there, you could never call anywhere else home. So Betts McGee was coming back to Charleston, was she? In my mind, Betts had been living *only temporarily* in New York for nearly two decades. Now she was coming home. Why? I wondered. For how long and what would it mean?

I knew Sela thought Betts and I should have married despite the odds. Part of her sided with me because she understood the profundity of my feelings for Betts.

Not to cast aspersions on my dear wife, but if I had married Betts and if sexual chemistry had any relationship to fertility, shoot, we probably would have had seven kids by now. Hell, I would have had me my own football team! Well, okay, maybe we would have had four or five children, or two or three. But the point is I would have gladly given Betts as many as she wanted. What I felt for her was the kind of love that only comes along once in a man's lifetime. Every time I thought about Betts, I was faced with the knowledge of how little I had.

I looked over at Valerie's head bobbing lightly against the passenger-side window like a wonton in a bowl of soup. I sighed hard. Not to sound like a whiny old woman, but long ago I had reconciled myself to a half-baked love life, and now I was facing the likelihood that children would not be in my future.

I blushed in the dark to realize how excited I was at the thought that I might see Betts again. I was having a moment of romantic foolishness and didn't care. What if I did see her? Would the heat still be there? Or would it be incredibly awkward?

You can imagine what happened between us. After her mother's death, she broke off our engagement and ran away from home. Since I had the luxury of long consideration, I know with certainty that the breakup was inevitable. Long ago my dad and I accepted the fact that my mother's behavior had been the catalyst for the entire debacle. Everyone acknowledged it . . . except Mother, that is. And let me tell you, my mother and I fought about the death of Adrianna McGee for years until there was nothing left to be said.

I guess that in the end, I dealt with the loss of Betts the same way Betts dealt with the loss of her mother. We both withdrew, except she took the added advantage of geographical distance. But one thing was certain. I would never allow myself to love anyone again as I had loved her. My long-standing marriage to Valerie was proof of that. For years I had been just going through the motions with her and working longer and longer hours.

But that night, knowing Betts was coming back, I relived it all. I relived it all. I was barely a kid back then, but I was so in love I couldn't see straight. Then that telephone call came. The next thing I knew I was looking for a dark suit and a clean shirt.

There must have been five hundred people at that wake and so many flowers that they spilled out into the hall. Somehow Betts and I got through that night, but we got through it separately. Betts stood at her father and sister's side, rooted there like a slim sapling. She was still wearing the diamond I had given her. But she was barely speaking to me or anyone else.

That was no surprise. The shock was immense. My parents made a brief and extremely uncomfortable appearance at the wake and the room fell silent. True, they sent a basket of flowers as big as a Cadillac, but it didn't change the facts. Everyone watched to see how the McGees would greet the Langleys. The McGees were stoic and looked right through Louisa and Big Jim as though they were invisible. Once again, my family had driven a stake through Betts's family's heart and every tongue in Charleston was wagging about it. Another generation, another blow, and the divide between our two families would widen again, this time perhaps forever.

The funeral was the following day. After the emotionally charged yet solemn service at her mother's family church, we drove in a long procession out to St. Lawrence Cemetery, where Betts, her sister, Joanie, and her father, Vaughn, visibly struggled to remain composed. To begin with, they were all as pale as cadavers. But the moment that the priest began to sprinkle the casket with holy water, any self-control they had just evaporated.

I think they call that kind of crying "keening," a piercing wail at such an acute pitch that you never forget it. It's still inside me to this day. It was so awful. So awful. Finally, by God's mercy, the interment ended and we made our way back to the grand old McGee home on Tradd Street for a reception. In true southern tradition, there was enough food for everyone on the entire peninsula and the liquor was flowing like water. The guests ate and drank aplenty, but the McGees had no appetite for anything but their own grief.

They were inconsolable. Vaughn blamed himself, telling anyone who would listen that if he had been better able to drive or if they had stayed at my parents' house—as my father had asked him to do, however insincerely—the accident would never have happened. Joanie was whispering and sneaking around the rooms, blaming Betts, saying she should have known the Langleys were a curse. Betts said little or nothing, but I knew she blamed my mother, thinking she was the worst kind of person there could be—disingenuous, manipulative, and rude to the point of indecency. Finally, when everyone was almost gone, Betts spoke.

"Why would anyone even want to *know* her?" she asked.

Her voice was weak, like someone who had cried so much that she barely had the strength left to speak. She wasn't accusatory. It was how she truly felt.

"Because she gives lots of money to charity," I said. "And that's the long and short of my mother's magnetism."

It was the worst damn day of my life.

The last time I touched Betts was when she removed the ring and put it in my hand, folding my fingers over it. Then she backed away from me and cried. I told her I understood and that I would never stop loving her. She said the same. At that point I believed that our families were truly cursed.

Until Valerie came along, I kept thinking that somehow we—that is, Betts and I—might find a way to get away from all the anger and be together again. Valerie. I looked over at her unconscious body, bouncing a little with every bump in the road. Valerie was a good-looking woman, no doubt about it. But she had been offered up like a turkey on a platter and I guess I had been hungry enough to go for her.

I had to hand it to old Louisa. Looking back, my meeting Valerie was another of her subtle "orchestrations." At least Mother had the manners to wait until the Christmas holidays to debut someone she thought was a suitable date for me, someone she deemed close to being worthy of the Langley name.

Betts was long gone to New York by then, a choice I never quite understood, but then volumes could be filled with the things about the fair sex that eluded the likes of me. Anyway, my parents were throwing a huge holiday cocktail bash to celebrate the Christmas season. I was in no frame of mind for a party, having just spent my first semester of law school studying all the time and moaning over the state of my personal life.

That fall I had lived in the condo that had been meant to be *our* home. Out of deference to my extreme misery, I had refused to do more than barely furnish it. There was a mattress and box spring on the floor of the bedroom with some cheap chest of drawers and an end table that I picked up at a yard sale. I had taken a desk and a chair with a lamp from a departing student. I never bought a sofa, just a recliner chair and a television that I put on a stand. If there had not been built-in bookcases already, my books would have been stacked against a wall.

Mother was appalled by the way I was living. It was a good thing she bought out the local Belks, or I never would have had a pot or a drinking glass. I just accepted whatever she brought to the condo and said thank you in the most civil tone I could manage. Throwing worldly possessions in my direction did not compensate for the evil of what she had done. Living like a bum and having the most minimal conversation with her as possible was my revenge.

The only thing I was happy about was that I was out of my mother's house. I didn't have to look at her face every day and constantly be reminded of what she had stolen from me. But there seemed to be no escaping Louisa. I would come home from classes and find her there, unpacking and putting away whatever she thought I couldn't live without. A wine rack. A wall clock. An area rug. She would make the effort to begin a conversation, but soon every word between us was filled with recrimination. *You need to get over her! How can I? You ruined my life! I did not ruin your life! Yes, you did!* Then, when she wanted to really stick it to me, she would pick up the framed photograph of Betts I kept on my desk and sigh.

She would say something really insensitive, like, "Why don't you just throw this away, son? She's out of your life now."

And I would say, "Why don't you mind your own business, Mother?"

"Don't you speak to me that way, J.D.," she would say.

I would curl up the corner of my mouth and shrug, an indication that I didn't give a damn what she thought.

"You're acting like a zombie," she would say.

"You made me one," I'd say.

When Mother and I weren't arguing, she pretended to be perky while I smoldered. I swear, in today's market, someone would have carted me off to some classes in anger management and some serious grief counseling. But years ago things were different. Back then I called a buddy, we just went out to the woods, bagged a deer, drank a bunch of beer, and I came home to smolder some more. Pitiful.

It's funny what you remember and what you forget. In those first months, I had tried many times to reach out to Vaughn and Joanie, but they wanted no part of me—or of Betts, for that matter. They told me they didn't have her address or phone number. They hadn't heard from her. Part of me actually believed them because everyone knew Adrianna's death had caused a terrible schism in their family. Even Sela advised me to stop trying to find her, saying Betts would find me if she wanted to find me. Betts had been all but officially banished from her family and she disappeared into Manhattan, becoming one of the anonymous swarm.

So there it was—my first semester in law school and life with Betts was behind me. The holiday season was in full swing, and I was unenthusiastically at home. Naturally, pretending that there was peace on earth, Mother had decorated the house from stem to stern. There were Christmas trees in almost every room, wreaths in every window, and candles burning on every table, or so it seemed to me. My toy train from childhood was running around on its track in the den and the old Christmas village was up on display in the sunroom.

The night was dark and unusually cold. Small fires flickered and burned in three fireplaces to take the chill from the rooms. Someone was playing a selection from Handel's *Messiah* on my parents' Steinway. If old Louisa knew how to do anything, she knew how to throw a party. Amazing to me, everyone she invited always came, and they brought their holiday houseguests. There must have been two hundred people in the house, beyond the catering staff. I figured this would be the occasion when Mother would slip in a ringer and she didn't disappoint me.

As commanded, I put on a tie and a smile and came downstairs, committed to being nice for a while. My plan was to eat a little, drink a little, and then disappear back to my room. My inner smart-ass taunted me, saying that my mother had planned this party with the singular mission of pissing me off, and it was working. I was feeling sour and cranky. Just then I spotted Mother in Dad's study, talking to someone. I went in to say hello and make my token appearance. As I came around the corner, I saw that she was talking to a breathtakingly gorgeous young woman around my age with more teeth than I had ever seen in one mouth. My mood took a sudden and dramatic rise. The red dress this creature wore had some kind of a treacherously low scooped-out neckline, with her . . . you know, propped up like a couple of flawless ivory balloons. Not one freckle. I must say, they were riveting. Was she for real? At that moment I did not care.

"Oh! J.D.! There you are, darlin'! Come and meet my new friend, Valerie! Her mother, Alice, is a trustee on the Spoleto board with me. Valerie, this is my son, J.D."

"Hey, J.D.," she said with a slow and dangerous breathy drawl. "Merry Christmas."

"Well, Merry Christmas to you, too," I said, thinking even a dead guy would sit up for this ripe morsel.

She was grinning and swaying back and forth the way girls do when their whole body is sending you a message. I figured I could get her panties off in about five minutes. Four, if we left the room. Gentlemen, set your timers.

Mother stepped away on the excuse that she needed to see about her guests. Bullshit. However, at the moment, it seemed to be the only right thing Mother had done in ages. Valerie watched my mother disappear into the throng of guests and then turned back to me in a way that reinforced her intentions, which were obviously to be my date for the evening.

"Your momma said you go to law school at Carolina. What kind of law you gonna practice?" She shifted from foot to foot, which I took to mean that either her shoes were too tight or that she wanted me to get the view from as many angles as possible.

Long blond hair, big blue eyes, perfectly matched orbs, and a gyrating pelvis. It was all I could do not to lick my lips. My best friend began to pulsate and twitch.

"Probably environmental," I said, trying to focus. "It's still a pretty new field, but it's growing. You?"

"Math. I'm still an undergraduate in Athens."

"Greece?" In that moment, as I gave her my most irresistible grin, Betts's face flashed across my mind. Guilt. Then the devil reminded me I couldn't carry that torch every night into eternity. Besides, here was a flagrant opportunity.

"No, silly! Georgia! I'm a Bulldog!"

"You don't look like a bulldog to me."

"Oh? What do I look like?" She actually batted her eyes and I actually found it charming.

"Valerie? Is that it? Valerie?"

"Yeah, that's me, hon."

"Valerie? You look like the angel on top of my momma's tree." I couldn't believe I'd managed to say that with a straight face.

"Ooooh!" she squealed with delight. "And I'm a thirsty little angel, too!"

"Well then, let's get you the proper libation to fit this momentous occasion."

I took her elbow and directed her to the bar in the dining room, thinking she might be excellent fun for a holiday romp. Well, she slammed down three cups of my dad's eggnog that I knew was half rum or bourbon and then asked me to take her home to her aunt and uncle's house where she was spending the holidays. Her parents were in Switzerland.

"The house is just a few miles from here, and Lord have mercy on my soul and body, this party's so boring, isn't it? I mean, not to be rude, but we are the youngest people here by at least thirty years!"

"The year Mother hired Hawaiian musicians was much worse. I swear."

Valerie giggled. I took her hand and steered her to the garage as quickly as I could before her virtue returned.

I remember that brief interchange like it happened yesterday, but I couldn't tell you what we talked about in the car, except that she was pleasant enough and not stupid. However, I recall with crystal clarity what happened when we got to her aunt and uncle's house.

We drove down quite a long dirt road and the house seemed to appear from nowhere, rising up from the darkness. It was large and white, a classic plantation house with porticos and Corinthian columns strung across the front, much like ours. Happily, no one was home. Things heated up pretty quickly during the requisite house tour. The next thing I knew we were upstairs and on her bed in a guest room. Four minutes, forty-two seconds.

Now, one thing I had learned during my puppy years was that humping was not going to bring about the desired result. So for starters at least, there was none of that. What we did was a lot of groping, slurpy kissing, and fast and furious mutual undressing. The sight of her scantily clad body nearly burned the corneas of my eyes. She was wearing very small red panties and, by necessity, a large red lace bra. I was, um, feeling eager. And like we say in law school: there did not seem to be any objection from the second party of the second party.

What a wonderful fabulous girl she was, crawling all over me like one of Santa's elves in red lace, and all that glorious hair! Okay, I'll admit, it was base and disgusting animal lust, but so what's the matter with animal lust?

The first round of sex was hot, sweaty, and fast. There was lots of moaning and that sort of thing. Then Valerie said,

"What about me?" She wanted more? This was better than a pony under the tree, I thought, thinking Christmas had indeed arrived early. The second round ended after a lot of rolling around and repositioning and by that point my heart was pumping so hard I thought I might die. I quickly calculated that I was too young for a heart attack, so I gave her all the gusto I had on the Big Bang theory and every trick I had ever learned from watching videos in undergraduate school. She loved it. We rested then, when all of a sudden the overhead lights switched on. There stood her aunt and uncle, returned earlier than expected, obviously, from my parents' party, instantly sobered, slack-jawed, and audibly gasping. Her uncle's hand was on the switch, which he quickly turned off, cleared his throat, and said, "Pull yourselves together!" With that, he closed the door and they left. Valerie and I were in some mighty deep feces and I knew it.

Here was the situation. We were old enough for consensual sex, but in the Lowcountry's polite circles, when one had consensual sex, it generally occurred in a frat house, a dorm, or someone's apartment. Not in the bushes, on the beach, or in the backseat of a car unless absolutely necessary. If someone were to discover you in flagrante delicto, it would normally be someone of your peer group, there would be a lot of snickering, and that would be the end of it.

Not so in the adult world. You didn't *do it* with some guy you just met a couple of hours ago, and at your aunt's house in the guest-room bed. Further, it was considered rude and crass to get caught naked and sweaty.

I could feel the onslaught of a shit storm in the air. I knew Valerie's aunt was going to pitch a fit, tell Valerie's mother, her mother was going to call her a slut, and it was going to get ugly. Very ugly. If only for the sake of the mores of the day, it was best for me to declare my affection for Valerie. So I did. I had never met anyone as happy to show off her lingerie as Valerie Pritchard of Athens, Georgia. For that reason, and the fact that she was gorgeous and in possession of a reasonably good brain, my best friend and I ran a mattress marathon with Valerie until Valentine's Day, when I gave her a diamond. If I couldn't marry Betts, at least I could have a good-looking nymphomaniac of whom my family approved.

My mother was as close to being thrilled as she could be. Perhaps because my engagement to Valerie meant that the McGee-family episode was finally behind us, or because, in appearance, Valerie was close to being a carbon copy of my mother, minus thirty years. But whatever the reason, old Louisa was so delighted to have a girl to mold she gave me my great-grandmother's diamond to give to her.

When I brought Valerie home wearing the ring, my dad looked at me askance and we both acknowledged in that one silent moment that Valerie wasn't who I really wanted, that I was settling for less. Later on he took me aside for a whiskey and a father-and-son talk, during which he said, "Things don't always go according to plan. A fallback position is a good idea." There was no enthusiasm in his voice, just resignation with a trace of pity.

I said, "Look, Dad, she's a sweet girl."

"J.D., if she makes you happy, I'll learn to love her." He looked down into his glass and up to me. Valerie was Mother's choice, not mine. Dad knew it. And he knew I was going along with it because something in me was dead.

Pathetic? Well, guess what? I was pretty sick and tired of being lonely and feeling remorse over something I could not have controlled, and Valerie appeared to everyone to love me to death. After the intense love I had felt for Betts and then lost in the blink of an eye, I would never risk that much of myself again. Too painful. Valerie was safe goods. She had some mileage on her, to be sure, but I didn't care.

It began to get around that I was engaged. I knew it was only a matter of time before Betts would hear about it and I wanted her to hear it from me. I mean, it didn't seem right for her to discover that kind of news from anyone else. What was I to do? I knew her father and sister would be useless, so naturally I went to Sela.

After Thanksgiving, Sela had returned to Charleston from

Atlanta, where she had completed some kind of cooking school with the famous chef Natalie Dupree, and had just opened her own restaurant. Too early for supper, it was about half filled with tourists and locals seeking an afternoon hydration experience. I sat on a bar stool and waited for Sela to spot me, which she did almost at once.

The conversation went something like this.

"Hey! Sela! Congratulations on the restaurant! It looks great! How are you?"

"Exhausted. We were here until two in the morning last night, doing the books and all that stuff. You?"

No one had ever accused Sela of being bubbly, at least not around me. But she was civil, which was more than I could say for Betts's family.

"Good, good."

"Can I get you a drink?"

"Yeah, sure. Whatever you have on tap is fine."

She poured out the beer and placed it on the counter with a thud. I could tell that she smelled something suspicious. Of course she did. Why else was I there?

"So, what's up, J.D.?" she asked. "You getting married to that little blond, um, *blonde*?"

I knew she wanted to say *whore,* but she did not and I was grateful for it.

"Uh, yeah, we just got engaged."

"I heard that." She paused and stared in my eyes so intensely it was unnerving. "Congratulations."

Hold your enthusiasm to a minimum, I thought.

"Thanks." We looked at each other and silently acknowledged that I had made a stupid, but almost unavoidable, decision. "Listen, I was thinking. I haven't spoken to Betts since, well, you know, since she left, and I just thought she should hear about this from me."

"You're right. Here's her number." She hand me a piece of folded paper from her pocket, which told me she had just been waiting for me to show up. "I always said you were a decent guy."

"Thanks. How's she doing?"

"Managing."

No point in elaborating, I thought. Sela had never revealed anything of consequence to me.

Meanwhile, customers continued arriving and gathering around the bar area.

She had to serve them, so I said, "What do I owe you, Sela?"

"On the house, J.D. See you soon."

I put the paper into my pocket and couldn't get to a telephone fast enough. My hands were shaking as I dialed Betts's number.

"Hello?"

It was absolutely her voice. I was certain of it. God, what a thrill to hear it!

"Hello?" she said again.

"Betts?"

"Who is this?"

"It's me. J.D."

Silence.

"Betts? I have to talk to you."

"Okay."

"Betts, I got engaged . . ."

"Really?"

Her voice was flat. No emotion. Not angry. Not congratulatory. Just flat as she waited for . . . what? An explanation?

"Yeah. I just thought—"

"Well, good luck, J.D. Nice to hear from you. Thanks for the call."

Click.

She'd hung up. Here's the amazing thing. I would have bet my life that I heard a cat mewing in the background. I was positively sure that I heard the distinct sound of a cat. But Betts hated cats! Who cared? I had her phone number and that was all that mattered to me.

Months later, right before the wedding, when I got cold feet, I called her again. I was thinking—desperately hoping, actually—that Betts would tell me to come to New York, we would get married, and just screw what our families thought. But I soon learned that her number had been disconnected and there was no forwarding number. I didn't have the gumption to go to Sela again, so I took this as a sign and married Valerie, knowing that in my heart I was still in love with Betts.

But that was eons ago and here I was at forty, rolling down Highway 17, with this pulchritudinous female who, I was almost sure, drank and self-medicated, and in whom I had almost no interest.

I pulled into our garage and gave Valerie a nudge.

"Come on, Val, time to wake up."

She stirred and then yawned loudly. "Golly! I must've dozed off!"

Dozed off. Sure. Call it what you want.

A few days later, Valerie and I were walking down King Street when I spotted Betts's sister, Joanie, coming toward us, half a block away. She was literally being dragged along by four of the ugliest dogs I had ever seen in my life. Giraffe-necked, bulging-eyed, flapping-tongued, crazy-faced dogs, loved no doubt for the first time in their lives, by someone with no career and no prospects of a future except for a modern-day version of *Life with Father*. She was, that is to say, still living at home with Vaughn, ostensibly in order to see about his care, but the truth was that Joanie had grown into a dumpy, angry, middle-aged woman with a negative opinion about everything. Who wanted to take *that* to bed? Not me, that was for sure. I remembered reading in the *Post & Courier* that she was raising money for a local animal rescue operation. It appeared she was taking the business to heart.

The closer she got, the fewer seconds remained for us to cross the street to avoid her. Naturally, as the demons of fate would have it, that was not meant to be. Valerie stepped into Stella Nova for her monthly fix of exotic hair products and soaps, the cosmic buzzer on their door went off with what sounded like a guffaw, and Joanie's menagerie all but knocked me down.

"Whoa, fella!" I said, and pushed the large wolfhound–slash–Heinz 57 dog's paws down from my shoulders. "Hi, Joanie. How're you?"

"Ugh," she said, as though she had just encountered a leper with open sores. "J.D.?"

Was that a rhetorical question or some kind of a half-assed greeting?

"How are you?" I repeated.

"How am I?" She cocked her head, which was as close as she was coming to one, and yanked her dogs to make them stay. "How am I? I am wondering why you bother to speak one word to me when you know how I feel about you."

"Jeez, Joanie. How many times am I supposed to apologize for something I didn't do?" I leaned down to scratch the basset-hound-slash-who-knows-what behind the ears.

"There are some things, J.D., that can be forgiven but should not be forgotten."

"How's your dad?"

"The same. Dementia. Worse all the time. He needs me."

"Well, I'm sorry to hear it. How's Betts?"

"That would be none of your beeswax, sir." Even Joanie knew that this was too rude, so she added, "Like I would know anyway? We haven't heard from Her Majesty in ages."

"Oh," I said, realizing that Joanie justified her otherwise meaningless existence by pretending that Vaughn was an invalid, and martyr that she was, she was sacrificing all prospects of finding a husband to act as her father's caretaker. Like there was a line of men carrying little velvet boxes extending from her front door all the way down the street to the Battery? Not. And where *was* Betts? Shirking her responsibilities to her father, that's what Joanie liked to think and say. Loudly. For years, according to the local gossip, Joanie railed against Betts at every opportunity.

At that moment Valerie stepped out of the store.

"Well, hello, Joanie. Don't you look, um, nice?"

Of course Joanie was dressed like a pioneer from the Oregon Trail and Valerie was outfitted like she shopped for a career, which, in fact, she did. I don't have to tell you she and Joanie had yet to find common ground much less each other's middle path.

"You, too," Joanie said as her eyes traveled the full length of Valerie's zillion-dollar designer ensemble. As if an effort to be attractive were a mortal sin punishable by an eternity in hell, Joanie shook her head in disgust. "I gotta go."

"What was *that* all about?" Valerie said, after Joanie and her canine entourage disappeared from view.

"You just saw what transparency looks like," I said. "That woman is made out of cellophane."

"You think so?"

"Yep. And I'll bet her house smells like a kennel."

All afternoon and into the evening I smiled because of Joanie's blatant hostility. Every thought she had was out in the open and plain to see. But here's what was interesting. She clearly did not know Betts was coming back to Charleston. The War of Yankee Aggression was a wienie roast compared to the pyrotechnics that were on the horizon. I just had to figure out how and where to position myself before the opening volleys were fired.

CHAPTER FIVE

Betts and Her Bundle of Joy

Good news traveled via jungle drums with respectable speed, but bad news took an SR-71 Blackbird, which, to the best of my knowledge, was still the fastest plane on the planet. It may seem strange that a gal like me was into airplanes, but I'll admit it. I was really something of a speed junkie. Fast cars? Not so much. I had a seven-year-old Toyota Camry in the garage that for the amount I used it, it would last for forty years. But fast planes that took me from one deal to another? Time was still money in my book. But most importantly, I loved the rocket-ship liftoff feeling you got from small jets.

ARC owned a G-4, which was a lumbering old hag next to the Citation X I flew when the G-4 was in use. The X could fly to Los Angeles in less than four hours at forty thousand feet and almost seven hundred miles per hour. But the Blackbird? Never been on one, but how's Mach 3.5 at eighty thousand feet? Imagine having breakfast in New York and arriving for an early lunch in Frankfurt with time to refresh your makeup.

So when I got a piece of good news, I was like the Blackbird, screaming into the air. Naturally, soon after I went through the mail and found the good news, I called Sela.

"What are you doing? Busy?"

"Signing checks for distributors as usual. Please. Interrupt me."

I giggled. Who liked to pay bills?

"Okay. Guess what?"

"What?"

"Adrian finally got off the waiting list and into Columbia!"

"Oh my! Glory hallelujah! Congratulations! How fabulous! Did you tell Aunt Jennie?"

"Are you kidding? First call went to Adrian—no cellphone reception, of course. Then I called Aunt Jennie. She's thrilled! Called you third. She's coming for dinner tomorrow night."

"You're *cooking*?"

"You have to take a cheap shot at my culinary skills because I called you third?"

"Sorry."

"Honey, don't you know New York is the world capital of takeout? We'll be feasting on Adrian's favorite sushi—fatty tuna and smoked eel—Aunt Jennie's favorite veal Parmesan, and my favorite ribs from Blue Smoke. Anyway, Adrian is going to be seriously out of his mind with some huge unmitigated glee."

"And you are, too . . ."

"You know it," I said. "Doing a happy dance over here! Ivy League is a very big deal."

"Absolutely. It absolutely is. Well, give him a big kiss from his auntie Sela."

"I'll do it!"

"I'm gonna send him something, too. Good grief, Betts, where does the time go? Seems like yesterday that I went up to Nantucket with y'all. Adrian was just a little squirt jumping waves and making sand castles."

"Right? Now he's six feet tall with a man voice, and a dead ringer for he-who-shall-remain-nameless."

"Nameless. You know what, girl? There's something so wrong with keeping so many secrets."

"I know, I know, but my tangled web was woven so long ago . . ."

"Adrian still thinks his father died in an accident with your parents, doesn't he?"

"What am I supposed to do, Sela, say, 'Oh, Adrian, by the way . . . remember that story I told you?' Be serious. It's better this way."

"Speaking of, did you call your father yet? To tell him you're coming to Charleston?"

"Ummm . . ."

"Um, yourself. You know what, Betts McGee? One of these days, all this lying and procrastination is gonna put your fanny on a barbecue spit."

"Okay. I'll call my father. Ah, crap. Can you imagine how *that's* going to go?"

"Probably a scream fest, but I'm just guessing here."

I was quiet for a moment, knowing that if I was to install Adrian in his dorm in two weeks and leave for Charleston in three, the moment had arrived, passed, and was long overdue to tell my father and sister I was coming back for a while.

"Betts? One lie breeds another . . ."

"And another. I know. I just keep remembering how crazy Daddy was when I told him I was leaving."

"Well, you didn't have that many options."

"No, I didn't." Sela was the only one who could understand how complicated it was. "I could have had an abortion, which I never would have done . . ."

"Because you're Catholic . . ."

"No, not really. Because my child was conceived in love and that one tiny fact changed everything, as far as I was concerned. And you know what, Sela? That baby was all I had then. I had lost everything. I did the only thing that made sense to me at the time. And to *you*, I'd like to remind you . . ."

"True enough. Well, thank God I *had* an aunt Jennie to save you from life in the streets."

"Truly. Sela? In all my life, I still have never met a more generous woman than her."

"Yeah, she's great. Thanks."

"No, she's not great. Jennie Moore's a freaking living saint. I mean, there I was on her doorstep with two suitcases and less than one hundred dollars. No job, nothing . . ."

"Fifty bucks of that money was mine."

"I never sent you a check?"

We had a good laugh over that.

"Anyway, she was so good to me, never a single judgmental remark. She's been like a grandmother to Adrian all his life. I just love her so much."

"Yeah; me, too. By the way, after all these years, I think we're unofficially related now."

"We should be. I'll claim you anyway."

"Me, too. Isn't it amazing how much good people can do for each other when you give them the opportunity to help?"

"Yes. That might be the needlepoint-pillow remark of the day, Miss Sela."

"No kidding. But think about it. You were just a few years older than Adrian when you went to New York."

"I was a certified genius, right? Incredible. A terrified, certified genius."

"You were a baby."

"That's for sure. A baby having a baby. Stupid."

"Maybe, but you know what, Betts? You have a wonderful son, you've had one heck of an adventure in your career, and . . ."

"And what?"

"And now your son is *going to college* and it's time for you to get a life for yourself."

"I have a life . . ."

"No, I mean one that includes sex."

"Oh. That."

"Yeah, that."

"Right. Well, I'll put that right on my to-do list."

Sela and I gabbed some more and then finally we hung up. The only time I'd returned to Charleston in all those years was when she married Ed O'Farrell. After all, she had asked me to be her maid of honor and I would have done anything to be there. I slipped into town like a stealth ninja, attended all the wedding festivities at Wild Dunes, and then slipped out again.

I always felt a huge twinge of guilt that I had made no attempt to see my father or sister, but every time I'd tried to contact them, I got a dose of my sister's wrath. Good grief, she had a temper! Daddy had to have known how Joanie carried on, but he never said a word about it to me.

After as many altercations as I could bear, I felt deeply abused and that's one reason why I stopped calling them. I sent my father and sister cards and gifts on the expected occasions, but at some point, I'd just stopped calling. They had to suspect that Sela knew where I was, but my every birthday and holiday went unremembered, and I cannot tell you how much that hurt. Being forgotten is one thing, but to be purposely overlooked over and over is very painful.

Joanie always seemed to conveniently dismiss the fact that I had lost my mother as well as the affection of my father, my sister, and J.D. But everyone looks at the world from their own point of view. Momma used to say that Joanie had been born angry. There was hardly such a thing as a pleasant encounter with Joanie for anyone as far as I knew. Sela thought I needed a sex life? Well, perhaps I did, but Joanie's need for some kind of a cure, sexual or otherwise, surely surpassed mine.

I looked at the clock. It was about six in the evening. Where was Adrian anyway? Then I remembered. That morning he had told me he was going down to the Village with some friends and then out to a movie. I decided to call his cell again.

Please enjoy the music while your party is reached . . . I then had the distinct privilege of thirty seconds of unintelligible noise that passed for music with Adrian's generation. At last, he picked up.

"Hey, Mom. What's up?"

"*Somebody* got a letter from the admissions office at Columbia University today."

I could hear the excitement in his voice as his breathing quickly escalated.

"And?" he said.

"*You're in!*"

"You're kidding! Sweet! Hey, guys! Guess what?"

The sounds of high-fiving and "Congratulations, man!" in the background was deafening.

"Adrian? Adrian?"

"Sweet! Awesome! This is some very awesome news!"

"Excellent! You got it made, man! Got it made! Awesome!"

If young people could not use the word *awesome* (and to a lesser degree, *excellent* and *sweet*), I feared their ability to communicate might be greatly impaired.

"Adrian?" I was calling loudly, as I knew he had lost interest in my end of the conversation. In fact, moments later, he closed his phone and we were disconnected. Kids. There was no point in calling him back. I supposed then that his acceptances to Colgate, Brown, and Penn were now a thing of the past. My basic mission was accomplished. He would be close to home and to me. When I got back from the trial of my life, that is.

I left him a note on his pillow, along with the acceptance letter, that said I was meeting two guys, McGrath and Pinkham, from ARC senior management for dinner at Del Frisco's. They had said they wanted to discuss business, but I knew their wives were out in the Hamptons and they were bored.

I told Adrian in my note that I expected to be home by ten. Funny, I never worried about him navigating the city. Ever since he was old enough to push a turnstile, Adrian had been using the subway like the map of it was imprinted in his genetic code. And he was with his friends, so he was doubly safe. They were all good guys who liked baseball, comic books, and electronic games. One of the many things I admired about my son was his innate practical sense about the world around him. Adrian was cautious but unafraid of almost everything. He reminded me so much of J.D. that sometimes, when we were together, I would think J.D. was in the room with us. Well, part of him actually was, and that gave me enormous solace.

I felt a little deflated that Adrian wasn't home just then so we could have shared a moment of celebration, but there would be time for that. He was out running around in the heat and having fun, as he should have been. Manhattan in late summer can be oppressive, with hot winds gusting on the cross streets. But at Adrian's age? Who cared?

McGrath told me to pick the spot. I had chosen Del Frisco's because besides the meat locker at Lobel's, it had the best air-conditioning I knew of in the entire city. More importantly, as was almost always the case, I was with men. I was just one of the guys. Men loved big steaks, big Bordeaux, and sexy female waitstaff. I was the babysitter who could vouch for their behavior and they could deduct the dinner if we talked about business. It didn't hurt that Del Frisco's wine list was phenomenal. Perfect choice, I told myself, admitting that I didn't mind a glass or two of great wine either.

I ran a brush through my hair, threw on a little black linen sleeveless dress with black-and-white striped sandals, and left my building as quickly as I could.

"Need a cab, Ms. McGee?" Sam, the doorman, said from the curb.

The heat of the day had broken and that warm breeze was wafting on the avenue.

"No thanks, Sam," I said, smiling at him. "I think I'll walk."

He gave me a little salute and I crossed over Park toward

Madison Avenue. I felt pretty happy at that moment. The big puzzle pieces of life seemed to be falling pretty neatly into place. I was healthy and financially independent, and my son was going to his top-choice university.

But what about the elephant in my date book? My assignment in Charleston began the third week of August. When you didn't want to deal with certain things, life had a way of throwing you on the battlefield anyway. The ten-block walk to the restaurant would give me more time to think that through. Daddy might be an old bear and Joanie might be wretched, but they were still my family and I hoped the Prodigal Son story would hold true for me. I would start with my dad, not Joanie. If I went to my father in a humble and apologetic spirit, perhaps we could find a way at last to put the unhappiness behind us and be a family again. Or at least take some first steps. Yes, that was what I would do. Of course I would tell them about Adrian at some point. I just didn't know how to open that Pandora's box. I mean, too many years had passed.

I knew it was very wrong of me to have kept my son from all of them, but once the die was cast, it became more complicated with each passing year to tell them the truth. I also knew—from Sela—that J.D. and Valerie had no children. Of course J.D. deserved to know he had a son, but some part of me took secret satisfaction in denying Louisa any knowledge of her grandson. Without a doubt, hiding Adrian's existence from them was the most evil thing I had ever done, but if Louisa Langley could live with what she'd done to my mother with no remorse, and my sister could blame me for it, then I could justify what I had done. Somehow.

So many times I wished J.D. and Adrian could know each other, with Louisa and everyone else left completely out of the picture. But there was no way to finesse that. And to admit to Adrian that I had told him so many lies? I simply did not have the courage. There was going to be a huge price to pay for all my lies. I knew it.

A glass of wine seemed like a brilliant idea just then.

I pushed the revolving door of Del Frisco's and stopped at the maître d's station, population four, to see if Pinkham and McGrath had arrived. They had not, so I asked them to say that I would be at the bar.

The bar area of Del Frisco's Double Eagle Steak House was as classic a New York bar scene as the imagination can conjure. Custom-tailored suits, "geek chic" glasses, and gelled hair were four deep. Beautiful young muffinettes, tanned and enhanced in every way their budgets could afford, squirmed and wiggled their way between the suits, searching for a life partner with a big wallet or at least another round of mojitos. Life in Manhattan was all about the accessories. You might live in a rat hole of a fifth-floor walk-up, but you wore a good watch and owned at least one Hermès tie or scarf or a decent knockoff from Chinatown.

In the world of cocktails, appearances mattered far more than acoustics. The bar was long and gleaming, but the whole area was loud. It was so loud you could hardly hear yourself scream.

I cozied my way through this mass of human ambitions and carnal longings and found myself next to a pair of cuff links that were attached to a smiling handsome fellow of Mediterranean origin. I smiled back. He seemed to be alone or perhaps he was waiting for someone, as I was.

I caught the bartender's eye and said, "Sauvignon Blanc?"

"Coming right up."

"Oh, no," the cuff links said. "A classy gal like you should be drinking champagne! A champagne cocktail! You know, with a raspberry or something like that floating around in it?"

The seasoned bartender who had seen two trillion pickups in his day looked to me for a reply.

"We got strawberries," he said. "No raspberries."

I could see that he was mildly exasperated and didn't have all day, and it wasn't his responsibility to broker my relationship with the cuff links, so I said, "Sure. Why not?"

What was the harm in one drink?

"What are you having?" I said.

"Martini."

I did a double take at his double old-fashioned glass: a martini is usually served in a tulip stem.

"I hate them sissy glasses," he said with a funny little laugh, packaged and couriered to Del Frisco's all the way from the worst neighborhood in Irvington, New Jersey. "So, please allow me to introduce myself."

The bartender put the glass holding a strawberry in front of me and filled it slowly, and I raised it to the cuff links.

"Don't tell me. Rolling Stones? You're Keith Richards?" I said. He was anything but Keith Richards. I was biting the insides of my cheeks to keep from laughing. Who was this two-hundred-pound lollapalooza?

"What? No, I'm Vincent Michael Anthony Braggadocio, but my friends call me Vinny."

We shook hands and I said, "Elizabeth. It's nice to meet you."

"It's nice to meet you, too. Oh! I get it!" It had dawned on him: "Please allow me to introduce myself" was the first line of that song the Stones had recorded decades ago— hence my Keith Richards allusion—and a grin spread across his face. "You're a smart one, aren't you? I like brainy broads. You got a last name, Elizabeth?"

"Yep." I took a sip of the champagne and put it down. "McGee. Actually, my friends call me Betts."

"So? May I call you Betts?"

"If you're buying me a drink, I suppose you're a friend, of sorts. So sure, call me Betts." Cuff links is the kind of guy I played with. He was safe.

"Is there a Mr. McGee?"

"Yep. Two." His face fell. Lawsamercy, this man was really a two-year-old. "My father and my son."

He smiled at the ceiling and then back to me. "Got a sense of humor, too. I like that. Besides, there's no ring. Gals like you would wear a wedding ring if you was married."

"You're right." I giggled, thinking he must have learned

to speak English watching old Jimmy Cagney movies. He was a handsome peacock, though. Deeply tanned but not too swarthy, beautiful brown eyes, thick black lashes, dimples, and perfect teeth. Manicure and pinkie ring. Okay, the last two details weren't so great—in fact, they be the go-button for a spew of spontaneous vomit—but then my imagination took flight. I wondered if he waxed his back or anywhere else? Did he wear his pinkie ring to bed? He had big hands and I wondered if that meant anything. You know, a correlation? What did his apartment look like or did he live in New Jersey in a glass-and-chrome house? With six kids? A humorless wife? And a violin case, home to something other than a Stradivarius. "You're not married? Come on. A guy like you?"

"Nah. Got close once or twice. But I just ain't the marrying kind. I guess it's best if you know that right off the bat, so to speak," Mr. Cliché said.

"Why? Ah, come on, Vinny. Are you already planning to break my heart?" Too much.

"No, baby, I got other plans for you."

Suddenly the bar area was thinning out. People were being escorted to their tables or leaving for dinner elsewhere. Vinny slipped off his jacket, hooked it over his finger, flipped it over his shoulder, and leaned back against the bar. Next, he crossed one leg over the other in such a way that one glance toward the protrusion directly south of his belt left little to the imagination about the, um . . . correlation? Let's just say he obviously thought he had reason to brag. He threw back the rest of his drink, jiggling the ice around for long enough to afford me the opportunity to observe that his abdominal muscles were rock hard. His shirtsleeves enshrouded the muscular perfection of his biceps. And he liked to chew ice. He was quite the specimen—a combination of tanning salons, casino savoir faire, and he clearly held a Ph.D. in phys ed.

"Plans?" The inside of my cheeks had to be bloody from all the gnawing I was doing. "What kind of plans?"

"You meeting somebody?"

"Yeah. Business dinner."

"You got plans later?"

"No. I mean . . ."

Laughing, he placed his glass on the bar, extracted a fifty-dollar bill from a wad the size of a deck of cards, put his jacket back on, and handed me his card. I frowned a little.

"Hey! Whatever. You either like what you see or you don't. Call me. I'll be free later."

"Thanks for the drink," I said.

"See ya, sweetheart."

Then my new friend Vinny, with an exit waltz worthy of a swashbuckling pirate, walked away and disappeared into the night. My jaw was hanging. What the hell was that all about? He was more brash and vulgar than any of the trashy underlings at ARC, but he was so cocksure, pardon the expression, that the entire episode teetered between hilarious and gross. If one of my friends had described this Vinny fellow to me, I would have called her a liar. I couldn't wait to tell Sela.

All through dinner my mind kept wandering, returning to Vinny. I was fantasizing about a well-dressed, over-pumped, shiny-fingered, probable thug. What was the matter with me?

"Betts? You with us here?"

"Yeah, sure," I said, and took a bite of my crabmeat cocktail. "Sorry. I was thinking about the subprime mortgage mess." Good one.

"Oh, yeah. What's our exposure there . . . something like ten billion, more or less," McGrath said. "Not quite that much. I started shorting the CDX back in February to hedge our position."

"Well, the market can't hold. The Commerce Department just reported another huge downturn in housing. And what about all those adjustable mortgages in the middle-income market? As soon as the banks adjust the rates up, forget it! Two points and all hell's gonna break loose. I think we ought to start dumping that stuff," I said. "Can I have a little more wine, please?"

"Sure," David Pinkham said. "Sorry."

"No problem. Thanks. So? Do we have a clue how bad the hemorrhage could get, how much is out there in sub-prime and 'no-doc' loans and how much money is adjusting up and when? I mean, how much is out there and who is holding it?"

Pinkham and McGrath stopped talking and eating and stared at me.

"A lot," Pinkham said. He turned the color of ashes. "I've been thinking about it, too, and trying to get some better research on it. Betts is right, you guys. We're in too deep for my nerves. I think we ought to dump."

"Talk about guts for the business?" McGrath said, and thumbed in my direction. "Scary."

"Thanks," I said.

I left the restaurant a little before nine-thirty and decided to walk home. Should I call Vinny? What was I? Crazy? I'd call Sela instead. I'd call Sela and she'd tell me to call Vinny. I could hear her voice in my ear. *The man thinks he's some hot Italian lover? Maybe he is! Call him.* Oh, a little fun is harmless, I told myself on the corner of Fifth Avenue and Fifty-eighth Street. And, sure that I was indeed losing my mind, I scoffed at caution, pulled out my cell, and punched in his number.

"Yo," he said on a speakerphone. "This is Vinny."

I know, hard to believe. But that's what he said.

"Vinny? It's Betts."

"Two hours, eighteen minutes. Took ya long enough."

"Don't be such a wise guy."

"Where are you? I'll pick you up. I'm in my car."

Within minutes, after much hoisting and pulling, I was in the passenger seat of an enormous Chevy Suburban, listening to Andrea Bocelli crooning his little heart out, and opening the window slightly as Vinny's Eau de Too Much was causing my throat to close up.

"So, where are we going?" I said, hoping the answer wasn't straight to his bedroom. I needed to gear up for that occasion, should it present itself. Ever.

"Brooklyn. The River Café. I figured let's have a look at Manhattan from over the river."

"Oh!" That was a relief. "Well, great idea. I've always wanted to go there."

"You've never gone to the River Café?"

"Honey, I've never been to Brooklyn."

"What? You're kidding me, right? How long you been here? And where're you from anyway? I hear something southern over there."

"Nope. Not kidding. Almost twenty years, and Atlanta, Georgia."

"You've probably never been to Jersey either."

"Yes, I have. Look, I don't have anything against Brooklyn, but why would you go there if you didn't have a reason? And, FYI, I fly out of Teterboro all the time."

"Teterboro? Well, well! What kind of a big shot have I got here?"

I giggled. "I don't own the plane; my company does."

"Oh, I see. But you didn't answer my question. What do you do for a living?"

"Private equity, hedge funds, that kind of thing. Boring stuff. You?"

"I got my fingers in a lot of pies. Hotels mostly."

"Yeah? Where?"

"South Beach, boutique hotels. Very cool. You'd like 'em."

We were passing Lord & Taylor and my mind began to race. South Beach. Mafia. Chevy Suburban. Didn't Tony Soprano drive one of these? That's television, I told myself, not reality. Plenty of nice people drove Chevy Suburbans. Still, he had a manicure, didn't he?

"Isn't that a lot of overhead? You know, housekeeping, constant maintenance, landscaping, liabilities? I've always looked at the hotel business and thought it would be tough to earn enough for all the effort it takes."

"Special events make money. You limit the guest rooms so it's always a little bit difficult to get a reservation. You know, the cachet of staying in a place and all that. Then you gotta have a pretty big restaurant with a brand-name chef and a big bar . . . that type of thing. Trust me; the orange is worth the squeeze. Besides, labor's dirt cheap in Miami."

"Bad boy. Don't tell me you're running your business with illegal aliens." I pretended to be shaken by the news.

"No. I got Harvard graduates changing the sheets and scrubbing down the showers. Whaddaya think?"

"Right." Vinny Whatever-his-last-name-was was so stereotypically mafioso I was waiting for Al Pacino to pop up from the backseat with a piano wire. "So why are you here? I mean, do you live in Miami, too?"

"Palm Beach. I got a gorgeous place there. If you're a good girl, maybe I'll take you down there sometime. I keep a place here 'cause I like New York and the family's here."

The family. Interesting.

"You mean like your siblings?"

He looked over at me, knowing exactly what I was thinking. "Yeah; them, too."

"And what does your family do?"

"They got a little business in South Jersey."

"Oh. Well, that's good." Atlantic City. I knew it. "And so you stay in Miami because you just want your space?" Space to launder money, I thought.

"Yeah, I went to Miami U, and after graduation I never really left. I love all that sunshine. Hate the frigging snow."

It was a crazy conversation filled with dangerous innuendo and I had been put on notice that I could play with Vinny but there were risks. Real risks. I had never met anyone like him in all my years of casual dating in New York.

We passed over the Brooklyn Bridge, and in less time

than it took me to reapply lip gloss, a parking attendant was trying to help me gracefully down from my seat in such a way as to prevent my dress from sliding up to my waist. I made a mental note to take my car the next time—if there was a next time.

The hour was late and the dining room was only sparsely filled. Vinny knew the manager, who rushed over when he saw us.

"Frankie, sweetheart! How are you?"

Vinny and Frankie actually kissed each other on the cheek. My imagination expected men in sunglasses and black clothes to appear and stand by with one hand in their armpit in case they had to defend Vinny's life. What a thought!

"Why don't you two sit by the window—sit anywhere you want—and I'll send you over something special."

"Great idea," Vinny said, and took my elbow to lead me to the table. "Thanks, Frankie."

It was a perfect summer night and the light show of Manhattan's twinkling skyscrapers opposite us was spectacular. The occasional boat floated by and I had to admit it was a terribly romantic spot.

"Beautiful here, isn't it?" he said.

"Yes, it is."

A waiter appeared with an ice bucket on a tray and two wineglasses. In the bucket was a bottle of Sauvignon Blanc. Apparently, Vinny wanted to please me by ordering a wine that I liked. I took that as a good sign.

"Know what, Betts?"

"What's that?"

"You shouldn't be getting in cars with strangers. I mean, you don't even know who I am."

"I've got a pretty good idea who you are."

"Yeah? Well, I know more about you than you think."

The waiter poured out two glasses of wine; we touched the rims and took a sip.

"Like what?"

"Like you live at 540 Park in a classic six, that you have a teenage son, that there's never been a husband, and that you drive a beat-up old car. You work for ARC, you are well respected, and there's not much happening in your private life. How's that?"

I was flabbergasted. And completely unnerved.

"How do you know all that?"

It was hard to believe those gorgeous eyes belonged to someone from the world of organized crime.

"Google," he said, and laughed. "And a couple of lucky guesses."

I smiled, not knowing whether to believe him or not.

"Oh, and by the way, you lied about Atlanta. You're from Charleston."

He winked.

CHAPTER SIX

J.D.'s Gone Fishing

Dawn. I was wide-awake. Wide-awake like it was three o'clock in the afternoon. I went to the window of our bedroom and looked outside to see what kind of a day it would become. Steam was rising from the grass. The brown patches on the lawn seemed to have spread overnight like a virus, slowly but surely devouring everything in its lethal path. The day would be brutal, but long ago I had learned how to navigate the heat. Dress light, drink a lot of water, stay inside during the middle of the day. How about just stay indoors in general? It was August in the Lowcountry of South Carolina. Of course it was hot. And with the kind of work I did, I didn't have the luxury of staying indoors all the time. To tell you the truth, heat was like anything else—you just got used to it.

I glanced at Valerie curled up in the bed in her pale blue eye mask and pale blue negligee and wondered if she was happy with her pale blue fluff of a life. She could not have been. Not at any deep level, anyway. Valerie had probably stopped thinking about happiness a long time ago. She would never have admitted it, but I thought she lived in a constant state of stress and worry that if my mother could do so, she would vote her out of the family, or that I would run away with a girl who could give me children. I wasn't going anywhere. That's not how we Langleys were wired.

I dressed quietly and went downstairs to make coffee. I loved this time of day best, before the world woke up and aggravation wound its way to my door. The pot dripped slowly and the air was filled with the rich smells of coffee from somewhere in the mountains of South America. I breathed deeply and told myself that despite my complaints, I was still a very lucky man.

It was time to get in my truck and go down the road to the mailbox to collect the morning papers.

Goober and Peanut were sleeping in their pen outside, but when they sensed my approach they roused, yawned, and began to bark.

"Shhh! Calm down, boys! Everyone's asleep!" I opened the gate and let them out. "You boys want to fish this morning? What do y'all say we go get us some bass?" I scratched them behind the ears and gave them each a dog biscuit. "Come on, get in the truck."

Goober and Peanut lived outside most of the time because they loved to roll around in dead things and Valerie said they reeked. They did, but not all the time. I would throw them in the river when they got muddy. Every so often I would slip Mickey twenty dollars to give them a real bath with dog shampoo. Wouldn't you know, as soon as they were clean, they would find something to roll around in again, like a decomposing skunk, and we would have to pour gallons of tomato juice all over then to kill the stench. Then we would toss them back in the Wappoo. A lot of people might say that dogs were too much trouble, but this was probably the only thing I had in common with Joanie McGee—love of animals. I loved my dogs. I sneaked them into the kitchen all the time, where they settled under the table by my feet while I read the paper.

Goober and Peanut—which, to the uninitiated and to the dictionary, meant the same thing—were two of the most optimistic dogs I had ever owned. They were always happy to see me. Always. And they were happy simply to be in my company, whether it was riding in the cab or the back of my truck or sitting on the boat while I fished. Goober was six years old, Peanut was eight, and they had never been on a leash, except to visit the vet for an annual checkup. So when they saw the leash in my hand, a little bit of running around ensued in order to get them in the truck. They were smart fellows.

I cranked up my white Ford truck, which also needed a wash, and we rolled down the avenue of miniature live oaks toward the street. I would be dead and buried for a hundred years before those trees would look like they should. Every time I passed them, skinny, wimpy things that they were, I was reminded that Valerie thought she and I were building something from *Gone With the Wind*. I had planted fast-growing pines in between them to play down their scrawni-ness, and I planned to cut those down at some future time when the live oaks grew to a respectable size. I had to tip my hat to Valerie's fantasy as she did to my practicality.

So it had become a habit to rise, set up the coffee, liberate my dogs, and go for a quick ride. Once, I had offered to pay a premium to the delivery boy to bring the papers up the drive, but he wasn't interested, saying if he did that for every-one, he'd have to cut his route in half, as many of the neigh-boring properties were set back as much as a mile from the road. He was right, of course.

Shortly after seven, as I was finishing up my third cup of coffee, and thanking the good Lord my name wasn't in the obituary pages, there was a rap on my kitchen door. The dogs got up with me and there was Mickey on the other side of the glass window. Goober and Peanut began to wag their tails. The advent of Mickey meant fun just might be on the agenda.

"I wanted to come over earlier," he said, giving the boys a scratch and a pat on their rumps. "Mom said don't do it. She said everybody needs a little time in the morning to get their motor going."

"Your mom is a very astute woman. Have you had breakfast?"

"Yes, sir. Four Eggos, a glass of orange juice, and a glass of chocolate milk."

It sounded to me like a prescription for major rumbling abdominal distress, but what did I know about the gastrointestinal constitution of young boys? Not much except that they were eating machines.

"Okay, then. Let me get my sunglasses and let's see what we can catch to feed the ladies tonight. Come on, boys."

As we collected our gear and walked down to the dock with the dogs, Mickey was a chatterbox.

"So, when I got up this morning I loaded the trap with a mayonnaise sandwich."

"Did you use the right bread?"

"Oh, yeah. Little Miss Sunbeam. Nothing but the best for our mud minnows."

"Good man! Tide's getting high, so I brought waders. Maybe get some bass."

"Mom's got a hankering for trout, but shoot, she'll take anything as long as we clean it!"

"Yeah," I said, "cleaning fish is man's work. Why don't you go check the trap?"

Mickey hurried ahead with the fishing rods, reels, and tackle box. We were going out in my Jon boat.

In my grandfather's day, you would get together with a couple of guys, your sons perhaps, and build your own boat. They weren't much to look at, just a flat-bottomed rowboat for scooting in and out of the maze of marsh grass. When I was just a little fellow, the remnants of an old oak one was permanently parked in the boathouse, alongside my father's treasured Chris-Crafts. As soon as I could toddle around, I remember my father putting me in it and I would pretend to be fishing with a bamboo pole. My love of water sports was hereditary.

Today, things were different. Who had time to build a boat? The Jon boat we used was made of welded aluminum, thickly painted olive drab, and had a Bimini top to avoid that sunburned skillet effect. In theory, it would hold five people, but in my opinion, two people and two canines were a full load. And for the convenience of all involved, I had added a twenty-five-horsepower outboard motor.

Off in the distance, I heard Mickey whoop with joy.

"We got us a mess of minnows, J.D.! Come see!"

It took a minute or two to get to the dock, as I was carrying the cooler and the waders. I dropped it all on the deck and had a look in the trap.

"They sure do love mayonnaise, don't they? What did you use? Duke's?"

"Is there any other?" Mickey was so proud you would have thought he had a great white on the hook.

"Come on. Let's get going," I said.

I ruffled his hair, and for the next two sticky and humid hours, we caught fish. Mickey got an eighteen-inch trout and six medium-size bream fish and I hooked four flounder.

"Look over there!" I said.

There was a lot of fluttering going on in the marsh grass and that meant one thing. The spot-tail bass were feeding on periwinkles and you could see their tails wiggling above the waterline. We started to laugh at the sight of them. There were so many I thought we could have just scooped them into the boat with a net.

"Look at these guys! They're suicidal!" They were practically jumping on the minnows. "So when do you start school?"

"Look at this one!" Mickey held up a fish for my approval and I nodded. "Next week. Ugh. Junior year. SATs."

"You're not really worried, are you? You did all right on the PSATs, didn't you?"

"Yeah, I did great, but that was a while ago and I need a scholarship, you know?"

"I wouldn't sweat that too much. There's always money around for a good kid."

Mickey gave me a lopsided grin. If you put aside his

youth and the thousands of freckles he had inherited from his mother, it suddenly seemed to me that there was almost a resemblance in his bone structure to a portrait of my grandfather that hung in Mother's house. Probably the heat, I told myself.

There was no way in hell the Langley money would not help Mickey go to the best college that would have him. I would see to that, although Dad had promised to take charge of Mickey's tuition. Maybe we Langleys weren't always the nicest and easiest people to do business with, but we believed in education and in taking care of our own. Mickey was practically family.

"It's getting hot," I said. "Think it's enough for one day?"

"Yeah, let's let 'em live," he said. "We got plenty for supper."

"Okay," I said, and we started back. "Listen, Mickey, I gotta go out to Johns Island to look at some houses we just finished. I'm meeting the architect and the construction manager. Wanna come? You might learn something."

"Sure!"

When we got back to the dock, we cleaned the fish, threw them in the cooler, and hosed everything down, including Goober and Peanut, who had chased a rabbit into the thicket, winding up in the plough mud.

"Damn dogs," I said, holding Peanut by the collar while Mickey brushed him with the boat brush and showered him with the hose. Plough mud was a very sticky and tenacious adversary, renowned for its stick-to-itiveness and fragrance.

"PU!" Mickey's face was scrunched up with disgust.

"You said it."

Funny. Neither one of us really cared about the bother and the fumes. For me, it was just nice to spend the time with Mickey. Each time I watched him ever so carefully reel in a fish, my heart would swell with a short blast of delight. He could have been my son.

Finally, when the dogs were passably clean, we let them

run back to the house. I divided up the fish and put them into Ziplocs, then handed him two thick packages. It was about ten o'clock or so.

"Mickey, you go on shower up and I'll meet you back in the kitchen in about half an hour. Is that long enough for you?"

"Yeah, sure."

"Make sure you rinse that fish good, okay?"

As he nodded and ran off in the direction of his house, I spotted my dad's SUV in my yard.

I put away all the tackle and moved up to the house. Through the windows I saw Dad clicking through the television stations from one news station to another. Big Jim loved to watch the news. He was all but retired, but he would not admit it. He was there to ride out to Johns Island with me and give the job his stamp of approval.

The kitchen door slammed behind me and Big Jim jumped, startled by the noise.

"Fish biting?" he inquired.

"They were practically throwing themselves in the boat."

Dad clicked the mute button, chuckled, and said, "Well, good. You'll have a good supper tonight. Rosie can flat-cook some fish, 'eah?"

"That's for sure. I've got some for you, too. You coming out with me to the island?"

"Well, that was the plan."

"Just give me a few minutes to clean up and we'll go."

"No problem. Take your time. I'm watching this idiot who's making all these dire predictions about the housing market. Incredible. Everybody's an expert!"

"That's for sure."

I checked the garage. Valerie's car was gone. Probably out shopping. I took the stairs two at a time to get to the shower. I could not have been gone more than fifteen minutes when I came back to find Big Jim napping in the chair.

"Dad?" I shook his arm a little and he stirred.

"What? Oh, I must have dozed off."

"You want to come or do you want to rest?"

"You know what, J.D.? It's hot as hell and I think I'm just gonna go home and have a little lunch. I'll go out there with you next time."

Dad was nearing seventy, but he had always been spry and eager to do anything, go anywhere, or to try something new. Lately, though, he seemed tired. Maybe it *was* the heat. But seventy on Big Jim had always seemed like thirty on me. Maybe I would talk to him about his health. There was nothing my parents appreciated less than a reminder of their advancing years. I would have to employ some severe diplomacy. Not my greatest strength.

"No big deal," I said. "I'll be out there every day this week going over the punch list. It's supposed to cool off by Thursday."

"Good. Maybe I'll go with you then."

"I'm taking Mickey out there today. Here." I handed him a bag of fish.

"Really? Why? Thanks."

Dad seemed annoyed for some reason.

"Well, he's a good kid and I think he gets bored out here in the sticks. I mean, there aren't any kids around, he doesn't have a license yet . . . what's wrong?"

"Nothing. I mean, it's just that Rosie is our house-keeper . . ."

"You say that like it's a bad thing."

"You're right. I'm just being a narrow-minded old fart. Take the boy. It's nice of you to do it. Besides, I gotta ride down to Hilton Head to see a buddy late this afternoon. Maybe I'll have a short nap."

Dad slapped me on the shoulder in a fatherly good-bye.

"Say hi to Mom," I said.

"She means well, son," he said, which was what he almost always said.

"Right."

Shortly after Dad left, Mickey and I were on our way, shooting the breeze.

"So, Mickey?"

"Yeah?"

"When are you getting your driver's license?"

"Six months, two weeks, and five days."

"You sound pretty sure about that."

"Unless Motor Vehicle is closed that day, I'll be in there when the doors open. I'm getting my permit this year in school. We all take driver's ed."

"You'll ace that."

"I've already taken the test online about fifty times."

"And?"

"I think I got it nailed."

I smiled. "Well you know what they say, Mickey, success is about ninety-nine percent perspiration and one percent luck."

"Yep. That's true."

I gave him a little shove in the arm. "You sound like a grown man over there, kid."

"Yeah, right."

We drove on for a while, air-conditioning on low and the windows open as well, enjoying the mix of hot salt cut with cooled air. It was good not to let your body become too chilled by the air-conditioning because when you stopped your vehicle and got out, the slam of the heat could almost knock you off your feet.

I was lost in thought watching the landscape and it seemed that Mickey was as well. We were crawling along Maybank Highway and had just passed the sign for the Angel Oak, which was thought to be around fourteen hundred years old. I remembered taking Betts out there when we were teenagers. I had just attained the same Holy Grail to which Mickey was counting down the days. My license was still warm in my wallet and I was driving my dad's car. We would walk all around Angel Oak, find a secluded spot, and I would coerce her into kissing and fooling around a little. Hiding in the shadows of a public place meant we could only go so far, but even at sixteen we knew we would wind up in a bed before we found our way to the altar. That was a fact.

"So, she's coming back," I said, without realizing I was talking out loud.

"Who's coming back?" Mickey said.

To say I gulped would be the understatement of the day.

"My, uh, mother. She's, uh, out at Kiawah, I think . . . at a ladies' lunch or something, and, um, I could have given her a ride home. Poor planning." I was a terrible liar. Well, not in all situations. Sometimes I could lie like a pro, but when caught by Mickey, I bumbled around like an idiot. I cared what he thought of me, I guess.

"Uh-huh. Right. Hey, J.D.?"

"What?"

"If my momma was in this truck, she'd tell you you lie like a cheap rug. I mean, it ain't none of my business and all . . ." Mickey started laughing, knowing he had me in a corner.

I thought about it for a minute, then against my better judgment, I decided to tell him a partial truth.

"Oh, Mickey."

"Sounds like a woman to me."

"How do you know that?"

"Because you said *she*. *She's* coming back."

"Ah, Mickey. When you're my age, you'll understand."

"Understand what?"

"That life's complicated."

"I think I already know that."

I had no doubt that he understood the many complications life could throw your way. But I said no more.

We finally reached the finest gated community Langley Construction had built. River Run. It was one of the projects of which I was particularly proud, except for the nasty business of fighting for dock permits and building setbacks and a long list of other details that had cost the family business plenty. At the end of the day, there was only so much water-front property in the world. My job was to identify what existed in our area, buy it, and develop it before anyone else did. And if some out-of-state developers, like Wall Street boys with buckets of money and upstate developers, beat me to the punch, my family's attorneys could make it very difficult for them to break ground, since, in such an eventuality, we would suddenly become great crusaders for the cause of conservation. Usually, if we threw enough money at the problem, it ceased to be a problem.

"Hey! How's it going?" I called out to the foreman, climbing down from my truck.

"Good, good. I think they sold the last unit today, but you'll have to check with Marianne over in the office."

"I'll do that. I'll do that today. Everything okay?"

"The usual—replacement motors for the faulty air-conditioning units not in yet, I don't like the size screws the men used to attach the shutters on the Dunes Villas . . ."

It was the normal list of problems we always faced before the owners would take occupancy, but this time we were thirty days ahead of schedule and that miraculous detail would please our family's management company to no end. You see, Langley Development bought the land, got the permits, provided the infrastructure—roads, sewage, and so forth—and built the houses and condos. Then we sold the entire kit and caboodle to my mother's cousin's real-estate company—Charleston's Finest Homes—who, in turn, sold the housing to individuals and dealt with everything from mortgages to upgrades on faucets, all the details I could not endure.

Dad's real job for the past ten years had been to manage our family's investments, something that seemed to come naturally to him. He took the profits of our construction business, deposited them in Langley Trust, which was a portfolio of every kind of holding you can imagine, from T-bills to an organic-herb communal farm. The earnings of Langley Trust that were not rolled over were the donations Mother made to charitable institutions. It was a very pleasant merry-go-round and only Langleys were allowed to ride it. So, in essence, as Mother liked to say when she was in her arrogant cups, we didn't really own Charleston, only the parts we wanted.

Mickey and I walked around and looked at some of the condominiums. It always amazed me that my opinion of necessary space could adjust itself so easily. At home, Valerie and I easily wandered five thousand square feet in the footprint of our house, but I could walk through a twelve-hundred-square-foot condo and tell myself that it was more than enough. Frankly, it was.

"What do you think, Mickey?"

He was staring out a large picture window that overlooked the Kiawah River. The water glistened like a billion shards of diamonds in the afternoon sun and the tall grasses scattered along the water's edge moved slowly in the quiet breeze.

"How much does one of these things cost?"

"Depends. You know, how many bedrooms and all that. Why?"

"Because I'd like to buy one for my mom. You know? Someday, that is. I'd like to go to college and get some great job and buy a place for my mom, so when she came home she could feel like this. Like I feel right now. You know what I mean?"

"Yeah, but how does it make *you* feel?"

He looked at me hard, his blue eyes so intent, filled with an adult seriousness I remembered in myself from his age.

"It makes me feel like it's worth it."

"What's worth it?"

"Getting up every day and doing what I have to do. If I could come home from school or work or whatever and look at this, I could suffer a lot."

I wasn't going to ask him if he thought his mother was unsatisfied living in our sharecropper's cottage. The question would have been inappropriate. Their housing came free with the job and was not exactly the Ritz-Carlton. It was adequate, airtight, leak-free, but no frills. And squeaking all of life into that space wasn't like stopping in your living room to look out at the sparkling waters of the Kiawah River on a perfect August afternoon.

"You hungry?" I said.

"Are you kidding? I'm a teenage boy. I could eat twenty-four/seven."

"Let's go get us a burger at the Sanctuary and figure out how you're gonna earn enough cash to buy you and your mom a place on the water."

"Sweet. I'm in."

In the parlance of the day, which required watching YouTube or the Comedy Network on a regular basis, Mickey meant he was amenable to the suggestion of lunch and the formation of a long-range plan.

"Do you want fries with that? Coleslaw or fruit salad?" a waitress, whose name tag read *Agnes Mae, Vidalia, Georgia,* said to him.

Mickey looked at me like she was an alien. *Of course* he wanted fries. To a young man of his years, a burger with fruit salad was a despicable, sissified blasphemy.

"Definitely fries," he said.

"Swiss, Cheddar, or blue cheese?"

"Blue cheese?" He made the face of horrors. "Cheddar's good."

"And how—"

"Medium well," he said, before Agnes Mae of Vidalia-onion fame could finish asking. "Just no blood."

"Got it." She looked to me.

"I'll have the turkey club with two slices of bread and fries. Extra pickle, please. Mayonnaise on the side. Thanks."

"I'll get that right out," she said, and walked away.

We stirred the lemon into our sweet tea and I decided to give him some sage advice.

"Want to know how to get rich, young man?"

"No. I want to know where I sign up for food stamps."

"Wiseass."

"Of course I want to know how to get rich! What's the secret?"

"Well? There are a couple of ways it happens. First, you're born into wealth. We call it being a member of the Lucky Sperm Club. Or, you can win the lottery. But the best way is to make a plan."

"Duh."

"No duh. Look, if you want to get rich, you don't major in third-century European history or spend your life studying the sex lives of newts. You go to business school or law school. You go into a field that's lucrative to begin with."

"Makes sense. What did you do?"

"Carolina Law School. I started out to study environmental, but then I switched my concentration to real estate . . ."

We talked on and on about real-estate development, iTunes, women, and the value of a really great burger. The bill was paid and Mickey was finishing off a slice of pecan pie, sopping up the last puddle of vanilla ice cream with the crust.

"I must say, Mickey, I have great respect for your ability to clean a plate."

"Thanks." He grinned as wide as he could. "Lunch was awesome."

"Good. So, what do you say? Want to ride around Kiawah and I'll show you some of the early buildings of Langley Construction? See how they're holding up?"

"Sure, why not?"

The temperature had passed its high for the day, and because we had lingered at the table for so long, when we stepped outside we got the immediate sense that evening was already approaching.

I loved to think about families ending their workdays with some satisfaction and coming back together for the night. Yes, although it was not yet four, people everywhere were looking toward supper. Housewives were already snapping beans, kids were climbing down from the high limbs of trees thirsty for a drink, and beachgoers were packing up their SUVs and knocking sand from their flip-flops. Goober and Peanut were probably sleeping in the shade dreaming about chasing squirrels.

We climbed into my truck and took off for the Sea Breeze Villas, Langley Development's first project on Kiawah Island.

"So what kinda wildlife they got on this island? Anything different from what we got?"

"They got more alligators, I think, and I've seen more river otters over here."

"Otters. Weird."

"Yeah, they're funny little devils."

Suddenly a distinguished-looking shock of white hair caught my eye. It was an older gentleman leaving his condo. Senator Hazelton. And a woman. Mother. It was Mother. There was no "ladies lunch." Clearly, it was a damn lie. My mother was screwing Senator Hazelton. Brant Hazelton, who also happened to be my father's partner in a dozen different deals.

My shock must have been apparent. Mickey said, "Hey! J.D.? Are you okay?"

"Yeah, I'm fine," I said. "I just remembered that I have to be someplace that I forgot about."

"Oh. No big deal. I got stuff to do, too."

I tried to look away from the senator and my mother, but it was like the train-wreck phenomenon—I couldn't tear my eyes away, and sure enough, I could have sworn that Mother caught my eye. I saw her step back under the building's overhang and reach for her sunglasses . . . as though I wouldn't recognize my own mother? I stepped on the gas to get away as fast as possible. Luckily, Mickey was fooling with the radio, cruising from one station to another, or he might have seen her, too.

I tried to be friendly and nonchalant all the way home and I thought Mickey didn't suspect anything. As the afternoon wore on, I struggled with my conscience. Should I tell Valerie? Hell no. What good would that do? Should I tell my father? Absolutely not. Had he not enjoyed enough skirts to fill a department store? Should I confront my mother? What possible good would that do? Zero.

It was six-thirty. Mother had not called. I wondered if she knew with certainty that I had seen her. Was she avoiding me? This was some bull. I mean, did she think that if she didn't mention it, she could pretend it didn't happen?

I was getting hungry. Where was Valerie anyway? I called her cell and got her voice mail. She would probably be home soon. I poured myself a bourbon. Rosie was in the kitchen, putting the final touches on supper.

"Looks good enough to eat," I said to Rosie as I glanced at the platter of sliced cucumbers and tomatoes.

"Thanks," she said, "and thanks for the fish."

"Your boy liberated them from their watery world . . ."

The phone rang and I picked it up in the kitchen.

"Hello?"

"J.D.?"

"Yes?"

"This is Brant Hazelton."

Well, I thought, I'll be damned. The old codger is calling to defend—or at least attempt to whitewash—mother's honor with some bit of hasty fabrication.

"Yes, sir. What can I do for you?"

"Well, son, I'm afraid it's not good news. I'm with your father down in Hilton Head. He's had a heart attack . . ."

My head started spinning. They were trying to stabilize him, he said. They thought he would be all right, but just the same, I had better come and bring Mother. I got the address, the senator's cell-phone number, and I dialed Mother. The phone rang and rang.

"What is it?" Rosie said.

"Dad's had a heart attack," I said.

"Oh no! What can I do?"

"Nothing. Tell Valerie when she shows up to leave her cell on once in a while." It wasn't Valerie's fault and I shouldn't have said that. "I'm sorry. I'll call as soon as I know anything. I've got to go see about him right now," I said. "Why isn't Mother answering the phone?"

I redialed. After five rings, Mother finally answered.

"Mother?" I tried to sound calm, but I was sure she heard the panic in my voice and took it to be the beginning of a lecture from me about her liaison.

"Now, see here, J.D.—"

"Mother? Brant Hazelton called."

"What?"

"Daddy's had a heart attack. I'm coming to pick you up. He's in Hilton Head."

I hung up and looked at Rosie, who was clearly upset.

"Please! J.D.? Give your daddy my love, won't you? Tell him I'll be praying for him with everything I've got?"

"Of course I will, Rosie. Thanks. I'll call as soon as I know anything."

In truth, I didn't care what my mother did in her spare time. After all, my father had been doing the same thing for as long as I had been aware that people had sex. But I was furious anyway and I didn't know why. Then I decided it was the lies that made me so angry. There were too many lies in our family. Most of the way to Hilton Head, Mother and I were silent, but as soon as we exited, I-95, we started to argue.

"You can judge me all you want, J.D. But just how do you think we got Bulls Island declassified?"

"I have no idea, Mother. Did the family's generosity buy the senator a new Maserati?"

"Don't be absurd. Besides, Brant could buy his own Maserati if he wanted one."

"Oh, I'm sorry. Like Dad never passed an envelope of cash to a building inspector?"

"Look, J.D. You really want to know what's going on here? I have enjoyed the friendship of Brant Hazelton for years and your daddy knows it. And guess what? He doesn't care! Your daddy does as he pleases, too, which is the most likely reason he's in the hospital right now. Brant's wife knows, too. And guess what else?"

"She doesn't care either. Whatever."

"Don't *whatever* me, young man. I am still your mother!"

"So fine, tell me how you managed to have Bulls Island declassified. I'm dying to hear."

"Well! He's ingenious, that's all. Brant buries it in the budget in a line item. You know, he says something like 'all islands west of this latitude and south of that longitude shall be offered for sale for specific use of the public good' or some such vague language. Who on earth is going to catch that in a big old boring budget document that's thousands of pages long?"

"Not even Sherlock Holmes, Mother. That's pretty clever. And you and Daddy snap it up before anyone else knows about the public offering, right?"

"That's right. We finalize the sale in the same moment the budget is signed."

I saw then that my father and mother were no better than common criminals. Highfalutin, modern-day opportunistic, greedy bastards with no conscience. And there I was, aiding and abetting common criminals. Nice family.

"So now we own Bulls Island."

"Yes, we do. We break ground in two weeks. ARC Partners is our partner. And I guess this is as good a time as any to tell you."

"Tell me what?"

"That Betts McGee is in charge of the project."

"That's nice," I said, but my heart started to pound.

If my father could indulge his weakness for strippers and my mother could have a semi-open affair with Brant Hazelton, could I have Betts? I struggled to focus on the fact that we were nearing the hospital where my father was possibly fighting for his life—fighting for his life with his strip-joint partner who was screwing my mother at his bedside. How many other secrets could my family possibly have?

Betts. Two weeks.

CHAPTER SEVEN

Dad, Joanie, and Vinny

It was Friday and I was thinking about enjoying the weekend. Aunt Jennie was coming for dinner, so I ordered a special arrangement of flowers for my foyer and for the dining-room table. I had a date with Vinny Saturday night. I had not yet decided how to deal with this budding relationship because he scared me a little. For some reason, that scary aspect of his personality was appealing to me, which was also scary. I guess I liked edgy living. And as you know, he fascinated me.

I had to start planning Adrian's move to his dorm and there was a long list of things he needed, linens and so forth, so we planned to melt the credit cards Saturday morning. But rattling around in the back of my mind was the fact that I had yet to give my father and sister fair warning that I was returning to Charleston. Deciding to face the worst music in the repertoire of my life, I took a deep breath and dialed Daddy's number.

Then I hung up.

I repeated the dialing process somewhere in the neighborhood of twenty times and quickly hung up each time, right before I could hear Dad's phone ring, behaving as though I were presenting some new variant of obsessive-compulsive disorder. I worried that perhaps the phone rang there before I could hear it ringing on my end or that my number appeared on their caller ID. Or, wait! Did they have caller ID? Were Joanie and Dad standing there watching the caller-ID screen and thinking I had truly lost my mind? Finally, I took a Lamaze-style breath, punched in the number one last time, and let it ring until, praise everything holy, I caught a karmic break and got voice mail. Joanie's recorded message drenched me in a cold sweat of relief.

You've reached the McGees. Please leave a message. Thanks.

No one had ever accused Joanie of being overly engaging or seductively poetic. I left the following message:

"Hi, Joanie. Hi, Dad. It's me, Betts. Just wanted to let you know that I'm going to be in Charleston for a couple of months on business and I hoped we might get together. Please call me. Thanks and I hope y'all are well. Love you both."

Perfect. I had sounded chipper and at ease.

I left my number, which I was positive they had somewhere in their possession in case they had to notify me of a catastrophe, and hung up, wiping my sweaty hands on my skirt. How long would it take them to return my call? What if they didn't call at all? I was determined to take the high road on this one. I had put them on notice that I was coming. If I didn't hear from them before I set up camp in Charleston, I would call them when I arrived. I would do the right thing even if they didn't. Sela was right. It was time for the nonsense to stop.

Most importantly, I wanted to see them in order to draw my own conclusions about Daddy's condition. It wasn't like Joanie held some medical degree or was an expert in geriatric care. But neither was I. If he seemed off-kilter, I would somehow persuade him to get a thorough evaluation from the best doctors I could find. But I suspected that Daddy was just perhaps going through the normal stages of aging, and like Sela said, Joanie used him as a crutch to avoid having an authentic life of her own.

I had finally concluded that I wanted to repair our relationship as much as I could. They were my family, after all.

In preparation for dinner, I started flipping through the delivery menus I kept in a drawer in the kitchen. Even though I had spent a fortune designing a hyperorganized stainless-steel gourmet kitchen that looked like a spaceship, my kitchen had a junk drawer like everyone else's. In it were an assortment of useless things I could never bear to discard in case of a terrorist attack or a blackout—candle stubs, matches, packets of soy sauce and saltine crackers, rubber bands from the mail, loose batteries that may or may not still work, coupons for free extra pizza toppings, long scraps of unwound ribbon, and enough scattered change to feed us for a month. And menus. One of these days, I told myself, I'm going to get this place organized.

I pulled out the menu from Fascino, which was the hot new Italian eatery owned by the De Persio family from Nutley, New Jersey—hot because their two sons, Ryan the chef and Anthony the manager, looked like a couple of movie stars. And because Ryan could do such magnificent things with tomatoes and macaroni that any one of the city's major food critics could be found there four nights a week, humming to him- or herself in satisfaction. Normally Fascino didn't deliver, but they did for me because they catered every recent ARC management meeting and we had a hefty house account there. Aunt Jennie would be thrilled with their veal Parmesan (not on the menu) and I also ordered her some fried zucchini flowers stuffed with ricotta cheese and a side of spaghetti marinara, plus a cannoli, a baba rum, and pumpkin cheesecake for all of our desserts.

Then I called my favorite Japanese restaurant, Dai Kitchi, and ordered California rolls, spicy tuna rolls, edamame, and a double portion of nabayaki udon with tempura shrimp. That mountain of Nipponese delights would surely catapult

Adrian straight to hog heaven. Speaking of hog, lastly I called Blue Smoke for a rare personal indulgence of baby-back ribs, a pound of pulled pork to stock the refrigerator's snacking department, two orders of baked beans, coleslaw, corn pudding, and a dozen biscuits. I knew Adrian would eat all the leftovers, and with my crazy life, it was easier to over-order prepared food than go to the store, schlep it all home, and cook it. Besides, if you paid me a million in unmarked twenties, I couldn't even make the broth for nabayaki udon much less the soba noodles that go in it.

Adrian came home around six, just as the deliveries began to arrive.

"Aunt Jennie's going to be here any minute. Want to set the table?" I said. "I'll get the door." I took three five-dollar bills from my wallet for tips.

"Sure! Hey, I saw the new Harry Potter film this afternoon."

"Thanks a lot," I said to the deliveryman, and closed the door. "How was it?"

"Awesome," he said.

"Of course it was awesome," I said, giving him a baby punch in the arm. "Everything in your entire *world* is awesome."

"Aw, come on, what did you say at my age? Groovy? Or 'far out, man'?"

"You've been watching that Woodstock documentary again, haven't you? FYI, we said 'cool.' "

"You still say 'cool.' "

"Because I *am* cool."

"Maybe. I mean, all things considered . . ."

"Rotten kid," I said. "How'd you get so tall?"

"All those asparagus you used to feed me."

The doorman buzzed again and I picked up the phone. "Delivery," he said. "Fascino's and Blue Smoke."

"Send them up," I said.

I picked up the two fives and went toward the front door,

passing Adrian as he set the dining-room table. He was moving around the table, placing flatware, and his back was to me. Something made me pause—the slope of his shoulders or maybe it was his posture. The sight of him gave me shivers because there he was—J. D. Langley in the flesh. Once again I was consumed with dark guilt over keeping his existence a secret from J.D. If I could have rebuilt the world from scratch, I would have populated it with only the three of us. It would have been paradise.

Adrian was already a young man and J.D. had missed his entire life. Adrian had never known a father. If they ever discovered the truth, J.D. and Adrian might kill me with their bare hands and no court of law in the land would convict them.

My doorbell rang and I snapped out of my gloom. J.D. and Adrian would never find out about each other because I would never tell.

It wasn't long before we were settled at the table with Aunt Jennie and an international feast. I was taken aback by how frail and stooped she looked, but after all, I reminded myself, she was nearly eighty. On the other hand, her faculties were as sharp as a blade of marsh grass.

"My word, Adrian, I just cannot begin to tell you how tickled to pieces I am for you! Columbia! My goodness gracious sakes alive! To think I changed the diapers of such an important man!"

Her blue eyes twinkled with youthful mirth despite their red rims of age. Behind those eyes there still existed a vital young woman, probably reliving a moment of her own teenage years. She reached across the table and patted his hand in a gesture of affection.

"Ah, Aunt Jennie. Thanks," Adrian said. "Edamame?"

"Who?" Aunt Jennie said. "You think I need a man at my age?"

Adrian and I had a fit of giggles, and Aunt Jennie smiled and said, "I guess my hearing isn't what it was."

"What?" I said, and we laughed again.

"Edamame is this soybean Japanese side dish that I could eat like a billion of," Adrian said. "See?"

He demonstrated for Aunt Jennie by popping one in his mouth, sliding the beans from the pod with his teeth, picking off bits of coarse salt. Then he passed the dish to her.

"Not bad," she said, after a tentative taste. "Kind of like boiled peanuts."

"And just as fattening," I said. "Everything good is bad for you, isn't it? Hey! Did I tell y'all that I'm going to Charleston on assignment for a couple of months?" It was as good a time as any to break the news.

"Awesome! Can I come visit? I hear the beaches are really, really good."

"We'll see," I said, fully aware that the only way Adrian was coming to Charleston would be to collect my dead body.

I could see the surprise register in Aunt Jennie's eyes, but she handled it with her usual aplomb. "Oh? And what will you be doing there, Betts? Charleston's such a pretty place."

I would call her later to discuss the details and seek her sage advice. "Yes, it is. I'll be building a very high-end gated community on Bulls Island."

"What the heck do you know about construction, Mom? I mean that with all due respect."

"No problem; but you're right. I don't know diddly-squat. I seem to have a long career of acquiring skills for the job as I *take on* the job. Crazy, right?"

"Not if you're well compensated for all the trouble," Aunt Jennie said, and smiled at me. I knew she wanted the details.

"My mom can do anything. Are you gonna eat that?"

"Here." I passed him some ribs. "Thanks for the compliment, sweetheart."

After Aunt Jennie got over her excitement about the news of my pilgrimage back to the land of my ancestors, the conversation limped along, but that limping wasn't for our lack

of interest in one another's lives. It was that our worlds were
so vastly different. Here was my Adrian, who lived in a high-
tech sphere, fueled by the noise of pop culture, and who was
on the verge of his college career. My world of calculations
and risk was so fast-paced, diversified, and complicated that
it was difficult to explain to an outsider what I did much less
why I was so addicted to it. And Aunt Jennie lived quietly
reading historical novels and biographies all winter and visiting gardens during the spring and summer. As much as we
loved one another, coming together was a reminder that
nothing lasted forever—Adrian's youth, my role as the heli-
copter mother, and indeed Aunt Jennie's days on earth were
all running neck and neck to some kind of invisible finish
line.

Before Aunt Jennie left, she reached for her purse and
took out an envelope. It was a greeting card with a check for
fifty dollars made out in Adrian's name. For some inexplicable reason, I wanted to burst into tears and it was only much
later that I realized that if my mother had lived, she would
have been the one writing that check. Sharing that dinner.
Hugging Adrian's neck.

"Now, you be a good boy in college," Aunt Jennie said
when she was at the door. "Do us proud. And if you need a
single solitary thing while your mother's away, you know
where to find me. And I have your cell-phone number, so I'll
be checking up on you!"

"Thanks, Aunt Jennie. Call me anytime and thanks for
the gift."

When we were alone we talked some more about me
leaving for the Bulls Island project and Adrian was fine
with it.

"Mom, don't worry about me. I'm sure I'll be studying all
the time—you know, except for when I'm doing lines and
getting drunk."

"Adrian!"

He started laughing and of course I knew he was fooling
with me, but the reality was, drugs and alcohol were as readily

available for anyone with the means as a soft drink was from a vending machine.

Then my big lug of a man-child put his hands on my shoulders and looked me squarely in the face.

"Mom," he said, "don't worry so much. I've been getting ready for this moment since the sandbox. I'm not interested in all that stuff. If I want to be president of the United States someday, I can't be doing drugs and raising hell."

"Since when?"

"Since when can't the president be a hell-raiser? You're kidding, right? Don't you know that Shrub—"

"No, no. Who cares about him? I mean, since when do you want to be president?"

"Well, I don't. But I know enough to understand that every single stupid thing I do is gonna haunt me forever."

I took a very deep gulp. My young Adrian had just dropped a truism of greater import than he could possibly have known.

"You are so right. You're a good kid, Adrian. Wanna help me clean up?"

"Sure. Who's gonna help you when I'm gone?"

"I don't know, baby, but I know I'm surely going to miss my boy being here."

"Don't worry. I'll bring my laundry home every weekend."

"Well, I can't wait for that!"

The next morning Adrian and I went to Bloomingdale's and spent a sentimental hour or so browsing the home-furnishings department, gathering together what seemed appropriate for a college freshman without resembling a layout from *Architectural Digest* that would put his sexual orientation into question.

"You know, Mom, if I show up with everything all brand new, my roommates are gonna think I've been away somewhere, like a really expensive mental ward."

"So what are you saying?"

"Well, I have to have a comforter or something for a

single bed because mine at home is like *huge* and the beds in Carman Hall take extra-long sheets, so we have to buy those."

"I get it. So, maybe what we should do is give you old towels to take to school and I'll buy new ones for the house?"

"Perfect. I just don't want to show up looking like Richie Rich."

"Gotcha. No monograms? Actually that's pretty smart. Who knows? Your roommates might be from some horrible third-world country, on a full scholarship. There's zero gain in rubbing our filthy capitalism in anyone's face."

"Exactly. I can always upgrade. I mean, it's bad enough that my laptop costs like a billion . . .'"

"Yeah, well, you'll have to keep your room locked or carry it around with you until you figure out how secure the dorm is, I guess."

"Actually, I register the serial number with the IT department, and well . . . you're right. Big deal. They could sell it on the street in about ten seconds."

"My point precisely. Hey? Do you want one of those little refrigerators?"

"Nah. I'll rent one and split it with my roommate. Who needs the hassle of moving it at the end of the year."

"Good plan. God, you are so smart!"

"Thanks, but I've read the admissions materials like over and over. Let's get this stuff and I'll make a pile of old stuff at home later. Can we go eat?"

I often wondered if my son had contracted some twenty-first-century mutation of a tapeworm that forced boys to consume their full body weight approximately once a week.

"Of course! You think I want you to starve?"

"Can we go to Nicola's?"

"Whatever you want."

"Sweet."

I knew there wouldn't be many more days like this one, shopping together, going out for lunch. We dropped our shopping bags off with our doorman and walked over to Madison

Avenue. Throughout lunch I was impressed by how magnificently Adrian had matured. While he babbled on about different professors he had been checking out on the Internet—apparently there was a website for rating professors—I quietly reminisced. He had seemed so young just a few short months ago, when he took his SATs and went to his prom. How I worried! I couldn't envision him grown so soon, looking like a man, mature enough to handle bank accounts, time management, and getting out of bed without someone giving him five more minutes. But here we were on the edge of a milestone and my boy couldn't wait to leap from the tiny bosom of Horace Mann School into the abyss of serious living. Where had the years gone? I felt a tightening in my chest. How would it be to live without him around? How cavernous would our apartment feel? I had been so busy worrying about getting him into college that I had never thought about how it would feel to have him gone.

"And there's this history guy from London, Simon Sch— You okay, Mom?"

"Yeah, baby. I'm just sitting here thinking that I'm gonna miss you, that's all."

"Mom? I can be home for dinner in fifteen minutes if I hop on the subway."

"I know."

We had a moment of recognition then and I felt my heart creak a little more. I didn't want my hesitation to dilute Adrian's happiness and anticipation, and I didn't want to shake his confidence. Let's be real here; I was entitled to an episode of hard-earned despair, but I knew it would be healthier for everyone for me to mourn privately.

"I'll be okay, Mom, and if living on campus is totally gross, I'll come home and take the train to classes."

"Adrian? I wouldn't let you do that. It's time for you to be out there. You're ready. But let your mother just give you one piece of valuable advice."

"What?"

"Get yourself a really obnoxious alarm clock."

"Good point."

After lunch, Adrian went off to meet up with some friends and I watched him disappear into the hundreds of people rushing up and down Madison Avenue. Everyone walked with such purpose in their stride, as though they were fully in charge of their lives and had to be somewhere five minutes ago. *Were* they so in charge of their lives? Was Adrian?

It never ceased to amaze me that with all the millions of people in Manhattan, everyone seemed to have their place of belonging. Unfortunately, for some it was a cardboard box in front of a church or on a side street. But everyone else sort of magically found their way through the maze of organized chaos back to their beds at night.

The bed I had not expected to find myself in was Vinny's. Before you get all judgmental, let me tell you how it happened.

I was to meet him downtown at Da Silvano's for dinner. It was right around eight-thirty when my cab pulled up, and looking inside I could see the dining room was mobbed with fashionistas, paparazzi, suits, and Robert De Niro having a quiet dinner at a table outside on the sidewalk with a friend. But no Vinny. There was an Italian car show outside against the curb. Ferraris galore. All around me, handsome, smiling Italian waiters dressed in black moved through the crowd with bottles of Pellegrino and wine and platters of gorgeous food. It was some scene.

Maybe, I thought, Vinny was in the Cantinetta next door, and sure enough, when I stuck my head in the door, I spotted him at the bar.

" 'Ey! There's my girl! Betts, come say hello to my buddy Gino."

The resemblance between them was so strong, Gino could have been Vinny's brother. Maybe he was.

"Hi," I said, "I'm Betts McGee."

"Look at you! How'd a bum like Vinny get such a gorgeous girl to have dinner with him?"

"Shaddup, Gino. Betts is crazy about me, ain't cha baby?"

"Crazy? Maybe. About you? We'll see . . ."

I mean, you had to laugh. Like a serious laugh the whole way from your toenails to the split ends on your hair. These two made me feel like I had stepped onto the set of *The Godfather* and we were poised to launch into a discussion on waste management and cement booties. Here I was in one of Manhattan's chicest watering holes with the Corleone boys. How about, it made me question my judgment? But somehow, Vinny had locked my imagination in overdrive and I couldn't get him out of my mind.

Vinny put a glass of vodka on the rocks with a twist in my hands, which was odd since I had never drunk vodka in front of him or recalled mentioning that I drank it, and I turned to Gino.

"So what do you do, Gino?"

"I'm the chief of heart-lung surgery at Columbia Presbyterian."

"Oh? I thought Dr. Oz was."

"Yeah, well, technically he is. But he's on *Oprah* all the time and traveling for his books, so I'm the guy watching the store."

"Gino here saved my old man's life," Vinny said. "Did a heart-lung transplant and now my dad's playing eighteen holes four times a week and he's seventy."

Still suspicious that Vinny may have procured and delivered the donor's organs, I had to admit that I had caught myself being an ass once again. Never judge the proverbial book by its Italian provenance, if you will. I soon learned that Gino was staying for dinner at Vinny's insistence, which was fine with me. They talked. I drank. Not a good plan if one wants to stay above water.

One vodka followed another and finally we were shown to our table. Vinny ordered for everyone. Grilled shrimp with a bottle of Pinot Grigio, penne all'arrabiata with more Pinot Grigio, osso bucco with a Barbaresco, and pretty soon I was stuffed and barely holding steady in the sobriety department. Thank God I wasn't driving. But Vinny was. Somehow he paid the check without my noticing and the next thing I knew we were in his big SUV heading for his loft in Tribeca. I objected, but it didn't register with him. Even in my cloudy state I recognized that Vinny was probably used to getting what he wanted. So rather than argue with him after a perfectly wonderful dinner and some of the most interesting conversation about health care I'd had in years, courtesy of Gino, I agreed to go look at the view from Vinny's terrace. It wasn't clear whether Gino was coming along, but it soon became obvious when he said good night, adding that he had enjoyed meeting me and calling Vinny a lucky devil. I smiled at that because had I met Gino first, things might have been different.

But I was draped on the arm of Vinny, and for the remainder of the evening that's where I would hang.

Vinny owned the penthouse of a loft building that overlooked the Hudson. The view was the single feature to recommend it. He opened the front door, flipped one single switch, and all the lights came on low and Tony Bennett started to croon from hidden speakers. The living room was enormous, with sliding glass doors everywhere. The sofas and chairs were white leather with chrome trim and the tables were glass with chrome trim. There wasn't a book or a photograph in sight. It could have been a rental.

"Here. Come see."

Beaming with pride, Vinny pressed a button on an electronic keypad that moved all the white billows of fabric back to reveal a wraparound view of the Statue of Liberty in the harbor and the Gold Coast of New Jersey. New Jersey was alive with the lights of so many lives and there stood Our Lady of the Harbor, the symbol of much of what we hold precious. It was magnificent.

"Let's go outside," he said.

"Absolutely," I said.

He grabbed a bottle of some kind of cognac and two

snifters. Well, I had already swallowed enough alcohol to fill my quota for a month, but I knew I wasn't going to say no to this either.

We stepped out onto the terrace and sighed as we took it all in. It was one of those kinds of nights that New Yorkers live for. Perfect temperature. Light breeze. And a dazzling view of every building.

He put the bottle down on the dining table—chrome, glass, with white pleatherette chairs—and poured out a moderate measure for each of us. We touched the edges of our glasses.

I said, "What or whom are we toasting?"

"I don't know, Betts McGee. Why don't we drink to us?"

Wanting to be the good sport, I said, "Why not? Here's to us and the magic of the moment."

Well, I guess he took that to be an invitation to initiate a mating ritual and he began making the requisite moves. What can I tell you? Blame it on the wine, Tony Bennett, and the Statue of Liberty. Blame it on New Jersey and the fact that he had a round bed and a mirrored ceiling. (Yes, he actually had a round bed, and all I could wonder was where he bought his sheets.) Something triggered my abandon, and for a while there I thought I had met the love of my life. Around three in the morning, when he was snoring lightly, and when I panicked to realize where I was, I slipped out of his apartment, caught a cab, and went home. I was a scandal and a disgrace and I could not have cared less what my late-shift doorman thought.

The next afternoon five dozen lilac and purple roses were delivered to my door—no small feat for a Sunday in Manhattan. Adrian took possession of the huge bouquet, opened the card, and read it aloud just as I was coming toward the door to answer it myself.

" 'I can't stop thinking about you. Vinny.' Who's Vinny, Mom?"

"Give me those, you bad boy. Vinny is this very nice crazy man I had dinner with last night and drinks one other time. He's just a friend."

"Yeah, right." Adrian laughed. "All your *friends* send you five dozen roses!"

"Why don't you go concentrate on your dormitory piles and I'll put these in water."

I dumped all the flowers in the sink, covered the bottom of their stems with water, and went searching for some containers under the cabinets, pulling out glass vases from old floral deliveries. Five dozen roses *was* excessive. As I clipped and stuffed them in between the greens, I thought, Isn't there some significance to lilac and purple roses? Vinny may have been the Dean Martin of our day, but he was anything but cavalier. I decided to Google the significances of the colors of roses, and sure enough, there it was. Lilac and purple stood for love at first sight, longing, all things mysterious, magical, and more symbolism than I was ready for on a Sunday afternoon when I was gearing up for work on Monday. Great.

I knew I should have called him immediately to thank him, but the profusion of flowers was overbearing and, frankly, a little creepy. Hadn't he ever heard of playing hard to get? A one-night stand? Did he think we had some meaningful relationship going now? Somehow, I was just going to have to tell him that there was a probable expiration date on this quasi love affair. In the first place, he was very inappropriate in every way. Not that it mattered. My career was reasonably secure and truly I could align myself with anyone I chose. Heaven knows, half my business associates, serial spouses almost to the last one, were married to bimbos. Vinny was inappropriate because I already knew his personality would wear thin and that he was one of those men who, although there was zero invitation on your part to be possessed, thought they owned you anyway. The roses were an omen of a proprietary claim. In their heady fragrance lurked his fantasy of a leash. Sorry, Vinny.

An hour later my cell phone rang. It was Vinny.

"Hey, thanks for the landslide of roses!" I said, trying to sound sincere.

"I thought it was important to make a statement." His voice was very serious.

"Well, I'm not sure what you were trying to say, but you sure said it!"

"I want to see you again."

"Oh! Well, sure! Yes, definitely!"

"You sound like you got some doubt about that."

"What? Oh! No. It's just the *when* part."

"Oh."

"You see, I'm putting my son in college and then I'm heading south for a few months . . ."

"Oh."

"But that's not for a couple of weeks so, yes! Let's try to work something out. Like next week? Tuesday? I think I'm free Tuesday night?"

"Sounds good."

"So what do you want to do?"

"Dinner, but let me surprise you. Figure, I don't know, seven o'clock? I'll pick you up?"

"Sounds great. Let's touch base that day just to be sure I'm on schedule . . . sometimes my days are a little crazy."

Silence. His silence implied he liked his women to be on call at all times. Another mild source of irritation for me. The only man on the planet to whom I would ever be so readily available was my son.

"Hello?" I said.

"Yeah, I'm here. I'll call you from the car, and if you're still at the office, I'll pick you up there."

"Sounds great." It did not sound great. I felt pushed. No. Not exactly pushed, just nudged. I didn't like the feeling, but I didn't dislike it enough to back out of our date.

I could hardly believe it, but I saw him almost every other night over the next two weeks. It began to feel like the beginnings of some kind of demonic possession. I did not like him choosing everything I ate, or that he was annoyed when I didn't take his calls during business hours, but for some crazy reason, at the end of the night, I could not resist him.

It had become a routine. After dinner, we would have one last drink on his terrace, drunk on night air, great wine, and the sheer magnitude and diversity of life all around us in the shimmering landscape of skyscrapers, water, and Lady Liberty. Juxtaposed with all that grandeur were his white leather interiors that led to a cardio workout in his beyond-the-pale gauche round bed with the tacky mirrored ceiling. Not only had good taste taken a holiday, so had good sense.

I continued coming home in the middle of the night and the next day more roses would arrive. The pink ones he sent to my home didn't bother me. They were beautiful, in fact. They were feminine and tender. Then the yellow ones arrived. Okay, I thought, these are cheerful. But when I was bombarded at the office with three dozen red ones after a night of breaking the world's endurance record for the Mattress Mambo Marathon, everybody had a comment.

"Are congratulations in order?" David Pinkham said.

"Yeah, who's the poor son of a gun?" Paul McGrath said. "When's the wedding?"

"You two are delusional," I said. "I'm never getting married."

"We used to call this a full-court press when I was a lad," Pinkham said.

McGrath wagged his finger at me. "*Somebody's* misbehaving." Then he winked at me and said, "Good for you!"

Somebody's exhausted, I thought. And I was.

For all the good my relationship with Vinny had done to relieve the anxiety of Adrian's departure and my return to Charleston, I also realized I had to quickly and efficiently put an end to it. That coming Saturday I was moving Adrian into his dorm room and I was leaving for Charleston on Monday. Needless to say, I had not heard from my father or my sister.

It was Friday night and Vinny and I were meeting for drinks. Afterward, I was going to have dinner with my son. Vinny and I were seated at a sidewalk table at La Goulue, one of *my* favorites for a change.

"So? Why can't I meet your boy?"

"Because it's not necessary, Vinny. There's no reason to complicate his life."

"How would that complicate his life?"

"Look, I never get my son involved with men I date. I like to keep my private life private."

"Oh! I'm sorry! Like I'm not part of your private life? What is this, Betts? Doesn't any of this, I mean, what we've been to each other, doesn't that mean anything to you?"

Vinny had been a diversion, a curiosity, a way to pass the time and exorcise the extraordinary stress under which I labored. He was also erotic in ways I had never known. The admission of his insignificance, however, would have been unkind and vulgar, and it would not have been entirely true. I would have loved to fall in love with someone—Vinny, Tom, Dick, or Harry. I just did not. Perhaps I could not. Naturally, I felt a certain amount of tenderness toward Vinny— probably a mélange of desire, loneliness, and fear of what waited for me in Charleston. But I did not love him. No, I did not love Vinny and never would.

"Oh, Vinny," I said, and sighed.

"What?" Vinny the Heartbreaker's cold heart of a hunter had fallen into the flames.

"Here's what I'm thinking."

He just stared at me and I watched his jaw set like a plaster mold. Vinny was getting angry.

"You're a wonderful man," I said. "A really wonderful man . . ."

"But?" A vein in his temple began to twitch.

"But timing is everything, isn't it? Look, we're not children here. You know, I'm leaving for a few months, my son's starting college . . ."

"So? I can't fly down there to see you? You won't be coming back? What are you saying? That I'm some kind of summer fling?"

"No! I'm saying that the time to bring my son into this relationship is very far away."

He calmed down immediately because what I said implied that perhaps there was a future for us. "Too soon?"

"Yeah. Too soon. What's the rush?"

"Yeah, you're right." He leaned back and drummed his fingers on the table. Then he smiled. "So you wanna grab a bite tomorrow night, after your boy is installed in his dorm?"

I thought about it for a moment and realized I might need the company. So, even though I recognized that accepting his invitation was a willful act of selfishness, I said, "Sure. Why not?"

CHAPTER EIGHT

Empty Nest

In raising Adrian, I had done everything right and everything wrong. I had been his champion in all academic and social arenas, made sure he stayed in excellent health, dressed him well, and loved him with all my might. And I had robbed him of eighteen Father's Days and every other kind of experience a boy has with his dad. How could I live with myself?

Adrian was taping boxes closed, packing up his life, the things that mattered most to him. Books, DVDs, CDs, socks, school supplies, sweaters, linens, a small assortment of kitchen and bathroom items, a reading lamp . . .

"I don't have a rug for my room," he said.

"Well, you're not going to college in Siberia, you know. And it's still hot outside."

We were both churlish and moody, unlike our normal selves. I knew that he was anxious to have the day over and done. By supper time he would know so much more about his immediate future and what it would require of him. Where were his classrooms? Would he get the professors he wanted? Would he like his roommate? Would he fit in? Could he handle it—a huge campus and so many strangers? And I was on the doorstep of a big bummer.

"True," he said. "I guess I should just wait and see what the deal is. I mean, I doubt if the floor is like just cold cement. I need a bulletin board, too."

"You can get one at the campus store, don't you think?" I said. "I'm gonna call the garage for the car."

"Yeah," he said, "I'm taking my clothes on hangers because I doubt if they have hangers."

"Good idea. Put a rubber band around the necks of everything so they don't go flying all over the road."

"Duh," he said. "Already thought of that."

"Right," I said, and thought this was not the moment to give him a reprimand for slinging a *duh* in my direction.

I didn't know what it was the moment *for,* except to press on as though it were a normal occurrence for my son to be moving out.

It was time to get the car. Our building was considered by Manhattan standards to have white-glove status, although it did not have a garage. I rented space around the corner, and because of the sheer volume of cars they juggled like sardines in their mine shaft of an underground garage, I always gave them about thirty minutes' notice when I wanted to liberate the Toyota. So I rang them and then called Sam the doorman to ask the superintendent to bring a dolly up the service elevator.

"He's not on today," Sam said. "Had a family christening or something. I can lock the front door and bring it up in a minute. How's that?"

"That would be great, Sam. Thanks."

I hung up the house phone and stopped again. Adrian had his expected level of reasonable anxiety, but I was beginning to panic. All at once I felt like something vital to my survival was being torn right out of my chest by the bare hands of a monster. I was not ready to let Adrian go. I didn't want to start hyperventilating, but I was already short of breath and could feel sweat on the back of my neck as I stared at the blue and gray tiles on my floor. My face was flushed and I wanted to sit right there at my kitchen counter and have a good cry. I cleared my throat and struggled hard to maintain self-control.

"Adrian? Bring the boxes to the kitchen and let's start stacking them up. Sam's coming with the dolly."

I picked up a framed photograph of Adrian and me that I kept on the kitchen windowsill, taken when he was about twelve. It must have been some important occasion—Aunt Jennie's birthday, I seemed to recall—and he was wearing a jacket and tie. So boyish and yet dressed like an adult. The signs of adulthood were there, like a sapling that already bore the look of the stately and solid tree it would someday become.

I stared again at the picture, and foolishly told myself that I hadn't changed much over the years. Each time I looked at this picture while doing dishes or chopping onions, each time I peered into it, thinking about how much my son meant to me, he was over on the sidelines, quietly growing into a young man. And now he was leaving me. As he should. It was right, yet I hated it. I was a selfish coward and I hated myself for that, too. I desperately wanted him to think well of me, but I reminded myself again that when the day of reckoning arrived, I would find myself floundering in a great lake of quicksand with no one to throw me a rope.

Thud! Adrian dropped a heavy box on the floor and turned to face me.

"You okay, Mom?"

"Yeah, I'm okay," I said, and took a deep breath. "Just thinking, that's all."

"Yeah, I know. Me, too. But like you said, I ain't going to Siberia."

At which point the back doorbell rang.

"Right," I said, and put the picture back on the sill. "Let's get this show on the road."

Adrian picked up the picture frame as I moved to open the door for Sam.

"You mind if I take this?"

"Of course not."

A part of me was deeply moved that he wanted a picture of me, of us really, for his room, and another part of me greatly wanted that twelve-year-old boy back in my arms. If we didn't load the dolly and get out of the building soon, I was going to dissolve into a puddle. Sam's presence was a godsend because I would never lose my composure in front of him. Sam and Adrian swung into action.

The next thing I knew, the car was packed to the hilt, Sam was shaking hands with Adrian, wishing him luck, and we were on our way up Central Park West toward the unfolding of my son's greatest dream. How could any mother worth her salt self-indulge in the face of that?

I was not surprised but still very relieved to see how organized the move was. Hundreds of volunteer students wearing identical T-shirts with a Columbia logo were on hand to help with everything. After Adrian checked in and got his key, the madness of unloading began. I waited in the car while Adrian and two nice-looking kids piled everything onto the sidewalk. Then I parked the car in a garage and returned to the designated spot. By the time I arrived, Adrian had secured a flatbed trolley and it was loaded to go. I followed him across the commons to Carman Hall. I hung back, letting Adrian chatter with the volunteers who were pointing out the student mailroom, theater, and Café 212, obviously named for Manhattan's area code.

Should I help him make his bed? No; I decided he would look like a baby to his roommates if I did. I concluded that the best course of action would be to follow Adrian's lead. At least that's what all the literature on the subject of "letting go" had advised. For one of the few occasions in my life, I was heeding the advice of others.

He opened the door of his room and pulled in the mountain of his belongings.

"Let's dump this stuff ASAP," the volunteer named Jacob from Milwaukee said. "They aren't enough trolleys to go around."

"There never are," groaned Mitzi, the bubbly redhead from Cleveland. "Move-in day is a nightmare," she said to me, and rolled her gigantic, unnaturally blue eyes.

Cosmetic contact lenses, I thought.

"I'll bet," I said, wondering if she slept around, and if she did, if she removed her lenses, and how much of her self-esteem was tied up in that shade of electric blue?

All the cartons came off the trolley; Adrian shook hands with his roommate, George Somebody from Richmond, Virginia, who had arrived yesterday; the trolley, Mitzi, and Jacob disappeared; and I had never felt more like a fifth wheel since high school.

"Okay! So, Adrian? What can I do to help?" I asked, with forced perkiness.

"I'm good, Mom. I can handle it."

He had no groceries, no books, and his bedroom resembled a catacomb. A very small catacomb. How would he adapt?

"You got money?" I said.

"Yep."

"You sure? Do you have your cell-phone charger? ATM card?"

"Yep."

"I just went through this with my folks yesterday," George piped in.

I wanted to say, "Listen, punk, I'm having a moment here and I don't need your advice," but I remained silent and just smiled serenely, remembering that my job was to make this transition easy for Adrian.

"Really, Mom. I'll be fine. I'll call you if I need anything. I swear."

"Okay, then. Give me a hug!"

I gave him something resembling a chiropractic adjustment and I could feel he was damp with perspiration. Nerves? The heat? Probably both.

"I'll call you tonight," he said.

"Okay, then," I said. I stopped at the door and took a business card from my wallet, handing it to George. "My cell's on there. If either one of you need a thing . . ."

"Don't worry, Mrs. McGee. I did two years at Avon in Connecticut. I'll show Adrian the ropes, and if anything goes bad, I'll call you."

He said this as though he had done a stint in the Big House rather than an exclusive boys' school.

"Thanks, George. Okay, then," I said for the third time. "Love you, son. Good luck!"

I wanted him to remember me smiling bravely on my departure so that later, when I died in a plane crash, he would remember me fondly, grateful that I had not mortified him and had let him go into the next phase of his life with some grace and dignity.

Walking down the hall toward the elevator, I decided that George the Wiseass might have had some redeeming qualities after all. That was how I made it to the parking garage without weeping like a fool. I told myself that George had learned how to live independent of parents. Everything was going to be all right.

Everything *was* going to be all right and I knew it, but I still had a serious case of the blues. The best thing to do in this case, I told myself, was to call Sela. I drove my car out of the parking lot, pulled over to the curb, punched in her cell number, and hit send.

"Praise God for cell phones," I said, sobbing when I heard her voice. "What if I couldn't find you when I needed you?"

"Betts? Is that you?"

"Yes, it's me! Oh God . . ."

"Honey? What's wrong?"

"I just left Adrian in his nasty, skanky dorm room! I

know it's stupid to be weeping like a fool, but I can't help it!"
My whole face was wet.

"Oh, crap. I forgot today was the day. Oh, shit, Betts. It's
not stupid. It's okay. Really it is."

"No! It's not!"

"I know . . ."

Witness another reason why Sela O'Farrell was such an
exemplary citizen of the world. She listened. She understood.
Her patience seemed endless. I ran on like dangerous white
water, my speech rapid and my thoughts jumbled, telling
her about everything from my family's unreturned phone
call to my serious reservations about Vinny to how it broke
my heart to leave Adrian.

"Look. You want my opinion?" she asked after I'd about
exhausted myself.

"Of course I do."

"I think putting your only child in college and returning
for two or three months to the freaking emotional quagmire
that you left behind in addition to dumping a possible thug
of a boyfriend *is* a lot for one week. Even for you."

"I have to tell Vinny tonight that it's over, at least for a
while, but I don't know what I'm going to say."

"Since when can't you unload a guy with some finesse?"

"Since now. I've never had one so determined to own me
as Vinny. Sela, he scares me a little. I know I'm gonna be
there in Charleston, somewhere, working or having dinner,
and I'll suddenly look up or over to see his face. No warning. Nothing. He'll just be there. And if I'm not thrilled out
of my mind to see him, he might get crazy. I don't think he's
ever been the dumpee. He's always the dumper."

"He's a hothead, huh?"

"Yeah. Big macho Italian ego the size of, I don't know,
Texas."

"Texas. Good one. If it was me . . . ? I'd let him down
easy and leave the future vague."

"That's what I'm figuring. But still . . . I don't know. I'm
probably being dramatic." I knew I was not being dramatic.

"Let me know how it goes. Well, you know, there *is* a glimmer of good news in all this."

"Tell it."

"I got you a two-bedroom condo on the water at Wild Dunes. It's such a score and it has drop-dead views."

"What would I do without you?"

"Probably die, but that's okay. I'll meet you at the airport and give you the keys."

"Oh, honey, you don't have to do that! Just leave them at the gate. You've done enough!"

"Right. The best friend of my life is returning to Charleston and I'm just leaving the keys at the gate. I don't think so. By the way, you flying commercial?"

"Can't. I'm packing like I'm going on safari. How's the weather?"

"Sopping-wet muggy? Blistering scorching heat? A travel brochure from the bottom floor of hell doesn't do it justice. Pack naked."

With that, we hung up, promising to speak the next day. I had finally stopped crying, and after hearing Sela's description of the weather, I actually found myself laughing, accepting the fact that my body and my hair were going to have some adjusting to do when I reached Charleston. And when I began to work in the savage jungles of Bulls Island, I was going to look like Nature Woman. Well, I knew it was good for at least a five-pound drop in weight.

It was around five when I pulled into the garage and walked back to my building. As I did so I noticed a man standing on the corner observing my approach. He flipped open his cell phone, made a speed-dial call, turned, and walked away. Was I being watched? The very thought of it made my skin run with goose bumps.

There were piles of clothes I intended to take to Charleston all over the bed in my room. Two months would be my minimum stay, and I thought, well, if I needed anything more than what I was packing, I could either fly home or buy it down there. It's not like I was going to Siberia, I thought, and that reminded me of Adrian saying he could be home for dinner in fifteen minutes, if need be. But given my business assignment in Charleston, I might as well *be* in Siberia as far as fixing dinner for my son was concerned.

Actually, where I was going was more a version of the Roman Colosseum than Siberia. I would be facing off against metaphorical man-eating lions and literal alligators, pretending to be businesslike and competent when all the while I'd be quivering with self-doubt. The timing of this trip was terrible.

Ben Bruton was always reminding me that developers were notorious crooks, payoffs were hidden in almost every aspect of the deal, and I'd need to go over every detail with a fine-tooth comb. If we ordered quarter-inch plywood, I had better carry a tape measure with me to check its width. Like I could really do this? But I would have to try.

I had plans to return for parents' weekend at Columbia, and no doubt I would, but what would happen between now and then . . . seeing J.D., my father and sister . . . These imaginings were the cause of so many stomachaches and restless nights, I cannot begin to tell you. *Anxious* had taken on new meaning. And what had I done? How was I, Ms. Sophistication and Righteousness, handling all of it? I had chosen the ostrich approach and buried myself in Vinny Braggadocio's bed. Pretty shameful. And now there was someone watching my comings and goings? Maybe I was going crazy.

My head filled with such thoughts, I took a shower and dressed for dinner, having arranged with Vinny to call for me at seven-thirty. We were having dinner uptown at Rao's, a wildly popular restaurant where customers had to die or move to Finland to make room for new ones. Vinny was very proud of the fact that he knew the restaurant's number by heart and that he could always get a table on Tuesday at eight. A good table, where he could be seen by celebrities and power brokers, all of them spellbound by the heady aromas of linguini with red clam sauce. I had never been there because it had always seemed like too much trouble, but I was excited to see the place.

Speaking of visiting new places, Vinny had yet to see the inside of my apartment, not that I would have objected if he had wanted to. But I knew there was some inexplicable bug in Vinny's psyche that prevented him from crossing the threshold of a Park Avenue co-op. In a way I understood this, because such buildings could be intimidating, but it wasn't like anyone would actually insult him or sniff at him. People in my building sniffed because of allergies to cat dander or because their deviated-septum surgeries had been unsuccessful. Their self-absorbed bubbles seldom deigned to make contact with their neighbors' self-absorbed bubbles. Had Charles Manson been in the elevator with them, they would have examined their cuticles just as they did with everyone else. Paradoxically, I found this kind of systemic arrogance one of the more appealing features of my building. Being invisible gave one a comfortable sense of privacy. It made my apartment building feel like a private house.

It was seven-thirty. When Sam rang to tell me that Vinny was downstairs, I was just turning off lights and checking to see that the stove was off, the normal list of things I would do before I went out for the evening. I had a lump in my throat because of the things I needed to discuss with Vinny. The discomfort I felt with him was growing, like an angry incoming tide across a shore. I was okay in my mind as long as there was a lot of beach between me and the water, but there loomed a great possibility that the ocean would soon cover the land and I would be drowned.

Vinny had no idea what I'd be facing in Charleston. We didn't talk about me very much. I thought, well, for the sake of honesty and integrity, such as it was, I would attempt to give him a reasonable explanation of why I needed time off for good behavior . . . On second thought, that term might ring too many bells with him.

I went down the elevator accompanied by the coiffed, emaciated corpse who lived in Eleven West. I lived in Nine

East. The apartments in the west line of the building were larger, implying greater wealth and importance. Therefore, according to the unspoken protocols, East did not speak first. East would nod, and if West wanted to engage, West would make an innocuous remark, and further remarks could then be exchanged.

West cleared her throat and said without emotion, "I heard your son's going to Columbia."

"Yes, he is. I moved him into his dormitory today."

"Yes, I know because the front door was locked when I came in this afternoon. Sam is not supposed to leave his station, you know. Co-op rules."

"Sam frequently locks the door to drop off your Sherry-Lehman deliveries."

Sherry-Lehman was the specialty wine merchant around the corner and West was a wino of house renown. West shot me a daggers-filled glance and I shot her one back. The door opened. We stepped out and sized each other up.

"Well, you must be very proud of your son," she said. "Congratulations."

"I am. Thank you."

She walked away. I walked away. In the building, everyone knew everyone and no one knew anyone. Perhaps life had given Eleven West valid reasons to polish off a bottle or so every night. You see, we put our garbage by the service elevator at the same time each morning and hers always made a distinctive clunk. It was always fascinating to me what you could learn just from the sound of someone's garbage.

Vinny was parked by the curb. Sam opened the door for me and I got in. Vinny was wearing so much cologne I thought I might have an asthma attack.

"Hey! You look good. So how did it go?"

"Like an amputation."

"Sounds like somebody could use a vodka with cranberry and a slice of lime."

"Isn't that how cosmos started?"

"Whodahell knows? Hey, we're going to a private party. Frankie's wife's birthday. Don't worry; I got her a bottle of smell swell."

"Oh. I didn't realize we were going to a party."

"This ain't like a regular party. You'll see."

I had preconceived notions of what dinner at Rao's would be like. I thought it would be like a mafioso hangout, a former speakeasy, or a funky joint, jammed with tables and old guys who all knew one another. Well, it had been all those things at one time or another in its history, but it turned out to be a good deal more than that. As we arrived we were greeted by one of the owners.

"Vinny! How are you? Thanks for coming!"

"Fraaaaan-kie. Like I'd miss your wife's birthday?" Vinny made a fake pout and then gave Frankie a little punch in the arm. "Who else could get you guys to open up the doors on a Saturday night? Here, I brought her a little something . . ." He handed the gift bag he was holding to Frankie, who handed it off to a minion.

"And who's this?" Frankie said, meaning me.

"This? This lovely lady is Betts McGee! I can't believe you two don't know each other."

"We go way back," Frankie said, addressing me and nodding toward Vinny. "My old man used to play stickball with his old man. That's a long time ago."

Frankie was a good-looking devil if ever I saw one. And Rao's? From the moment we stepped in, we went hurling back in time to the 1920s or maybe the 1950s. You could hear Jerry Lewis telling a joke and Frank Sinatra humming a tune. It was as if every person who had ever been there had left some piece of themselves behind in the time warp that was Rao's.

We made the rounds, saying hello to everyone who seemed to know Vinny well, and smiling widely, all the while I was worrying about my dreaded conversation with him. Obviously it would have to wait. But if all these well-heeled folks seemed so honestly happy to see Vinny among them, maybe I was acting in haste to say it was over between us.

We were seated at a table with another couple, older, who knew Vinny's parents, and they began to tell stories about the old days, the street festivals at Our Lady of St. Carmel's and how, during Prohibition, Rao's had run homemade wine from the building next door through a hose in the basement and sold it for a dollar a bottle. We began to eat and drink and all the while people came and went from our table to the next, spreading goodwill, while I faded into the paneling, which was perfectly fine with me. The food was absolutely delicious, the toasts were heartfelt, and whatever snippets of conversation I managed to have with the older lady next to me were perfectly charming. Unknowingly and without preparation, I had stepped into Vinny's world at its best, and had a wonderful, warm, boisterous evening whose only agenda was to have a great time feting Frankie's wife.

Crazy Vinny. Maybe not so crazy after all. I began to doubt my judgment and thought it might be better to leave things as they were and deal with Vinny on an as-needed basis. I would go to Charleston, and if he wanted to visit, I would find a way to wiggle out of it. He would get the message. He might be crass, but he was no dummy.

But it wasn't to be that easy. On Sunday we had brunch downtown at Pastis, and over Bloody Marys and eggs Benedict, he began to ask the impossible questions.

"So, you're leaving tomorrow?" he said.

"Yes. Three o'clock wheels up."

"When am I gonna see you again? You want me to fly down next weekend?"

"Vinny . . . I'd love to show you Charleston, but I have a pretty complicated agenda in front of me." I swirled a piece of the English muffin around in Hollandaise sauce, hoping he would just let the subject drop.

"So whaddaya saying?"

I looked up at him with what I hoped was an expression that said, *Please try to understand, without making me spell out the details.*

Lockjawed and clearly angered, he slammed his napkin on the table, got up, and walked out.

CHAPTER NINE

Betts Is Back

I could deal with any burly honcho from a teamsters' union without flinching. I could do an assessment of a hundred-million-dollar company that was hemorrhaging cash, roll a few heads, and turn it around to a profit without breaking a sweat. I could deal with all sorts of things in the world of business and never lose sleep. But as my plane approached Charleston and the Corporate Wings jet strip and we waited for clearance to land, the hard ball of a knot I had in my stomach was killing me. I was terrified.

We came to a quick stop, my right foot touched the steps, the humidity grabbed my hair, and the heat slammed my whole body. The porters blithely unloaded my luggage onto a trolley as though it were a perfect spring day. My hair was turning into corkscrew pasta on steroids. Fusilli Head. That was me.

After my conversation with Sela, I hadn't really packed all that much, but I knew enough to bring clothes to layer, as the weather in Charleston was very changeable during hurricane season. Hurricane season. Yeah, boy, I was back in

Charleston and small-craft warnings were in effect until further notice.

Through the glass doors of the terminal, I spotted Sela waving, a welcome deliverance from my inner turbulence. I picked up my pace to greet her. May as well get the show on the road, I said to myself, thanking God she was there. And to think I had not wanted her to go to the trouble to meet me. What had I been thinking?

She pushed the door open and stepped out onto the tarmac. Her whole face was smiling.

"Hey you!"

She threw her arms open wide for a sisterly bear hug, complete with backslapping and giggles. I hugged her back and thought, Good grief, it felt like I had not seen her in a thousand years. It had been a long time, but to my surprise, she had not changed in any significant way.

"Look at you! You look fabulous!" I said.

"Oh, please, I'm an old thaing . . ."

"Then what does that make me?"

"Girl? You got so much on your plate you don't even know it!"

"What?"

We were going through the tiny terminal at a clip, my luggage piled high behind me.

"All will be revealed. I'm parked right out front."

"Great. More problems to deal with? Worse than facing my father, my maniac sister, my once-future mother-in-law, and oh, let's not forget the father of my child? What could be worse than that?"

"Um . . . you're right."

"So, who cares? No matter what's happening, it can't be any worse than what I've dealt with in the past. Lemme tell you, it's tough out there in the world. Gosh, it's good to see you!"

"You're right. I should relax. I forgot that you're a Xena clone."

"My costume is in the hanging bag."

We loaded my four suitcases, laptop, duffel bag, and hanging bag and in minutes we were off, headed for the Isle of Palms.

"So, okay. Read these. And did I tell you that Big Jim had a heart attack?"

"No! Is he okay?"

"Of course! Honey, that man is gonna bury us all."

Sela handed me a manila envelope containing a small stack of recent op-ed pieces and articles from the *Post & Courier* and the *State*.

"Still, that's too bad. What happened?"

"Let's just say it could have been embarrassing, as he was in a compromising position, but of course the long arm of Langley spin control put the kibosh on details. I heard it from my good friend who's an ER nurse at MUSC."

"Figures."

I began glancing through the articles. To say that public sentiment was against the development of Bulls Island would be putting it mildly. It appeared that every organization from the Nature Conservancy to the South Carolina Coastal Conservation League was vehemently opposed to it. Every single solitary suddenly-green-thinking local- and state-level politician jockeying for reelection had grown a conscience overnight and was foaming at the mouth, rabid with outrage at the prospect of a further rape of the land.

"Boy, there's nothing like a little development project to get the South to rise again, is there?" I asked.

"Hmmph."

"How come no one complained this loudly about developing Daniel Island or Kiawah?"

"Dunno. Perhaps they were blissful in their ignorance at the time? Who knows? Listen, you're walking into the cause du jour and I'm just giving you this stuff as heads-up."

"Great. Thanks. Well, maybe someone will buy Capers Island to develop and divert attention from this."

Sela shot me a sideways glance that said, Yeah, sure.

"Well? One can dream?"

"You're right. You're dreaming."

We continued chatting away like long-lost girlfriends do. Her business was doing great. Ed was fine, but she worried about his safety constantly. He had just broken a major drug ring that was importing cocaine from the Philippines in tightly wrapped Ziplocs concealed in five-gallon jars of mango puree.

"How bizarre!" I said. "Mango puree?"

"Yeah, for ice cream and margarita mixes, I guess. Anyway, there was something funky about the X-rays, so they notified Ed, who notified SLED, who notified, I don't know, the freaking FBI? Yeah, it was all over the papers. But he scares the hell out of me sometimes." [SLED was the acronym for South Carolina Law Enforcement.]

"Scares me, too."

"Right? But then, you know Ed! He gets to talking about when he played for the Falcons? God, these men love to relive gridiron glory, don't they?"

"All men are boys."

"Isn't that the truth? But he says there's nothing scarier than a three-hundred-pound linebacker raging toward you, planning to rip your head off with his bare hands. I guess it sort of puts risk and danger in their proper perspective. This stuff was just in a container shipment. To him it was no big deal. But that's not what I worry about."

"What do you worry about?"

"I worry about guns. I worry about guns a lot. And homemade bombs and stuff like that."

"What a world."

"You can say that again."

I looked out the window at the gorgeous landscape, thinking about what Sela had just said. It was true that Ed didn't walk a beat or drive a patrol car, but he was in a big enough position that somebody with a grudge and a gun could try to end his life anytime they wanted to. Scary.

The marsh on either side of the road was so beautiful. I thought about that and the wildlife and was more than a little apprehensive to be involved in its destruction. Although the first shovel of dirt had yet to be lifted, it was clear that the Bulls Island project was going to need a serious PR campaign and the entire project needed a comprehensive review.

Soon we were pulling through the security gate of Wild Dunes, and within minutes I was dragging my suitcases, bumping up each step to my new home for the foreseeable future. Sela, with a duffel over her shoulder and a rolling bag in tow, opened the front door and tossed me the keys.

"Welcome home," she said. "I even bought you some groceries!"

"Sela? I'm going to have to give you a kidney or something. This is gorgeous!"

It *was* gorgeous—for a rental, that is. At the far end of the living room were sofas and chairs, the requisite metal-framed sliding glass doors that opened to a reasonably sized balcony overlooking the ocean. On the close end of the room was a glass-top table with eight armchairs on wheels, and behind that was an open kitchen that was more than adequate for the amount of cooking I would probably ever do. I guessed whoever owned the condo had chosen a decorator's prefab package because no part-time resident would have been able to find the wide range of Wedgwood-blue fabrics that covered every upholstered surface or so much distressed-bamboo furniture. It wasn't my taste, but for a temporary home, it was just fine.

"The master bedroom is over here and there is another bedroom upstairs with a storage room that I guess could have been a third bedroom, but who knows? Maybe they have their old crazy aunt Tillie locked up in there."

"Well, this *is* the South," I said, and we laughed at that.

"Actually, Mizzy Betts, we don't do that anymore down here in God's country. We Dippity-Do their pin curls, buy them a new housecoat, and send them off to *Jerry Springer.*"

"Think about those poor people. Disgusting." There was a desk in the living room and I was already unpacking and hooking up my laptop and the chargers for my BlackBerry and my digital camera.

"Seriously. So tell me, did you ever talk to your dad?"

"Nope. He never called me back. Can you believe that?"

"No kidding," Sela said, and shook her head. "What a sin."

"I know. That tells me a lot."

"Maybe. Or maybe your crazy sister picked up the message and never even told him you called."

"Possible. Why in the world would Joanie do that?"

"Well, let's see. There are two possibilities. One, she's the one with dementia, or two, she didn't want him to know you called."

"I've got a hunch that I should go with knucklehead," I said, knowing in my heart that she hadn't told him I called.

"Good choice. Just call him again, then. If you run into him without him knowing you're here, it would be very embarrassing for both of you."

"You're absolutely right. I've been in a petulant funk about it, but unfortunately I think you might be on to Joanie."

"And, FYI? Your sister? I've seen her around town with much older companions lately."

"Oh Lord. She just can't get that daddy-worship thing of hers under control, can she?"

"Who said they were men?"

"Holy crap. Sela? You think she's gay?"

"I think she's a lonely dowdy frump who would be grateful for any and all attention."

"I'll add her to my list of puzzles to decipher. Good grief."

"So when are you going to see *himself*?"

"You mean J.D.?"

"No, I mean freaking Kaptain Kangeroo. *Yes,* I mean J.D.!"

"After I get my hair completely flat-ironed and find some makeup that won't melt. That will probably be Wednesday." Two days from now. I said it as though seeing J.D. would be nothing of consequence, but Sela knew better. We had been reading each other's mind for over twenty years.

"Umm!" she said in a cautionary tone, and wagged a finger at me.

"You said it. You know it's so funny because part of me can't wait to lay eyes on him and another part of me is dreading it."

"I'm sure. Small prediction here . . ."

"What?"

"Your hormones and your conscience are about to get a workout. Come on, drive me back to the city."

On the way to the island, Sela insisted that I use her SUV during my stay, saying she and Ed had four cars that just sat around all day and it was stupid to blow the money on a rental. I didn't want her to know that I had an expense account the size of our national debt, so I accepted. It was another very thoughtful gesture. I would send her flowers for the restaurant every week.

We talked constantly on the short ride back to the city, trying to squeeze everything into the short time we shared. Topics were skimmed over. Like how did I really feel about J.D.? Hard to say. Was I ever going to be emotionally prepared to see him? No. We both knew that to be true.

When I dropped her off in front of her restaurant, I got out to give her a hug.

"Thanks for everything, Sela. Really."

"Ah, it was nothing. Why don't you come back for dinner?"

"Oh, gosh. Thanks for the offer, but I want to get unpacked, check my e-mail, call Sandi and Dad, and start bracing up."

"Well, you're welcome here every night, if you can stand the fare! The food's about the same as it's always been."

I got back into the car and closed the door. "It's the company and the seal of the confessional I'll be needing," I said in my best Irish brogue.

"Anytime!" She waved, blew me a kiss, and disappeared through the doors of O'Farrell's.

All the way back to the beach, I sort of blanked out and let myself fall under the spell of Charleston and its natural grandeur—the smells of the marsh, the clusters of snowy egrets, the sparkle of the Cooper River. Charleston was the quintessential chameleonic dowager queen of cities if ever one existed. Over three hundred years old and every bit as beautiful as the day she was born. In fact, she was more interesting for all she had seen and all she knew. She was sultry, determined, cultured, and wise beyond any other American city because the sons and daughters of Charleston knew what mattered—taking care of their mother. Mother Charleston was going to tan my hide if I allowed the Bulls Island project to turn out like some others had.

The first thing I did when I got back to the condo was call Sandi. She was at her brother's in Summerville. I had grabbed Sandi from Human Resources for two reasons. She understood everything like a true psychic and, by coincidence, she was from South Carolina, the land of my people.

"Ah! So you've arrived," she exclaimed. "Great! We have about a bazillion and one things to go over!"

"I'm sure! But I'm just as sure you have it all under control. I'll see you first thing in the morning . . . unless you need me now?"

"Nope, I copied you on some e-mails, but not to worry, just get yourself squared away because the work's not going anywhere."

"What's on top of the agenda?"

"Gatorzilla and trying to catch the sucker. Ever since the Department of Wildlife guys began looking for him, he's been hiding. But they've already moved over a hundred alligators to Capers. And a mess of cougars or bobcats or some kind of killer cat."

"A mess of? You're acclimated!"

"Still! Who wants that job? Can you imagine trying to humanely capture critters who would just as soon eat you for lunch?"

"Nope, but well, it's a noble beginning. I'll see you in the morning."

I hung up wondering if the natural habitat of Capers could sustain the alligators and made a note to check it out. It probably could, but I wasn't sure, and should their numbers begin to decline, that was the kind of detail that would kill the project. Alligator lovers would unite and come after us with a vengeance. Worse, what if they could walk back to Bulls Island at low tide like you could walk from DeBordieu to Pawleys? I wasn't even going to bring that up to anyone.

I opened my hanging bag and began to put my clothes in the closet, shaking them out, as the incredible humidity had crept its way in between all the zippers, turning every piece of linen into a slightly damp dishrag. Suddenly I could smell all the dry-cleaning fluids in my clothes and it made me gag. It couldn't be healthy to have all those chemicals on your skin, I thought. I wondered then if I would even wear any of the clothes I had brought because they all looked wrong.

Next my curiosity took me to the pillows, the linens on the bed, and the towels in the bathroom. I threw back the bedspread—blue swirls on beige with nylon batting to provide backing for the quilting. The backing was covered with picks and pulls. Not okay. The sheets were so thin you could read a book through them and the pillows were lumpy fiber-fill foam, slept on by a thousand heads. I knew even before I tried one that the bath towels couldn't cover the backside of a four-year-old. It was no surprise that there was no soap dish, bathroom glass, or tissue-box cover. Renters have a reputation for stealing everything, so what is usually supplied is of the lowest reasonable quality. And everything wears out so quickly because who's there to tell them not to take the bedspread to the beach or to use the pots to make sand castles?

If not tonight then tomorrow, I was headed to Bed Bath & Beyond to drop a few dollars because I freely admit that at this point in my life, I wasn't going without some basic creature comforts. Rental linens were not even remotely as nice as hotel linens. Besides, when the job was all over, I could give whatever I bought to Dad, assuming he would even accept a contribution from me, or I could ship a box home.

I wasn't fooling myself. It was already after six o'clock and I was doing everything in the world to avoid picking up my cell phone and calling Dad. But on reconsidering the possibility that my sister was the cause of his silence, my warrior gene became inflamed. I dialed his number. He answered right away and my anxiety dissolved. I was thrilled and relieved to hear that his voice sounded so robust.

"Dad? It's me, Betts. The prodigal daughter?"

Gasp and then silence. Not a good sign, so I just plunged ahead.

"I know you probably don't want to see me, I mean, I knew that when you didn't return my call—"

"What? What call?"

"I called you a couple of weeks ago."

"I never got any message from you. I . . . I mean, you say you called a couple of weeks ago?"

"Yes. I did."

The silence that hung between us told him that there may have been other occasions when I had tried to reach out to them. Of course there were. Anything else would have been unnatural.

"Betts, I don't know what to say . . ."

Without uttering a single word, we knew it was Joanie who had thwarted my efforts to reach him. Then I thought with a rush of nausea, What about his side of the story? Had he given Joanie birthday cards over the years to mail to me that she had simply thrown away? Christmas gifts? Letters? Had she denied knowing my cell-phone number or my office number? What kind of despotic megalomaniac had she really become?

"Just tell me that I can come see you, Daddy. I want to see you."

I could hear the whole truth in his long sigh of surrender and disappointment.

"Of course you can. I have missed you, girl. Missed you with all my heart. I thought you had . . . I thought you stopped loving me."

"Oh, Daddy! No! And I thought you had stopped loving me."

"Never."

The hourglass had turned over and the sands were now running in my direction. It was my time to receive my father's love again. But regaining his affection and trust was not going to happen with the snap of my fingers or his. I hadn't been available for all those years. Had he tried to find me? Ever? I did not know. Maybe he had. Perhaps he had given up when his efforts to find me were met with no response. It was clear that we were going to have to confront Joanie.

Joanie. The family terrorist. Perhaps Daddy had developed some minor version of the Stockholm syndrome, but now in this conversation, from one second to the next, I could feel his defenses coming down like a house of cards that was waiting for a strong wind and would have settled for a breeze.

"Are you in Charleston?" he asked.

I told him yes, I was, and that I would be for a month or two or maybe longer. I could hear him sigh again, but it was a sigh of possibilities. He asked me when I wanted to get together and I suggested dinner at O'Farrell's the following night. He said he would be there at six and then he started to cry. He was silently admitting that he knew Sela had always known where I was. The ugly truth was that he had made no effort to contact me through her and had allowed Joanie to take over his life. But in deference to the many unknown facts, I said nothing. What was the point?

"I thought I had lost you forever, Betts. Those damn good-for-nothing Langleys and all the heartbreak they have caused. I hope they all burn in hell." He had conveniently shifted the blame to the Langleys and I did not argue the point. We would sort out the truth at a later date . . . somehow.

I choked up and then sniffed loudly. "Well, Daddy? I hope they *all* don't burn in hell, but I've got a short list of candidates if the Lord wants to know."

He sniffed, too, and then he sort of chuckled. "Starting with that no-good Louisa, am I right?"

"Yes, sir. She'd scare the hell out of the devil himself. Daddy? I can't wait to see you."

"Me, too, sweetheart. Me, too."

"Want to bring Joanie?" Loaded question.

"I'll ask her and we'll see."

We hung up and my mind was racing. Had he become so dependent on Joanie that he would have gone to his dust without ever asking Sela to tell him where I was? What possible motivation could he have for such inaction? Once more, I decided to put it all aside.

Tomorrow night, I would start by telling him that I loved him and that I wanted him back. Those words had not been a part of my plan because, first of all, I had no plan and, second, that statement would probably lead to other painful revelations. But I had not expected him to become so emotional or so accepting when we spoke. Hearing his voice crack—just hearing his voice at all after so long—nearly made me fall to the floor with weakness. Joanie aside for the moment, he was all I had left, and just as important, he was all I had left of my mother.

How could we have let this terrible separation happen? Had we been so overwhelmed by the drama of the moment? Yes, *I* had been, but how could I have let so many years go by, years of my stupidity, my fears, my frustrations . . . no, it didn't matter anymore because the most important step had been taken—the first one, the one where I did battle for myself.

Joanie or no Joanie, Langleys be damned, he was still my father and we could redraw the terms of a new relationship without anyone's permission or approval. I burst into tears and sat down on the ugly worn comforter that covered the lumpy bed, the one where I would doubtlessly struggle to find sleep. I wept. But these were tears of relief. The first major obstacle had been cleared—maybe not like an Olympic champion, but cleared nonetheless.

Finally, I got up and continued putting things away, but I stopped when I opened the closets and smelled the musky scent of salt in wood. Nice for a candle, not so great in lingerie. I added shelf paper to my mental list. I emptied as many suitcases as I could until I could no longer ignore the growling of my stomach. I was famished.

I put my makeup and toiletries in the bathroom and looked in the mirror. I had a long road ahead of me, but wasn't it worth it? Yes, I told myself it was. I washed my face, reapplied a little makeup, grabbed an apple, and left.

I should have been exhausted, but I was strangely invigorated, like I'd caught a second wind while running a marathon. Deciding that order and familiarity would make me happiest, I swung around over the connector bridge to the Towne Centre Mall. I knew I would find everything I needed there. Within an hour, Sela's SUV was loaded once again and now I was truly ravenous. So without going home, I took Rifle Range Road to Coleman Boulevard and headed for Sullivans Island. They say that when in doubt, you should retreat to the familiar, so I did.

Monday night on Sullivans Island was pretty quiet, even during the heat of the summer. I had no problem finding a parking spot in front of Station Twenty-two Restaurant. I locked the car and went inside. One of the other nice things about the islands was that I didn't have to worry about theft. The car had an alarm system and what self-respecting thief wanted pink sheets and towels anyway?

They were just closing the kitchen, but because I must have seemed a little pitiful, they seated me anyway. Jessie, the very attractive manager, took one look at me and knew I was from out of town.

"Can I get you something to drink?" she said with a smile.

"Yes, thanks. Ice water and a big glass of Sauvignon Blanc."

"Had yourself a day, huh?"

"Unbelievable. I haven't been here in twenty years. I think the last time I was here this place had just opened."

"I'll get that drink order right away. We're out of the crab cakes, but the flounder is fabulous. I'll be right back." She handed me the menu and walked away to the bar.

I looked over the offerings. Aunt Mattie's Crab Cakes, Crispy Whole Flounder, the Paradise Burger, Island Fried Seafood, hmm—it all looked good, but one thing was certain, for dessert I knew I was blowing the diet on Uncle William's Brownie Fudge Pie.

"Did you decide?" Jessie said, placing the glass of wine in front of me.

"It all looks great, but I think I'll go with the flounder. I haven't had flounder in forever."

"Well, you won't be disappointed," she said pleasantly, and took my order to the computer to enter it.

She had great bone structure in her face and I thought, Wow, I'll bet when she's seventy she's going to still look fifty. Lucky!

After I practically Hoovered the fish, all the vegetables, two pieces of hot cheese bread, and Uncle William's fudge pie, I paid my bill and waddled out. Fabulous, fabulous.

I drove back to Wild Dunes and to my lovely condo and threw the new sheets and mattress cover in the washing machine. It was around ten. Too early to nap on the couch and I wasn't a big fan of television. I called Adrian and he was studying, could he call me tomorrow? And, yes, he was fine, please don't worry.

I decided to open the balcony doors and step outside. It was a gorgeous night, the ocean was roaring and the sky was lit with countless diamonds. I decided then that like all the islands that dotted the coastline of South Carolina, this had to be the sexiest and most hypnotic place on the planet. I stood there for a while just listening and watching the stars winking at me, telling me the roller coaster was waiting, did I have my ticket?

CHAPTER TEN

Remember Me?

Triangle Equity. That's what we were calling ourselves for the Bulls Island Project. We had formed a separate corporation whose principal stockholder—actually, the *only* stockholder—was ARC. I was on my way to the office, which was rented space downtown—just three rooms, but I was excited to see it.

Traffic was terrible. When I was a teenager I could fly from the end of Isle of Palms to the cradle of Charleston, also known as the Holy City, in twenty minutes and now I was crawling along Highway 17 South like a turtle commuter on the Long Island Expressway. What was this boom of traffic all about? I mused over this and then remembered reading somewhere that Mount Pleasant was the seventh or tenth fastest-growing town in America. All you had to do was look around to see what it meant. Live oaks, hundreds of years old, were being destroyed and every kind of wooded area mowed down in the name of housing developments and shopping malls. It bothered me.

In fact, the whole thing bothered me and I didn't know why or by what wave of a magic wand I had grown such a grand social conscience over Bulls Island and housing developments. Maybe I just wanted to come back to Charleston and find everything the same as it had been when I left. Wasn't the whole mantra of Charleston and indeed of South Carolina to preserve, preserve, preserve?

I didn't understand why there had to be a fifty-thousand-square-foot grocery store flanked by a string of chain stores everywhere I turned. No question I was sensitive to grocery stores because of my family's mercantile history, but every time I passed a branded mall I wondered how an immigrant today could come to America and live his dream, make a profit, support his family, or be a part of a neighborhood. Maybe there were still places even in the Charleston area where one could set up shop, but I had yet to see them and did not expect to.

I was sickened by the visual blight I was passing on Highway 17, with frontage roads and strip mall after strip mall. There was something so wrong about it. I could remember when Mount Pleasant was a little fishing village with charm and personality. Who had planned this mess? Obviously someone with no regard for the face and fabric of the town. Where could a mother roll a stroller, stop for a sandwich, or run into a friend? Where was a shaded area? Where was the landscaping? A little park? No, there was nothing. And was I any better than the ruiners of this town if I was involved in the Bulls Island Project? I had better be.

Again I remembered my first conversation with Ben Bruton and how flabbergasted I was that Bulls Island had been sold. It hadn't seemed possible. But if anyone had told me twenty years ago that Mount Pleasant would come to this, I would have had the same reaction.

As I drove along the highway, I tried to sort out my feelings. My primary reason for hesitating to take on this assignment had been nervousness over returning to Charleston. The magnitude of the emotional problems I faced knowing that I had to deal with the Langleys reduced my issues with my father and sister to a teaspoon of chopped chives. At first, the thought of confronting J.D. or Louisa or Big Jim gave me the cold sweats, but after reading the newspaper articles Sela had given me, I began to think differently. If this project was going to have the support of ARC and Triangle, then every detail was going to be scrutinized and rescrutinized until I was satisfied that we were doing our absolute best for the environment and the protection of natural habitats. The Langleys may have been the well-financed local muscle, but Triangle would be the wallet with a voice of caution and morality.

Finally moving past the traffic jam, I began to cross the Cooper River on the glorious new bridge. You could ask anyone and they would tell you that the other ancient rattletraps connecting the islands to the mainland had given legions of drivers some stupendous white-knuckle experiences. But this new bridge, named for Arthur J. Ravenel Jr., was a brilliantly executed piece of engineering. Its suspension coils reminded me of an angel's harp. I was surprised to learn that the night-lights had been lowered to protect the fish and crustaceans that lived below it. The Ravenel Bridge was proof that when people of noble purpose put their minds together, good things could happen.

I didn't know yet how J.D. felt about environmental issues, but I suspected he was the same as he had always been. I could hear the speech! They loved the land and the Lowcountry, but as I had witnessed for myself, the out-of-control building of new housing and commercial properties was inevitable, so they might as well reap the benefits from it. They were the pragmatic destruct-icons.

I pulled into the parking space reserved for my car and found the offices without a problem. TRIANGLE EQUITY. The sign looked good. We had leased the first floor of a Charleston house and I liked the idea that our building had a porch, some history, and some character. I wondered for a moment who had lived there in the past, what their lives had been like, and I marveled at how short they must have been as I reached to turn a doorknob that was substantially lower than any I'd touched in years.

I turned it and stepped right into the reception space.

"Well, hello, Miss Sandi! Look at this glorious little camp we have here! This is great! How are you?"

Sandi stood up from her chair, smiling to see me. She was around thirty, pretty, but as buttoned up as a nun. Except for the Prada logo on the side of her eyeglasses, you would never know who made her interchangeable wardrobe of jackets, skirts, and low-key professional attire. She was the epitome of geek chic. But she was in possession of a quick dry wit. Quick and dry was my favorite style of funny.

"It *is* great, isn't it? And I'm fine. Glad to see *you*! Come see! But it's gotta be a quick tour."

"Lose the gum," I told her with a wink.

"Sorry," she said, with a shrug and a pseudo-Brooklyn accent, discarding it into a tissue.

I hated gum chewing.

"Sorry to be such a stickler."

"No biggie. Come see!"

The rooms were laid out railroad-flat style. Sandi was positioned in the center space with her desk, two upholstered chairs and a small table, a reading lamp, and a stack of current magazines. To the left was the conference room with a round table and eight chairs, probably more than we would ever need. The left wall had French doors, and a nonworking fireplace was in the center of a sweet view of Wentworth Street. The panes of the windows were warped by age and opened and closed by pulleys.

"Look at this," I said, pointing out the mechanism.

"Cool, right?"

"Very."

A powder room and kitchenette had been constructed behind the reception area. The kitchenette would be handy for late nights or lunch meetings. My office was to the right of the front hall and could be accessed either way. My space, which overlooked a small garden with a fountain, also had French doors that opened onto the porch and a nonworking fireplace that Sandi had filled with a basket of eucalyptus branches.

"This smells good," I said. "Nice touch."

"Thanks. I have dried hydrangeas coming for the conference room."

"Good idea. Warms up the place."

I suspected that at one time my office had been a dining room because the ceiling was hand-plastered in a design of fruit and flowers. And there was a chandelier in the center. Something grand had perhaps once hung there, but its replacement was an inexpensive job from someplace like Lowe's.

Behind my office was a locked room with an outside entrance that the building's owner had reserved for himself.

"I think he's an artist because I can smell oil paint in the morning," Sandi said. "He's never here during the day."

"Who cares? This is completely charming! Where'd you get all the furniture?"

"Well, some of it was here, like the rugs, but I got the chairs and the curtains at Pottery Barn. I found your desk at an antiques store for like no money and got it polished up. The conference-room furniture is leased. My desk is leased, too. So are the phones. I bought the palms and the artwork is on loan."

"The owner's work?"

"No, I got a gallery to give it to us for ninety days. It's all for sale, though."

"I'm sure. Well, kiddo? You did a heckuva job. You'd think we had been here forever."

"That was the general plan, wasn't it? You said you wanted it to look stately and serious like Charleston. But I think we need tchotchkes, you know, to give it a little more personality. Maybe some blue-and-white ceramics for the mantelpieces? An umbrella stand?"

"Don't worry yourself. We're not going to be here forever."

"I'll raid my brother's house, see what he's got we can borrow."

"Oh, how's he doing?"

"Fine. He's a vet out in Summerville, you know."

"Married? Kids?"

"Widowed. My sister-in-law died two years ago. Breast cancer. She was only thirty-six."

"What? Oh no! That's horrible!" How did I forget these things? Was I going senile?

"They were going to have kids, but she found out she had cancer at thirty-two. She fought it like a tiger, but it was this very rare rapid-spreading thing that was all in her lymph nodes and liver and everywhere by the time they even found it. I thought you knew all of this."

"Know what? I'm sorry. I probably did, but there's so much breast cancer around that I hear about another case almost every week."

"It's okay. But I mean, who gets breast cancer at that age, right?"

"Unfortunately, a lot of people. Gosh, you have to be so vigilant these days."

"It's the truth. So listen, we need to talk about approximately one thousand things."

"Yeah, I know. My friend Sela gave me this little mountain of newspaper articles." I rattled the manila envelope in the air. "We're in some deep trouble in our public-relations department."

"I'll say. Hey, I didn't know you had friends here. I thought you were from Atlanta."

"Sandi? There's so much that nobody knows about me, you'd go running out the door if I started talking . . ."

"I doubt it."

"Anyway, let's send Sela a huge arrangement of flowers once a week for her restaurant, O'Farrell's, okay?"

"Sure. No problem."

"Well, maybe I'll tell you a long story, but for now let me get unpacked and settled and let's figure out what to do about this lovely fiasco we are facing."

I went into my new office, dropped my laptop case on the desk and my briefcase on the floor along with my handbag, and plopped myself into my chair. I was completely worn out before I had even begun the day.

Sandi, whose shopping gene had to be jacked up on mega vitamins, had seen to it all. There was a beautiful desk blotter, a lamp, a pencil cup, a stapler, and small dish of paper clips right next to a funny-looking little monkey wearing a fez that held a platter of business cards. Sandi had even printed up business cards with our logo, a triangle naturally, our Charleston address, phone number, e-mail, and it appeared that my whiz kid had constructed a website for us as well. She was amazing at details and it was a good thing she was because that was the most important skill I needed at the moment. My stomach was doing somersaults.

I heard the phone in the outer office ring and a few seconds later Sandi buzzed me.

"You want to talk to J. D. Langley? He's called three times."

Did I want to talk to J. D. Langley? No, I did not want to talk to J. D. Langley. Strangle him, perhaps, run away with him maybe, but there was no reason to talk to him except in a professional capacity. Wait. This *was* a professional capacity. My feelings were clearly conflicted. Should I talk to him now or put it off as long as possible?

"Take a message? Tell him you're on another line?"

Talking to J.D. meant that I had to be ready for anything. I wasn't ready for anything.

"Hello? Betts? You there?" Sandi was quiet for a moment. "How 'bout I just tell him you're on with New York."

I saw the light on the phone go dark and within two minutes my door opened. There stood Sandi.

"Look," she said, a little at sea over how to deal with my peculiar behavior, "you don't have to tell me anything you don't want to tell me, but is there something I should know?"

"That was put about as diplomatically as the ambassador to France would say it. Sit."

Sandi took a seat, and for the next forty-five minutes she

listened. I told her everything, almost, because the time of secrets had to come to an end. I needed her on my side, and if she was to really *be* on my side, and be of any use, she needed some facts. I did not tell her about Adrian, but if she did the math, she would probably figure that out anyway.

"Holy Mother! What are you going to do?" she asked when I'd finished my story.

"I was hoping you might have a thought or two on this," I said, hoping for a tone of gallows humor. "Actually, until I see him and his parents and hear their position on all these environmental and conservation problems, I don't know what I'm going to do. Ideally, I would like them to be sensitive and for all of us to find a way to make this happen peacefully and profitably."

"Tomorrow is the groundbreaking."

"Swell."

"Press like crazy, hard hats and gold-plated shovels, catered event under a tent, the whole nine yards."

"That's why I'm here."

"You could put off talking to him until tomorrow. But you know that."

"You're right. But I'm no coward. Get him back on the phone and let's see what we've got."

"Okay. Done." She turned to leave and then turned back to face me. "This is going to be *really* interesting. I mean, this could be like a soap opera."

"You're right, but you know what they say—truth is just a whole lot stranger than fiction."

She closed my door and buzzed me a few minutes later.

"J. D. Langley is on one."

"The plot thickens," I said, and took a deep breath, pressing the button to take the call. "Well, hey, J.D. How're you?" Benign enough, right?

"Betts McGee. Betts McGee. It seems that destiny wants to screw with us one more time, doesn't it?"

"Yep, looks like it. So, how are you?"

"'Bout the same, a few grays here and there."

"Still dressing up in camouflage and killing stuff on the weekends?"

"Nah. I'm lucky to drop a hook in the water. Or catch a Clemson game. How about you? How are you?"

"Fine! You know, good. Yeah, I'm good."

I wanted to say, "How am I? I am terrified of seeing you, that's how I am!" But I didn't because the warrior in me was determined to maintain a completely inscrutable stance.

"Good. So where do you want to start? Wanna have lunch or something?"

"Sure. Why don't you come over here around noon and I'll bring in some sandwiches. How does that sound?"

"Fine. Perfect. I'll bring the blueprints?"

"I've got a set."

"Okay, then. I'll just bring corrections. See you at noon. This should be weird."

"I'll say."

I could only hope that he had lost a few teeth. Or that he was paunchy and bald. Or that he had unbelievable, incurable halitosis. Maybe he had become a chronic nose picker, crotch scratcher . . . something! Anything!

Sandi stuck her head in the door.

"You know I listened to every word, but I could only hear your end of the conversation. How does he sound?"

"Halloween must be early this year because I'm scared to death. How's my hair?"

"Not the best I've ever seen it. But there's rain-forest humidity around here, so what are you gonna do? I mean, do you *want* him to think you had a makeover for the occasion?"

Really, Sandi was right. It was probably better for J.D. not to think that I had gone to a lot of trouble fixing myself up just to see him. I looked in the mirror and decided I didn't look so bad for someone who had just stuck her tongue in a lightbulb socket. Fear and poor pallor appeared to travel hand in hand. My anxiety levels were swirling around the Space Station Mir.

"We gotta get lunch in here," I said in rapid fire.

"Handled. East Bay Deli. Pastrami, corn beef, pickles, and cookies."

"Great. Are they good? Because it has to be good. I mean, this is important."

"They deliver. It's the deli everyone around here uses."

"Oh? Okay, then."

"So, Betts? I have a flatiron and a whole set of Bare Minerals makeup, including lip gloss and mascara. You want to maybe fool around with it?"

"Um . . ."

"Gotcha. I'll be right back. Go wash your face."

I washed my greasy face and stared at my splotchy complexion in the mirror. For so many years I'd avoided J.D. so carefully . . . and now he was coming over for pastrami on rye? And then there was the fact that I had aged. Nearly twenty years. Did it show? Of course it showed. Just for good measure, I aged five more years on the spot.

When I got back to my office, there was a layout of war paint and the hair straightener was warming up. It was eleven o'clock. One hour until liftoff.

"Down here you can't wear liquid foundation with any oil in it unless you've got lizard skin. But you should know that. Put that stuff in the bottle on first. It holds the makeup on your skin."

"Gotcha."

"I'm gonna section off your hair and flatiron the back for you. Then you can do the rest and I'll show you how to use this stuff."

"Fine. I think I'm going to throw up." I couldn't hold a thought in my head.

"Betts? I know you're my boss and all, but I think *I'm* gonna throw up, too! This particular stress was not mentioned in my job reassignment. And I thought the part about the alligators was sort of crazy . . ."

"Sorry. I knew I'd forgotten to tell you something . . ."

Sandi ironed the back of my hair section by section until

it appeared to have grown four inches. I had some serious frizz going on.

First, Sandi applied something all around my eyes called Well Rested, which was something I certainly wasn't. But when I looked in her compact mirror, it appeared that I was. Okay, I thought, this might work. Then she brushed small amounts of a powdered foundation all over my face until I was blotch-free and my skin looked really good. Then came the contour and blush, eyeliner, and mascara, and voilà! Not a pore in sight. I looked about ten years fresher than I had when I walked in the door.

"We're doing big eyes and a natural mouth, okay?" Sandi said.

"You're the Svengali here, not me. Whatever you say is fine." When we were all done, I looked in the large mirror over the mantel. "Well, this is quite the transformation! Where'd you get this stuff?"

"Stella Nova, right around the corner on King Street. They are like a one-stop shop for everything you ever wanted in your life to make you happy."

"No lie?"

"No lie. Well, except shoes." She started cleaning up my desk, smiling to herself.

"Right! Hey, Sandi?"

"Yes'm?"

"Thanks."

"He's gonna drop dead when he sees you, Betts. I'm telling you, dead on the floor."

"Good."

Lunch arrived, and Sandi was in the conference room setting it up while I pored over the newspapers, pulling out articles and letters to the editor protesting the proposed development of Bulls Island. The next thing I knew, I looked up to see J.D. walking through the door with an architect's tube under his arm.

"Hey," he said, and took a deep breath.

"Hey, yourself," I said, and stood.

He was gorgeous.

"So are you," he said, hearing my thoughts.

But wasn't that how it had always been?

Our eyes were locked on each other's face, our minds roaring backward over the years, looking for recognition, old affection, broken hearts, lost time . . . there we stood, waiting for the other to make some kind of mysterious first move, something that would turn anger to forgiveness, bring us together, make the job we had to do together possible.

It would never be. All the old memories, the dormant but still white-hot passion, the ache of wanting without having, burst into flames, and in just minutes, all these emotions raged like a blast furnace into a swirl of confusion. It was going to be impossible for me to stay away from him . . . and, I could see, for him to stay away from me. I had known the risk of being in J.D.'s company from the moment I had agreed to return to Charleston. I should have remembered that our attraction to each other was as powerful and predictable as the tides, as sunrise and sunset, as any phenomenon in nature. Actually, I *had* remembered this . . . but had foolishly chosen to test my own puny strength against it.

"Oh God." I said. My body temperature was rising and I knew I was blushing every shade of red in the spectrum.

"What are we gonna do, Betts?"

"I don't know what you mean. But if I did, I would say that we're gonna tough it out. This is just business, J.D." My eye began to twitch.

"Sure. Whatever you say."

At that moment Sandi stuck her head in the office and said, "Lunch is ready. What would y'all like to drink?"

"Iced tea," I said. Cyanide, I thought. And some strips of duct tape discreetly applied to my twitching eyelid would be good, too.

"Tea's fine for me," J.D. said.

We had not touched each other yet—no hug, no shaking of hands. Sandi, who had an expected smirk on her face, left to get our drinks and J.D. stood aside so I could pass through the door. I carefully avoided any contact with him as though he were covered in vines of poison ivy. But I could feel his breath as I moved by him and that was all it took for me to break a sweat.

It probably sounds crazy, but J.D.'s scent dropped me into a state of complete distraction with a silent plunk. It wasn't exactly musk and it wasn't sweet or salty. I assumed he wore cologne and it was probably one whose fragrances I had inhaled hundreds of times. But mixed with his body oils or skin, it made him smell like something else, something that could make me drunk. Insatiable. Blind. Irrational.

"What's for lunch?" he asked, clearing his throat.

Trying to focus, I said, "Corned beef, pastrami, and a pile of op-ed pieces from every newspaper in the state."

"Oh, that. Big pain in the behind. That whole ruckus, I mean."

"Well, some of it may have merit," I said.

"Maybe."

We took a seat at the conference table and passed the platter of sandwiches back and forth, unwrapping them, taking halves of each. We began to share lunch as naturally as we had ever shared anything—except the last nineteen years.

"Big maybe. We have to talk about everything, but first, tell me how Big Jim is doing. I heard he had a heart attack."

"He did. But you know him, he's fine, the moose. Thanks for asking."

"And your mother?"

"Still mean as a junkyard dog, but mellowing somewhat around the edges."

"Valerie?"

He looked over his right shoulder as if there might be someone else listening and then he looked back to me. He just cocked his head to one side and said, "She's the same."

"Good answer," I said.

"Yeah, well, your eye's twitching like a sail in a gale-force wind."

"Shut up. You're as nervous as I am."

"Yes, ma'am. You're right about that. And for good reason."

"Amen. So, J.D.?"

"What?"

"Let's talk about Bulls Island."

"What do you want to know?"

"How'd you get it declassified?"

"Ask me something else."

"So, the Langleys are still up to their usual games, huh? Working the system?"

"Tell you what. You can ask my mother to tell you the story. This was her pet project. I just make sure the buildings meet code and that the customers get what they pay for."

"This is a little more complicated than that. You know what Bulls Island means."

"Yep, I do. But that's all changed. Right now we're working with the South Carolina Department of Wildlife hunting down alligators, fox, and deer, and moving them over to Capers. And we're working diligently to diminish the snake population."

"Nice." I shivered. "How's that going?"

"Pretty good. But we really won't know until spring when they hatch again."

"Ew. Gross."

"Your eye's still twitching. You're still afraid of snakes?"

"Screw you, J. D. Langley. No, I'm not afraid of anything . . ." My eyelid was acting like a strobe light from a cheesy dance club.

"Really?" He grinned in a most appealing and dangerous way that one hundred years ago might have left a young innocent girl to feel that her virtue was possibly compromised.

"Okay. Almost anything, but I wouldn't want to spend ten million dollars on a home and then find a copperhead knocking on my front door."

"Good point. Well, we're keeping the loggerheads and over two hundred species of birds. And we're dealing with a helluva lot of vandalism to the earthmovers and our ATVs."

"I hadn't heard about any vandalism . . ."

"So far we've been able to keep it out of the papers. No point in stoking the fires of the crazies out there."

"You're right, I guess. You'll have to fill me in on that. Anyway, there are a couple of questions I've got about the comparative environments of Bulls versus Capers."

"Like what?"

"Well, for example, does Capers Island have enough fresh and brackish water impoundments to support the additional reptile population?"

J.D. wiped his mouth with his napkin and was quiet for a minute.

"What? Did I just ask a stupid question?"

"Betts?" J.D. shook his head with such incredulity that I knew what he was going to say before he said it.

"What?"

"Betts? What's this about? Did you go off to New York City to work in private equity with the biggest reptiles on the planet and come home a freaking tree hugger? What's going on here?"

"I just worry, J.D. That's all. No, I am not a *freaking* tree hugger, thank you, but I also know I won't have my company involved in a project that's in any way irresponsible."

"Irresponsible?"

"Environmentally irresponsible."

"Well, thanks for the clarification. Number one, we are not touching the impoundments and we are building no bridges. The chemistry of the water impoundments of Capers is identical to Bulls. Two, the contract is signed and the check has cleared the bank, so you're *in this,* unless your firm wants a lawsuit. Number three, you come waltzing in here after all these years and you don't know the first thing about me and how I work. I was a boy the last time you saw me . . . the time you walked out on everyone. My family may have a reputation for doing business in an unorthodox manner, but that's not how I operate."

"I apologize. I didn't mean to imply—"

"Yes, you did. You did mean to imply . . ."

"It's just all these articles . . . they say such terrible things."

"Yes, they do, but let me tell you something, okay?" He balled up the wrapper from his sandwich and threw it on the table. "We've got more salt marsh and brackish water than we have uplands over there by almost eight hundred acres. Needless to say, there are more varieties of bloodsucking bugs than all the noodles in China. In addition, Bulls Island has the largest loggerhead nesting refuge outside of Florida . . . and *I* have a personal commitment to protect it. And to top it all off, we have nut jobs picketing at the dock by day and slashing our tires every night. Between you and me? I never would have touched Bulls Island. But Mother got her hands on it and it's a helluva lot better for me to develop it than a pack of Yankees with no conscience!" He stopped and took a breath. "Now, do I have a partner or do I have an adversary?"

"Um, it appears that you have a partner who's a half Yankee with a raging conscience. And her partner seems to have become a man with a formidable temper."

He leaned back in his chair and stared at me. I had made him angry because I had not chosen my words well, and I had assumed that he was in it just for the money. I was wrong all the way around. The tension in the room was palpable.

"I guess you grew up okay," he said. "Principles and all that."

"You, too. I guess. You want a cookie? Sugar might sweeten you up." How principled I was remained to be seen.

"No, thanks. Trying to quit."

"Coffee?"

"Never touch the stuff."

"Yeah, me either. So, let's have a look at the plans, I guess, right? I'll just clear this stuff up."

He unrolled a stack of architectural drawings and I could tell he was looking around for paperweights to keep them flat.

"How about coffee mugs?"

"That'll do 'er."

I grabbed four mugs from the kitchen area and anchored the drawings with them.

"Okay," he said, "first of all, we need a meeting with the architects, the contractors, and the wildlife guys to really examine the specifics, but to get started, let's look at this aerial view of the island, because the natural geography presents some special challenges."

"How big is the island? I mean, square miles?"

"A little under eight. But it's about six and a half miles long. Anyway, in stage one of this, we're only planning to develop about two hundred acres for private housing—single-family structures, two to an acre—and then a clubhouse, one small hotel, a golf course, a general store, and an emergency medical facility. The primary question, of course, is what to keep—I mean, whatever is of historic value should be kept, don't you agree?"

"Of course. I mean, you're talking about things like the Dominick House, right?"

"Yep, and the shell middens and the old fort and so forth. But most importantly, we want this to be as green a project as possible. We want hiking trails and nature trails and so forth."

"Hey, J.D.?" I asked.

"Yeah?"

He looked up at me and I could feel blood rushing to my face again.

"This is very exciting. This project, I mean."

"I've thought about this a lot, Betts. If we couldn't build a life together for ourselves, at least we can build one for somebody else."

J.D. was twisting my heart with almost every word he uttered. How was I going to make it through the next few months without falling in love with him all over again?

He gave me a broad outline of each area of the project and I began to see exactly how much time and thought had gone into every segment of the job—how to run power over there, sewage, freshwater—the problems of providing for basic needs had been carefully studied. When we got to the drawings of the golf course and the clubhouse, I could see that Bulls Island was going to be magnificent and that the Langleys' intentions were that it would remain basically unspoiled in spite of development. But I had my suspicions still because people had a tendency to screw up the world no matter their good intentions, so why would this be an exception?

When it got to the point that we were becoming bleary-eyed from trying to take in the enormous scope of our work, J.D. suggested that we call it quits and I reluctantly agreed.

"I'm having dinner with my father tonight," I said, standing next to the table as he rolled up the drawings.

He cleared his throat at my remark. He had not asked me anything about my personal life and he surely knew that I had not been in touch with my father or my sister.

"Your sister is as crazy as a mattress fulla bedbugs, you know."

"You're telling me?"

Somehow, we said good-bye. Somehow, we did this with professionalism and courtesy. But we both knew that it was a matter of *when* not *if* trouble would find us.

CHAPTER ELEVEN

Dirt on Everyone

*H*e's pretty fabulous," Sandi said after J.D. left and my mental and emotional equilibrium had been partially restored. "If you don't mind me saying so."

"I don't mind, and that's the problem."

"He's married, right?"

"Yeah, to a complete nincompoop."

"They got kids?"

"Nope."

"Does he know that you do?"

She had guessed.

"Nope, and let's keep it that way, understood?"

"Understood."

"Sandi? Wonderful as you are? Indispensable as you are to me, especially now? Letting that news hit the streets would be an instantaneous deal breaker for us."

Sandi removed her eyeglasses and stared at me while she cleaned them with a tissue.

"I have no knowledge of your personal life," she said. "No knowledge whatsoever."

"Right. Okay, it's after five-thirty. I'm going to meet my father for an early dinner at O'Farrell's. Why don't you get out of here and go have a nice evening?"

"Good. Thanks." She pulled open her bottom drawer to remove her purse.

"And Sandi?"

"Yes?"

"Thanks for everything—the office, the makeover, the lunch, your discretion . . ."

"Look, this is a great deal for me. I get to stay with my brother, even though he lives like you don't want to know. And decorating was actually fun. Who doesn't love to spend somebody else's money? But your makeover? That was like doing a rescue mission—"

"Stop! You're so fresh!"

"Ha! Gotcha! Lunch was just a phone call, and that discretion thing? I don't know what you're talking about."

I gave her a wave and left the office for the first time that day. The heat had broken and the skies threatened to burst. Classic. I knew we would be bombarded by rain and crackles of lightning for an hour or so and then it would seem like midday again. I couldn't have cared less.

I drove Sela's car over to the parking lot closest to her restaurant. As I made the turn onto King Street, I looked in my rearview mirror and saw a man in a car across the street staring at me. What the hell? Was I being followed? Was this the long arm of Vinny following me around through the cellphone camera of some hired thug? How stupid! What did he expect to learn? I told myself it was all my imagination and to get over myself.

The first pelts of rain began to fall as I pushed open the door to Sela's place. She was behind the bar.

"Hey!" she called. "I haven't heard from you all day! How's it going?"

I climbed on a bar stool and gave her a half hug across the bar.

"Whoo! I came early because Daddy's meeting me here at six. I thought we could grab a fast glass of wine or a Coke or something."

" 'Daddy's coming at six.' Um, you said that like this is an everyday occurrence for you. So you called him, huh? White wine? Bottle with a straw?"

I laughed at that and nodded in agreement. "Sure. White's good. Anything. I don't care as long as it's got a big splash of alcohol in it. Oh, Sela. What a day. I feel like I've been here for a year."

"I'll bet. So, start from the beginning. How was your dad on the phone?" She put the goblet in front of me and filled it with an unfamiliar Chardonnay. "Do I have to beat it out of you?"

"You know what? It's a big fat mess, but we'll get it straightened out. He was a sweetheart. Cheers!"

"Cheers, yourself! See?"

"Yep. You were right, as usual. But we have a lot of fences to mend and it's not all going to happen over one dinner."

"No, I imagine not. So, how's the new office? I can't wait to see it."

"J.D. liked it. At least I think he did."

"Um, I think I'll have that scotch now."

"I'm telling you, Sela, this has been a day out of Hollywood."

"Details, please?" Sela poured two fingers of a rare eighteen-year-old single malt into a tumbler. "I'm just gonna sip this if that's all right with you."

"Sip. Yeah, he called, I called him back, he came over for pastrami on rye, and we went over the plans."

"JMJ, girl. Aren't you the cool customer? So how was it? Electric? Terrifying? I mean, is there heat?"

"What the hell do *you* think?"

"I think that this is gonna be the hottest summer on record."

"If I can get through this assignment with my virtuous reputation intact, it will be a miracle."

"Holy crap. Did he put the moves on you?"

Her face looked so solemn and her wording of the question was so dated that I burst out laughing.

"Put the *moves* on me? Heavens, no! He was the perfect gentleman, I'm happy to report."

"Well, I'm sorry to hear it."

"I'm not. Being in the same room with him was just about all my nerves could handle. You know, I haven't seen him in a while."

"Truly. So what did you think?"

"I think—" I felt a tap on my shoulder.

It was Daddy, shaking out his umbrella and smiling from ear to ear.

I jumped down from my seat and threw my arms around his neck. He hugged me back so hard I thought he might have cracked a rib. At that moment nothing mattered, all the years, all the lies . . . we would figure it out. Sela had stepped away, probably to give us a moment's privacy, I thought.

Finally, we stood back and had a look at each other.

"You look wonderful, Daddy. Really wonderful. I can't believe my lucky eyes are finally so filled with you! Oh my God! How are you?"

"Well, I'm afraid I've become an old coot. But look at you! You're a woman . . ." His eyes filled with tears and he reached for his handkerchief. I had forgotten that he used handkerchiefs. "I promised myself I wasn't going to . . ."

"It's okay, Daddy, I cried all last night. Oh! Gosh! It's really you! This is a very big deal." Thankfully, Sela returned at that moment.

"Come on, Mr. Vaughn, I've got a special table for you two."

We followed Sela through the restaurant, back through the kitchen, and to a storage room that served as her wine cellar. She had quickly set up a small table for two with flowers in a Coke bottle, votives, and cloth napkins spread out to serve as a makeshift tablecloth.

"Well, it's not exactly Per Se—"

"Oh, Sela! It's perfect!"

"Can an old man give a young woman a hug?" Daddy said, and hugged Sela politely.

"Mr. Vaughn? I'd love a hug! I'll be back," she said, and left us alone.

"It's a little chilly in here," I said.

"I guess it has to be," he said as he held my chair for me.

"Still the gentleman . . . thanks."

I snapped my napkin across my lap and looked at him as he took his seat. He had aged quite a lot, but the changes in me were probably much more profound in his eyes. As J.D. had observed, the last time we had seen each other, we were practically children.

"Always a gentleman," he said with a smile. "Some things such as good manners still matter. Well, to me at least. So tell me, my beautiful Betts, where do we start?"

I reached across the table and took his hand in mine. "I think I'd like to start by saying how sorry I am, Daddy. I am so sorry and I hope somehow, by God's grace, you will find a way to forgive me—"

"No, baby, I'm the one filled with regret. That I let all these years pass and never came looking for you. Well, it's just completely reprehensible and—"

Just then, the door opened and a waiter put a bottle of champagne in a cooler on our table. He quietly removed the cork with barely a hiss and poured for us. Another waiter followed with a platter of some very yummy-looking hors d'oeuvres, broiled shrimp impaled on toothpicks with tiny onions, crab cakes nestled on toast points, garnished with tartar sauce and a minuscule sprinkle of mustard sprouts, and baked marinated citrus olives stuffed with almonds. This was very fancy fare for O'Farrell's, even if we were in Sela's cellar, the newly appointed hideout for extremely dysfunctional-family reunions.

"Well, Daddy, either we're going to spend the whole evening apologizing for things we can't change—"

"Or we're going to make a fresh start. What do you say? I think we should make a fresh start."

"I say we have both been a couple of knuckleheads and we should leave the past—"

"Behind us where it belongs!"

We touched the edges of our glasses and silently toasted the future.

"So, what about Joanie?" I asked. "I take it she didn't want to come?"

"Joanie is the other knucklehead in the family. I don't know what to say about your sister."

"Well, as I hear tell, she has some concerns about your health." I popped an olive in my mouth and was surprised at how good it was. "Here, try one of these. It's incredible!"

"Thank you." He took one, ate it, and raised his eyebrows in surprise. "Imagine that! I thought olives were only for martinis!"

"Live and learn, right? So, you were telling me about your health?"

"Betts, the reports of my ill health are greatly exaggerated. I've never felt better in my life. My only problems are the normal ones that accomp'ny advancing years. I creak a little in the morning, but as soon as I get moving, I do just fine. As a rule, I walk her crazy dogs down to the Batt'ry. You know, to take the air?"

I loved that he said "Batt'ry" instead of "Battery." And "accomp'ny" rather than "accompany." He had traces of that old Charleston accent that I had not heard in ages, and on hearing it again, I was flooded for the umpteenth time in twenty-four hours with waves of nostalgia and sentimental feelings.

"Joanie is complicated, Daddy. She always was and she always will be."

"I think she would be a lot happier if she fixed herself up, you know, made an attempt to dress like a lady. Then she might actually find a romantic interest, you know what I mean?"

"Well, romance isn't for everyone, is it? You're still single; in fact, we all are."

"Yes, that's true. I mean, I can understand in some ways why you never married. Your mother's death was very traumatic for you and for all of us. But like most parents, I had always hoped to have grandchildren, you know? A little scamp to take fishing? A little girl to take to the fair or out for an ice-cream cone?"

I was so close to telling him about Adrian that I had to clench my jaw.

When he saw me withdrawing, he said, "Oh, listen to me rambling on . . . what's the difference? I have *you* back and that's more than good enough for me! This is a night for celebrating what we have, not for wanting more."

"It's human nature to always want more. It's okay."

"So, tell me why you're here? You didn't tell me."

The door opened again.

"Menus? We have a couple of specials tonight that are not on the menu . . ."

The hyperpolite waiter rattled off a pasta dish, some kind of mahi-mahi concoction that sounded awful, and a special stuffed pork belly that I wouldn't eat for love or money.

"Do you know what you'd like to have, Betts? I'm going to have the chicken potpie."

"Me, too."

"It's the best thing on the menu," Daddy said. "Sometimes, when I can escape your sister's eye and Sela's disapproving glares, I sneak in here, sit by myself in the back, and have one. Although I must say, I usually don't wash it down with champagne."

"What do you normally have?"

"Oh, you know me . . . or you've probably forgotten . . ."

"Or I never knew. Just tell me. Let's not dwell . . . please?"

"You're right. Well, I like a Manhattan, but I like mine made with Maker's Mark and two cherries. After that, I usually just drink water or tea. But I still like to have a cocktail."

"A Manhattan. There's nothing wrong with that."

"So, you haven't told me."

"Told you what?" I thought, told you a thousand things that would probably send you right into cardiac arrest?

"Why you're here?"

"Oh! Gosh, yes. There are a few stories to tell. Well, I work for ARC Partners, which is a . . ."

I gave him the general picture of what I did and he seemed quite proud. Most importantly, he absolutely seemed to understand every aspect of my business. Joanie was a liar. Daddy was not senile in the least.

"So what exactly are you doing in Charleston?"

"Do you want the long answer or the CliffsNotes?"

"CliffsNotes first, details later."

"Developing Bulls Island with the Langleys, J.D. specifically. How's that for weird karma?"

Daddy leaned back in his chair, inhaled for a long time, and then exhaled even more slowly.

"Well, that's one way to enter the city. I hope you weren't expecting a parade in your honor."

"Daddy? That's pretty chilly coming from you, especially given the occasion. Seriously, if what you rely on for facts and information comes from what you read in the papers, then you would be grossly uninformed."

"Enlighten me."

I told him how I had been chosen for the project in the first place so that he understood that declining the assignment would've meant certain death for my career at ARC. Then I went through what J.D. had presented to me.

"Look, they could ruin the whole island if they wanted to, but they don't. Out of the two thousand plus acres they could develop, they're only developing housing on two hundred right now."

"You're gonna expect me to believe that they could put up four thousand houses, but they're only going to build four hundred? How's this boondoggle supposed to pay for itself? I think you may be naive on this one, Betts. You know the Langleys. They are the greediest sons of bitches I ever knew, pardon the expression. And that 'sweet boy,'

J.D.? Hmmph. He's just like his old man. Big Jim Langley could talk a dog off a meat truck. I wouldn't believe a daggum thing he says."

All my alarms went off again and I became suspicious of J.D. Maybe his intentions were honorable, but would Louisa override them?

"And that's exactly why I'm here. To protect my company's investment."

"Well, you sure have one deep and tough row to hoe. Hmmph. Anytime you need a sounding board, and I *mean* this, call me. I can smell Langley bull like a boykin can flush out a dove."

"He swears they're not touching the wetlands."

"Perhaps, but this is a bottom-line game here and either they're building more houses than he's telling you or they're going to charge some exorbitant membership fee for the golf club. Or something. I'd be *very* wary if I were you. And you realize how seriously unpopular this entire development is. Public sentiment despises developers, even if Al Gore himself is a paid consultant."

"Bringing Gore in might not be a bad idea. At least to ask him to give it all a cursory glance."

"What was that?"

"I said, bringing Gore in might not be such a bad idea, you know, just ask him to give it all a look." Apparently Daddy was a little hard of hearing, but who wasn't?

"I thought that was what you said. Well, I don't think so. It's not what he does best. Besides, if you love Al Gore, as I suspect you do, you wouldn't want to jeopardize his reputation with any of the Langley shenanigans."

There and then we had found a sliver of common ground. My father would be my resident guru if I needed one. Maybe.

We made our way through the potpies and then picked over two slices of apple pie à la mode until it was obvious it was time to say good night.

"Do you want to come back to the house?" Dad said.

"Joanie's there?"

"Most likely."

"Know what, Dad? I just saw you for the first time in almost twenty years, and J.D., too. If Joanie wanted to see me, she would've been here."

"Now, don't go starting trouble with your—"

"I'm not starting anything. I'm exhausted."

He looked at me and saw me not as the ill-tempered woman my sister had become but as a reasonable adult who had taken enough bullets for one day. As the old warriors would say, the day had been "target rich" for the other side.

Outside on the sidewalk, after Sela refused to let us pay for dinner and we had thanked her profusely, Daddy and I hugged and lingered in the embrace long enough to be satisfied that we were on the road to some kind of certifiable reconciliation. Hopefully—hopefully—it would improve with each day. Until he found out what I had been hiding from everyone, that is. I hoped with everything I had in me that I could build a base of love and trust that would be solid enough to support me when Adrian eventually arrived.

"I'll call you tomorrow?" he said.

"Sure. Here's my cell, and the office number's there, too, and my e-mail . . ."

He looked at my card and then looked into my eyes.

"Your mother would have been very proud of you, Betts. I know I am."

"Thanks, Daddy. I love you, you know."

"I know you do. And in my own stubborn way, I love you. Oh, my goodness! It's been such a long time since I spoke those words."

"It's okay."

The rain had cleared up and night was finally on our heels. Somehow, when it was dark I gave myself permission to relax and I could feel my shoulders drop back into their natural position. I watched my father walk away. I had offered him a ride home, but he had declined, saying the exercise was good for him, and it probably was. He strolled up the empty block, tilted a little to the left, but he did not lean on the umbrella for support. Suddenly, as though he could feel my eyes on his back, he stopped in the middle of the next block, turned to me, and blew me a kiss. I blew him one back and thought I had been through all I could take for one day without dissolving into a pool of my own tears.

On the drive back to the Isle of Palms, I thought of calling Adrian. What would I say to him? That I had seen his father and grandfather that day? The ones he thought were dead? That they were fine and happy? There was a lump in my throat and I knew I was going to have a hard time sleeping that night. But to my surprise, I woke at seven, having slept the sleep of the dead.

I threw back the rubberized blackout curtains and was nearly blinded by the sun's reflection on the water. It was going to be a gorgeous day. Groundbreaking, in fact. What to wear to a groundbreaking ceremony?

Wardrobe fiasco.

If I wore something like black trousers, a white T-shirt, a jacket, and loafers, I would look like Miss City Slicker who in all likelihood did not know diddly-squat about what I was doing except ruining Bulls Island to make money for some unseen suits up north. And I would perspire myself into a dangerously low electrolyte count. Fainting at a press conference would not do.

If I wore a khaki safari jacket, jeans, and a cotton shirt with a Kaminski straw hat, I would look like Clem Kadiddlehopper, who *definitely* did not know diddly. A dress was out of the question. Or was it?

Digging through my closet, I found a black cotton-jersey wrap dress that I would wear with black-and-pink-print low-heeled Pucci-esque pumps. I had a thin pink cotton sweater that I could wrap around my shoulders to ward off the sun or use to swat bugs. I remembered I had packed a great-looking triple-strand necklace of baroque pearls, earrings, and large black sunglasses. These details would send a serious message. It probably wasn't perfect for the terrain, but it would photograph well. A girl had to keep her priorities straight.

Sandi and I were to meet everyone at the Awendaw dock at three in the afternoon. We spent the morning at the office rehashing the prior night, straightening my hair again, and running around to Stella Nova for my own cache of mineral makeup and other products that suited the climate. And sunscreen. Oh, and bug repellent. I bought a wildly expensive black patent-leather quilted tote bag to hold everything. I thought I was looking fashionably in-the-know. I hoped.

At the office, Sandi chattered away, probably because hearing more about J.D. and my father was too much to process.

"My brother Cam's house is a wreck. Boy, does he need a woman or what? I spent last night looking around to see what I could beg, borrow, or steal and he's got nothing but big wads of dog hair all over the house. His yard looks like a hillbilly lives there. He needs a maid, a landscaper, and I don't know what all. Plus, he's miserable."

"He sounds perfect for my miserable sister, Joanie. She's the queen of animal rescue in Charleston. And morbidly single."

"Seriously? Maybe we should introduce them. How old is she?"

"Thirty-four—no, thirty-five. How important are looks to him?"

"Well, the age is right, but he's as shallow as, I don't know . . . he thinks he's gorgeous or something."

"Yeah. They all do. Maybe they should both clean their mirrors and then take a good look."

"Truly. We'd better get a move on if we want to be there on time. Traffic, you know. Seventeen is brutal."

"You're telling me? It appears that the town fathers need some guidance in their infrastructure planning. It took me almost forty-five minutes to get here today."

"Crazy, right? Let's go."

"Sandi?"

"Yeah?"

"Lose the gum."

"Sorry," she said, and used a tissue to discard it. We both laughed.

We took Sela's car and drove along the highway without the benefit of the radio. My mind, which I thought was a million miles away, was apparently wired into Sandi's.

"Is his wife coming?" she asked.

"Whose wife? J.D.'s?"

"Uh, yes. Who else? What's her name?"

"Valerie."

"Well, too bad for her."

"Yeah, why?"

"Because you ain't never looked this good as long as I've known you."

"That would be a mere two years?"

"Two years at ARC is a looooong time!"

I made the right turn at Seewee's Restaurant to travel down the long road toward the government dock at Garris Landing.

"It's a lifetime. Who's catering this shindig?"

"Tidewater Foods. Fabulous. Cam took the day off to help them set up. Best barbecue, I don't care what anyone says."

"Seriously?"

"Yep. You'll see."

"Why did I even ask? Of course this entire soiree is managed down to the embossed napkins, am I right?" I said.

"I wanted to surprise you!"

"You never cease to amaze me."

I pulled into a parking spot and saw the noisy crowd, milling around on the huge dock. The farther we walked toward them, the farther away they seemed. It had to be a dock constructed to hide battleships in case of a national emergency, but as far as I knew, it only ran the Coastal Expeditions' ferryboat back and forth between Mount Pleasant and Bulls Island.

When I got close enough, I saw that there were almost a hundred protesters with signs. They were chanting something about saving the red wolves and migratory birds. Then

I spotted Joanie among them, but she didn't see me. She was dressed like a slob in baggy khakis and a T-shirt with a German shepherd on it, blinged out with press-on fake stones.

"That's my sister," I said to Sandi, pointing as discreetly as possible.

"You're kidding, right?" Sandi lowered her sunglasses and squinted.

"I only wish," I said. "Will the mortification never end?"

I had two choices. I could greet her, give her a hug, and be a lady about finding her in this most unfortunate circumstance. Or I could ignore her, get on the ferry, hide behind a pole, and hope she hadn't seen me. I opted for decency and bravery. Knowing that Louisa Langley was on the island, waiting to sink her teeth into my neck, made saying "Hello, Joanie" seem pretty minor.

I worked my way through the crowd to her side. She did not recognize me as I approached. I took off my sunglasses and tapped her on her shoulder.

"Is this my little sister?"

"Betts?" She lowered her sign and her jaw in the same moment.

I smiled and threw open my arms to give her a hug.

"What? What are you doing here?" She gave me the most impotent of all hugs in return.

"I called you and told you I was coming, Joanie."

"I never got a message from you," she said with a straight face.

"It's not nice to lie to your family, Joanie," I whispered.

Silence.

"I had dinner with Daddy last night."

More silence.

I looked around and put my sunglasses back on. Although it was deep in the afternoon, the ground where I stood still radiated heat.

"So, I see you're politically involved. That's good! It's good to have a cause."

I didn't think I sounded patronizing, but she apparently

thought otherwise because she tilted her head to one side and gave me a look that would melt the remains of the polar ice cap.

"Well! I'm not surprised to see that you're on the *wrong* side of the cause," she said, and actually snarled. "As usual."

This was very stupid and we were not going to get anywhere as a family if she was going to paint a line down the middle of the road when the mood struck.

"Joanie, Joanie. I'll tell you what. Why don't you come over to the island with me, as my guest? Put aside your doubts for the moment and just listen to the plan. I think you'll be pleasantly surprised by what you might learn. Come on. What do you say? We're having a big barbecue and it will be fun."

"Is that all you think about? Making money? Ruining the environment? Having fun?"

"No. You know what? You're being gratuitously nasty, Joanie. I am extending a perfectly civil invitation to you that your activist cohorts here won't enjoy, and you just stand there and hurl insults at me. Not nice. I haven't seen you in nineteen years. Don't you think you might give me a chance?"

She looked at the ground and then she ran her hands through her hair.

"Okay." She handed her sign to someone next to her and said to a very unattractive woman, "I'm going over to Bulls with my sister. She's a partner in this morass of bull."

"Oh!" her friend said, and stepped back as though I were spreading Ebola.

I appraised her friend, this specimen of the Ugly Stick phylum, thinking even the most inexpensive moisturizer would do her a world of good. I turned to Sandi, who was just completely bewildered that my sister was as she was in appearance and attitude.

"Sandi. This is my sister, Joanie."

"Hi! It's nice to meet you." Sandi was cool and reserved, as though she were meeting a top account executive and could she get them a cappuccino.

"Is she your partner?"

"No, Sandi works for me in New York and she's here to help me get this job done right."

"Meaning?"

Who knows what Joanie was thinking? I decided to disarm her with nonstop charm from that moment forward.

"Well, today you'll see a lot of what Sandi does. I'll bet you leave here thinking you've just met the most organized woman on the planet! Let's go."

The ride over on the ferry was very pleasant. A nice breeze was coming up and the temperature seemed to be cooling off somewhat. There were twenty or so people on board and Joanie kept her distance, staring out at the spartina grass so that she didn't have to engage in conversation. That was all right. We would have been too easily overheard, possibly by someone from the press, and there would be plenty of time to talk about the past and the future. I knew that reestablishing some kind of family bond with Joanie was going to be a slow and arduous process.

We disembarked and wandered toward the tent that had been set up for the event. I had the fleeting thought, Oh Lord, why did I make Joanie come? I have enough to deal with without another layer of hostility added to the mix.

But Sandi, who was still shell-shocked by Joanie's overall demeanor, read the panic on my face and came to the rescue.

"Joanie, why don't you come with me? I'd like to introduce you to my brother, Cameron. He's a veterinarian and Betts said that you have done a lot of rescue work, haven't you?"

"Why, uh, yes . . . I have. Okay."

Sandi led Joanie off to the cooks' tent and I breathed a sigh of temporary relief. I looked around. The main tent was set up with picnic tables and benches, buffet stations on both sides, and two bars, one in the back and one in the front of the tent. There was a riser with a podium and flip charts to unveil the plans and a small table of brochures and press releases. Everything seemed in order.

Then I spotted Louisa, J.D., a young man I didn't know, Big Jim, and a woman I assumed was Valerie as they simultaneously lasered in on me. I swallowed hard.

Louisa was the first to worm her way through the throng to my side, *worm* being the operative word.

"So, well, well. Goodness me. Look who's back in town," she said.

"Yes, I'm back."

"Well, that's nice. Ahem. I know you think you have some authority here, but I think it would be important for you and all y'all from up north to know that this is a *Langley Development* project."

I sighed. Did the woman not have one stitch of charm?

"I'm afraid you have your facts wrong, Mrs. Langley. Langley Development has an equal partnership with Triangle Equity. That would be a fifty-fifty split in all decision making, profits, and losses."

"Do you mean to say that you all think you can call the shots?"

"No. Only half of them. But I'm sure J.D. and I will find a way to settle any differences of opinion."

"J.D.? J.D.? You listen to me, Betts McGee, this is *my* project. J.D. wouldn't even have a hand in this if it weren't for me. He's my son, after all!"

Lawsa, as we are fond of saying in the South, she certainly was one feisty little Chihuahua, wasn't she? I just stared at her, and after what I thought was a meaningful length of silence, I smiled and said, "I'm certain of that. It's nice to see you, too."

I walked away toward J.D., leaving Louisa Langley marinating in her outrageous and insufferable hubris.

As my endless good luck raged on, more outrageous and insufferable hubris approached. Valerie Langley.

"So. You're the notorious Betts McGee?"

My immediate thought was that *notorious* was a pretty complicated word to be used by someone whose reputation and appearance spelled total ignoramus.

"I am indeed. I assume you are J.D.'s wife?"

"I am."

She stared me up and down and I matched her, designer detail for designer detail. Sunglasses. Shoes. Handbag. Diamond studs. However, I wore pearls and subdued makeup and was dressed in casual business attire. In my opinion, she had on too much of everything—gold jewelry, lip gloss, mascara, and cleavage, and her mane of blond highlighted and low-lighted hair was overprocessed within an inch of its life. It was a showdown of sorts and could not have been more ludicrous. My outfit should have been the least of her concerns. She blustered and huffed and I held back a giggle.

Clearly something about me ruffled her cool. What did she think? That she was the only one with the wherewithal to spend too much money on her clothes? The difference was I *earned* mine, and earned it by being able to think on my feet. She'd married hers, and didn't have to think about much except lying on her back.

Oh, pull in your claws, I told myself. To be fair, I had made a career and a whole life around being unflappable. Valerie had Louisa Langley for a mother-in-law, a barren womb, and no profession to buoy her up should her marriage hit the skids, except some kind of financial settlement that, given her situation and the formidable panel of greed meisters with whom she would have to contend, would never cover the expenses of her elderly years. All these conflicting and admittedly unkind thoughts ran through my mind and finally I remembered my manners.

"Well, it's nice to finally meet you. I've heard a lot about you."

"Yes. And I have heard all about you as well," she said, and walked away.

I noticed something funny about her eyes—her pupils were pinpoints, and I wondered if the cause of that was sunlight or something else, like a medication.

"So, I see you've met up with Valerie and my mother," J.D. said.

"Yeah. Charming."

"Well, my dad wants to say hello to you and I want you to meet Mickey."

"Sure. Who's Mickey?"

"Housekeeper's kid. Over there. He's like my long-lost son."

My heart skipped a beat and my left eye twitched.

"Oh! Really? Oh! Jeez, J.D., he sure looks like you . . . what are you saying?"

"What? Oh Lord! Oh! That's rich! No way! His mom's a nice gal but definitely not my type!"

"Right. Whatever you say. So, are we ready for this pack of hellhounds?"

"I think so. Come say hello to Dad. He always loved you, you know."

"Yeah. I loved him, too."

I said hello to Big Jim, asked him how he was. He took both of my hands in his and told me how wonderful it was to lay eyes on me. I thought I would break down and cry. But I didn't. Too many years had passed and I was only too acutely aware that J.D. was no longer mine to have.

The barbecue was laid out and people began filling plates and tables, talking among themselves. Joanie was helping Cam, who was helping the caterer fill chafing dishes over Sterno. She was actually smiling. And Cam, who was the total antithesis of Sandi, seemed quite entertained by Joanie— well, as charmed as a well-fed grizzly bear could be when enticed by a hungry lioness. His fat ego, though, still seemed to have room for a sandwich.

Cameras flashed all over from the time we disembarked until the last person had been satisfied with lunch and it was time to make our presentation. Surprisingly, Louisa and Big Jim decided to let J.D. do all the talking for Langley Development. Why, I thought, would Louisa make that choice?

Could she have wanted us to appear in the papers together? Or perhaps, despite her bravado, she and Big Jim were less involved in the project than she made out. Or maybe she wanted Valerie to think she had some competition. Who knew what devilment was stirring the pot in her muddled brain.

J.D. took the microphone, thanked everyone for coming, introduced his parents and Valerie, and made his remarks about how sensitive Langley Development was about preserving Bulls Island and that the only thing they intended to change was to move the alligators and other predators safely over to Capers Island. He talked about how they intended to use only natural pesticides and how fertilizer would be so carefully applied and how all around the borders of the ponds there would be swales and vegetation to absorb any nitrogen that might come off the golf course. He told the crowd that they had hired a marine biologist from Greenville, a fellow he introduced who was recently retired from the Department of Health and Environmental Control, to be our conscience in all areas but most especially to protect the impoundments and habitats that attracted so many migrating birds and their beautiful songs. You would have thought J.D. was some kind of evangelist. All my alarms began to go off. Then he introduced me.

I simply agreed with all that J.D. had said and of course acknowledged the great pride of Triangle to have the privilege to be involved in such an important undertaking, adding that there would still be a public dock, that schoolchildren engaged in environmental studies would still be welcome, and that Triangle's commitment to the sensitive nature of this endeavor certainly matched Langley Development's.

I could barely get these words out of my mouth as I stood by J.D.'s side. J.D. and I seemed like natural partners, standing there together. The cynical members of the press were actually smiling at us and taking more pictures. And then there was the groundbreaking itself.

Big Jim, Louisa, J.D., and I put on hard hats, took gold-plated shovels, and lifted a shovel of dirt at the same time, symbolically beginning the official construction. Cameras flashed again.

When it was over a member of the press stopped me, asking if this didn't upset me in some way, to see Bulls Island become just another beach resort.

"You know, when I was a girl and I wanted to know what heaven might look like, my daddy would bring me here."

"So then you understand why Charleston is so up in arms about it?" he said.

"We intend to give the preservation of the natural beauty of this island every consideration," I said.

"So you're saying that negative changes are inevitable?" he said, taunting me.

"I can't comment on that," I said, thinking he must have been a moron to try to entrap me.

Then J.D. appeared from nowhere and took my elbow, which sent shock waves through me and, I am embarrassed to admit, made me actually weak in my knees. He whispered in my ear, unknowingly evoking a powerful tidal wave in my southern climes.

"Don't talk to this guy," he told me in a chiding tone. "Notorious radical environmental confrontationist."

At that moment I would have done anything J.D. wanted and I was sure it showed all over my face.

The "notorious radical environmental confrontationist," who happened to be from a syndicated press service, snapped our picture in what turned out to look like a lot more than a professional moment—read: lusting for each other like wild jungle animals in desperate heat—and the next morning it was on the front page of every paper in the state and many others across the country, including the national section of the *New York Times*. The headline read, SOME BULL TO CONSIDER!

CHAPTER TWELVE

Catching Bull

Y ou're not going to like this," Sandi said when
I arrived at the office the next morning.

"What?"

She followed me into my office with a stack of newspapers and a mug of hot tea.

"Louisa Langley has already called four times, J.D. has
called twice, and there have been so many hang-up calls, you
wouldn't believe it. Like his Sparkle Wife thinks you answer
the phone here and we don't have caller ID? Jeesch!"

I flipped through the papers and saw one photograph after
another that made it look like J.D. and I couldn't find a bed
fast enough. I broke beads of mortification just looking at
the pictures.

"Bruton's not gonna like this."

"Oh yeah, he called, too."

"Great. Let me see what the articles say . . ."

"Whatever. Doesn't matter. A picture is worth a thousand
words, you know."

"Thanks for the tip. Hold my calls for about an hour,
okay?"

"You're the boss."
I sat down to read:

Triangle Equity, a subsidiary corporation of ARC Partners of New York, has teamed up with Langley Development, the well-known real-estate developers of
the Lowcountry of South Carolina, to execute one of
the most egregious scams in recent memory. The pil-
lage and plunder of Bulls Island all in the name of . . .
what else? Greed.

Bulls Island, also called Bull Island, once home to
the Seewee Indians, was named for Stephen Bull, an
English mariner who realized its charms back in the
seventeenth century. The island's history includes
pirates and Civil War blockade runners who found its
coves and inlets to be perfect hiding places.

In 1925, a northern investment banker, Gayer Dominick, thought that having his own hunting preserve
seemed like a good idea, and he bought the entire island. Whether it was the alligators or the bugs is un-
clear, but Mr. Dominick returned ownership to the
Fish and Wildlife Services in 1932, under whose aus-
pices it has flourished until now. Bulls Island has been
called the Jewel in the Crown of the Cape Romain
National Wildlife Refuge. But if this development is
allowed to continue . . .

As I read on, I ticked off every negative thought anyone
had ever had about commercial development. No remark
was made about the inappropriate stance of the partners in
the picture, but no remark was necessary.

Then I hit a quote from me that was a complete fabrication.

Betts McGee, originally from Charleston, who is the
chief operating officer of Triangle Equity, questioned
the morality of the project herself, saying it was a

shame to see a place that was her childhood heaven come to this ruination . . .

"I *never* said that!"

My body temperature went up to at least a hundred and four. I dialed J.D.'s cell phone and he answered on the first ring.

"Betts?"

"Yeah, it's me. Where are you?"

"Out on Bulls."

"Seen the papers?"

"That's why I'm out on Bulls. I'm hiding with Blackbeard in Jack's Creek. We're shooting craps with shark's teeth."

"You're a riot. Do you know that?"

"My, ahem, *wife* doesn't think so. Valerie was actually throwing stuff around this morning. Cups. Plates. A box of Honey-Nut Cheerios. Do you know how many of those little O's can fit in one box?"

"I'm guessing here, but I'm gonna go with *a lot*?"

"Yeah. Mother's raising hell, too, calling you a harlot. I just hate that. Women. So unforgiving."

"You'd better look out. 'Yo momma' might be right."

"Really? Is that hood speak?" He cleared his throat.

"Maybe."

"Well, it's still the best daggum news I've heard all day."

"Yeah, you wish . . ."

"I *do*. What are you doing?"

"Right now?"

"No, tomorrow night at eight."

"Oh, then! Putting on a French maid's costume and waiting for you on a waterbed in Goose Creek." Why did I say that? "What do you think I'm doing? Trying to figure out how to solve this PR mess in the papers today!"

"Why don't you bring some lunch out here and we'll figure it out together. And some bug spray. I'll get one of the guys to pick you up at the dock and I'll meet you at the Dominick House."

"Okay. What do you feel like?"

Pause.

"Anything. Just come."

We both knew his thoughts were soaked in mortal sin. Well, I was *assuming* his were, but mine? Definitely. He was probably just teasing.

"I'll call you when I'm fifteen minutes away," I said, and hung up. "See you later," I said to Sandi, who stood in the doorway of my office, as I started packing up my briefcase. "I'll be on my cell."

"Where are you going?" she asked nonchalantly, knowing I'd been on the phone with J.D.

"I'm going to hell."

"Oh, okay, and your sister called."

"Tell her I'll meet her there."

"In hell? Well, not quite yet. She wants you to come to the house for dinner tonight."

"Really? What time?"

"Seven?"

"Call her back and tell her I said okay, will you? Thanks."

I passed Sandi, went outside, closed the door behind me, and started down the steps toward my car when realized I hadn't asked the important question, so I went back inside.

"What'd you forget?" Sandi said.

"How did Cam and Joanie get along?"

"Like two walruses in a peapod."

"Perfect. Well, there's a lid for every pot, right?"

"I imagine so. See you later. What do you want me to tell Bruton if he calls?"

"Tell him that everything is fine. I'll try to call him. Or he can call me on my cell."

· "Whatever you say . . ."

It didn't take long for me to swing through Whole Foods in Mount Pleasant and pick up chicken salad in a pita, tuna salad in a pita, three bottles of tea, and two brownies. I had bug spray and sunscreen in Sela's car and threw it all in a Whole Foods canvas bag. I bought the bag in an effort to appear green, wondering how many other things I could do to appear as though I was making an all-out, sincere, and knowledgeable effort to minimize my carbon footprint.

I raced to the ferry, grateful that the humorless lawmen of Mount Pleasant seemed to be occupied with other matters that afternoon. I tried calling Ben Bruton several times, but I had no reception or the call was dropped. Truly, it was just as well. All I could think about was being alone with J.D., having wild crazy hot steaming sex, and getting it over with so we could figure out how to have a professional relationship that did *not* include sex. I knew there were some flaws in the reasoning of that plan, but at the moment it seemed to be the only sensible course.

I slammed on the brakes as I drove over the gravel of the parking lot and came to an abrupt stop. My breathing was irregular, the back of my neck was sweaty, my eye was twitching like mad, and when I looked in the rearview mirror, I saw that my pupils were dilated. Dilated pupils without the object of my desire even present were frightening. I put on my sunglasses and got out of the car, doing emergency yoga breathing exercises to calm myself. *Center! Center! Be in the moment!*

All the way down the dock, I chastised myself for having insanely Tantric erotic thoughts about J.D. He was married, I reminded myself. So what? said the imp on my left shoulder. Valerie was merely his fallback position, as far as the imp was concerned, but I also knew that calling her this was a horribly immoral position for me to take. But too bad, he was the father of my child, and I had never loved anyone else. This was a quagmire of self-deception, indecency, and rationalization the likes of which I had never experienced before. And there was no rule book to follow . . . well, not one I wanted to know about anyway.

As I hopped onto the boat and we made our way across the water, I decided that I would let J.D. be in charge of this nonaffair affair. He would set the pace. I was too crazed to plan strategy for a water-balloon fight, much less a total emotional collapse.

"Beautiful day, isn't it?" said the captain.

"Yes, it is." A beautiful day to steal a few minutes or an hour with someone you love.

"Mr. Langley says you're from here."

"That's right. I moved away years ago."

"Well, I'm sure you had your reasons, but I can't understand why anyone would ever want to leave a place like this. This is as close to God as I think you can get on this earth. Just so beautiful, isn't it?" He peered out over the water, pointing out an American eagle in flight that I had spotted as well. "Look over there!"

This lovely gentleman, this naturalist, was right about the heavenly aspects of the open water, the marsh grass, and so forth, but he had no clue that Satan himself was hiding all over the oyster banks, in the osprey nests, between the blades of grass, snickering patiently, waiting for me to surrender.

We docked and the captain helped me off the boat. I called J.D.

"Your caterer is here," I said, trying to manage a lighthearted tone.

"Good. I'm starving," he said, and I could feel the warmth in his voice.

"See you in a few minutes." It was like I had never left him. All the familiarity, the easy camaraderie, was still there. I just hated it. I just loved it. For all the risks and dangers of seeing him again, he made me feel alive, alive in a way I had not felt in so many years I could hardly remember it. I had spent almost all my adult years resigned to fulfilling my responsibilities and all my passion had been directed toward our son and to our very support. And to weaving my cocoon of deception.

While I waited for the truck to pick me up I called Ben Bruton again. The call would still not go through. I thanked God because I wanted to talk to him about as much as I wanted to spend a spa weekend with Louisa and Valerie.

Oh, and throw in Joanie, for the ultimate getaway experience. No, I just wanted to see J.D. and hear what he thought about the articles and the picture in the paper. And to smell him.

An SUV with a Langley Development logo on its side appeared from the thicket and in minutes we were bumping along the hard-packed dirt road.

"I'm Bill," the driver said.

"I'm Betts," I said.

"I know," he said.

It seemed I had the Clint Eastwood of Charleston County for a chauffeur, which suited me fine, although I should have requested a cardiologist.

We came to a stop and I climbed out, taking my briefcase and tossing the tote bag over my shoulder, gathering up every shred of strength I had to appear cool. J.D. was there clicking away on his BlackBerry, sitting on a picnic table like the sun god on a Mardi Gras float. He looked up and waved at me. Could he have known that the afternoon sun would enshrine him in streams of majestic light? It was as though the hand of God were holding him high on display in a luminous monstrance. I took this as a sign to let my heart proceed.

"Hey, you!" I called out, blinking my eyes, and yes, the left one was still twitching.

"Hey, yourself! Need a hand?" He got down from the table and came toward me.

"No, I'm fine. How are you? Want to eat here?"

"Nah, let's take my truck and go out to Boneyard Beach. It's low tide. And I can show you where the second nine for the golf course will be."

"Sounds good. Who's designing it?"

"Rees Jones. He's the best."

"Jeesch. Even *I've* heard of him!"

"You don't play golf, then?"

"Excuse me, but I'm not old enough for golf. It's an idiotic sport. Besides, it's not the best use of my time. Do you play?"

"You think I'd admit it now if I did?"

He got in his truck and started the engine. I just followed him and threw my stuff on the floor of the cab, and off we went. It still seemed odd that we did not embrace as old friends or shake hands as colleagues. But perhaps we unconsciously recognized that physical contact of almost any kind could be hazardous. It didn't matter because you couldn't fight fate. I could hear our sighs and groans approaching like a train from a nearby town, rolling down the inevitable track.

I tried to concentrate on other things, like the surprising amount of low-hanging branches that hit the windshield on my side, startling me, causing me to jump. J.D. laughed every time I did.

"I'm bringing gardening shears next time," I said.

"You do that."

Finally, we came to a stop and he got out. I was about to let myself out as well when I saw him there, ready to help me down from the high perch of the seat in his truck.

He took the tote bag from me and then my briefcase and put them on the ground. I had my right foot on a ledge and was trying to turn around so that I could find the ground safely while holding on to a handrail. It was a good thing I had worn pants that morning. And flats. There was no dignified way to climb down from a truck.

"You don't need your briefcase out here, do you?"

"No, it's too breezy, I think. We can go back to Dominick House to go over the papers, right?"

"I think so. If we need to." He tossed the briefcase back in the truck and slammed the door.

Carrying lunch and a blanket he retrieved from the depths of the storage containers in the back of his truck, we climbed the natural berm that separated the land from the dunes, and right before us was the spectacular curiosity known as Boneyard Beach.

It should have been called the Eighth Wonder of the World.

Hundreds of oaks and loblollies were spread all over the gray sand for miles like a spooky sculpture garden. Storms and erosion had left them all dead. Some were askew and some upright, in every position, bleached to a stark white by the intensity of the beach's southern exposure and the heavily salted air. It was a surreal landscape.

"Well, this sort of puts our relative importance in the cosmos in perspective, doesn't it?" he said, sweeping his arm across the expanse.

"I'll say. It's madness to think we have a say in the planet, isn't it?"

He spread the blanket on the soft white sand and we sat.

"Yep. But that's exactly what we're trying to accomplish. Feed me."

"Okay." I unpacked the bag with what I thought was nonchalance, as though we had lunch alone on a blanket on an abandoned beach every third Tuesday. "Chicken or tuna?"

"Wanna go halves?"

"Sure. Tea?"

"What are my options? Is that French-maid thing you mentioned one of them?"

"Yeah, sure." I lifted my sunglasses and rolled my eyes. "Look, J.D., that was a very inappropriate remark and I knew it as soon as I said it. I could make that same stupid comment to a hundred other guys I know and they would laugh it off. You? You're still thinking about it. We're in trouble here."

"Why are we in trouble?"

"Because I'm thinking about it, too. Not the French-maid outfit, but you know, us in general."

"Hmm. I think you mean us *specifically*. Well, that's why Valerie was so pissed. She can smell trouble, and seeing you in action made her feel very insecure."

"Seeing us in the paper made her even crazier, right?"

"Yes. The Langley women were not pleased."

But I was pleased that they were irked. So, shame on me.

We were quiet then, watching dolphins play in the water

and pelicans dive-bombing for fish. After devouring my lunch, I decided to lie down and look at the clouds above us; surprisingly, so did he.

"Remember that game we used to play as kids? What does that cloud remind you of?" I said.

"Yep."

We were lost in our own thoughts; one of mine was how absolutely lovely it was to lie next to him, even though we were not touching each other. He was probably thinking about how a certain cloud formation resembled his favorite dog.

"May I ask you a question?" I said "I mean, one that's absolutely none of my business?"

"Sure. Why not?"

I hesitated for a moment and then said, "You and Valerie? Y'all get along all right?"

I heard him laugh, but it was an incredulous laugh, as though I had just asked a dying man what he was looking forward to.

He rolled over onto his side, propped himself up on his elbow, and stared at me. I could almost hear the wheels of thought turning in his brain, raking his thoughts together like a pile of leaves to present them to me neatly in a stack.

"If you asked me, 'Do we get along all right?,' the answer is yes. She drinks vodka like water, pretends to suffer from migraines, and goes from one doctor to the next collecting prescriptions for OxyContin. You can't fight with someone who's stoned out on drugs and alcohol all the time. So, technically, we get along. But that's not what you're asking, is it?"

"No. But that tells me a lot. Was it always like this?"

"What do you mean?"

"I mean, you must have married her for a reason."

"I married her because Mother wanted me to marry her. It was a long time ago. Anyway, after a number of miscarriages and other issues, whatever bloom there was is long off that rose."

"You're going to tell me that your mother *made you* marry her?"

"Not really. Of course not. I was supposed to marry *you*, remember? And after your mother died and you left, I just didn't care about very much, outside of getting an education and somehow getting very far away from my family, a plan that failed miserably. Obviously. I even called you to see if maybe you'd had a change of heart, or something. Do you remember that?"

"Vaguely. I mean, I remember you calling. But I sure don't remember you asking me to run away with you."

"Because I was so young and stupid I thought you hated my whole family after what happened."

"Well, I did. I always liked your father well enough, but your mother? She's yours and you can keep her. She had a lousy attitude toward my family . . . still does. Who needs it?"

"That bull goes back for generations. It should be ancient history . . ."

"Except that it seems to keep repeating itself," I said. "And I was innocent enough to think we might have been the generation that stopped all the craziness."

"Well, maybe this project for Bulls Island will build something good between all of us."

"Aren't you the optimist? There's a lot of bad ink out there, you know."

"Yeah, I saw the papers. Look. We will just prove them wrong, that's all. One issue at a time. We'll have a series of feature articles or something placed in the press that shows how sensitive we are to the island's fragile ecosystems. Maybe some public lectures. I was thinking of hiring a publicist for the short term. What do you think?"

"A publicist. Might not be a bad idea. How much?"

"A couple of thousand a month. Not terrible."

"Well, while we're working on image, can we get someone to undo that picture of us? Jeesch!"

"Why? I love that picture. Screw the Langley women. Moody bunch. I'm just glad to have the chance to see you again, Betts. You have no idea how many times I have thought of you."

Here it came, I thought, a little seduction on the beach. Finally!

"Um, me, too. You know that without me saying it. But pictures like that just don't look good, J.D. And you know it."

"Well, it's not like we're having an affair, Betts."

"J.D.? It's not like we aren't on the brink of one either."

"Well, I won't let that happen."

"Really? You're lying there looking at me like this? Honey, your mouth is saying one thing, but your eyes are saying something entirely different."

He was very quiet then, just staring at my face. He smelled so good that I wanted to wipe my hand on him to take some of that scent home. If you don't think the sounds of surf pounding on the shore and the squealing of gulls, the sight of J. D. Langley's eyes, and the feel of a salty breeze floating across your face are an aphrodisiac, please tell me what is.

"Betts? You're right *but,* and this is a very big but, there are two things a life of mediocre satisfaction teaches you. One is to lower your expectations and the other is how to control yourself. I am the unfortunate master of self-control."

I sat up then, no longer feeling the rush of anticipation I'd felt on the drive here. In fact, I was let down. And annoyed.

"Well, bully for you," I said, "and your 'masterful self-control.' I guess my question is *why*? You want to kowtow to a drug addict and alcoholic, that's your business. Have a happy life. Now let's see those golf-course plans."

"Hold on there, partner. Aren't *you*?"

"Aren't I what?"

"Entitled to personal happiness?"

"Who says I'm not happy? And besides, what's happy *worth* if making yourself feel better makes everyone else feel worse? Doesn't it become some kind of exercise in narcissistic self-indulgence?"

"I don't know, Betts McGee. These are the kinds of questions I've been avoiding for years. Let's get moving."

"No, wait. Are you saying it's better to just 'keep the evil that you know'?"

"I don't know, Betts. I don't know."

"Whatever. 'Master of self-control' sounds like 'big fat wimp' to me."

"Ooh! Betts! Them's strong words! That sounds like a challenge."

He was actually smiling at me—and I could feel my temper rising, so I backed off to recoup my composure.

"Take it however you want," I said. I'll admit that the smile on my face was a forced one, put there in order to veil the bruise to my ego.

He had no intention of seducing me.

We cleaned up the remains of lunch in weighty silence and walked back to the truck. J.D. cleared his throat and pulled out a folded piece of paper from his pocket.

"Okay. Are we speaking now?"

"Of course we're speaking."

"Good! All right. Look."

He showed me how the second nine holes would wind around Boneyard Beach, using the existing freshwater impoundments as water features. I had to admit, it was a brilliant plan.

He infuriated me.

We talked for a while at the Dominick House then rode to the northeast end of the island, where the most expensive houses would be constructed. Our conversation was focused on plans and budgets, and then, before we knew it, it was time to go back to the mainland as it was getting late.

"So, you think a publicist is the answer?" I said, still fuming.

"In the short term."

He looked at me with an expression that gave me no personal satisfaction whatsoever, except that I knew from our meeting that I could report back to Bruton that we had a fair partner in Langley Development. He knew his business inside and out. So far.

We headed back to the dock, and despite the fact that there were no protesters that day, I was surprised at the depth of my own petulance. In my fantasy world, J.D. still loved me, we would have a blazing-hot affair, maybe he would or would not dump his wife, and I didn't know what else. I was very confused about everything except that it had seemed fair to assume that my return to Charleston would rock his world a little harder than it had. I felt like a fool, that I had revealed too much of my own feelings, that he was confident that I wanted him, and that it would give him just as much pleasure to tell me no as to tell me yes. What kind of masochistic nonsense was this from him? Worse, what kind of a woman was I to contemplate interfering in someone's marriage, no matter how ill matched they may have seemed?

We rode across the water in silence, stealing a glance at each other now and then, smiles of resignation passing between us. I just kept thinking how different things might be if he knew about Adrian, but I wasn't going to use Adrian as a weapon to get what I wanted. If J.D. had no desire for me, there was no reason to tell him about his son now. I knew in my heart that the time was coming closer when I *would* tell J.D. about his son, but not yet, not now. We had a huge job to do first. A very lucrative job. Seven hundred million lucrative.

When we docked, I climbed off the boat with the help of the boat's captain and J.D. was behind me. He followed me to my car—Sela's car—and he caught my arm with his hand as I went to open the driver's-side door.

"What?" I said.

"I'm stuck, Betts."

I looked in his eyes and knew exactly what he meant. He was in a loveless marriage with nothing to keep him there except his sense of duty and honor. And where would he go anyway? To me? And where was I? I had raised our son, he had gone off to college, and now who was there for me? No one. I was one of those people who was excluded from all the alleged joys of marriage and a traditional place in my community. And why? Because of three choices I had made almost twenty years ago during the worst trauma of my life—to leave Charleston, to have my baby, and to keep that child a secret. It didn't seem fair. But life, the universe, fate—call it what you want—the Force did not seem to be particularly concerned with an equitable distribution of happiness.

"So am I, J.D. So am I."

We stood apart from each other and sighed. I was certain he didn't know why I thought I would be stuck in any *way* or in any *thing,* but he accepted what I said as though if I believed it to be so, therefore it was.

"We should get together tomorrow," he said. "Why don't you come to my offices?"

"Sure. What time?"

"Well, I'm meeting with the power-and-gas guys out here at ten. I should be back by two or two-thirty, so why don't you come at three? I'll bring you up-to-date on our plans for waste management."

"Do you need me to come out here for that?"

"Nah, just come to my offices at three and we can go over everything."

"Okay. Sounds like a plan."

Neither of us moved an inch to get into our cars. We just stood there, like a couple of discombobulated teenagers, waiting for the other one to say, "Don't worry, things will be fine, just go about your business. Don't worry." Or something, some words of solace or encouragement.

"What are we supposed to do, Betts?"

A crack in the wall had finally appeared.

"You're asking me? Well, I'll tell you, then. We are going to build the most amazingly smart and gorgeous development in the history of the world and then we will see where we are. I guess?"

"If you say so."

"You said so, Mr. Master of Self-Control." I smirked at him and he shook his head.

"Touché."

I finally clicked the button to unlock my door.

He opened it for me and I climbed in.

"Hey? J.D.?"

"What?"

"I'm having dinner with my sister, Joanie, tonight. Jealous?"

"Please. I have my own personal hell, you know."

"Your choosing! See you tomorrow!"

We were laughing then, at the impossibility and the stupidity of our own lives. At least we were laughing together, and if nothing else, we had reestablished a friendship within the confines of what was acceptable behavior.

Later, as I dressed for dinner, I relived the day I'd spent with J.D. What had I gained? Well, first and most importantly, I knew for sure that his marriage was in rigor mortis but he had no real intention of doing anything except to honor his vows. Gentlemen like J.D. did not go sleeping around. It was cheap and reprehensible. No. It also appeared that J.D. had taken over his family's business to a great extent, because, I'd noticed, he never mentioned his parents' names in the context of business. Finally, I was greatly reassured that he understood and agreed on how critical it was to keep Bulls Island's ecosystems intact.

"Isn't it odd," I said to Sela over the phone, "that I worried so much about seeing J.D. again? Being with him is the easiest thing in the world."

"It sure looked like it in the *Post & Courier*. Besides, remember he doesn't have all the facts."

"I know. I know. But I mean, I thought he would be hostile or something. Not that Louisa wasn't and that Valerie wasn't . . ."

"Do not underestimate the power of those two. They can make your life a living inferno, you know. Valerie would love to scratch your eyeballs out, even though their marriage is a joke."

"Do you think so?"

"For sure."

"Hey! Did you ever hear of a drug with *cotton* in the name?"

"No. Why?"

"J.D. says Valerie is a vodka hog and that she takes these pills that I can't remember the name of except that it has *cotton* in it."

"Listen, I'm concentrating on learning about Napa and Sonoma. But I can ask Ed. He knows all about drugs."

"Yeah, ask him. I'd love to know what that little snit is up to."

Then I ran a brush through my hair one last time and attempted to muster the strength to go downtown to my childhood home. I had not been there in so many years; I couldn't help but wonder how many memories it would raise from the dead.

CHAPTER THIRTEEN

Home

It was as if I were floating inside a taupe-colored bubble filled with some kind of malaise—which is to say that I was feeling disoriented. I stopped the car in front of the house. First, Daddy's and Joanie's cars filled the two parking spaces. There was no place for me to park in our driveway, so I had to park on the street. *No space for you. Out in the streets with you.*

With a bottle of red wine under my arm, I climbed the three steps to the street door, opening it the same way I'd done millions of times. The door seemed to be more crooked than I remembered. I thought, Well, the house is old and probably continuing to settle, and after all, the foundation of the peninsula of Charleston is nothing but plough mud.

The overabundance of ancient wicker porch furniture was exactly the same as it had been in my grandmother's day, but the crumpled cushions had been changed and things were rearranged enough to feel odd and unfamiliar. I felt out of place before I even went to the house door. The next thing that happened was that I almost knocked. Stopping my arm in midair, I realized I was hesitating about simply walking into my own childhood home. To bypass that awkwardness, I opened the door and called out, "Knock! Knock!"

"I'm out here!" Dad's voice called from the direction of the kitchen.

He sounded cheerful, and that allowed me to put my discomfort aside for the moment and go in search of him. But I had this overwhelming urge to inspect the house first. On the left was the living room, and at first glance I thought it looked exactly the same as it had the day I left. Mother's portrait still hung over the fireplace and the red-and-yellow chintz prints that covered the sofas and chairs were the same. Her collection of Staffordshire figurines still stood in the bookcases. Their number appeared to be unchanged. In fact, every single detail of the room seemed to be exactly as it had been years ago.

The dining-room furniture stood in their original positions, but in the dim light of early evening, I could see that everything was covered in a thick layer of dust. The room had not served its purpose in aeons. At that moment I figured we would be eating dinner in the kitchen, which was fine with me. I was right.

The kitchen table was set for three with straw place mats, paper napkins, and stainless flatware, but with mother's best china and crystal. Daddy probably couldn't face cleaning the dining room, Joanie would have refused to iron linens or polish silver in my honor, and apparently Daddy no longer employed any domestic help. I decided it would be best to keep these observations to myself. Daddy had made his best effort, no doubt without a finger of help from my sister.

There was a platter of seasoned steaks and a bag of prewashed mixed greens for salad on the crowded counter. How they managed to put together meals with so much clutter was baffling to me. I hated disorder. Especially in the kitchen.

The back door was open and I could smell charcoal and lighter fluid. Dad was in the yard fanning the grill with a folded section of newspaper.

"Hey, Daddy! Need a hand?"

"Nope! I've got it all under control. Come give your old man a kiss!"

I hugged him and gave him a noisy smooch on the cheek. Beyond the grill area, the backyard was filled with dog pens and dog toys and dog paraphernalia from one side to the other. At least the animals slept outside, or so I assumed.

"This looks great!" I lied. "You know, I can't believe I'm actually here."

"Neither can I. Long overdue, to be sure!"

"Where's Joanie?"

"Out walking her brood. You won't believe this, but she's been cleaning up all day because you were coming."

"Really? Gosh!"

"She even gave the dogs a bath. Much needed, I'd like to add."

"Gee whiz, Daddy. Why does she have so many dogs?"

"She's a softie at heart."

"So was Hitler," I couldn't stop myself from blurting.

"Well, dogs are better than snakes. And she went to the beauty parlor."

"You're kidding. The beauty parlor?" Holy cow.

"Yep. How do you like your steak?"

"Medium rare, more rare than medium." I could only imagine what the house and yard had looked like before I got there. The day after Armageddon? But I kept a smile on my face and followed my father inside. "What can I do to help? Anything?"

"Yes. You can watch me make a perfect Manhattan. Would you like one?"

"Sure, I'll sip on one of those. I brought some wine, too."

"Good, good. Thank you. So, tell me. How was your day? You look sunburned."

"I probably am. I spent most of it out on Bulls with J.D., going over the plans."

"Joanie told me she was at the groundbreaking."

"Actually, Joanie was with a bunch of screaming protesters on the dock and I took her over to Bulls to try and show her the other side of the coin."

"That's your sister. She said it was interesting. And she said she met a veterinarian? Now, where's the vermouth?"

"Right here." Of course it was right in front of us. "Yeah, he's the older brother of my assistant, Sandi. Lives out in Summerville."

"Think there's a spark there?"

"How would I know?"

"Two cherries?" He had them ready to drop into the glass.

"Who would I be to mess around with tradition?"

He raised his eyebrows at that: I was the very embodiment of someone who messed around with tradition, and we both knew it.

"Cheers!"

"Cheers. Yeah, well, I like cherries anyway. All that red dye and sugar."

"This whole meal is unhealthy—cooking red meat over charcoal, loading up potatoes with butter and sour cream, salad that's probably absorbing chemicals from the bag itself—you can't worry about everything all the time. Sometimes I just like to eat what I want. Life's too short!"

"That's for sure."

We could hear dogs barreling across the front porch and out to the backyard and Joanie hollering after them.

"Julius! Slow down! Hang on! Let me just . . ."

She took all their leashes and came in through the back door.

"Whew!" she said. "Hey, Betts. Hey, Daddy. Whew! Crazy dogs. What're y'all drinking?"

"Manhattans. Can I pour you one?" Daddy said.

"Whoo-hoo! Betts, I usually don't drink any booze, but since you're here, I might need it to fortify myself."

"Have a double," I said, staring at her new haircut, which was something between a topiary and a mullet, " 'cause I'm not leaving anytime soon."

"All right, girls," Daddy said.

"She started it," I said.

"How old are you?" Daddy said.

"Right. Sorry," I said. "So, um, Joanie? Who cut your hair?" Edward Scissorhands? I managed to beep myself from asking.

"I went to one of those walk-in places. I don't think I like it," she said. "Too chopped up. What do you think?"

"Weeell? You won't be able to tell until you wash it and blow it out yourself, but I probably would have taken a little more length from the back."

It was nearly impossible to believe that Joanie had actually asked my opinion about anything, but even with zero knowledge of the beauty industry, she knew enough to know her hair didn't fit the rest of her.

Daddy handed her a drink and she took a long gulp on the way to the dining room to check herself out in the mirror that hung over the buffet.

"Looks like complete hell," she wailed from the other room.

"No, it does not," Daddy called back, and then whispered to me, "Who do we know that can rectify the situation?"

Joanie came back into the kitchen and rummaged around in the junk drawer until she found a rubber band. She scooped her hair up into a ponytail, except that the front layers hung there like so many feathers.

"I don't know why I even bother to try," she said. "What's the point?"

I almost laughed, but instead, realizing this hair debacle had most likely occurred in the name of Cam the Vet, I said, "I've got a wizard who can turn you into a certifiable Cinderella."

"Really? Well, I seriously doubt that 'cause you know you can't make a silk purse out of a sow's ear." She took another extended swallow.

She was saying this about herself?

"Oh, don't be so hard on yourself, sweetheart," Daddy

said. "I'm gonna put the steaks on the grill. You girls check the potatoes, okay?"

My dad really was a prince. I would've already smacked Joanie once and told her to shut up twice.

"If you want, I'll see if she can squeeze you in tomorrow."

I had recently invested so heavily in the inventory of Stella Nova that the last time I was there, the owner, Ginger Evans, came to the store from her salon to say hello and thank me for my business.

"Oh, Aunt Fanny's fanny! Why not? I can't go around looking like who did it and ran, now can I?"

I wanted to say "Well, you always have," but I didn't. I cleared my throat while rummaging around in my brain for a sensitive response.

"Look, there comes a time in every woman's life when she has to make the most of what she has. I say go for it." Before I could stop my tongue, I added, "If you want, I'll take you shopping, too."

"Really?" She was polishing off her Manhattan like it was a glass of iced tea.

I stuck a long fork in each of the potatoes in the oven. They were beyond done. "These babies are vulcanized." Grabbing a towel to substitute for a pot holder, I pulled the baking sheet from the oven and pushed aside the salad to rest it on the counter.

"Who cares? A potato is a potato. Well, as far as shopping? As you can probably tell, I pretty much dress in whatever can withstand globs of dog slobber."

My appetite took a cruise to the Caribbean with that remark.

"Because you deal with dogs all day. Makes sense to me." Joanie was making no movement toward putting the salad together, so I popped open the bag and dumped its contents into a bowl. "We have a tomato in this house?"

"Windowsill," she said, and pointed to a row of tomatoes sitting up there like the Rockettes, ripening in the filtered light.

Lord, and this was prayer, she was so insecure, lacking every kind of poise and in urgent need of professional help! I didn't know if I was up to the task. Or if I possessed the motivation. Then I realized I was judging Joanie by my standards when any improvement at all would probably thrill her.

"You know how to use a corkscrew?" I asked, putting the bottle and the tool in front of her. Her Manhattan had vanished and she was chewing ice cubes, another most unattractive habit I just daggum deplored. Daggum? My inner southerner seemed to have announced her hoopskirted return.

"Honey, if you lived *my* life"—she pointed to Daddy in the backyard—"you'd have one attached to a string around your neck. Watch this."

And much as you might envision how the swarmiest female wrestler on the circuit might liberate an enemy's head from his neck, she yanked the cork with a determined guttural sound.

"Wow," I said. "Impressive." But not in a good way.

I handed her two goblets and she poured a healthy measure for both of us.

Daddy came inside with the steaks and put them on our plates. Somehow we made it through dinner without Joanie and me having any kind of showdown, which was miraculous, as I had fully expected them to grill me about my life and all that had gone on over the years. Oddly, I seemed to be the one carrying the conversational ball. I asked Joanie about herself and she babbled on. Daddy had a comment here and there, but mostly Joanie lectured us about the cross she was doomed to carry.

It was as though I were a stranger interviewing them for an article on modern martyrdom. From their perspective, I was the one who had missed everything and my life was uninteresting to them beyond the politest of queries—where did I live, did I really love living in New York, why had I never married, and indirect inquiries about my salary and position.

Joanie liked wine and she liked to talk about herself. I matched her gulps with sips and Daddy drank tea.

We were having a bowl of ice cream with Pepperidge Farm molasses chip cookies crumbled on top when Joanie found it impossible to restrain herself any longer.

"So. Nice picture of you and J.D. in the paper this morning. I'll bet his wife laid him out in lavender-and-purple paisley and plaid for the way he was staring down your blouse, huh?" Joanie, poor thing, was wobbling along the shores of Vino Creek.

I decided it was time to clean up, so I rose from the table and took Daddy's bowl with mine to the sink.

"I don't think he was really staring down my blouse, but I saw the picture. I agree. It appeared, um, a little too familiar for my professional blood. But I couldn't tell you what Valerie Langley had to say about it. We don't chat."

"Hmmph," Daddy said with a satisfied grin, delighted by my deadpan delivery. "Why not? She seems like such a nice lady."

"She'd probably like to see you dead," Joanie said.

"Don't say that," Daddy said.

"She'd have to get in line behind Louisa," I said, slightly irritated by Joanie's remark. "Y'all got any soap for the dishwasher?"

"Just scrape off the food and run everything on the scrub cycle," Joanie said. "Cascade! That's *one more thing* to put on my list for tomorrow! Jeesch!"

Nasty. How long had my father been eating from dirty dishes?

"Oh. Okay," I said, gagging a little.

"I gotta go walk my babies," Joanie said, declaring her intention not to help us finish the cleaning-up.

"No problem!" Daddy said. "We're almost done here anyway."

Daddy and I restored order in the kitchen in the best way we could and neither of us commented on the ruckus outside as Joanie bridled her pack of animals for their evening stroll.

When the barking of her dogs could no longer be heard, Daddy and I settled ourselves on the porch in the old rockers with glasses of water, the sounds of cicadas and the pleasant hum and intermittent creaks of the rusting overhead fans the only sound track. The weather was warm but not unbearably humid. After a day in the heat of Bulls Island, I'll admit I was aching for some heavy-duty air-conditioning, like in the confines of my condo rental. But there I was on the porch of my childhood home with my father, wondering why in the world he was living as he was.

"Daddy? Can I ask you something without offending you?"

"Well, I can't answer that until I've heard the question, now, can I? But go ahead."

"Well, it's just that . . . oh, shoot! Listen, Daddy, you're a very wealthy man. Why don't you have a housekeeper?"

"Because your sister can't get along with anyone. I've hired them one after another. They all quit or she fires them. Seriously. It's ridiculous."

"What's ridiculous is that Joanie is sort of holding you hostage in your own home with her funky dogs, when you should be entertaining ladies, spending your money, and having fun."

There was a long pause from the direction of my father's chair. Then I heard a sigh that seemed to come from a place so deep inside of him, it was as though he had spent the last decade dreading the question I'd just asked. I waited for his response.

"Betts. Here's the truth. After your mother died, I never looked at another woman again."

"Why? Are you serious? I mean, I understand that mourning is normal and all that, but it's been so many years."

"Yes, it has. But like you, I imagine, the days just turned into months, and then, you know how it is in this town—people stop calling, and well, I don't mind this life."

"Daddy? Don't you want to travel? You know, go on a safari? See Cambodia? Mexico City? Paris?"

"Oh, Betts. It's not that I wouldn't like a change of pace from time to time. And I realize that Joanie living here isn't exactly optimal for either one of us. But this is the life I've gotten used to. She has as well. I think it's too late to change things now."

"There's something more to this and I know it. I mean, take Joanie for starters. She's just a mess!"

I could see him smiling slightly in the faint light, that knowing look of agreement and acceptance on his face.

"Well, she *is*! And you deserve more, Daddy. You really do. You worked so hard for so many years . . ."

"Deserve? What do I deserve? I don't deserve anything."

"What do you mean? You deserve anything you want!"

He became very quiet then and there was a long silence before he spoke again.

"If I could have anything I wanted, Betts, it would be to have your beautiful mother back. Her death ruined our lives."

"Daddy, it was an accident. What are you saying?"

"Perhaps it was an accident, but it was *my* fault."

I could tell by the insistence in his voice that this was something about which he was absolutely resolute. I hesitated a moment, and in that moment I thought about my own sins.

Finally, I asked him quietly, "How could it possibly have been your fault?"

"Because I was the one who insisted on leaving the Langleys' that night. If we had stayed another ten minutes, just even another five minutes, that truck would have rammed into a tree instead of plowing into us."

"There was nothing to be done about that, Daddy. That's like saying if you could've seen the future, you would've bought tons of Microsoft on the IPO! The accident was pure fate. Not one bit your fault."

"Ah! But if I had not had so much to drink, I would have been driving, not her. That was a choice I made, not fate, and look where it led. Look where it led."

"Oh, Daddy."

I reached out across the distance between us and put my hand on his. Despite the warm night, his hand was chilled. I had noticed earlier that his hands were spotted with age and that his skin, once tanned and manly looking, was now thin and crinkled like crepe paper.

"Well, sweetheart, it's getting late and I need my rest if I'm to live another day and deal with your sister. She really means well, you know."

"She's delusional," I said.

To my surprise he actually laughed a little.

"Aren't we all?" he said. "Now, you go give those Langleys hell and don't let the press catch you looking at J.D. like that again, you heah me? It's not nice."

"Yes, sir. Loud and clear."

The whole way back out to the beach, I thought about Daddy denying himself the simplest pleasures of life because of his imagined guilt over my mother's death. Of course, if I had been in his position, I would have questioned myself over and over, too. But as I said to him, he didn't have a crystal ball. Worse, because I was such a poor excuse for a daughter, I had not been there through the years to encourage him to get back to the business of living. I had work to do on changing Daddy's mind-set. There was so much for which I needed to atone and I had no idea how to begin. Would anything I said or did make a difference to him?

I called Adrian, got his voice mail again, and left a message. Then I decided since I was having such poor luck contacting him, I would start an e-mail campaign. Under the veil of e-mail, I could choose my words judiciously. I worried then that if I got him on the phone, he might hear some trace of anxiety in my voice, and because, like Sandi, he could practically read my mind, he would suspect something was dreadfully wrong and then accidentally begin somehow to discover what a colossal liar I was.

As I undressed for bed, I continued, of course, to worry about Daddy. There was no voice of reason in his house—

only the chaos brought about by Joanie's madness, her insistence on painting herself as a martyr and some sort of rescuer, whether it be of Daddy or those dogs. Or seeing herself as a righter of every wrong in the world by getting involved in protesting development projects she didn't even understand.

My feelings about developing Bulls Island were changing. The pragmatic side of me knew that the Langleys were going to build on every available square inch of the island because they were in the business of making money. But the side of me that loved J.D. believed that he would be careful not to destroy the natural beauty of the island. Especially if I kept an eye on him, which would be my greatest pleasure.

I hate to admit this, but in every private moment, my thoughts were about him. At one turn, I was ashamed of my feelings, and at another, I was exhilarated by them. Was I really such a terrible person?

It was about ten-thirty and I was turning in early so I wouldn't have puffy eyes when I saw J.D. the next afternoon. Just as I reached over to turn out the bedside light, my cell phone rang. It was Sela.

"Hey! You sleeping?"

"Nope, not yet. Hey, Sela, thanks again for dinner last night. It was so sweet . . ."

"No problem. Listen, remember you asked me about a drug with the word *cotton* in it?"

"Yeah, why? Did Ed know what it was?"

"Yeah, I kept forgetting to ask him, and when I did he laughed his head off. He's not a Val Langley fan. It's Oxy-Contin."

"Well, who is? So what's OxyContin?"

"It's this highly addictive painkiller that people are robbing drugstores and killing pharmacists to get their hands on. It's like morphine. They call it hillbilly heroin. It's got street value. I mean, seriously, is Valerie taking this stuff?"

"That's what J.D. said. And drinking vodka like water."

"Wow. Betts? Valerie is in big trouble."

"You think so?"

"Listen, after Ed told me, I Googled it, and you can't believe what's on the Internet about this stuff. You can extract oxycodone from it if you prefer the intravenous mode. It's totally gross. What's she doing messing with something like this?"

"Migraines."

"Migraines. Yeah, sure. See? It just goes to show you. You never know who might be a drug addict or an alcoholic."

"Gee whiz. Wow. Poor thing." I actually felt sorry for Valerie.

"Poor thing, my big fat pink behind! Louisa Langley probably drove her to drugs and booze, but nobody made her keep doing them. I wonder how much she abuses."

"I'll find out from J.D."

"How's that going?"

"So far? We're at the gate of the Garden of Eden and I can see the snake. No apples so far. I'm seeing him tomorrow."

"Who? What snake?"

"Let's not go to metaphor land tonight. Maybe he's just a good smoke."

"Call me tomorrow."

"You know it, sugar."

That night I dreamed I was falling from bridges and tall buildings, that I was dead, no one knew, and I was not able to tell anyone, that I was half naked and in public. Finally, when I woke at six, I decided to get up, take a shower, and have breakfast. What did these dreams mean? Falling—I hated the feeling of it. Did that mean I was losing control? Death? Was I going to fail? Or that I worried that no one was listening to me? What about being unclothed in public? Was that about the picture of J.D.?

After I showered, I read the *New York Times* from cover to cover, drank endless cups of tea, and was relieved to see that nothing about my work was in the paper that day. There was one letter to the editor from some nut who had lived in a giant sequoia or something for a year in order to protest all developers in the universe, but nothing else.

The sun was up, rising in the eastern skies as it always did, and I decided to go for a walk on the beach. It would help me focus, cover me in salt spray, and I could shower all over again. Who cared? Half the population of Charleston County was covered to some extent by salt spray. I pulled on a pair of shorts with a T-shirt and flip-flops and walked toward the water's edge. There was every sign that it was going to be a gorgeous day. The incoming tide was peaceful and rhythmic, washing the shore. I began to relax and let my mind drift.

I couldn't wait to see J.D., and the thought passed through my mind that perhaps I would just go out to Bulls Island anyway, instead of waiting for three o'clock to roll around. But that could only send two wrong messages—one, that I was desperate to be in his company, and two, that I didn't trust him to talk to the South Carolina Electric and Gas guys without me. I had to make myself busy until then. I walked on, unconsciously picked up a sand dollar, and picked away the caked-on mud with my fingernail.

Finally, when I'd had my dose of sand and salt, I turned around and went home. I placed the sand dollar on the porch railing to let the sun bleach it and went inside. I was thinking it might be nice to pick up a shell with every stroll and see how many I could collect.

It was eight o'clock and there were messages on my cell phone. Adrian and J.D. had called. I returned Adrian's call first.

"Sweetheart?"

"Hi, Mom!"

"How's it going?"

"Great! I mean, I love it! I mean, it's a lot of work . . ."

"No! I'm sure! Well, I'm so glad . . ."

"When are you coming home?"

"Soon! Do you need anything? How's your roommate?"

"You mean George? Oh, he's fine. I never see him. He's

got this girlfriend and he's always with her, which is fine with me because he's a partier and I like my quiet. Plus he's a slob . . ."

We talked for another ten minutes and then he had to go to class, so we hung up promising to talk just for a few minutes at least every other day. I could see his face and hear his breath and I missed him so badly I thought my heart would break. But I was careful not to let him hear that in my voice.

I just said, "Okay, baby, if you need a single thing . . ."

"I'm fine, Mom, I swear!"

He sounded so grown up.

"Okay, then. Love you!"

"Love you, too!"

I hung up and called J.D.

"Hey! Where were you?"

"Walking on the beach."

"Oh? Alone?"

"No, actually, I was with Tom Cruise and Alec Baldwin. They're fighting over me. How embarrassing is that?"

"Very." I could hear him chuckling.

"A day without humor is a very dreary day, J.D."

"Indeed. So listen, SCE & G canceled, so why don't you come downtown earlier. I mean, we can get together earlier than three. I have a stack of architectural plans I want to show you."

"How's eleven?"

"That's fine. See you then."

It wasn't long until I had reshowered, blow-dried my hair, and dressed in something only slightly provocative. The black skirt and jacket were well tailored and very conservative, but the little white blouse was something that might have made Lolita blush. Did I dare wear this to a business meeting? Oh, why the heck not?

J.D.'s offices were located right next to Saks Fifth Avenue, which was very convenient, as they had a parking garage. Parking was always at a premium downtown. I arrived at his offices, opened the door to the reception area, and smiled at the receptionist. The reception area was beautiful—dark wood paneling, Lowcountry artwork adorning the walls, thick area rugs in deep plum and gray—it was inviting and all business at the same time.

The receptionist led me to J.D.'s office.

J.D. had rolled up his sleeves and rolled out the plans. He was in the midst of explaining what six to eight million dollars, before landscaping and outside lighting, could buy someone to build their ultimate dream home on Bulls.

I tossed my jacket over the arm of a chair and I knew I was looking pretty good. I could tell by his breathing, which alternated between breathy, uneven inhalations and steaming sighs that shouted old-fashioned lust. Or was it love? Two compatible people of like minds who are wildly attracted to each other and had been all their lives?

"Well, here we are, J.D." I just said it, knowing he would understand exactly what I meant.

"I know. I'm willing to admit it, even if you're not. I'm in love with you, Betts. I always have been. All that stuff I said yesterday on the beach? I thought about it last night and I know this. I let you get away once. I'm not letting you get away again."

"J.D., you know I'm still in love with you. God help me, but it's the terrible truth. But there are problems, J.D. You have a wife. And I won't be your mistress."

"I'm not asking you to, Betts . . ."

Then there came the shrieking voice of Valerie.

"Well then, J.D., just what are you asking her to do? I can't believe it! Your mother was right!"

We didn't know how long she had been standing there and we were uncertain how much she had overheard. What was the difference? In just a few sentences, J.D.'s commitment to his marriage had begun to unravel, and I had been so very willing to pull the first thread. I began shaking all over.

Valerie's face was bloodred and I think that if she'd been

in possession of a pistol she would have blown our brains out. Instead, she turned on her heel and stormed out.

My cell phone rang. By sheer force of habit I answered it, although I was in no condition to talk to anyone. It was Ben Bruton and he was not happy.

"I've got a plane waiting for you out at Corporate Wings. Wheels up at three. I want you on it. Understood?"

CHAPTER FOURTEEN

J.D. Speaks His Mind

Betts was visibly shaken by the one-two punch. We weren't positive what her boss was so angry about, but we were reasonably sure it was the newspaper article. And before that, there had been the advent of my lovely wife. I wasn't exactly looking forward to the warm loving glow of a home-cooked meal that night, even if Val had been a cook, which she was not.

With Betts gone to New York and Valerie very likely positioned up on the chimney with a shotgun to kill me dead when I pulled into the driveway, I decided perhaps it would be best to spend happy hour in other company. I called my dad. In times of trouble, it's best to stay loose and keep out of the corners.

"Feel like a bourbon, son?" Dad said when he greeted me at the back door. "I never heard of a little trouble with the wife that can't be resolved with a double shot of O Be Joyful on the rocks."

"Where's Mother?" I followed him toward his study. I didn't want to deal with her.

"At your house consoling your, ahem, *wife*."

"Is Valerie, um, hysterical?"

"I would say *hysterical* sums it up quite nicely."

He opened the glass door over the bar and removed two tumblers, put a handful of ice from the ice bucket in each of them, and covered them generously with Virginia Gentleman.

"This is the best whiskey in America, son. Let your old man hear the story."

"Where to start? Okay, here it is. I'm still in love with Betts, Dad. It's pretty straightforward. Haven't seen her in almost twenty years, took one look at her, and knew right away I was still dead in love with her."

Dad settled himself in his favorite armchair and I sat on the sofa.

"Hmmph." He raised his glass to me and said, "Cheers. Are you sleeping with her?"

"No, but I intend to. In fact, I intend to sleep with her for the rest of my life. Do you know what kind of bull is going on with Valerie? Is anyone here even vaguely aware of the nonsense that's going on in my life?"

"I am well versed in the ways and wiles of the fair sex. There's not much you could tell me that would surprise me. But divorce is a horse of another color, son."

"What do you mean?"

"I mean to say that every now and then a man has to do what he has to do. I'm not saying that infidelity is right, but it happens. Great God! Look at the Italians! They're having sex every five minutes! And the French, too! Wasn't Mitterrand's mistress there at the funeral consoling his wife? It was all over the papers! This country is so puritanical and unrealistic about human nature that it's downright scary."

"So what are you saying? Just stay married to Valerie and have an affair with Betts?"

"I think if you are discreet, Valerie will reconcile herself to it. I'm pretty sure that Valerie doesn't want a divorce. Women don't want to get off the gravy train in middle age, J.D. Surely you realize that a divorce would bring about a serious fall from the Langley loft for Valerie. What would she do with herself?"

"Probably what she's doing right now—sloshing down vodka with pain pills."

"Well, that's not good. Not good at all. How are you and Valerie in the, you know, the bedroom?"

"Not much to report. I mean, I'm not into necrophilia, if you get my drift."

"Hmmph. Well, she should've known that withholding her favors would lead to something like this. Can I freshen up your drink?"

"No. And nothing led up to this except what's real. Thanks, though. Do we have anything to eat? Suddenly I'm starving. Do you believe that? I'm sitting here up to my throat in trouble and all I can think about right now is my stomach."

"We're men, aren't we? Rosie's got the night off. Mickey's got a football jamboree or some such thing. Why they play football in this heat is a mystery to me. Why don't you and I go in the kitchen and see what we can rustle up? It's amazing those kids don't drop dead."

"Yeah, seems crazy. Maybe just a sandwich."

I pulled him up from his chair because I could see that he was struggling. Ever since he had his heart attack, Dad had begun to age. Not a lot, but there were signs here and there of weakening strength.

"Thanks, son. I'm falling apart at the seams."

"No, you're not. That chair is deep."

"You're a gentleman to say so."

We inspected the insides of the refrigerator together.

"Well, it's slim pickings tonight. I thought your mother was going to make us something, but when Valerie called, she ran off to her instead of going to the grocery store."

"Mother's compassion surprises me."

"Hmmph. I'll say. But she loves drama."

"Some people do. We have eggs. There's some cheese. Want me to make an omelet?"

"You know how to make an omelet?"

"No. But how hard can it be? Isn't there a cookbook around here?"

"Yep. Right on that shelf."

I flipped though the pages and found a recipe.

"Here we go." I put the open book on the counter and ran my fingers down the list of ingredients. "So, Dad, if you could live your life over again, wouldn't you make some changes?"

"Absolutely. I just hate the idea of divorce, that's all."

"Are you saying that if you could stick it out with Mother all these years, then I should stick it out with Valerie?"

"I think I'm admitting that I have fallen in love over the years with other women, but I stayed with your mother in spite of it."

I knew he stepped out on Mother, but fell in love? And to tell me so nonchalantly? I went back through the refrigerator and found some mushrooms, half a red bell pepper, and some scallions. I found a cutting board and a butcher's knife and began chopping it all up.

"So, there's some honor in simply sticking it out? Even when all the love is gone?"

"Maybe. But then, it was different for me because we had you."

"You know, I have never asked you why you didn't have any more children."

"Well, that was a bone of great contention between your mother and me. I wanted more and she didn't."

"So that was it? You just didn't have any more?"

"I didn't say that."

The recipe said to sauté all the chopped-up vegetables separately in two tablespoons of butter, but mine were mixed all together and I couldn't see how it would really make any difference. So I threw a chunk of butter in the pan and turned the stove on to a medium heat, which seemed sensible.

Wait! *What* did he just say?

"Dad? What are you saying?"

"I guess I'm saying I don't want to see you make the same mistakes I made."

"No, I'm sure you don't. But are you telling me I have some siblings hidden in the woodpile somewhere?"

"Do you want toast?"

"Sure, but are you going to tell me?"

"Tell you what?"

My confusion turned to anger. It was bad enough that Mother had been sleeping with Senator Hazelton for years and that Dad was his partner. Did Dad know? Of course he did! And here he was telling me I should stay with Valerie because of a piece of paper when he knew she had an alcohol problem and probably a drug problem, too. We had no children, never would, and now he was implying that there *was* another child somewhere? Whose child? What child?

"You know what?"

"What?"

"This family stinks."

"Every family has its own peculiar smell."

We were quiet then. Dad put some bread in the toaster and set the table. I cracked some eggs in a bowl, fishing out the little pieces of shell with my fingertips. Then I threw in some salt and pepper and some milk, stirred it up, and poured it over the vegetables. I chased the whole concoction around the pan with a spatula and was well aware it didn't look like any omelet I had ever eaten.

"I could have another heart attack and die, you know . . ."

"Yes, and your dirty little secrets would go to the grave with you."

"They aren't dirty and they aren't secret." He sounded angry.

"Look, ever since I got here, you've been talking in circles. I come here, and tell you the honest truth. I *am* going to divorce Valerie and I *am* going to marry Betts . . . if she'll have me, that is. I *am not* going to engage in some sordid affair with the woman I have always loved and stay married to a woman I feel less for than my *dogs*! Now, why can't you level with me?"

"Mickey? Rosie's boy?"

"What about him?"

"He's mine."

There was a long pause while the news traveled the airspace and settled into my conscious mind. I thought he said that Mickey was my half brother.

"Seriously? You and Rosie?" I almost fell over. "She's like *my* age, Dad."

"I know. Silly as it sounds, we fell in love. She used to be an exotic dancer in one of my clubs. She doesn't come from much, you know, but I found her completely charming and I fell head over heels for her. I wanted to leave your mother and marry her when we found out she was pregnant, but your mother wouldn't hear of it."

"Is that when Mother . . ."

I suddenly realized that the eggs were burning. I picked up the frying pan and put it in the sink and dinner sizzled its way to its dismal demise.

"Yes, that's when she began fooling around with Brant, trying to make me jealous."

"And somehow you wound up with Rosie living here on our property and raising Mickey under Mother's nose?"

"It was the easiest thing to do. What Rosie and I did wasn't Mickey's fault. I wanted to make sure he had everything he needed and that she was all right. By the time Rosie's condition was apparent, your mother was so heavily involved with Brant Hazelton, I could have fathered ten different children with ten different women and built a compound for them right here! She wouldn't have cared."

"Dad, this is some very heavy stuff you're telling me."

"Well, I've wanted to tell you for some time, but the opportunity never presented itself. All I'm saying is that life can be damn complicated and you will figure this out. Would I prefer living in that little cottage with Rosie to living in all this grandeur with your mother's viperous tongue? Yes, some days I would. But it wouldn't be fair to Rosie to be stuck with an old goat like me. As soon as Mickey goes off to college, I think Rosie will be moving to Charleston. I'd like to see her find a nice young man."

"So, Mickey is my half brother, then."

"Yes. Yes, he is."

"Great God."

"I need to be sure he is always taken care of, J.D. He's a wonderful boy."

My head was absolutely reeling with the news, which, actually, I was strangely happy to know. I loved that kid.

"I give you my word on that . . . but, Dad? How did Mother allow Rosie to cook for us and clean the house all these years?"

"Your mother? She thought it was divine justice to have Rosie clean her house."

"Good Lord. Figures. And poor Rosie! How did she accept all this? I mean, it had to be a bitter pill, right?"

"Not really. She didn't have many options. We were really in love and both of us desperately wanted the baby. Somehow, it seemed reasonable at the time. And it's worked out."

"Well, this is amazing news, but it still doesn't solve the problem I have with Valerie."

"Which one?"

"Yes, there is quite a menu, isn't there?"

"Well, speaking of menus, it seems tonight's dinner has been canceled."

"Yeah, sorry about the eggs. Dad, if I go home, she's going to go crazy when she sees me. She might shoot me!"

"She might, although I doubt it. I think you have to get her in a sober moment and just ask her for a divorce, J.D. I mean, if that's what you really want."

"And you'll support me?"

"Of course I will. I know you've always been in love with Betts."

"It's true. Mother won't like this, you know."

"Don't worry about her. She'll come around. She just likes playing the champion."

"Since when?"

"You know what? You're right. She just likes the soap-box, that's all. Come on, let's see if there's a pizza in the freezer."

"Nah, thanks. I think I'm just gonna go home and face the music. Maybe Mother has already run interference for me."

Dad slapped me on the back and said, "A man can dream, can't he? Be careful, son. You want some advice from an old pro?"

"Why not?"

"Don't bring it up. Be very quiet and listen to what she says."

"If I don't come in the house all apologetic and all that, she'll go ballistic."

"Then you can tell her that her irrational behavior is a big part of the problem."

"That's usually what happens anyway. Okay, Dad. Thanks for listening. And thanks for telling me about Mickey. Hey! Does he know the truth?"

"About what?"

"You know, there's so much wrong with this family it's not even funny. A good shrink would have a field day with us."

"I asked Rosie not to tell him. He's too young and it's too complicated."

Withholding the facts made him culpable for another lie. And a huge one.

While I drove home I thought about Dad's life. I admired his affection for Rosie and Mickey, but I would not have stayed with Mother if I had been in his shoes. What kind of marriage could they possibly have? Was I being too idealis-tic? But maybe that was what love could do to a man—make him really see the sham, the absurdity, of his existence and motivate him to want to throw it all out and start over again. Betts had certainly made me see the absurdity of mine. I thought then that the real reason Dad had not left Mother and married Rosie was that he knew that if he did, despite the depth of their affection for each other, it would have hurt too many people and destabilized too many lives. In his mind, he had done what was in the best interest of everyone, but I still thought that Mickey deserved to know his father's identity. Who could withhold that kind of information?

As much as I dreaded going through my front door, I was relieved to have the truth on the table. I pulled my car up to the garage next to Mother's car and left it outside in case I had to make a fast getaway. The dogs barked when they saw me, so I went over to their pen and scratched their ears.

"Your dad's in deep trouble," I said to them.

Good old Goober and Peanut. They looked at me like they truly understood my plight, and somehow I felt sure that they did. It wasn't the first time I'd whispered my troubles to them and it probably wouldn't be the last.

I turned around and went in the back door.

Mother and Valerie were in the kitchen. I could smell freshly brewed coffee. Valerie was in a state, to put it politely. She actually hissed at me.

"You! How could you *do this* to me?"

"It's not about you, Valerie."

Mother stood when I came in, shaking her head and rolling her eyes. Somebody was engaged in mixing strong talk and caffeine in the hope of bringing somebody else's blood-alcohol level back into the neighborhood of sobriety. It was a hopeless endeavor.

"Ah'd like to have *ah* word with my son, Val'rie. Will you 'scuse us for a moment?"

As always, Mother's accent reverted to extreme southern when the hour demanded an Oscar-winning performance.

Valerie just threw her hands up in the air and I followed Mother through our dining room to the living room. Every few steps Mother looked back over her shoulder to see if Valerie was following us. I knew better. When she found herself in this condition, Valerie sounded like a rhino on a full-blown charge. She moved through rattling the china cabinets, banging into chairs, and talking to herself or apologizing to houseplants and furniture.

Mother looked over her shoulder one last time, grabbed me by the elbow, and whispered, "Maids are May when they are maids, but the sky changes when they are wives!"

"*As You Like It,* but not as I like it, Mother, and yes, there are stormy skies in the marital chamber."

"Very good. My clever boy."

"No need to whisper. She won't remember what she hears anyway."

"Son? What *evah* are you going to do? Mercy! I had no idea she was so—how do I say this politely? So *dependent*! And how dreadfully unfortunate of you to get caught with that McGee girl! Now the applecart is all upset! Do you know Valerie's mu'tha just gave Spoleto one million dollars? All because *I asked* her to! Now what am I to do? Your timing couldn't be worse! What will I *say* to her?"

"I don't know. Why not start with something like this. 'Your drug-addicted, alcoholic daughter who has given us no grandchildren has proven to be an unsatisfactory spouse for our only'—oops, can't say that anymore—'our son, who will be seeking a perfectly justifiable divorce and we fully support him.' How's that? I mean, we can work on it. Surely we can come up with something appropriate. Some party line."

I watched my mother's face transform from her milquetoast version of a maternal coconspirator to that of a very angry woman.

"*What* has your father told you?"

"Um, that I have a half brother?"

Mother simply stared at me for a long time and finally said, "Well, there it is. Now you know."

"Someone might have told me."

"Why? What purpose would it have served?"

Now I was angry, too.

"You're kidding me, right? What you really mean is that it would have embarrassed you and Dad if the truth got out. God! How can you live with yourselves? It's just incredible to me. Incredible."

She knitted her eyebrows and frowned, and in that instant my mother suddenly looked like a troll.

"What *evah* do you mean to dare speak to me this way? I am the matriarch of this family! I have given you everything I have to give, and you repay me by questioning my character? You, young man . . . you don't understand how complicated things are!"

"I think—"

"Don't tell *me* what you think! I am utterly uninterested in what you think until I hear an *apology* from you!"

We were going nowhere and I realized it was too late in the game to make my mother see the world from any other point of view but her own.

"'Manhood is melted into curtsies,' Mother. I apologize."

She smiled then and peace was restored. I kept a little Shakespeare up my sleeve for emergencies, you know.

"But, darlin'," she purred. "This is not really *Much Ado About Nothing.* You've had a shock tonight; I'll admit we probably should've told you about Mickey."

That was Mother's version of an apology.

She continued: "But your big trouble is in your kitchen. What-evah *are* you going to do? Is she like this all the time?"

"Not quite this bad. Lately she seems especially prone to overdoing it."

"Well, these diseases are progressive, you know. You've got to get her some help."

"Mother? I think the *help* has been the *problem.* Her doctors are too quick to prescribe medications. Obviously it has become habitual. It's awful."

"My poor *deah* boy! Well, it's a vile business."

"Anyway, when she sobers up, I'm going to ask her for a divorce. No. I am going to tell her that I am divorcing her. There's plenty of money for everyone and we can certainly take care of her . . . maybe send her to Promises, or that Cirque Lodge or some other rehab place. It's not really my problem. It's hers."

"And then I imagine you think you'd like to marry that McGee girl?"

"No, Mother. I *am* going to marry Betts McGee. So you may as well get used to the idea right now."

When she saw that the course was set, she backed down.

"Honey, your mother is the most flexible woman you will evah know. I'm going home to your father now. He's probably half starved to death."

"Sorry about the mess in your kitchen."

"Oh? Did you two try to make something to eat?"

"Maybe Dad threw the pan out. I would have. Anyway, thank you for listening to Valerie rant and rave. I'm sure there's more to follow."

"I'll steel myself for high winds. We've never had a divorce in our family, you know. Couples have lived separately, but never divorced. There was my mother's fourth cousin . . . was it Marjorie? Yes, I think—"

"Come on now, Mother. Let's move. I have to go see about my lunatic wife. Divorce might be the only possible failure we have yet to enjoy. Let's try to get the most fun out of it as possible."

"Listen to you! You're terrible! Just like your father! Well, just try to keep the hullabaloo within the dictates of good taste. For the sake of the family's name, you know."

"Come now, Daddy's waiting on you . . ."

"Son?"

"Yes, Mother?"

"I'm sorry about all this . . . I mean, that you have to go through all of this. It's just such a shame."

"Well, Mother? It's essential to recognize when it's time to fish or cut bait."

Then Mother did the most out-of-character thing I'd ever seen her do. She stood up on her tiptoes and kissed my cheek. She had not kissed my cheek in a very long time, but then Mother was not exactly the hallmark of demonstrative affection.

"You deserve better, son. I'm just not sure it should be a McGee."

Louisa the Merciless was back.

When we reached the kitchen, Valerie was passed out cold on the floor.

"Lord!" Mother called out. "Mercy!"

I knelt down and felt Valerie's pulse. My human Timex was alive and ticking.

"It looks like she just slipped out of her chair." I felt under her head. "There's no blood."

"Well, what should we do? Should I call 911?"

"Shoot, no. I will haul her bahunkus to the sofa in the den, roll her on her side so she doesn't choke on her own vomit, and cover her with a throw. I'll turn the television on, put the remote next to her, and tomorrow she'll think she fell asleep watching *The Colbert Report*. I've done this before."

"Clearly. I'll call you in the morning," Mother said. There was a trace of disgust in her voice. She went to the back door and turned around to face me. "Let her sleep on her back."

"Mother! You horrify me."

"No, I don't, and we both know it."

Then Mother was gone. Louisa Langley, mistress of a United States senator, the reigning queen of secrets and lies, judge of all mankind, few of whom met with her approval, disappeared into the night uttering words of unfortunate truth.

I scooped Valerie up like a hundred-pound sack of kibble and carried her to the sofa. She didn't even stir. I went back for her shoes, and by the time I returned and placed them where she would think she had left them, she was snoring like a wildebeest.

Suddenly I wanted to slap her face, but the urge passed as genuine pity set in. I felt a rush of sympathy for her. She had not asked for infertility. And it wasn't as if we had never enjoyed a special affection for each other. I didn't hate her family and she didn't hate mine. We were simply not meant

232 | DOROTHEA BENTON FRANK

for each other and that was the end of it. Adopting a child never would have made things better between us. She had turned to drugs and alcohol to deal with her problems and I had buried myself in work. Suddenly I felt very guilty and very empty. What kind of a man was I to ignore all the signs I had seen as Valerie began her downhill slide? It didn't say much for my sense of noblesse oblige, did it? Valerie was a poor but lovely duckling who never expected the queen swan to come swim in her pond. Surely I could do better for her than this.

What a day it had been. I was exhausted and wrung out. And this was a sorrowful state of affairs.

As soon as I left Valerie and began turning out lights, my thoughts turned to Betts. I wondered how she was doing, if her flight had been safe, if she felt the same way about me as I did about her. And then my thoughts returned to my pitiful wife.

While I was brushing my teeth I decided to take a tour of Valerie's medicine cabinet and all her handbags. My "pharma-hunt" yielded some interesting bounty. She had bottles and bottles of pills. Many of them had been prescribed within the same month. OxyContin. OxyContin. I flushed them all down the toilet. So much for Valerie's meds.

In the morning I was going to call her doctor. In fact, I was going to call every single doctor she had ever seen and demand that they stop prescribing all this crap before they killed her. I was going to tell them what other doctors she was seeing in order to let them know they were all giving her the same drugs to be used within the same time period. Shouldn't there have been something in the system to prevent that? Everyone was going to be put on notice.

I didn't want her dead. I just wanted a divorce.

Morning came before I was fully prepared to greet the day.

"What have you done?" Valerie was standing at the foot of our bed and screaming at me

I said nothing.

"Answer me! Where is my medicine? I need my medicine!"

Remembering my father's words of advice, I got out of bed and was silent. I went to the bathroom and closed the door. After my brief ritual, during which she banged and banged on the door, cursing and swearing at me to open up, I came out ready to begin dealing with her madness.

"Valerie? Let's go downstairs and get some coffee and try to be rational, okay?"

It seemed like a good, even generous suggestion to me—in the same position, I was sure many a husband would have dumped her bony behind in the dog pen for her behavior—but I was soon to learn what happens when you call someone irrational. It gets ugly. Fast.

I pulled on a pair of khakis, a knit shirt, and a pair of boat shoes. I thought when the storm had cleared, maybe I would take my brother fishing. While I dressed, Valerie continued carrying on.

"What did you *do*, J.D.? *Where* is my medicine? I have a *terrible* migraine! I *need* my medicine! I could just *kill* you! What have you *done*? *Where the hell is it?*"

I stopped in my tracks and faced her on the second-floor landing.

"Are you threatening me, Valerie? Tell me now. I just want to know if my life is in imminent danger, okay?"

"No, of course not. But what do you expect from me? Breakfast? Eggs and grits? Homemade biscuits? Why don't you get your girlfriend to make it for you?"

"I want a divorce, Valerie. Get a lawyer. Call your doctors for refills. I don't care. I've had enough of this charade."

"What? What are you saying? Divorce? No! No! No! Never! I will never give you a divorce! Never!"

When talking to someone who is raging, it is best to maintain a steady tone of voice. Do not be emotional in any way. Don't fan the flames of their anger. I filled the coffeepot with grounds and water and pressed the start button.

"That's not how it works in South Carolina, Valerie. I can and will divorce you. And you should consider rehab for the sake of your own life. There's plenty of money. We'll work that out. You can have the house. I don't care, but I'm all done. All done."

"I can't believe my ears! What's this about? That woman Betts? Your mother warned me about her! She was right! She's nothing but a whore!"

"Valerie? Don't you ever call her a name like that again. Do you understand me?"

"I'll call her anything I want to call her! She's a home-wrecking whore!"

"Really? What kind of a home is she wrecking? One with a drug-addicted, alcoholic wife? You call this a home? Pretty loose definition if you ask me . . ."

Then she sat down at the table, shaking with anger or early signs of withdrawal—I didn't know which—and began to cry. Really cry, as only a woman could. Big, gulping sobs.

"What can I do? Please don't leave me, J.D.! Please don't leave me. Don't. What will I do? Please let's work this out! I'll get help! I swear!"

"Okay. Get help."

"And then will you stay and start over?"

"I don't know, Valerie. We'll see."

There was no nice way to break this kind of news, but I was determined to get out of my marriage.

CHAPTER FIFTEEN

Betts in New York

I didn't even stop at my apartment. I just went straight to ARC. I decided that with all the anxiety I was feeling, it was better to face what was waiting for me and get it over with.

We landed at Morristown because the air traffic around Teterboro was thick enough to cause at least a thirty-minute delay, although it ended up taking the same thirty minutes on the ground to pass Teterboro on the way to Manhattan. But you never knew what was really happening with Air Traffic Control these days. That thirty-minute delay could easily turn into two hours. The airspace around the metropolitan area was ridiculously crowded, anytime, any day of the week. Maddening.

I had spent the last two hours rehearsing my speech for Bruton and I was anxious to see him face-to-face in order to plead my case. I felt confident that my history with ARC would well make up for any mistakes I'd committed or was assumed to have committed—confident except for that bile trampolining from my esophagus.

I grabbed my overnight bag and hopped into the waiting black car. Traffic was light, and before I knew it, I was arriving at the offices of ARC, with the intention of heading straight for Ben Bruton's office.

But outside the building, standing right there as though he had an appointment with Bruton, too, was Vinny Braggadocio. He smiled and held up a newspaper with the picture of J.D. and me. What in the world was he doing there? Talk about unnerving!

"Nice picture, sweetheart," he said. "Nice comments, too."

I walked right past him, but he came up from behind and grabbed my arm.

"What do you want, Vinny?"

"You don't walk past me like that, you understand?"

"How did you know I would be here?"

He threw down my arm and his face turned to something menacing and evil.

"I can find out anything I want to know, Betts. And I'm just warning you. You're in danger. That's all."

He started to walk away.

"What does that mean?" I said, calling after him over the horns of rattletrap taxis and other vehicles and the buzz of the crowd—everywhere around me, I saw men in dark suits screaming into their cell phones, shoppers and teenagers shouting to one another, North Africans hawking their wares—mostly copies of Gucci bags, Burberry scarves, and the like—over all of this noise and humanity, Vinny had said I was in danger. What kind of danger?

"Wait!"

He did not wait. He dumped the newspaper that featured the incriminating article into a garbage can, and try as I did to follow him, he disappeared around the corner.

Danger? What was he talking about? Some environmental zealots? I couldn't think about this at that moment. I had, like we say in the South, other fish to fry. Vinny was probably jealous because of the picture or something stupid like that. What an ego! What arrogance! I made my way into the building and took the endless elevator ride while trying to bring my breathing to a more normal state.

Darlene, Bruton's secretary, was looking a little too smug for my nervous system, and when she said in the special tone she reserved for the doomed, that he "was waiting," I aged a full ten years in a matter of seconds.

"Thanks," I said, and let myself into the sanctum of fear and terror.

As he had been doing during my last "papal audience" with him, Bruton stood looking out his windows, down at Rockefeller Center and over the thousands of people below, who were hurrying in zigzags like so many ants on amphetamines. His hands were behind his back, clasped in some kind of fervor of contemplation. His fingers were white from the pressure. I noted this in the same way someone climbing to the gallows would recall the patina of the hangman's shoes.

"Hi!" I said, attempting to sound nonchalant.

"Hi," he said, turning to greet me. "How was your trip?"

"Fine, thanks."

Niceties over.

I would not say that his expression was one of anger or disgust, but I would say his mood bordered on the bubbling fury of every devil in hell. Kerosene with a match to restore the fires to their most effective level. Human barbecue to follow.

"Sit," he said.

Like a good dog, I sat. He went around to his side of the desk, sat in his chair, leaned back, and looked at me long and hard across the dry gulch of silence between us for a very uncomfortable and excruciatingly long few minutes. Then he leaned forward, shoved the newspaper toward me, and leaned back again.

"You've seen this picture and read the article, I assume?"

"Yes, I have. Very stupid."

"Very stupid of whom? The photographer? The reporter?

238 | Dorothea Benton Frank

You? You know, when this came across my desk, it struck
me as odd. Really strange. There was something wrong here,
something that was out of character for you, at least for as
long as I have known you."

"I never said those things."

"Okay." Pause. "I believe you if you say so." Silence followed by more silence. "It's none of my business what you
do on your *own* time, but it is most definitely my business
what you do on the *company's* time. With our money. And
how you watch our investments. And our reputation. Obviously, I have to know what's *really* going on here. We have
huge bucks in this. The other partners, even Pinkham and
McGrath, are not pleased by what this picture implies, and
more importantly by what this scoundrel of a pissant jour-
nalist says you think. And before I cancel this entire deal,
I'd like to hear an explanation from you."

Bruton was predictably furious.

"It's complicated."

"Apparently. Betts, I'm not saying that you're not entitled
to a personal life, because you most definitely are. Love is
fine. But in business it's better left at the door. You get involved, you start to buy into the other guy's priorities, suddenly you exist in your own deal outside of your company's
best interests, and the next thing you know you are compromised in a way that's unprofessional. Even lethal. *You
know that.* You're too smart for some dirty little office affair, so what the hell is going on here? Before I cut our losses
and throw this whole deal out of the window, I'd like some
facts."

"How much time do you have?"

"All the time we need. Now, let's have it." He leaned forward and crossed his arms on his desk in the most attentive
position I imagined one could assume. But his brow was
drawn in deep furrows and I knew it was going to be difficult to explain the situation in a way he would want to hear.

"I'm not sure where to start . . ."

Forty-five minutes later, Ben Bruton knew all the environmental issues as well as I did and understood why close communication with J.D. was so important to the deal. I couldn't endorse decisions on ARC's behalf if I didn't understand the local politics and the real problems with pollution, erosion, and the disturbance of habitats.

"So there was quite a learning curve on this one, is that what you're telling me?"

I could sense that he was starting to relax, as there was a moderate change in the clench of his jaw from a Great White to the claw of a blue crab.

"Yes, and there's more. Obviously."

Soon he knew the history of my relationship with the Langleys. He asked all the right questions and I answered him honestly, choosing my words with care. But there was still a sense of uncertainty, that famous Bruton hard edge that had no problem putting a sword through a blueprint. He was on the verge of pulling me off the project, and if he did, my career would go up in flames. I could sense his temptation to do this in every nerve ending.

"So, you're satisfied you can handle the public's, shall we say, extreme displeasure?"

"Yes. Well, to be completely honest, we have had frequent problems, daily almost, with vandalism, but nothing more serious than slashed tires, green spray paint, and that kind of thing."

"Maybe it would be a good idea to go down there, you know, pay a visit. Do a PR splash?"

"Can't hurt. We're actually hiring a publicist."

Then, after a considerable pause, came the bomb.

"And what about J. D. Langley? Your boy is his, isn't he?"

What? What did he say? I felt the blood and sweat drain from my whole body and I was sure that if I looked in my seat and on the floor, I'd see it all there in a pool. The room began to turn and I thought I would faint right then and there. I didn't know what to say.

"He doesn't know, does he?"

"Know what? Who?"

"J. D. Langley. That your boy, Adrian, is his son?"

"How? How did you find out?"

"Two phone calls. And the picture on your desk. Great God, Betts, he's practically a *clone*."

We stared at each other. Finally, fighting back an ocean of tears, I found my voice.

"Why are you asking me this?"

"Why am I asking you this? Perhaps it might make a difference if I share the details of my personal life with you?"

"I don't know."

Bruton stood, faced the bookshelves behind his desk, picked up a photograph of his wife and children, and stared at it, taking a deep breath.

Then he turned back, put the photograph down, leaned across the desk, and said to me in a very quiet, extremely angry voice, "Because my mother left me in a laundry basket on the steps of a church when I was just hours old. How clichéd is that? It's like something out of an old black-and-white movie, isn't it? In fact, that's probably where she got the idea. Who knows? But the punishment? I never knew her. Or my father. All my life. No mother. No father. Never knowing, thinking they didn't even care. And they didn't. Grew up in orphanages and foster homes. Here I am with all this, and guess what? They don't know. No one to slap me on the back and say, 'Good job!' You want to do that to your son?"

"No, of course not, but—"

"You see, Betts, in this lousy world, here's what means everything. Integrity. That's the stuff that makes and breaks lives. You're a smart woman. So, even though this is technically none of my affair, I want to *know* that you're not going to do to your boy what my mother did to me because it's *so, so wrong*. What's your plan?"

"To continue working on the Bulls Island project—"

"And figure out how to come clean? I am no longer so worried about the project. A good campaign can clear that up. You know, another stab at informing the public that we aren't the evil developers."

"Even though we are."

"Everything is point of view."

"Hey, I'm on the side of the house."

"I know that. Betts? Listen to me, the sooner you tell J.D. he has a son—"

"He's married."

"Of course he's married. But he doesn't have to make a public announcement about an illegitimate son, does he?"

"He's getting a divorce."

"That's what they all say. Let me tell you something, okay? When there's shocking news to deliver, it's best to just put it out there. The person hearing it will need time to process it anyway. That's the truth."

"I don't want to use Adrian as a tool to expedite his divorce."

"Don't flatter yourself, McGee. He's a man. He's going to do what he wants."

"Don't go sugarcoating it for me, Bruton. Thanks a lot." I stared at him, a little angry and insulted. But it was true, wasn't it? It was all true.

"I don't like this stuff in the papers, Betts. It's garbage."

"Neither do I. I agree."

"Let's not have this happen again. Got it?"

"Got it."

"Okay, do you have plans for dinner?"

"I was just going to go back to my apartment and throw up."

He actually laughed.

"Okay, then. I just thought you might like to join a group of us at Sparks. We're starting a new fund to invest in the operating turnarounds of mid-market companies."

"Bor-ing."

"You're right. You could've handled that in the ninth grade, but I'm just guessing." He clicked his mouse on his computer screen and brought up his calendar. "Let's see here. All right. Looks like I could come to Charleston in three weeks. Is three weeks sufficient time to execute a plan to move the public-awareness-campaign rock up the hill?"

"Could you use another word besides *execute*?"

He smiled again.

"Actually, I thought I might surprise my son with dinner or something. He doesn't know I'm here."

"Good idea. Listen, I haven't told anyone else that I was thinking he was Langley's boy. That's your secret to tell, not mine."

"Thanks." So he *didn't* actually know! That son of a . . .

"So you weren't actually sure?"

"I play poker on the weekends."

"Ah. Well, it does my heart good to know you have a vice."

"Go call your son."

I stood, knowing I was dismissed. "Right. Hey, Ben?"

He had already reimmersed himself in the three computer screens on his desk, watching numbers.

"Yeah?"

"Thanks for listening and for—I don't know—understanding."

He looked up at me and I had the feeling our relationship had moved away from the red zone and closer by a notch to green.

"Life's complicated," he said. "Try and keep it simple. Don't get all sappy on us and stay in touch, okay?"

"You know it."

I let myself out, passing Darlene with a serene smile for her to interpret and distribute along the gossip machine. *Bruton did not eat her alive.*

I stopped in my office and went to my desk. I took the framed photograph of Adrian and dropped it in my purse. Seeing no other items that demanded any attention, I tossed all the junk mail in the wastebasket and left. I had almost left the building when I felt another hand on my elbow. Dennis Baker, Elevator Annoyance. Ew.

"Hey! I thought you were out on assignment. What are you doing here?"

"Had a meeting with Bruton."

"Everything okay?"

I just looked at him and wondered if that now renowned newspaper article had been posted on the company's website or SmokingGun.com.

"Of course everything is okay. Like it's any of your business?"

Dennis backed up and threw his hands in the air, feigning innocence.

"Hey, I'm just being a friend, you know, happy to listen or help out. Whatever."

"Oh, Dennis, Dennis," I said as I pushed the revolving door to the street. "There is no *whatever* between you and me."

I didn't look back, but I could feel his cynical smirk groping my derrière, which had been the target of his weasel eyes from day one.

I pulled out my cell phone and pressed Adrian's number on speed dial.

"Mom? I'm in the library," he whispered. "Can I call you back?"

"Sure, but I just need a sec. I'm in town. Wanna have supper?"

"Um, sure! Seven okay? Meet you at home?"

"Perfect."

I hailed a cab, got in, throwing my overnight bag across my seat, and gave the driver my address. When we pulled up in front of my building, Sam the doorman was there.

"Well, Ms. McGee! I wasn't expecting to see you today. Welcome home!"

"Thanks!" I said, giving the driver a ten-dollar bill. "Keep it," I said. I was feeling generous since I had not been fired in disgrace. "How are you, Sam? Everything quiet in the building?" I handed him my bag.

"Yes, ma'am. Quiet as can be. We like it like that."

"Yes, we do, Sam. Quiet is good."

He went ahead of me into the lobby and pressed the elevator button. When it opened, he held the door for me. I stepped in and he placed my bag at my feet.

"Anything else I can do for you?"

"Nope, that's great. Thanks, Sam!"

The door closed quietly and I pressed the button for my floor. For some reason, the elevator seemed small and claustrophobic. And I thought for the moment about how my surroundings seemed to change dimensions every time I left them for a while. The door opened and I stepped out, fumbling for my keys. The day's mail was stacked on the hall table and I was sure there was a mountain of it inside.

When I was out of town, my housekeeper brought the mail into the apartment for me and piled it on the kitchen counter, next to where I had the garbage cans tucked away in a lower cabinet. We had known each other for so long, she even knew which catalogs to discard. Bills had their own pile, Bergdorf's and Saks catalogs had theirs, just in case there was something I wanted from there that I couldn't live without even though I could walk to either one of them in twenty minutes. Anything that was hand-addressed or that looked like personal mail was placed front and center so that I would be sure not to miss it. I gave that stack a cursory flip and decided it could all wait until later.

My apartment felt lonely. I went into my bedroom and decided when I caught a glance of myself in the mirror that I looked lonely, too. Maybe I was.

"You need a shower," I said out loud to no one, and began taking off my clothes.

I let the water in my bathroom run and run until the air was thick with steam. A hot shower always lifted my mood and Adrian would be there soon. I would order sushi or whatever he wanted. We would get caught up. I missed him then, something fierce, and I couldn't wait for my arms to be around his neck.

The time flew by, the mail dropped into the trash, and soon Adrian was there, ringing the doorbell.

"Hi, Mom! Where are you?"

He had rung the doorbell and also let himself in, calling out so he wouldn't scare me to death.

"Hey! Where's my boy? Come here, you!"

It seemed that he had grown taller and older, more mature in the few weeks since I had seen him, and I marveled at the changes.

"Mom! Wow! You look great!"

Maybe I had a bit of a suntan?

"Thanks! So do you! Who is this strapping young man before me? Oh! Sweetheart, I missed you so!"

"I missed you, too! Strapping? What's for dinner?"

"Just like a male, always thinking of your stomach!" I said. "Get the menus!"

"Nothing like a home-cooked delivery!" he said.

"You know it!"

Soon we were eating sashimi, shrimp tempura rolls, and all sorts of Japanese delicacies.

"So tell me every detail of your college experience, baby. How are your classes? Your roommate?"

"Classes are wicked hard. It seems like all I ever do is study. George the Slob is good. He's from like this really huge family. Must have a zillion cousins or something. On parents' weekend—"

"Parents' weekend? Did I miss that?"

"It's okay, Mom. I called Aunt Jennie and she came. I wasn't going to drag you all the way back here for something that lame. I mean, it was stupid and it wasn't important to me."

"I feel terrible! Adrian! You know I would've come! I just didn't remember . . ."

"I know that! Jeez, Mom, don't fall apart over it. It was this really huge waste of time anyway. Seriously!"

"Still! I mean, I never missed a class play or anything and now I blew this? Your first parents' weekend?"

"There's another one on the calendar. If you want to blow a perfectly good day sitting in an auditorium listening to a bunch of academics who are so boring you could kill yourself . . ."

"When you find out the date, I want to know, okay?"

"It's on the website. But anyway, I gotta tell you, Mom, the only thing that sort of got to me was that George has such a huge family! Seriously! I mean, there's just us? Don't we have any cousins or *anything*? Any old ladies in nursing homes? We're from Atlanta, right?"

We're from Atlanta, right? His words were slamming all around the inside of my skull like bullets ricocheting on the walls of a steel vault. Was this the moment to tell him? No. I quickly decided it was not. News of that importance deserved a well-thought-through revelation, not some slapdash "Oh, by the way . . ."

"Adrian, I wish I could tell you we have more family, but well? What can I say?"

"Well, I Googled 'McGee' and 'Georgia' and there are massive amounts of them in every county. It's just a little hard to believe we don't have anyone on the planet besides us who is a blood relative."

"I know. But there it is. We don't have one single relative in the entire state of Georgia. Maybe some of them are distantly related, but I never knew them." I was deceiving him again. This could not go on forever, but I couldn't help myself.

"Not even one hillbilly hiding in the mountains of Tennessee? Somebody with a still and no teeth and pet pigs?"

"If we do have relatives like that, I wouldn't be claiming them and you know it. So tell me about your professors." My left eyelid began to twitch.

"My professors? Interesting question. They cover a wide range. I think my algebra teacher is like an alien or something . . . Mom? Are you okay?"

"Sure, I'm fine. What do you mean?"

"Your left eye is, like, going nuts over there. What's bothering you?"

"Me? Oh, nothing. Just a little stress at work." My traitor-ous eyelid!

"Must be 'cause I know the signs! So, how is Charleston and what's up with that thing you're doing?"

"Developing Bulls Island. And Charleston is hotter than the hinges on the back door of hell. The bugs! And it's mug-gier than the—"

"Okay! Got the picture! But other than the tropics, how was the play, Mrs. Lincoln?"

"Oh, shoot. Adrian? It's a rough project. Unpopular be-cause Bulls Island was always this pristine little oasis. Now it's gonna have homes for multimillionaires and the radical environmentalists are flipping and—"

"Sounds like a battlefield."

"Pretty much."

"Hey, Mom?"

"Yeah?"

"Whatever happened to that guy you were seeing? The one that sent you all the flowers?"

Now, for the first time ever, my *right* eyelid began to twitch. I had a regular duo of Judas Iscariots harmonizing smack in the middle of my face.

CHAPTER SIXTEEN

The Envelope, Please

It was Monday morning and I was back in Charleston. Sandi had been e-mailing me like mad to let me know that Louisa Langley was waiting for me in the office. She had been there for an hour. And the prior Friday, while I was having my confession heard by Bruton in New York, she had parked herself in my office, not believing Sandi that I was gone for the weekend, and in the process making Sandi a nervous wreck. When you realize that Sandi was something of a female fortress to begin with, you get some idea of how relentless the imperious Louisa Langley could be given the opportunity to bare her fangs.

I e-mailed her back: *Throw her a raw piece of meat. I'll be there in ten minutes.*

I wasn't looking forward to starting my day with a confrontation with Louisa Langley, but I wasn't afraid of her either.

Just after nine o'clock, I pulled into the office parking lot to discover that Louisa's big old Benz wagon had commandeered my spot. Good grief. She was worse than a male dog marking the neighborhood and just as childish.

I pulled into the visitor spot, turned off the ignition, and took a deep breath. What would I say to her? And what accusations of transgression would she hurl my way? I got out and went inside.

There she was in her navy-blue-and-tan Lilly Pulitzer print dress and jacket, wearing pearls and embalmed in makeup.

"Good morning, Sandi. Messages? Good morning, Louisa."

Yes, I took the liberty of calling her by her first name.

Sandi handed me a stack of pink sheets with various names and phone numbers on it. I made my way toward my office, talking over my shoulder.

"Do you want to come in, Louisa? Have something on your mind?"

She followed me in a bluster and dropped her purse on my desk. I went around to my side of the desk and silently stared at her purse and then at her. She picked up the offending Gucci and put it on a chair adjacent to the desk. I inhaled, admittedly puffing myself up over the small victory.

"Would you like coffee? A cold drink?"

"No, thank you. I don't drink coffee."

"Neither do I."

"One of the very few things we have in common, I'm sure."

"Indeed. Won't you sit down?"

She sat, shifting around in her seat until her bony rump was comfortable.

"So, what can I do for you, Louisa?"

"Well, you can go on back up to New York City and get out of our lives, for starters."

I looked at her and smiled the same serene smile I had given Bruton's secretary.

"Can't do that and I won't do that. Is there anything else?"

"You certainly have become a brazen thing, haven't you, now?"

"I'm not sure what you mean by *brazen,* but it surely sounds accusatory and very impolite, considering that you burst in here—and not for the first time—uninvited and unannounced." I said this to her in the detached tone I reserved for the Dennis Bakers of the world. Another point for me.

"Betts? My son has enough to deal with without you sashaying in here like something from a bandbox and turning his head." Half point.

" 'Bandbox'? 'Turning his head'? My, my, Louisa. I didn't know you found me so attractive." Full point.

Her face and neck turned scarlet and I knew I was winning.

"You had better just listen to me, Betts McGee. There are greater forces at play here. An oath taken before God, a very sick wife, and a hound dog for a son. Did you know my son has announced his intentions to marry you? Did you know he has asked his wife for a divorce? Don't you feel any remorse?"

That was all news to me. But . . . remorse? I leaned back in my chair and just looked at her, thinking loudly enough for her to hear, I feel no more remorse than you did for being the indirect cause of my mother's death and I don't really care what you think.

What I said aloud was: "For your information, not that it's any of your business, J.D. and I are not involved."

She pulled the newspaper article from her purse and slammed it on the desk in front of me.

"Perhaps," she said, "but any fool can see it won't be long before y'all *are* involved."

"What do you want from me, Louisa?"

"I have given this a great deal of thought and it is a complicated and terrible situation all around. I think many things. First, it's patently obvious J.D. still cares for you. Loves you, in fact. Second, his wife, his good and loyal wife of *many* years, is dreadfully insecure and appears to have some rather serious health problems. I would like to see J.D. help her get back on her feet and then you all can go fly to the moon on a wooden horse for all we care. It's not right to kick Valerie in the teeth while she's in this precarious situation. It's not nice."

"You of all people have some nerve to decide what's nice and what isn't nice."

"That may be true, but Lord in His heaven, Betts, the poor girl is a disaster and your presence has simply exacerbated her problems. She is saying and doing all manner of crazy things. I am afraid for her mental health, and to tell you the truth, I am afraid for her life."

. . . afraid for her life . . .

She had me there. Game, set, match. The horrible old biddy was right.

"Listen," she continued. "I can see with my own eyes what's happening here and so can the whole world. I'm just asking you to back away from J.D. until we can get Valerie under control . . . you know, stabilized, that's all."

"This isn't a contest, Louisa. But I happen to agree with you. When you marry, you make a deal. He owes her that much, to try and help her overcome her problems, that is. I will tell him that."

"Then we all have nothing else to discuss."

I stood to let her know she could leave then, that she might have won the day, but that I was still someone to be reckoned with, not a coward, but a reasonable woman who would play fair in a time of crisis.

She stood and looked at me long and hard, relieved that her point was taken, but it was clear that to be spoken to in such plain words had disarmed her. No one spoke to Louisa Langley without a bow and a kiss for the ring first.

"I appreciate your candor, Louisa."

"Well, I am relieved that you do. I imagine that soon the day will dawn when we will have to find our way to getting along again, won't we now?" She spoke with such a long-drawn-out southern accent you would have thought she'd grown up at Tara.

"Yes, but not now. We can save our mutual admiration for another day."

"Thank you, Betts. Big Jim always said you were a *decent* person."

Decent person? That was the best she could manage? I let it slide. I wasn't going to argue with her any more than I already had. It wasn't worth it.

I watched her leave my office, and when I heard the front door close behind her, I went out to Sandi to collect the other messages that had come in.

"Holy cow," she said.

"Did you hear what she said?"

"Of course I did. But you have more drama to deal with this morning."

"What now?"

"J.D. called. There has been a major disaster out on Bulls. Most of the big equipment has been damaged and one of the guys involved was seriously attacked by an alligator. Lost most of one leg and his whole arm. He almost bled to death, but somehow they got him out of there and to the hospital. Needless to say, he's in critical condition."

"What? Are you kidding? Oh no! Oh Lord! This is terrible! Who knows about this?"

"The immediate world."

"Were the police called in?"

"Of course! It's trespassing, destruction of private property—"

"Get J.D. on the phone."

As Sandi started dialing she said, "He's already called four times—"

"Why didn't you tell me? Interrupt me?"

"Because I figured ten minutes one way or the other wasn't going to change the facts, and you had your hands full with his mother."

She was right, of course. There was enough madness in the air already; an interruption from J.D. would only have made Louisa more insane . . . and perhaps that was what Sandi had been thinking. It didn't matter.

I went back to my office and dropped into my chair. It

wasn't even nine-thirty and I felt like I had worked a ten-hour day in the hot sun.

"J.D. on line one," Sandi called.

I picked up the phone and somehow, the very second I heard his voice, I felt better.

"Got those public-relations folks on the payroll yet?" I asked.

"I wish. This is some mess," he said. "These idiots took a sledgehammer to everything. You might want to come out here and bring a camera with you."

"Did you call the insurance guys?"

"Of course. But the *Post & Courier* is here, and the *State* as well. Every local network affiliate is on its way with a crew—"

"I'll be there as fast as I can." Great, I thought. "I'll be on my cell," I said to Sandi as I sailed past her and out the door.

"Is there anything I can do?"

"I'll call you . . ."

In my car, I looked in the rearview mirror before I backed out of the parking space. Wait! Was it the same man who had followed me before? Was that him across the street sitting in his car pretending to read a newspaper? Yes! What did he want? It occurred to me that he could be a friend of Vinny's. Why would Vinny care what I did? What was the matter with him? Apparently, Vinny was not going to go quietly into the mists and disappear. I would have to call him and ask him nicely to call off the dogs. Yes, that's what I would do. As soon as I had resolved the problems at Bulls Island and the endless stream of trouble this entire development was causing.

All the way out to Awendaw I worried. First of all, someone had to put a stop to these incidents of vandalism. Maybe we could put a guard or even two on the island overnight in a secure area, free of man-eating reptiles. Then there was the PR problem. Who would want to live in a multimillion-dollar house on an island that was infested with hungry alligators? I had thought most of them or all of them had been moved over to Capers Island. Clearly, they missed one or two.

I pulled into the parking lot and hurried to the dock. J.D. had the company boat there waiting for me with a captain. Three or four reporters were also on the dock, posted there to see who would show up, but I wasn't talking to them until I spoke to J.D.

They recognized me.

"Excuse me! . . . Ms. McGee! . . . Do you have a comment on the break-in last night? . . . Do you know that the victim's life is hanging by a thread? . . . Do you know if they successfully reattached his arm?"

No comment! No comment! No comment!

Even though *we*—Triangle Equity and Langley Development—were the victims here, we were going to have to endure more scrutiny and criticism and I knew it. Fine! Let the entire citizenry of the state of South Carolina come have a look!

I boarded the boat as quickly as I could and escaped the inquisition of the stringers from the press. But more of them were waiting on the landing at Bulls Island. Maybe we needed to hold a press conference. I could feel my chest constrict, then my eye started twitching, and I just wished it would all go away. All I wanted to do was develop the island with sensitivity to the pertinent issues, make my money, and get the hell out of town. But then there was the matter of J.D. Well, I couldn't focus on J.D., except that at some point we would have to have some discussion about Valerie. What was *really* going on with her? I wondered.

As soon as the work site came into view my priorities reordered themselves. First, somebody had to clean up the destruction. There was broken glass all over the ground and machetes hanging from the tires of earthmovers and backhoes with smashed windshields. Every piece of equipment had been spray-painted with peace signs, dollar signs, and slogans like STOP THE MADNESS! KILL GENTRIFICATION! TAKE

BACK THE EARTH! I sympathized with the sentiments, but the reality was that you couldn't stop progress of this type. Moreover, the world was better off with someone like J. D. Langley in charge of developing Bulls Island than with any number of disreputable butchers out there who would do much more harm than good.

"Morning, Betts," J.D. called out to me.

"Nice little disaster we've got here, huh? How's the guy that the gator bit?"

"He's in a medically induced coma. Lost half his blood, I heard. Can't talk to *him* for a while."

"Good Lord, that's awful. Even if he is a criminal. They didn't catch anyone else?"

"No. The three fellows who got him to the ER just took off and left his arm in a cooler filled with ice and vitamin drinks right in the middle of the admissions area."

"Fortified with guava and pomegranate, but running like sissies?"

"Yep. Probably afraid of the cops. Maybe somebody got a plate number; I don't know. We got a couple hundred thousand dollars' worth of damage here. Maybe more. The foreman is trying to put some numbers together for the claims adjusters over there." He pointed to two men in khaki pants and knit shirts with cameras, talking to one of the foremen and some other guys from Langley. "We're supposed to be running power and sewage lines this week and this fiasco is probably going to delay that. How many barges do we have in Charleston that can get us new equipment on short notice?"

"Good question. Well, there's just no good news anywhere, is there?"

"No. Apparently not."

J.D. took off his sunglasses and I took off mine. We looked at each other long and hard. Each of us was confident of the other's ability to stay cool while we got everything straightened out.

"J.D., we need a plan to secure this place. Pronto."

"Got one. My guys are bringing two trailers over on a barge. We were gonna do that anyway, for office space. But I got four of the guys to agree to start sleeping out here and they have shotguns. We're gonna post signs and run fencing around the equipment with barbed wire around the top. And of course the SC Wildlife men are gonna do another gator roundup."

"Yeah, I thought the gators were all gone to Capers."

"They were, but somebody forgot they can swim."

"Clearly. Right. Of course they can. Did you talk to the press?"

"I just told them that Langley and Triangle deeply regretted the terrible trauma caused by the criminal actions of the radical environmentalist group who destroyed our private property. And I told them that we had not decided whether or not to press charges. Personally, I think he suffered enough. What do you think?"

"I think it would be seriously lousy to put that guy in jail. But the ones that ran away? I say, let 'em hang."

"Whoo! That's cold, Betts. Better let me do the talking. You know, in the interest of public support?"

"You're right. That's probably best."

Oddly, the press was not that interested in talking to us. I watched as the reporters spoke to their cameras, pointing to the spot where the alligator had attacked the trespasser. Their eyes grew wide with excitement as they recounted the event, gesturing to the marsh and the birds of prey overhead. It seemed that they were more concerned with the *human-interest* story of the poor idiot who almost lost his life in the name of industrial sabotage. And they were clearly painting Bulls Island as a dangerous place. I had little doubt we would be thoroughly vilified in tomorrow's papers and on the evening news. But they pretty much shot their footage, got back on the ferryboat, and left.

I took some digital pictures to send to Bruton so he would be in the loop before the story went out on the wire. I could have sent him pictures from my phone, but they wouldn't have really explained the situation as well as an e-mail and a phone call outlining the steps we intended to take to correct the problem. I knew Ben Bruton well enough to know he wanted his problems to be delivered soaked in solutions.

J.D. was busy with the construction foreman for a while.

"How long is it going to take to clean all this up?" he asked.

"Well, we gotta get a barge over here. That's gonna take a day, maybe two . . ."

"Then we have to wait for new backhoes and trucks?"

"Yeah. That's not gonna be all that complicated. We already made some calls."

I listened, and soon, when it was apparent there was nothing more we could do until replacement equipment arrived, it was time to leave. We got in a Langley truck for the short drive to the dock.

"Well, this is a setback," I said.

"Yeah, but almost predictable. So, listen," he said, "you haven't told me anything. How was your trip to New York?"

"Almost as much fun as my impromptu get-together with your mother this morning."

"What? Where did you see her?"

"She was waiting at my office this morning when I got there."

"What did she want?"

"She wanted us to remain celibate until your wife is completely stable. J.D., what's going on with Valerie?"

"Ah, shoot." He cocked his head to the side, screwed his lips up, and I knew he was going to take a minute before he continued. "What did she tell you?"

I told him and he said "ah, shoot" under his breath about ten times.

"Look, here's what happened. I flushed all of Valerie's medications down the toilet and she went crazy. Totally, completely, lost it. Ever since then she's been screaming, blaming you and me, saying we're ruining her life. First, she promised to go seek help and then she apparently changed her mind. Over the weekend, she was out till all hours and it appears that she has acquired another source for her drugs—probably from some street dealer because I found a bunch of pills in a baggie."

"Did you throw them out?"

"No, it was just this morning that I found them and then the phone call came about the vandalism, and besides, it wouldn't do any good because she has a new source. She'll just go buy more. No prescription required. I have to think this thing through."

"Well, it's not going to help Valerie get her bearings if we appear to be involved in any capacity other than professional. My firm was not pleased by the papers from last week."

"I'll bet. So what did you tell them?"

"That it was not the sordid business it appeared to be, but pretty much I told my boss the truth."

"So is your job in any kind of jeopardy?"

"No. He's coming down with two of the partners. He wants us to launch a full-fledged campaign for public awareness and education. Talk about a timely idea? Wait till he hears about this flipping alligator almost eating this idiot alive! They're not gonna like this at the home office, you know."

"As if it was my fault?"

"J.D., no one blames you. I'd say Mother Nature takes the hit for this, right?"

I reached over and patted his hand the same way I would any other colleague and he stopped the truck. Of course we *had* arrived at the dock, so it made perfect sense to stop the truck, but he took my hand in his and started to pull me toward him.

"Betts?"

"Not now, J.D. I . . . I promised your momma."

"My momma?"

Then we started to laugh more from nerves than anything else. And once again, the anticipation of being together had been ratcheted up to a higher level. One way or another, we

would find our way through the morass of weeds and traps
and we would be together. Maybe.

I had to wait to see what toll honesty would take. Waiting.
Waiting for the players on the chessboard to assume their
new positions, castles to tumble, knights to make a wrong
turn, the king to fall, the dark queen to be captured . . . the
future had become a terrible balancing act between confusion and surety. The stars were almost perfectly aligned, but
so far there was no relief in sight.

On the boat ride back to the mainland, we would look at
each other and say "your momma" or "my momma" and
shake our heads, incredulous that Louisa had the cheek to
take a moral stance about anything. The rest of our conversation was punctuated with groans over the man in the hospital and how this additional trouble was going to play itself
out. Would some environmentalist group perhaps file a mo-
tion for an injunction to stop the work? Or for a civil suit
against us? After all, Gatorzilla did constitute the epitome of
a hostile work environment. Nah, we agreed, too far-fetched.
But somewhere out there, we knew there was a lawyer trying to scheme an angle to make money out of this.

"What an awful mess. I guess I'll see you later?" I asked,
climbing out of the boat.

"Sooner is better than later," he said. "What do you say
we just happen to bump into each other at Sela's? Have a fast
drink around six?"

"I say let's not tempt the devils. We've got enough trouble
as it is. Besides, I promised Dad I would bring them dinner.
So after I give New York the news, send them updates on
everything, and close up the office for the day, I have to run
to the butcher and the grocery store."

"So you can cook, too?"

"Cook? Me cook? Of course I can cook! I can cook anything!"

"Liar. Your eye is twitching."

"Shut up!"

"Well, it is . . . see you tomorrow?"

"I'm sure of it."

"Try not to poison your family!" he called out as he got back into his truck.

"Yeah, and that's not an option with yours either!" I called back. Too bad it isn't, I thought.

Given the nightmares of the day, we were in pretty high spirits.

That is until about fifteen minutes after Bruton got my e-mail and my phone rang.

"McGee? I am beginning to doubt the worthiness of this deal. I mean, are people so opposed to the development that they would be willing to die for it?"

"It's a small group of radicals. I'm sure of it. Ben, obviously I've been thinking about this all day, and I think we have seen the last incident of this type. The good news is that everything is covered by insurance and that there are more backhoes in South Carolina than you can count. We'll have them all replaced this week. We will only miss a day or two."

"So, you think the risk–reward factor is still there?"

"Yes, most definitely. And listen, we've still got Gatorzilla on our side."

"Some secret weapon. That poor son of a gun. Last time he'll go vandalizing a work site. Think he's gonna make it?"

"Who knows? I wonder if he'll even *want* to make it when he realizes what's happened to him. I'd sleep with a light on for the rest of my life, at the very least."

"Okay, then. Thanks for the update and keep those memos coming."

We hung up and I looked at my watch. Somehow the day had slipped away and it was after four. I called Joanie on her cell.

"Hey! It's me."

"You think I don't know your voice?"

"Right. You still want Ginger Evans to straighten out your haircut?"

"Oh, why not? It can't look any worse than it does."

"I'll call you back."

"Whatever."

I could tell you why Joanie had never been within spitting distance of an altar and it would be a very brief conversation.

"Okay. Stand by."

I clicked off and looked at the phone. Then I called Sandi.

"Please, do me a small favor, will you? Call the spa at Stella Nova and ask if Ginger has had any cancellations for a cut and a blowout. Tell her it's for my sister and she looks like the mad professor whose head got struck by lightning. Twice."

"Really? What happened?"

"Don't ask. She went to the wrong groomer. I think it was inspired by meeting your brother."

"The German shepherd? The thought of him having a relationship with anyone is so bizarre . . . this weekend he asked me for Joanie's number, by the way."

"Ah, come on. He's a nice guy. I hope you gave it to him."

"Of course! Yeah, he's nice enough, but he lives like a dog. Anyway, I'll go make the call . . ."

"Thanks."

I was having an attack of narcolepsy from reading an engineer's report on water and sewage when Sandi buzzed me.

"If she gets over there right now, they can take her."

"You're an angel!"

I dialed Joanie and told her to move herself as fast as possible.

"Oh, who cares?" she said.

"Listen to me, you want Cam Wilkins to romance you? Move it!"

"He called me."

"Good. I want to hear all about it. Meanwhile, people drive here from Charlotte and Atlanta to see Ginger Evans and it takes *months* to get in, so hurry!"

"How did you—"

"You're wasting valuable time. I'll tell you tonight. Now go! Run!"

I hung up on her so she couldn't tell me to cancel the appointment. Honestly, besides Louisa, Joanie was the most frustrated and the most frustrating woman I had ever known. Ever. Really.

A few hours passed and then I was back in my dad's house with sacks of groceries. I had bought the ingredients for a Bolognese sauce, salad, and garlic bread. Soon the air was perfumed with garlic and onions, sautéing in olive oil. I set the kitchen table the same way I had seen Joanie and Dad do it, not wanting to offend anyone by suggesting we clean up the dining room and use it as the good Lord intended.

"Can I make you a drink?" Dad offered.

"I think a glass of wine would be better for the sake of the cook's sobriety. I bought a Barolo. It's a pretty good one."

"Well, thank you. Now, where is my jigger?"

"Right here, Dad."

Of course it was right where it had been the last time I was in the kitchen. But just because he didn't see it at once didn't mean he had dementia.

"Ah! Thanks."

He was mixing his drink and I could see by his expression that he was worried.

"What's wrong, Dad?"

"Nothing. Why?"

"You have an expression of concern on your face. That's all."

"Well, I heard about that whole ballyhoo out on Bulls Island and I was just thinking that I hope you are being very careful, that's all."

"Don't worry about me, Dad. I'm very careful and safe."

I added some chopped bell pepper to the sauce and stirred it around, giving it a shake of salt and a couple of grinds of pepper.

"Okay, if you say so. Cheers."

We touched the rims of our glasses and he looked at me with watery eyes.

"You look so much like your mother, do you know that?"

"Thank you. I'll take that as high praise."

"You're welcome. Just seeing you brings her back to life. Do you know that?"

"Sure. I get that."

"Can you imagine what it's been like for me to live out my life without the only woman I ever loved?"

"Better than you might imagine, Daddy."

I thought about how I had comforted myself over the years with Adrian's resemblance to J.D. and I knew exactly what he meant. I was a thief, no better than the criminals who'd smashed up our construction site. I had robbed Daddy and myself, too, of so much. I had cheated Daddy, Joanie, J.D., and Adrian in innumerable ways. With each passing hour, I knew the time for honesty was growing closer, and the closer it crept to me the more I trembled inside. The innocents would side with one another and I would be shunned. Wouldn't I? I certainly deserved to be punished and I freely admitted it, but only to myself. I couldn't help it, but tears began sliding down my cheeks and Daddy noticed.

"What's wrong, honey?"

"Nothing. I'm fine."

He rubbed my back while my tears fell into the sauce I stirred, and I wondered what to make of us all, certain that my father was having the same thoughts.

"Do you want to talk about it? Is it J.D.? The alligator?"

"It's everything."

"I understand."

"I know you do, Daddy. Oh, shoot! It's just been a lot, you know? These past few weeks? It's a lot to handle."

"I'm sure it is, sweetheart. Don't worry. Everything's going to be okay."

And that was when I broke down and wailed in my father's arms until I was all cried out. He had said everything would be okay. Did he have any idea how long it had been since anyone had even implied to me that things might actually work out?

"Go wash your face," he said.

"Right. I don't want Joanie to see me like this."

"Oh, come on now. We're family, aren't we?"

When his eye caught mine, the absurdity of the truth brought on a blast of laughter and I knew that for the moment, everything actually was all right.

Soon Joanie was there with a much-improved haircut and we were eating dinner like it was old times.

"Your hair looks terrific, Joanie. And your makeup."

"Are you wearing makeup?" Daddy said. "Look at me; let me see . . . so you are! Well, you look very nice."

"Oh, Daddy. Thanks to Betts and that genius. Boy! She was really nice! I thought it was gonna be some stuck-up place like, I don't know, some highfalutin beauty parlor, but she was so daggum nice!"

"Well, of course she is! She owns the business, too."

"Really? They sold me a whole bunch of stuff. I hope I can just remember what goes where and for what."

"After dinner, let me see it and maybe I can help you figure it out."

"Really? Thanks. By the way, this is very good, Betts," Joanie said.

"Well, thank heaven, because it's about the only thing I know how to cook."

They smiled at that and I took it to mean they were glad I wasn't accomplished in every quarter. It made me more like them.

The meal went off without an unkind word. As we were cleaning up, Joanie went out to the dining room to get her shopping bag, which was on the chair with my purse. I saw her peek in my handbag and didn't say anything. But when she lifted out the framed photograph of Adrian that I had yet to remove to a safer place, my heart almost stopped. Just as I was turning away I saw her smiling in recognition. What was I to do?

There was no way to get her to wipe the sneer from her face, so before I left, I went to her on the porch, where she was brushing her nasty dogs.

"Joanie?"

"Somebody has a big secret," she said, reverting back to her old mean-as-a-snake self. "Oh yeah! A big one."

"Somebody had better keep her mouth shut about it, too."

"And why wouldn't I do that? Are you threatening me, Betts?"

"No. I'm *guaranteeing* you. One word and you'll regret it."

"We'll see."

I remembered then why I didn't like my sister.

Later, at two in the morning, when I still had not found a wink of sleep, I took a Tylenol PM. In the morning when I crawled out of bed, it took me a few minutes to recall that Joanie had been added to the list of "Those in the Know." History had proven that it was going to be extremely difficult for her to keep the secret to herself.

Joanie was horribly outspoken and had been all of her life. When we were children, she would always be the one to report who had cheated on a test, and later in high school, she'd been known to tell a girl who wasn't necessarily a friend of hers that she had seen her boyfriend kissing someone else. Maybe she thought that delivering these infomercials would somehow endear her to the recipients, but it never did. If anything, she was viewed as a vicious blabbermouth and was very unpopular. You would think she would have learned something about discretion by the time she hit thirty-five, but there was precious little evidence of maturity in her judgments. I knew she was probably champing at the bit to tell Daddy and perhaps even J.D. or Valerie, or anyone who cared to listen about what she'd just learned about me. Great.

As soon as I got to the office, not looking like Miss America, I'll admit, I called Sela.

"You busy?" I asked.

"No, Ed's gone to work and I'm just getting a massage from Russell Crowe. *Yes! Right there!*"

I couldn't help but grin despite the seriousness of my call.

"Thank God you're so crazy."

"Thank you. So, what's going on? I saw all the mess in the newspapers this morning and on the news last night. Gatorzilla is hungry again and on the move!"

"He swam over from Capers for a midnight snack."

"Gross."

"Truly. Well, that's what that poor SOB gets for wrecking private property. It's somewhat like terrorism."

"You know what? It is. It's environmental terrorism, isn't it? It's out of Ed's jurisdiction, but if you want, I can have him look into it."

"Sure! If he could help in any way at all, we would be thrilled."

"No problem, he's got tons of friends on the Mount Pleasant and the Isle of Palms police forces. So, what else is going on in your crazy world of high finance and corporate intrigue?"

"Um, you're not gonna like this because I don't."

"Let's hear it."

"Joanie found a hand grenade and she's about to pull the pin."

"Meaning?"

"A framed photograph of Adrian that was resting in the top of my open purse."

"Holy crap. What did she say?"

"Oh, she's just way too smug and I could see that she was about to burst the news to Daddy. Basically, I threatened her life."

"Think she'll listen to you?"

"In the short term, but I know her. She'll choke if she can't spill the news to someone whom it would nearly kill with a heart attack."

"Betts? Betts?"

"I know, I know . . ."

We talked some more and I told her of my plan to tell J.D. about Adrian before I left Charleston. She was mollified by the news that I had moved closer to telling the truth, but not convinced that I would follow through. Frankly, she was right, because a true best girlfriend could hear your chicken feathers when they ruffle.

At that moment Sandi buzzed me. J.D. was in the outer office.

"Send him right in."

Sela and I said good-bye, the door opened, and there stood J.D., looking like he had suffered a long night. He wasn't disheveled—southern gentlemen are rarely disheveled—but his eyes were bloodshot and he oozed crankiness.

"What in the world happened to you?" I said.

"And I might say the same about you."

"Look, I'm excused today because I had dinner with Joanie and Daddy last night."

"If I told you what happened to me last night, they could make a movie out of it."

"Really? Tell me."

"Well, first of all, here's a copy of all the insurance claims and the police report. I thought you would want them for your records." He handed me a manila envelope.

"Thanks. That was very thoughtful because in all likelihood New York would have asked. You want some coffee?"

"Yes, thanks. Coffee would be good. Half-and-half, if you have it, no sugar."

"Don't you know I have half-and-half? This is a swank outfit, Mr. Langley." I buzzed Sandi and asked her to fix tea for me as well. "FYI, I drink my tea with half-and-half, no sugar. I'm sweet enough."

"I don't know if *sweet* is quite the most appropriate adjective to describe you, but okay."

"What would you say would be, then?"

"Betts, I'm trying to honor your promise to my momma, so let's not go there."

"Yo momma! Good grief." We smiled at each other then, recognizing the sheer physical exhaustion in each other. "But you still haven't told me the story of last night."

"Where to begin?" J.D. looked up at the ceiling and then back at me. "Okay, so it's midnight and Valerie is nowhere to be found. She's not answering her cell and I have no idea where she is."

"Not good."

"No, definitely not good. And I think I told you that over the last week her behavior has been very erratic. Nutty talk, delusional really, and mood swings. All that kind of stuff. Then I found the pills and knew she was buying on the street. Not good."

"No. That's seriously dangerous."

"Right."

Just then Sandi appeared with a tray, put it on the table, and started to serve.

"You know what, Sandi? I can do that. Thanks."

"Sure."

Sandi knew the code for "leave us now and close the door," which was exactly what she did, knowing she would hear it all anyway at a later time.

"Thanks, Sandi," J.D. said.

"You're welcome," she said, and closed the door behind her.

"So, it's getting very late, naturally I'm getting concerned, and then the phone rings."

"The dreaded middle-of-the-night phone call . . ."

"Exactly. But it's not the police calling, it's the bartender from a private club downtown. He tells me that my wife is there and in no shape to drive. Somehow he talked her into giving him her car keys, don't ask me. Anyway, she's sitting up there at this bar with two guys from New York, drinking vodka, and she's completely stoned on something. I say, hang on to her and I'll be there as fast as I can."

"Not like you live next door," I said.

"Right, but I figure I'd ask O'Farrell for mercy if I get a ticket for speeding."

"Ed would understand."

"Well, that didn't happen, but I was racing hell-bent for leather the whole way there. Sure enough, I get there, she's bombed, we haul her butt out of this joint after tipping the bartender on the very generous side and take her home. This morning she doesn't remember a thing, like, where is her car? So, without a word to me, she takes my SUV and goes off again, presumably back downtown."

"J.D.? What are you going to do?"

"I have talked to her about rehab, but I'd say at the moment she's not interested in that."

"Obviously. She's in über-indulgence mode."

"Good name for it."

"So, who were the two guys from New York?"

"Some guy who owns a string of boutique hotels who told me not to feel bad, that this kind of thing happens."

Vinny!

"And the other one?"

"Some punk who works for him. Or used to work for him. It wasn't clear. Seemed very nervous. He was giving the hotel guy an envelope of pictures or money or something, said it was personal. The hotel guy is probably tracking down a bad debt. Who knows?"

How small was the world?

"Did they seem to know Valerie?"

"No, they were a few seats away. Well, actually, that's hard to say. The punk seemed familiar with her. But they helped me get Valerie out to the car and we talked for a few minutes. Why do you have that look on your face?"

"This might sound crazy to you, but I have a hunch that I know those two men. They didn't give you a card or anything, did they?"

"No, nothing."

"Figures. That just figures."

CHAPTER SEVENTEEN

The Best-Laid Plans

I was in J.D.'s office, settled on a couch, wishing I had the chutzpah to say something very naughty to him and seduce him right there, but we were waiting for Ed O'Farrell to arrive so we could go over the Bulls Island vandalism with him. It wouldn't do for the chief of police of Charleston to find us twisted up like a couple of undulating pretzels. Just a thought.

"What's the latest with Valerie?" I said, since Ed had not yet arrived, and I felt compelled to ask about her, as I had just experienced a vision of my hips under her husband's. Guilt.

"I don't know. Terrible, I guess. When she's home, she's usually sleeping, and frankly, we aren't talking much. When we do speak, it's ugly. She is one very angry woman. I mean, I can't blame her. But she's dangerously ill, at least in my opinion, and she doesn't want any help, so it's very frustrating for me."

"Great. But she thinks she has reasonable cause for her rage. She doesn't know how well behaved we are."

"True. I'm sure she imagines us having this huge love affair."

"Meanwhile, we're like Saint Francis and Saint Claire, Abelard and Héloïse . . ."

"Exactly. Meanwhile, every time I see her, she's as tight as a tick or stoned to the bone or some combination of the above. I can't seem to have a rational conversation with her. Yep. Welcome to my world. Nice, right?"

"No. It's awful. I feel sorry for her."

"I'm sure she wouldn't welcome your pity."

"I'm aware. Maybe I should say that I feel empathy for her."

"And why in the world would you sympathize with *her*? What about me? I'm supposed to be helping her and she won't let me. I get to worry about her driving drunk, maybe killing somebody. I keep taking the car keys from her, but that only causes more arguing. I mean, at some point I'm just going to have to sit her down and tell her it's rehab or it's really over between us because I can't live like this forever."

His words stung so badly it was as though he had slapped me with all his strength. I thought he had already told her he wanted a divorce. Now he was waffling. Wasn't he? My face got so hot I was sure he could see it. All I wanted to do was to run from the room. How could I have failed so miserably to get the correct read on his feelings? It was all I could do to appear calm and centered.

I cleared my throat and said in the most cavalier voice I could manage, "Well, I guess it's true that you can't always get what you want in this life."

"There's a song in there somewhere . . ."

He was completely unaware of how deeply he had upset me. How crazy was I to be so unnerved? Wasn't he merely doing the thing he had promised to do? And why was his attention to his wife's illness and this new ultimatum he was planning give her making me so insecure? Because, my love for my son and a few friends aside, I didn't trust the blazing emotions that seemed to accompany affairs of the heart, that's why. I had once trusted them, and they had pulverized my life; and for all the years since then, I had sworn that I'd never trust my feelings again. All those mighty and mettle-testing proclamations . . . yet as soon as I saw J.D. again, I had let myself believe that our love was still alive. Apparently, he had not arrived at the same conclusion.

As those thoughts rushed through my head, J.D.'s intercom buzzed and his secretary announced Ed O'Farrell.

For some crazy reason, I found myself indulging in some ridiculous juvenile behavior. For example, Ed was wearing a suit and I had to say he looked very impressive and even intimidating, perhaps because I knew there was a gun somewhere in his pants and I wondered where it was. What was the matter with me? I needed serious hormone adjustment and a Dutch uncle's advice.

"Hey, Ed! Good to see you!" I stood up and gave him a kiss on the cheek. Then I blushed.

"Hey, girl!" He gave me a kiss, too, and then shook J.D.'s hand.

"Come sit down," J.D. said. "You want coffee?"

"Nah, too hot. You got a Diet Coke?" He patted his rock-hard abs and said in his Irish brogue, "Gotta be watching me girlish figger, you know."

Returning to my senses, I smiled, thinking how lucky Sela was to have a loyal gorgeous husband, and all at once I wished I had one, too, perhaps because it seemed like such an impossibility. Well, I wasn't dead yet, and if J.D. really did eventually dump Valerie, perhaps, well then . . . well, what? You see, it only took one or two minutes and my mind was trying again to envision myself at J.D.'s side.

It was best to stay focused on the moment, I told myself, and just put those fantasies in a sealed box in my attic.

In minutes, J.D.'s secretary placed a Diet Coke over ice in a glass tumbler in front of Ed and I said to her, "Know what? Do you have mineral water? Suddenly a cold drink seems like an excellent choice."

"Me, too," J.D. said to his secretary, and then took his seat behind his desk. "So, Ed? What's the news?"

"Unfortunately not much. But I called in a few favors and this is what we got. Work-shoe imprints that match a particular model widely sold by Wal-Mart, fingerprints that match nobody on God's green earth, and tire-tread prints that match a 1971 Volkswagen van. They called every auto body shop and every detailer in the Charleston area and the whole way up to Columbia, and there are no reports of anyone bringing in a bloody van to clean. The hospital says the victim's only visitors are family members and he hasn't regained consciousness to be questioned. Now, there *was* a surveillance video from the ER delivery area, but it's too fuzzy to make out a face or a plate number. So, unless this dude wakes up from his very long nap, we got nothing."

"How's he doing?" J.D. asked.

"Not well," Ed said.

"Probably having one nightmare after another," I said. "I would be."

"I'll say," Ed agreed. "Anyway, looks like he's gonna be in the ICU for a very long time. Apparently, he had some sort of a stroke or a brain bleed."

"You have to wonder," J.D. said. "You have to wonder if this guy ever thought his politics could bring him to this. I mean, alligator attacks?"

"Usually they grab little dogs," Ed said. "That gator must have been highly threatened to attack an adult human."

"The poor guy was most likely in between the gator and the water," J.D. said. "Usually they grab their prey, drag them into the water, and drown them. Then they eat them—"

"Okay! That's enough! Ew! Gross! I may never eat again!"

"Well, Ed, thank you for this highly informative session," J.D. said with a laugh.

"If I hear anything remotely useful, I'll call one of you." Ed stood and drained his drink. "Gotta go back to fight the good fight and save us from whatever evil lurks!"

"Give Sela a kiss for me," I said.

"You know it." He shook J.D.'s hand. "Thanks for the cold one. Sorry I couldn't tell you more."

Ed left and J.D. went back to his chair.

"It's one of the mysteries of life, isn't it?" I said. "How people get so wrapped up and passionate about something, and in a heartbeat, their whole life changes in the most unbelievable ways."

"Hmmph."

"What? What do you mean, *hmmph!*"

"Where passion can lead? Like ours? Like the car accident that killed your mother? One night, one storm, one truck?"

"Good example. Yeah, that's really true. The whole world changed in that instant. But may I point out that it wasn't our passion that caused my mother's death?"

J.D. was quiet. Excuse me, but five minutes ago he was telling me how he was going to lay it on the line with Valerie, and now he was mooning at me all hangdog, with guilt over his mother's disastrous behavior all over his face? What was the point? To elicit some understanding from me? I didn't think so. I continued talking, trying to fill up the awkward silence.

"It happens all the time, I guess. Like this poor misdirected soul who met up with Gatorzilla. I mean, he might *die* because he thought he was doing the world a favor. It's so wrong."

"Yeah, well, you're right."

"Glad I'm right about something. Um, which part am I right about?"

"That it happens all the time. Speaking of events that change your life and the dangers of passion, and I don't know why I am feeling comfortable enough to tell you something I haven't even told Valerie, but there it is. Big Jim told me a story that would make your hair stand right up on end."

"Tell me."

"Take it to your grave?"

J.D. arched his eyebrow at me and I knew he was being very serious.

"Of course."

"It seems I have a brother. Actually, a half brother."

"What?"

"Yeah. I do. I have a half brother."

"Good grief! What does that mean?"

"What does it mean? Let's see." J.D. looked up at the ceiling and then back to me. "For one thing, it means my mother gets her jollies every time his mother cleans our toilets."

"Wait. Your housekeeper is the mother?"

"Yep. How do you like that? Seems she used to be an exotic dancer in one of Dad's clubs. Dad had a roving eye back in those days—you know, a love-'em-and-leave-'em kind of deal? But this time he really fell in love. Anyway, when they discovered there was a biscuit in the oven, he wanted to marry her. But Mother, as you might imagine, flat refused to give him a divorce. So, Rosie—that's her name—moved into one of our caretaker's cottages and has been there for fifteen years. You know, it's funny, I had always thought that Mickey looked like my grandfather."

"J.D.! You mean that kid you brought to the first event out at Bulls?"

"Yes, that's the one."

"What a story! You just found this out?"

"Yep. And I'm sworn to secrecy not to tell Mickey, who doesn't know. It seems that no one has the balls, pardon the expression, to tell the truth anymore."

The room took a swirl and I took a slide to the floor. Who in my shoes would not have fainted?

The next thing I knew, my head was in J.D.'s lap and he was politely slapping my cheeks—the ones on my face, thank you.

"What happened?"

"You fainted."

"I never faint!" My skirt was way up my legs and one

shoe was missing. I must have looked a sight! "Oh, gosh! Help me up!"

After some fumbling around, I made it to my feet and found my shoe, straightened my skirt and my hair, and sat down again.

"Whew!"

"Well, at least the color is coming back to your face. You okay?"

"Yeah. I don't know what happened!"

"We were talking about Mickey being—"

I held up my hand. "Right. I remember now. It's okay. I'm fine. Maybe I'll drink some water."

"Are you sure you're feeling all right?"

"Of course! It must be the heat. You know, I'm not so used to all this heat and humidity. Then Ed giving the gory details of gator kills . . . too much for me." Playing the magnolia would excuse me.

"Did you eat breakfast?"

"J.D.! Stop! I'm fine! I swear!"

He walked around his desk and took his seat, staring at me as if keeping an eye on me would restore perfect equilibrium. Then he called his secretary to bring in some water, which she did.

"Okay. Are you able to talk a little business?"

"Of course!"

It wasn't true. I was hardly able to keep my mind on anything he said because the discovery that he had a half brother did not seem to have made him as happy as I would have imagined. In fact, the deception made him angry. His half brother was only a few years younger than Adrian. I racked my brain trying to envision a good outcome. A family reunion? A holiday dinner? I could not see it. And the fact that J.D. had entrusted me with the information and not Valerie was an indication that he was dealing with a marriage in its death throes, not one that was being revived. The problem was that he was not ready to admit this. Or maybe I was dreaming again.

He rattled on and on about the public-relations event, saying that our companies should share a full page in the *Post & Courier* inviting the public to come see for themselves. We would do a PowerPoint presentation on six big screens. There would be brochures to take home and a website to track the progress and give the public ongoing information. We would compare Bulls Island to the great successes that had come before us, like Spring Island and other communities that had worked out so beautifully and pleased the environmentally sensitive leaders. We needed a slogan; J.D. was thinking of a few and wanted me to ask New York for their thoughts, and did we have an advertising agency that we worked with that might have an idea about this?

We reconfirmed the date with Bruton, two weeks from Saturday, and decided we would ask Sela to cater. We would also ask Ed if he had some off-duty officers who could be there just in case there was trouble.

It seemed like a reasonably good start. We had a plan, and once the plan began to become reality, I knew I would feel better about the future of Bulls Island.

"I'll call Sela," I said, "and put together a menu and a budget. Should we serve alcohol? Beer and wine? Cash bar?"

"Normally, I would say no, that this was a business event. But maybe some beer would soften them up. What do you think?"

"I think it's probably not a good idea, now that I'm thinking about it. There are the issues of liability to consider and that many more portable potties to rent . . ."

"Yeah, you're probably right. Okay, see what you can cook up with Sela and we can plan a nice dinner for afterward for your guys from the big city. Peninsula Grill? How's that?"

"That's perfect. A postmortem while it's all still fresh. Where should I put them up?"

"Charleston Place. There are loads of B and Bs around, but I'll bet they're the types who will want room service and all that, am I right?"

"Definitely, and the *Wall Street Journal* on their pillow."

"Got it. You want me to make the reservations?"

"No, thanks. I'll do that . . ."

The next hour or so was spent on the mundane details of the event and we divided up the workload between us. We had sandwiches brought in and worked through lunch, and finally around two, I felt the next step was to just go get busy laying the groundwork.

When I was leaving, J.D. said, "Are you sure you're okay?"

"Yeah, I'm fine." I gave him a weak smile.

"What's bothering you?"

"It's nothing."

"You sure?"

"Yeah, I'm sure."

Sure, nothing. First, you tell me you want me, then you tell me you're back in there with Valerie, then you pluck my heartstrings about ten more times, and then we plan a barbecue.

I called Sela on my cell to see if she had a little time to talk about the Bulls Island Rally, as I was calling the PR event at the moment, trying on a name to see how it felt.

"Come right over," she said. "We're in between lunch and dinner, so it's a great time to do this."

I was at the restaurant in just minutes and we sat at a back table.

"So what are you thinking of for food?" Sela asked.

"J.D.'s muscles slathered with guacamole."

"Umm, umm. Girl, aren't you allergic to shellfish with raging lunatic wives?"

"Right. I forgot. How about loin of J.D. on pumpernickel?"

"Ummmmm? Ms. McGee? What's going on with you?"

"Just that I have come to the realization that my whole fantasy about having J.D. is probably hopeless. So it's okay to trivialize the remains of my love life with carnal humor while I entertain a probable next career as a country-music singer."

"So that's the cause for your twang?"

"Yeah . . ."

I told Sela about Louisa's visit, J.D.'s remarks about Valerie, the possibility that J.D. had met Vinny Braggadocio in a bar, and under the seal of the confessional, I told her about J.D.'s discovery of his half brother.

"Whew! You've had a helluva twenty-four hours! What's up with Vinny maybe being in Charleston? And meeting J.D.?"

"Right? J.D. was hauling Valerie's drunk ass out of a bar in the middle of the night. I swear to you on a stack of Bibles that he described Vinny and that little rat who's been following me."

"What little rat?"

"I didn't *tell* you this?"

"Um, I think I would remember something like you being followed."

I gave Sela the lowdown on Vinny and the goon and she said, "I'm telling Ed."

"Oh, don't bother him. Maybe I'm being paranoid."

"Maybe, but just because you're paranoid, it doesn't mean you *shouldn't* be! I'm telling Ed today and I want his guys all over this."

"Maybe. So to ice this cake, J.D. seemed *way* more bothered by the fact that he had been kept in the dark than he was happy to discover he had a half brother."

"Well, speaking as an heir . . ."

"No, I don't think money had anything to do with his attitude about it. I think he was seriously provoked that his father and mother had hidden the facts from him. That his respect for them has been greatly compromised by the lies upon lies upon lies."

"I think you're dead wrong because you're just caught up in your own guilt. I'll bet you anything in this world that J. D. Langley has been gunning for his parents since the day you left town."

"You think?"

"You know what? Here we are together again after twenty

years. You and I still fit. You and J.D. still fit. Ed and I still fit. Valerie doesn't fit and never did. Even if she wasn't a pill-popping sot, she wouldn't fit in with the Langleys for one big fat reason and that reason is you. How many times do we have to go over this?"

Sela's patience appeared to be wearing thin. Maybe she was suffering from some unusual stress or I had been so selfish, talking about my issues so incessantly that I was wearing her out. Probably the latter, I surmised, blushing again.

"You're right. So let's talk food. No booze."

"Mini-quesadillas, chicken satay with a peanut dipping sauce, slider burgers, curried shrimp on toothpicks, fruit skewers with a mixed-berry yogurt dipping sauce, mini–ice-cream sandwiches, mango smoothies, sodas, tea, and iced water. Twenty dollars a person, not including rentals, service, tax, and gratuities. I'll send you a list. Done!"

"No pigs in blankets?"

"I'll go out to Sam's Club and get tons of them. Happy?"

"You've done this before?"

"Uh, yeah. Just a couple of times."

I started to laugh then. "You amaze me, Sela O'Farrell! You're the only woman I know who can trim my sails and pull a party for five hundred out of her pocket in five minutes."

Her expression turned grim. "Five hundred? Wait. You didn't say anything about *that* many people."

"Oh! Wait! Don't worry. We'll enlist the troops to help. I'll call Joanie, and Sandi will help and her brother—that's three more people right there."

"Don't worry. I'll get Ed to give us some day-passers from the county cooler on the work-release program." I must have looked at her in horror because she broke up laughing. "Good grief, Betts! I actually had you! Wait till I tell Ed . . ."

I got up and hugged her as hard as I could. "Thanks, Sela."

"Don't forget, I'm not such a saint. This is how I pay the bills."

"Then throw in a shrink's fee!"

"Seriously!"

I blew her a kiss, and by the time I walked back to my office, a faxed proposal was on my desk.

"I don't know how she does it," I said, holding the proposal up in front of Sandi.

"Must have a template," she said.

"She must. Okay, come on inside with me."

"So what's going on?" she asked.

I gave her all the preliminary plans for our No Bull Today (new possible event title) and she took a lot of notes.

"Can you think of anything we're missing?"

"Additional water transportation?"

"Good point! Thanks. Anything else?"

Sandi loved planning events more than anyone I had ever worked with. They were her chance to shine and shine she did.

"I see lots and lots of visuals—you know, canvas blow-ups of photographs of the plans, all on easels around the tent. You know, we have people enter, get a drink, amble along in sort of a serpentine fashion after a receiving line so they are almost forced to look at the different stages of development on the easels? I mean, let's walk through this in our heads. They get off the boat and onto what? A bus?"

Sandi and I had planned and executed scores of successful dinners and special events. I trusted her judgment completely, whether it was to set up temporary offices or arrange a dinner for a thousand.

"Yes, buses. We have to have this in the clearing, by the Dominick House, where the bathrooms are. The ground is very level there."

"That makes sense. What about ADA compliance? Is there a handicap-access bathroom?"

"Don't know. I'll have to check."

The next hour was spent recounting and expanding the outline I had put together with J.D. In the end we talked about the ad.

"Even on short notice like this, we still need to reach out to the whole community."

"What about radio and television?"

"If you could line that up, anything at all, it would be great."

"I'll make some calls. What about the mayor?"

"Joe Riley? Well, it is in Charleston County. Absolutely. Let's ask him to say a few words."

"Great idea."

"And what about the content for the ad?" Sandi said.

"I'll work on that and all the logistical stuff, too. J.D. has resources for transportation and whatever we need in that department, I'm sure . . ."

The two weeks flew by so fast I didn't have time to do anything except sleep, eat, and plan the Bulls Island event, which was now called simply "Bulls Island—Open House."

Sandi and I took Sela and her chef out to the island with the tent and rental company to do a walk-through. J.D. and I did an appearance on *Lowcountry Live,* a local morning television program, and we raced up to Columbia to tape an interview with Walter Edgar for *Walter Edgar's Journal,* which aired on the state's NPR affiliate. Our letter ran in the *Post & Courier* twice and we were getting tons of phone calls. The website got hundreds of hits and I began to worry that we would have more than five hundred people.

I called Sela about a hundred times that week and the last phone call had been about crowd management.

"Don't worry," she said. "I'll get Ed to ask the Isle of Palms Police Department to post an officer at the dock with a counter. When he clicks five hundred and fifty, not counting our people, obviously, he won't let any more folks go over to the island. Done!"

"Brilliant! You'll have food for five hundred and fifty people?"

"Honey, I'll have food for the army and the navy."

J.D. had his hands full with Valerie, and when I saw him

on the Thursday before the open house, he told me he hadn't seen her in the last twenty-four hours. Naturally, he was frantic. Then he got a call late that night from one of Ed's officers, who'd found her sleeping in her car in a parking lot on St. George Street, behind Bob Ellis Shoes. Her pulse was dangerously low, so they rushed her to the emergency room. She'd taken an apparent overdose. So they called J.D., pumped Valerie's stomach, and admitted her for a twenty-four-hour observation and a psychiatric evaluation.

"I hope like hell they can talk her into a rehab program," he said. "I told the admitting doctor everything I knew."

"So, was he shocked that somebody wearing a billion dollars' worth of diamonds could indulge in that kind of behavior?"

"Half a billion. Not in the least. He gave me her jewelry and her purse and I took it all home. She was steaming mad. And I mean *steaming* mad. But she can sign herself out anytime she wants, and she probably will."

"I'm sure. You don't think she's going to let us throw this big shindig without her, do you?"

"You're right. She won't."

"My dad and sister are coming, too, to see if they can lend a hand."

"Like Sela is gonna let your sister touch the food?"

"Right? Not without a hairnet and gloves. But Joanie's looking pretty good these days."

"Really?"

"Boyfriend. Sandi's brother, Cam the vet. He's coming, too."

"Joanie with a man. Well, if you live long enough, you see everything, don't you?"

"I guess so," I said.

"My parents are coming. And my new brother, Mickey, who doesn't know I'm his brother."

"Poor kid. Well, I expected Louisa and Big Jim would show. Sorry, but yo momma never missed a single solitary photo op in her whole life!"

J.D. burst out laughing.

"Well, I may have come across a brother I didn't know existed, but with any luck, Mother will finally get the daughter-in-law she deserves!"

"What?"

"You heard me."

The cat-and-mouse thing with J.D. was exhausting. At that point I'd believe J.D. when I saw a divorce decree and the ring, and not sooner.

Bruton was arriving Friday night, and although I had offered to pick him up at the private airport, he declined, saying he was coming in with McGrath and Pinkham and they had other matters to discuss and would work through dinner. I was to meet them for breakfast Saturday morning at eight.

At 7:35 that morning, I was in the Charleston Place lobby restaurant reading the paper, enjoying my first cup of tea of the day. I don't know why I wasn't worried or nervous. You would have thought the biggest thing on my agenda was a manicure. But somehow, having Ben there along with my favorite partners was calming. I was anxious for them to see the island because I knew they would fall in love with it.

Most importantly, J.D. would take care of the appropriate Lowcountry wooing. He would squire them over to Bulls Island on his precious Chris-Craft Riviera. He would have the chef at Peninsula Grill make some special seafood concoction for them that would have them begging for more. By the time we put them back on the plane, they would think of themselves as honorary good old boys and J.D. would already have made a date with them to go fishing the next time they came down. I was confident and fully prepared for my meeting with them.

I spotted McGrath first and waved at him. They ambled over, winding around other tables, smiling in my direction.

"Hi! How was your trip?" I asked Bruton.

"Boring, just like I like all airline flights to be. How's everything here?"

"Back on track and moving ahead, just the way I like work to be! I'm so glad y'all are here."

"Hmmph," McGrath said. "That's some bull."

"He's been making bull jokes for two days now," Pinkham said. "He thinks he's Henny Youngman."

I had no clue who Henny Youngman might be, so I looked at them with a questioning face.

"Before *our* time," Bruton said in my direction. "Catskills comedian, I believe."

"Ouch," said McGrath and Pinkham in stereo.

"I want you to be my Trivial Pursuit partner," I told my boss.

"I don't play games," Bruton said.

"Whoa! Tough guy!" McGrath said in a sissy voice.

"Yeah. Oooh!" Pinkham said in a girlie voice. "Scary!"

Apparently these three enjoyed a healthy sarcastic repartee outside the office. No matter how important men became, inside them beat the hearts of boys.

We had our sensible breakfast of oatmeal, fresh fruit, poached eggs, and juice, talking about the order of events for the day. When the bill was paid and a generous tip was left for our very officious waiter, we walked over to the Triangle offices, where Sandi was waiting.

"Well, look at this," McGrath said. "Looks like this place was built a hundred years ago."

"Longer," I said. "And it's for sale. One million six hundred thousand, and there's not a right angle in the whole building."

I brought them inside and Sandi jumped up from her desk to greet them. More coffee was served after they had the tour and everyone paid Sandi the compliments she deserved.

Detail by detail I took them through the work and its progress and soon it was time to head out to the island, where we would meet J.D. and his team of architects, foreman, and so on. Needless to say, I knew that Big Jim and Louisa had been prepped by J.D. for the occasion.

"Well, despite the unforeseen rhubarbs, you've done a fantastic job, McGee," Bruton said. "So far."

"But we knew you would," McGrath said.

"Because we have just a few bucks riding on this one," Pinkham said.

"Thanks," I told them, and meant it. "But never fear, we're gonna make so much money on this one, you won't believe it."

McGrath, who I thought was feeling rather chatty, piped up again. "Yes, on the plane coming down here, Ben showed us the projected earnings, and I must say we were mighty impressed, weren't we, David?"

David Pinkham nodded and his blue eyes twinkled. He had eight children. How anyone with eight children managed to retain a bit of twinkle in their eyes was beyond me. His wife, Amanda, was Superwoman and Mother Teresa rolled into one. When I thought about families like theirs, my private life felt so meager and miserable. But if I could find my way to the light of truth, maybe all of that would change.

We loaded Sandi's car with materials for the presentation and I took the men in Sela's car. Soon we were on our way.

Sela had been on the island since early that morning, getting ready. J.D. arrived early, too, to oversee, setting up the riser and the sound system, and checking any other details, like the "Absolut" arrival of his vodka wife.

I called J.D. on my cell when we got to the dock, and as I knew he would do, he brought over his beloved boat with his captain, Smitty, to deliver the men from New York and me to Bulls Island in style. There must have been a hundred or so people waiting for the ferry, and those who knew boats pointed at J.D.'s when it pulled up alongside the dock. For a split second I thought I saw Vinny's weasel in the crowd, but I decided I was mistaken. Besides, I wasn't going to allow any thoughts of Vinny to ruin the moment.

It was a gorgeous late September day and the famous

South Carolina brilliant blue sky and water were living up to their reputation. The marsh grass was still green and scores of birds, Snowy Egrets, gulls, and terns, were everywhere to be seen, watching us watching them.

J.D. got off the boat to shake hands with everyone and it only took a minute for me to see that we weren't all going to fit comfortably on his little boat.

After shaking hands and exchanging polite remarks with Bruton, Pinkham, and McGrath, J.D. turned to his captain and said, "Take the men over. Sandi, Betts, and I can jump on the ferry. We'll see y'all there in a minute."

"I've always admired these boats," Ben said. "Is this a Capri?"

"No, this is a 1953 Riviera," J.D. said with pride. "My dad gave it to me when I graduated from college."

"Fantastic," Ben said.

"He's on the island waiting to meet y'all," J.D. added.

"Great!" McGrath said, and Pinkham nodded in agreement.

Ben Bruton sat in the back with McGrath, and David Pinkham got in the passenger seat next to the captain. They pulled away from the dock at a sporting clip and we followed them a hundred yards behind, lumbering along on the old but faithful ferry.

It's incredible what you remember in a time of crisis. I remember I was looking into J.D.'s eyes with such pride when we heard the explosion. We watched in stunned horror as his boat burst into flames. I saw McGrath and Pinkham fly up into the air and land in the water, but his captain and Ben Bruton seemed to have simply disappeared.

"Help! God, help me please! I'm hurt!" Paul McGrath screamed.

"Can't swim!" Pinkham called out in terror.

The ferry captain stopped our boat, and three men, then three more, dove right into the water to help save them. They threw out a dozen lifesavers and Pinkham and McGrath each managed to grab one, then all the men gathered at the side of the boat and pulled my colleagues on board.

"Where the hell is Bruton? Where is he?"

I realized I was screaming.

"And Smitty? Oh my God! Call Sela, Betts! Tell her to tell Ed!"

J.D. and Sandi rushed to McGrath and Pinkham's side to assess their injuries and I dialed Sela.

"We saw it from here," Sela said. "Ed just called the IOP police and they're on the way. So are ambulances. Try to stay calm. What's their condition?"

"Sela? Bruton is missing! So is Smitty, J.D.'s captain! What if . . . what if they're dead?"

"Don't even think it. Get ahold of yourself! Do you hear me? Stop panicking!"

"I'm going in," I said, and hung up.

While I was pulling off my shoes, I knelt to speak to McGrath and Pinkham.

"It's going to be all right," I said, knowing otherwise.

"They're okay," J.D. said. "Just banged up, and McGrath has a nasty gash on his leg."

"I'm going to find Ben."

Before he could stop me, I jumped over the side of the boat, feetfirst, as I was unsure of the depth of the water. It was deep and cold and the first few seconds were jarring. But I couldn't see underwater. The boat was in pieces all over the place and still burning. I began to think that perhaps I should have left this to the professionals, but I could not stand by and wait. What if Ben was unconscious but still alive? Time was precious! If I had the chance to save him, shouldn't I do it? I dove again and tried to see what I could, but the water was so murky I couldn't see ten feet ahead.

Thirty seconds later I heard J.D.

"Betts! Wait!"

He was swimming toward me.

"Betts! Stop! This won't work! We need divers with sonar!

There're a dozen of them on the way. And fire and rescue, too! Come back with me! We have to get McGrath and Pinkham to the hospital!"

I hung there, treading water for a minute, trying to think and to process what he had said. I was almost paralyzed with fear and thoroughly shocked by what had just happened. If I left, I could be leaving Ben to die when perhaps he could have been saved.

I screamed, "No! J.D.! I'm not leaving without Ben! I can't!"

He reached my side and grabbed me under the arms and started swimming back to the ferry with one arm.

"Ben's gone, Betts. So is Smitty. People saw them . . . people saw what happened. I'm sorry. Just relax now . . ."

I felt myself go limp and then I began to weep, sobbing all the way back to the ferry and as we made our way back to the dock.

The dock was loaded with people waiting, trying to get a glimpse of us. Needless to say, the press was arriving in full force and I noticed several ambulances.

"Where are you taking them?" I said.

"East Cooper," said one of the team loading McGrath onto a stretcher.

"I want to call Sela. Oh my God. I just can't believe this!"

"Ah, crap," J.D. said as I pulled my waterlogged cell from my pocket. "We'll get you a new one tomorrow. Sandi?"

"You okay?" she said to me, handing me J.D.'s cell, knowing I was anything but all right.

"Yeah, I'm *going* to be okay. Just not yet. Do you know where the hospital is?"

"I can follow them."

"Okay, do that and I'll see you there in ten minutes."

Walking away from them to a quiet spot, I dialed Sela's number and she answered.

"You're not going to believe this," she said.

"What?"

"Valerie is over here . . ."

"I knew she would be."

"Well, she's so whacked out on whatever it is she's on that when she heard there were only men on that boat, she didn't even ask if J.D. was okay. She was so completely discombobulated that she blurted out, 'What do you mean? Betts was supposed to be on board!' Do you understand what I am telling you?"

The implication of her words didn't register in my mind as it normally would because I was still reeling.

"No, what do you mean?"

"Simple. If they find explosives in the remnants of that boat or anywhere in the area, Valerie's going up the river, honey. We're talking murder."

CHAPTER EIGHTEEN

Shock Waves

I would never get over the shock and the pain of losing Ben Bruton in so incomprehensible a manner. He was an icon, fearless and brilliant, and in addition, probably the most highly respected man I had ever known. His wife and children had to be just absolutely, completely inconsolable. It was no exaggeration to say that the world suffered a great loss that day. In the financial world, where greed is a cunning mistress, ethics were sometimes most easily achieved through government seizure of one's fortunes, the promise of public humiliation, and/or an invitation to be a "guest of the state" for the rest of one's natural years. In that world of high stakes and continuous temptation, Ben's reputation was impeccable.

What I knew of Smitty was that he was quiet and polite and knew how to handle a boat; J.D. was heartbroken because he had known him for years and loved him. All Smitty wanted to do was please the Langley family and ride the rivers of the ACE Basin and the Intercoastal Waterway. He was a simple man with a loving patience for all, J.D. said, and certainly every meeting I had had with him rang true to J.D.'s description of his character.

I couldn't help but think about what you left behind when you died. Here were two men, polar opposites in many ways, whose legacies were strong moral character and a commitment to a code of righteous behavior. Certainly there was a large lesson there for all of us to learn.

Was Sela right? Had the explosion been meant to kill me? Was Valerie involved somehow? I decided not to repeat Sela's story to J.D. because it sounded like hearsay or gossip, and during those first hours, there was no shortage of hysteria in any quarter. The truth would eventually become apparent. At that moment what mattered most was making sure that Pinkham and McGrath were okay. And finding Ben's and Smitty's bodies.

The local media, who were already at the dock to cover the event, suddenly seemed to be swarming like angry bees because this was real news. Given the amount of energy in the air, I was convinced that it would make national news, too.

The first thing J.D. and I did was update Ed by cell phone, and then we rushed to the hospital in J.D.'s truck. The air was thick with screaming sirens, anxiety, and desperation. *Get out of the way! Time is critical! Every minute!* Every kind of emergency vehicle was arriving on the scene as we were driving off.

When we got to the hospital, we found Sandi in the admitting area. She reassured us with the news that McGrath and Pinkham were being treated and would be released shortly.

"Can we go see them?" I asked.

After some convincing, the medical staff let us go into the examining rooms. J.D. and I must have looked frightful, with our wet clothes clinging to us and trauma plastered across our faces. I was shivering so badly that a nurse gave me a blanket, then another. Pinkham and McGrath's injuries were minor, but their emotional states were understandably shaky. We were all very shaken and suffering various degrees of shock.

Pinkham, who was slightly senior to McGrath, had already

called Doug Traum, the chairman of ARC Partners. They decided it was appropriate for Traum to make the call to Bruton's widow.

"He's flying Carol down here in an hour," McGrath said. "If they find his remains, she wants to take them home for burial."

"Just what in the hell happened out there?" Pinkham asked.

"We don't have any idea," J.D. answered, "but Ed O'Farrell, our friend who's the chief of police for Charleston, and four other officers who were on Bulls with him, are questioning everyone. The rest of the force is all over it. They're compiling a list of 'persons of interest.' And their divers are already arriving on the scene. I'm sure that what's left of the boat is being gathered up and they're searching the marsh and the wooded areas with bloodhounds for any pieces of evidence there might be."

It occurred to me again that in this world of competitive TV networks, so desperate for any kind of news story, this would definitely be of interest to the larger markets. I knew at once I had to warn my son.

"Hey, J.D.? Can I borrow your cell phone?"

"Sure," he said, and handed it to me.

I walked outside to the parking lot to call Adrian so he would know that I was unharmed. Of course I got his voice mail.

"Hi, sweetheart," I said, struggling to sound upbeat. "It's Mom. Listen, there's been an accident down here, and should you see it on the news, I just want you to know that I am fine but my cell phone is broken. But I am one hundred percent fine. Didn't even break a nail. Okay? Love you and I'll call you as soon as my phone's fixed."

Then I called Sela again. No answer. Well, I thought, she was probably frantic, trying to pack up and leave the island. (One didn't use the metaphor "up to one's eyeballs in alligators" on Bulls Island for fear it might come true.) Our eco-friendly picnic was now a crime scene.

As I walked back into the hospital J.D.'s phone rang. I answered it and it was Ed O'Farrell.

"Hey. Is J.D. there?"

"Yeah, sure," I said. "I'm just walking back inside now. I'll get him."

"You okay? The others?"

"Yeah, I guess. I mean, I've never been though anything like this before. None of us have. I can't believe what happened, can you?"

"No. Incredible. Like a war zone or something."

I reached J.D.'s side and handed the phone to him.

"Hey, Ed. It's me. J.D. What's up?" He paused for a minute and then said, "What? She said *what*?"

His face was incredulous. Aghast. Red and then ashen.

"What?" I said.

He held his hand up to me, asking me to be quiet for a minute. His brow was knitted in concern and he was shaking his head back and forth. What was Ed telling him?

"Of course I'll call our lawyer! Could you please tell her just to shut the hell up until she has a lawyer at her side? Oh, they are? Well, that's good." There was a long pause and then J.D. said, "Thanks, Ed. I appreciate that. Of course! Pick them all up and let's get to the bottom of this! I agree. I agree with you completely! Thanks. Of course. Okay, we'll talk later."

"What happened?"

"It seems my wife is part canary."

"Meaning?"

"She started singing, screaming actually, when the boat blew up. And she said all kinds of really incoherent and stupid things to implicate herself in the explosion."

"Such as . . ."

"Such as: 'This wasn't supposed to happen! I didn't tell him to do it! Oh my God! All we did was have one conversation about it! He promised me! And where the hell is Betts? She was supposed to be on that boat! Why did I believe him?' You can imagine that Ed was just a little bit curious about who she was referring to, so he's taking her downtown for questioning. Thank God my parents are there. They're going with her. Here's the second part of the kicker. Turns out she also admitted that the guy she was talking about is the same fellow who has been supplying her with her pills. Apparently, there's some suspicion on Ed's part that they've become an item."

"Well, that's disgusting, but sometimes the simplest explanation is the truth. Good grief. Do you think she was fooling with him so he would give her what she wanted?"

J.D. was so thoroughly shaken by the news from Ed that he became uncharacteristically sarcastic. "I'm unfamiliar with the relationship between drug dealers and their clientele. But I'd venture a guess that he would be able to convince Valerie that she would find it easier to procure what she wanted in a timely fashion if they were intimately involved."

"Well, that's one way of putting it."

"Innocent or not, she's in big trouble. And here's the most despicable detail. She didn't want to give him up to Ed because if he goes down for possession and distribution of illegal narcotics—not to mention possession of a deadly weapon with intent to commit murder—where is she going to get her next fix? How self-serving is that?"

"Very. But she told him?"

"Yeah, and she told him about some other guy, too. Apparently there are two men involved in this. Maybe more. But Ed's going to bring them all in for questioning."

At that moment Paul McGrath and David Pinkham appeared, dressed in their damp clothes and looking completely bedraggled.

"Y'all okay?" I asked.

"Glad to be alive," McGrath said.

"Me, too," Pinkham said.

"Well, thank heaven you are! Sandi? Why don't you take them back to the hotel and we'll meet you there as soon as I get cleaned up. J.D.? Do you mind running me back to the dock? I can pick up my car there, go change, and meet you at the hotel."

"Okay, that sounds fine. Until Traum arrives with Carol we should stay together."

I gave McGrath and Pinkham a hug around their necks and felt tears rising again. I had shed more tears on that day than I had in years.

"I'll see y'all soon," I said, and left with J.D.

We walked in silence to his truck and drove back in near silence to the dock.

"What's gonna happen now?"

"I don't know, Betts, I don't know. This is so much to think about. I mean, is Valerie completely insane?"

"I'd say yes to that. Are you going to put her in rehab?"

"That's up to her. One thing is for sure, though."

"What's that?"

"I'm all done with her."

"I don't blame you, J.D. No one would." It was at least the third time he had said he was through with her, but this time it had nothing to do with me.

"I think you're right."

We pulled into the parking lot and just stared at each other then. The enormity of the day's events was pressing on us, the senseless loss of Smitty and Ben, the heart-break it would bring to their families, Valerie's shocking vengeance—it was a lot to absorb.

"What are we going to do about Bulls Island? The project, I mean?"

"Well, I don't know. I think a lot of that decision will depend on why this horrible tragedy took place. For all we know right now, it could've been another ecoterrorist incident. We have to gather the facts and then we can decide. Which is why, when I let you off at your car, if you get spotted by the press, don't talk to them."

"I think it's a good idea for none of us to speak to the press or it might compromise the police investigation."

"Yeah, I don't want to be the one who could've put a

criminal behind bars and then doesn't because of a careless remark."

We drove through the enormous parking lot and finally came to my car. There were media trucks everywhere, but by God's grace, we went undetected. I looked at J.D. for a few moments. What was left to say?

I got out and, turning back, said, "Thanks, J.D. I'll see you soon."

"Sure thing."

I despised the uncertainty that the tragic events of the day had left in their wake. As I drove back to the condo, I was remembering a less complicated time, being young with J.D., lemonade and the fragrance of roses in the heat of late day, walking hand in hand on the beach, warm sand and no shoes, the way his eyes sparkled in merriment, the way it felt to be next to him. All the elements were still there, but everything had been sullied by Valerie's admissions and the horrendous loss of Ben and Smitty. More than anything, I wanted to roll back time, and of course that was not to be. That could never be.

I showered and changed, mentally preparing myself for a long night, and drove back to downtown Charleston and the hotel.

Not long after I arrived, Doug Traum and Carol Bruton called us to say they had just checked in and were on the way to our suite as soon as they unpacked.

McGrath and Pinkham had showered and changed into fresh clothes and so had J.D. The hotel had sent us several carafes of coffee and platters of sandwiches, all on the house. But no one showed any signs of an appetite except Sandi, who was devouring a chicken-salad sandwich.

"Well, that was very nice of them," I said to Pinkham, pointing to the food.

"They knew we had endured an extraordinary day," he said.

"That's for sure," McGrath added.

"I keep a few things at the office," J.D. said. "And Sandi

picked up dry shoes and socks for me at Dumas." He had the most peculiar look on his face, but I decided it could have been for any number of reasons and kept myself from trying to interpret it.

"Sandi's a good woman," I said.

"Thanks," she said.

I asked, "Did we hear anything else from Ed or Sela?"

"Not yet," McGrath answered.

The five o'clock news was on television. When pictures of the dock flashed across the screen, McGrath raised the volume and we fell silent.

Regrettably, the first face we saw was Joanie's.

"Yep!" she was saying to a reporter. "And my sister, Betts McGee, jumped right off that boat to try and find her boss! I didn't know she was so brave but she's a hero today!"

"She certainly is," the perky reporter replied. "Two people are reported dead and the cause of the incident is under investigation and still unknown. Anyone with information about this terrible tragedy should call the Charleston County Police Department at the number shown on your screen. Now back to you, Bill . . ."

The likelihood of Joanie's being shown on any national news show was slim, but I wanted to know for sure so I could sleep that night.

"Can you switch to CNN, Paul? I think it's on Channel Ten."

"Sure."

He lowered the volume and we all continued to watch in a numb state of disbelief as the events of the day played out on every single network, with my crazy sister revealing my identity to the world. I could barely breathe. All Adrian would have to do was turn on a television to discover he had a crazy-as-a-loon aunt, one who was living and breathing.

The doorbell rang and Doug Traum entered the room with Carol Bruton at his side. Carol, always elegant to a fault, wore a black Armani pantsuit with a black-and-red Hermès scarf at her neck and tons of gold jewelry, encrusted with stones. Her thick strawberry-blond hair was held back with quilted Chanel sunglasses. What could you say? Despite swollen eyes, she was as stylish in widowhood as she was on any other day.

They went around the room shaking hands with everyone and thanking them for being there and for their prayers. When they came to me, Carol took my hands in hers and began to cry again.

"I heard what you did," she said. "Absolutely heroic! So brave. Thank you. I just wish . . ."

"So do I, Mrs. Bruton, I would give anything to have found him . . ." My eyes welled up again. "I'm so desperately sorry. We all had such great regard for your husband."

"I know that and I thank you for it. And you, Mr. Langley, thank you. This is such a terrible shock for me . . ."

"Come, let's sit," Doug Traum said, in a surprisingly soothing voice. This great bear of a man, who generally bellowed every word he spoke, was suddenly so gentle and touching. After they took their places on the large sectional sofa, Traum took a deep breath and said, "So tell us. What's the latest news?"

"We expect to hear something before dark," J.D. said. "They'll continue to search with night-lights, but it becomes more dangerous . . . you know, the environment out there is still pretty rustic."

The majority of us knew that meant the night hunters would be on the prowl, but no one said anything specific. I knew there was the occasional bobcat, more snakes than Saint Patrick ran out of Ireland, and yes, those deadly gators. There was no point in risking more loss of human life.

We recounted what we knew for certain over and over, leaving out the Valerie part, but until we heard from Ed, there was nothing new to discuss. Finally, around seven, his call came. He was in the lobby, he said, could he come up?

"By all means," McGrath said to him on the hotel's phone, and then hung up. "I have to get a new cell phone right away."

"So do I," Pinkham said, adding, "It's amazing how dependent we've become on them, isn't it?"

"Make that three," I said. "Gosh, I hope he's got news."

The bell rang and J.D. opened the door.

"Come in, come in."

Ed looked all around the room and recognized at once that the other woman in the room had to be Bruton's widow. He went right up to her, introduced himself politely and solemnly, and took her hand in his.

"I am so dreadfully sorry for your loss, ma'am. First, I want to tell you that we have found your husband's body. He is intact. In fact, we found both men. Once you make a positive ID, we can have him prepared to go home."

"Praise God," she said quietly. "Thank you."

I was standing right next to them and I thought how difficult it must be to tell someone you have found the body of their loved one and it *wasn't* intact. Having to mention its state at all had to be extremely difficult, but Ed had twenty years of practice and he was graceful and sensitive.

"Why don't we all sit down," Ed said.

Everyone took a chair or settled on the sofa while Ed stood.

"First of all, here's the most important news. It was an accident."

"An *accident*? How can that be? What about what Valerie said when—" I began.

"We'll get to that. The first thing I did, because of my wife Sela's tip this week, was put a tail on the man who was following you, Betts. His name is Louie Genega. He's a small-time drug dealer who used to be in the employ of one Vinny Braggadocio, your friend from New York."

"Oh my God," I gasped.

"The guy in the hotel business?" J.D. asked.

"Yep. That's the one," Ed replied. "It seems Valerie met Louie through an exchange of goods for cash and she told him about you, Betts. Apparently, she wanted you gone and out of her life."

I had to sit down. Knowing the depth of her hatred for me made me feel ill.

"Gone like . . . dead? Or just back to New York?" J.D. asked.

"Interesting point," Ed said. "According to Mr. Genega, Valerie was apparently very high one night in a club and was ranting and raving about you and how you were trying to take her husband away from her."

"Is that true, McGee?" McGrath said.

"Well, I . . . J.D. and I were engaged once upon a time. It would be easy for her to leap to that assumption, I imagine."

"Balls, McGee. I wasn't sure you had them," Pinkham said quietly, and perhaps because of the occasion, no one laughed, but they did smile.

"We never even thought of you as a girl," McGrath said. "Pardon the oversight?"

"It's a long story," I said.

"So, Genega starts following Betts around because he's lovesick for Valerie and definitely smitten by her glamour."

"What's he going to find out about me?" I said.

"Not much. But he's baiting her with pictures, telling her how wonderful she is and how she deserves better than J.D. He starts wining and dining her. And getting her high."

"Hmmph," J.D. said. "Tramp."

"Only thing is," Ed continued, "that Louie boy can't afford the romance. So he calls his old boss, Vinny, to ask him to help finance his new love life, thinking he's gonna get you out of the picture by wooing her out of her marriage, she'll get half of whatever J.D. has, and he'll be on the gravy train. Vinny didn't know yet that Betts was the target.

"So Vinny feels sorry for him, gives him twenty grand, and Louie doesn't pay him back. Vinny comes to Charleston, figures out what's going on, and—"

"I knew it!" I said. "I *knew* Vinny was a bad guy!"

Everyone, except Ed, looked at me, wondering what in the world I meant.

"Um, actually," Ed said, "Vinny's not a *bad* guy. I mean, he's not the Archbishop of Canterbury, but he's got some good qualities. It wasn't so nice what he did to Louie's eyes and nose, but when he found out Louie was considering blowing you up to impress Valerie, he pounded him into the ground. And think about this. If J.D. had been in the boat, Valerie would have been that much richer, right? So I think it's fair to say that Louie was considering it, but so far there are no facts to prove he *did* do it."

"Vinny *did* warn me. Oh Lord."

"Well, I'd like to hear about that. So, early this morning we got the judge to sign a warrant to search Louie's apartment. We've had our eye on him for some time. Four of Charleston's finest paid him a visit and found C-four charges and enough OxyContin to ease the pain of everyone in town."

"C-four charges? What are C-four charges?" I asked.

"Explosives. Like Play-Doh. You can attach it anywhere and blow something up with a cell phone."

"So, is that what happened?" J.D. demanded. "That's what blew up the boat and killed Ben and Smitty?"

"No, not at all. Believe it or not, the boat hit an old Civil War mine. All the dredging your men have been doing to run electric conduits and sewage pipes must have stirred things up. Forensics isn't complete, but they're pretty sure what it is."

"I'll be damned," J.D. said. "No foul play, then. Is that right?"

"Not as far as the explosion goes. It appears that it was a complete accident. Of course there will be a more thorough investigation, but this is what we suspect is the case. And that's all the news for tonight."

"Except that somehow Valerie is involved in this evil, am I right?" J.D. said. "Valerie had some conversation with Louie about a *hit* on Betts? Is that what I am to understand?"

"No, it was more like speculative daydreaming, but understand this, our friend Louie was looking for a home run. Valerie was the closest thing to financial independence he had ever seen. If he could have been rid of both of you, it would have been twice as good for him." Ed took business cards from his wallet and handed them to Carol Bruton, Doug Traum, Pinkham, and McGrath. "In case there's anything to report or if you have a question. Mrs. Bruton, if you'd like, I'll go with you to the county morgue . . ."

"I'll come along," Doug Traum said.

"You need us?" Pinkham asked.

"No, why don't you wait for me in the bar downstairs," Traum said with a wry smile. "I'll bet you guys could use a shot of something."

"Yes, well, um . . . okay, then."

Sandi said, "Unless you need me, Betts, I'd like to go out to my brother's house. Call you in the morning, Betts?"

"Yes. Fine. Sandi, thanks for everything."

Sandi left.

J.D. stood and then I did, too. What else was there to say?

"Come on; let me walk y'all to the door, Ed," J.D. said. I followed along to listen. "Where are my folks?"

"They went back out to the plantation. After we released Valerie, she asked to be returned to MUSC for detox."

"Well, how about that?" J.D. said. "At least she's still got the sense to recognize the end of the road when she sees it."

McGrath and Pinkham were suddenly behind us.

"Wait up, Ed, we'll ride down the elevator with you. You staying, J.D.?" McGrath asked.

"No, I'll be along in a minute. I just need to ask Betts something in private."

"Oh! Okay," McGrath said.

"All right, then," Pinkham added.

"We'll see you later." J.D. closed the door.

He looked very somber and took the longest breath I had ever seen him draw, exhaling, it seemed, every detail of the night. Except one.

"What's the matter?" I said.

"Your son called."

"He did?" I was so shocked I didn't know what else to say.

"Yes, your nineteen-year-old son named Adrian for your mother, Adrianna, saw his aunt, Joanie McGee, on CNN and was wondering who else was down here in Charleston whom he might like to know."

"What did you tell him?"

"I told him that I expected there were many people who would like to know him. I gave him my credit-card number and told him to get on a plane. He's arriving on Continental at nine-thirty. Would you like me to pick him up for you?"

"Um, I don't know. I mean . . ."

"I think I'll come along in my truck. Just to make sure you get there okay."

"Um, J.D.?"

"Yes?"

"He's yours, J.D. That's all you need to know."

"Look, Betts. You've had under one minute to think of what to say. I've had several hours. It's an unfair advantage, so we're not going to play a game about this, okay? I hate games anyway. Come here to me."

I started to tremble and couldn't stop, and then the tears began to flow. He put his arms around me and I leaned into him. I felt his chest rising and falling and knew he was crying, too. It was too much to bear in such a short time.

"All I can do is wonder what you've been carrying on your shoulders all alone all these years. Betts? Didn't you know you always could have come to me?"

"No! I didn't know that! Oh, I don't know what I knew, J.D., except that I had a son to raise and no family to help me. I did the best I could to cope. It was so hard . . ."

"I'm sure it was. Ah, God! I should have tried harder to see you, Betts. I am so sorry."

"And I should have told you, J.D. And Adrian. And Daddy and Joanie. But it was so complicated and I was so afraid everyone would reject us. It was easier to say nothing. Somehow it was easier to live the lie than to face you, your parents, my father . . . I mean, it's *never* been good between our families! Something *always* happens! I figured I would just disappear . . . so I did."

"But you didn't. And here we are. And somehow, by the grace of God, the world has finally cleared the way for us to be together . . ."

"Not without more than a few casualties along the way . . . but I can't even think about that now." I smiled then.

"You're right. There will be plenty of time to think about what kind of relationship we're going to have. Tonight, the battlefield is rife with carnage. Let's go to the airport and meet my son."

"Let's go meet *our* son."

We owned our lives for the first time in our lives.

A little while later, we pulled into the airport, parked, and went inside the terminal to wait. Adrian's flight was late. Of course it was. Everything out of New York is always late.

"Want a beer?" J.D. asked.

"No, but I think a glass of wine might be the ticket. I think I earned it."

"Maybe two."

We walked into the airport's watering hole, and who was sitting there on a bar stool all alone? None other than Vinny.

He turned and saw us, then turned away. I went straight up to him and stood right in his line of vision.

"Whatcha drinking, Vinny? Can I buy you a bona fide mint julep and a glass of Huge Apology and Forever in Your Debt on the side?"

He looked up and down and then at J.D. Then he looked back to me and smiled. Naturally, he turned to me and naturally he tried as hard as he could to look irresistible.

"Ah, Betts. Where'd you get that hair?"

"Swimming."

"What's to be done about Betts McGee?"

"Be my friend, Vinny. Every gal needs a true friend like you."

"I always was your friend. Always had a soft spot for

magnolias, you know." He turned to J.D. "You must be J. D. Langley."

"I am indeed." J.D. stepped forward to shake Vinny's hand.

I said to Vinny, "My son is J.D.'s boy. Sort of an engagement baby." Then I turned to J.D. "Vinny and I dated for a while."

"And the truth will set you free," J.D. said. "What are you drinking, Vinny?"

Vinny looked long and hard at us and said, "Dinner."

Who could fault that choice, given the last twenty-four hours?

We talked for a few minutes and finally Vinny said, "So, Betts? Are you coming back to New York?"

"Well, I'll be in New York for Bruton's funeral and then I guess I'm coming back here for a while at least, depending on what happens with the Bulls Island project. What are your plans?"

"Don't worry about Vinny," Vinny said. "I got more plans than time." He looked at his wristwatch. "I gotta go to my gate."

"Hey, Vinny?" I said. "I owe you."

"You don't owe me nothing," he said. "Just plant one right here." He pointed to his cheek. I stood on my toes to give him a solid kiss. "Take care of her, J.D. Don't make me come back down here and start that war all over again!"

"Don't you worry. I will take excellent care of her." J.D. shook his hand soundly.

I loved hearing J.D.'s sentiments, however premature they might be. We watched Vinny walk away.

"He's got some swagger," J.D. noted.

"Hey, that's Vinny Braggadocio."

"And just what does *that* mean?"

"He is one hundred percent Eyetalian good old boy!"

"I think I understand," J.D. said. "Come on, let's check Adrian's flight."

It had arrived and we went quickly over to the security

area where he would be coming out. A few very exciting minutes passed, then I spotted him before he saw us. My heart was in my throat.

"That's him," I said to J.D. "That's him in the blue sweater. The tall lanky one."

"Oh my God," J.D. breathed. "That's my boy."

Adrian ran up to me, giving me a bear hug. Then he stood back and looked at J.D.

J.D. said, "Son? I'd know you anywhere. Come here!"

J.D. was hugging Adrian's neck so hard I thought it might snap, but then he dropped his hold, choked up with tears, and covered his face with his hands.

"Mom?" Adrian was blushing and thoroughly confused.

"Adrian? I don't know what to say or how to say this, but . . . this is your father, J. D. Langley. You'll probably have a few questions."

BACK AT MY CONDO, after a lot of rapid conversation, and before the hour grew too late, we called Daddy and Joanie to say we were all right and asked if they could meet us at Sela's Sunday night for dinner at six. They said yes, of course, and I gave them the facts about the accident, as I knew them, leaving the details about Valerie and Adrian's arrival for another time. Joanie wanted to know if Cam could come and I said absolutely, yes. I was sure there would be more information about the accident the next day and we finally said good night.

Then J.D. called his parents and got an earful of Valerie's long sad tale of woe. No one cared about Valerie's weeping and moaning and that was exactly what made her long tale truly sad. But yes, they said, they would meet us at Sela's for dinner, too. Six o'clock. And by the way, would they bring Mickey and Rosie? Well, why not, they said, unsure of why but suspecting J.D. had something up his sleeve.

The night didn't end until almost two in the morning, with J.D. on the sofa bed, Adrian in the guest room, and me staring at the ceiling in my room for hours. I didn't care that I couldn't sleep. I really didn't want to sleep, as I was struggling to remember every detail for a memoir I planned to write someday. Surely this story was worth a book?

Morning finally came, and the day that ensued was a logistical nightmare. First, we had to get the county coroner to sign off on Ben Bruton's certificate of death in order to release his body to Carol. The entire incident was still under investigation as a crime scene and his body was technically evidence. But given the strength of the fact that no crime had been committed and Ben's high-profile stature, the judge was very agreeable and signed the necessary papers.

Then there was the sorrowful task of putting him on the plane. J.D., Ed, Adrian, and I all met at the airport. Doug Traum brought in the largest plane the company had at its disposal, but it barely had room for Ben's casket. We all hugged and kissed Carol, and J.D. and I offered to take the ride with her, knowing how horrible it would be for her to be on that plane with her husband's remains. But she was resolute in her refusal, saying that with Traum, Pinkham, and McGrath at her side she would be fine.

"He looked so peaceful, you know? He was so good," she said. "I'm okay. Really I am."

"As soon as the arrangements are made, please let us know," I said.

"Depend on it," Traum said. "We'll talk tomorrow."

I knew he meant that he was thinking about the project and wavering about a decision to pull out. I would call him first thing.

After that horrible task was done, we were all feeling the blues.

"I've got to get back to work," Ed said.

"Right," J.D. said. "Well, I guess I'll follow Betts and Adrian to the phone store."

"Drowned my phone," I told Adrian.

"It's okay. It was for a worthy cause," Adrian said.

"I love this kid!" J.D. declared.

After I had a new cell in my hands and we were back at the condo, J.D. made an announcement.

"I'm leaving home," he said. "I'm moving in here."

"When I go back to school, you can have my room," Adrian said innocently.

"And you're going back on Tuesday, probably with me," I said. "And, J.D., I think you moving in here is something we might want to, I don't know, discuss?"

"I'm giving Rosie and Mickey my house."

"Well, that's very generous of you, but what about Valerie?"

"I'll move all her stuff to the caretaker's cottage and give her a cash settlement. Listen, whatever, I'll work that out."

"J.D.? Good. You work that out. But, no. You're not moving in here. I'll find you a condo nearby or something downtown, but we're not living together until everything is settled. It's too much. Besides, who said I was staying? This condo is on loan."

"Oh," he said, "okay." He looked at the floor and then back to me. "Right. Well then, can I stay for a night or two?"

"Yes, on the couch." I looked at Adrian and giggled. "He's really forceful, isn't he?"

"You two are so weird! What's the rest of my family like?"

"The rest of the family? You know those dioramas at the Museum of Natural History with the cavemen?" I said. "Dragging their women around by their hair?"

"Well, that's a gross exaggeration," J.D. put in, "but when you throw us all in one room, an anthropologist can have a field day. You'll see. Especially my mother."

"Especially my *sister,* your aunt Joanie. I'd better call Sela and warn her."

"Good idea. So, Adrian, want to drive out to the plantation with me to get some clothes and things? Plus I gotta get Goober and Peanut."

"Dogs?"

"Not just dogs. They're my best friends."

"Can I go, Mom?"

"Why not? It's your ancestral home, too. Sort of. I'll see you two at Sela's? Six o'clock. Don't be late, okay?"

"Deal." J.D. nodded. "Can I have a key?"

"Adrian can have a key. You may not have a key."

I got an extra key from the drawer and threw it to Adrian.

"Don't let him make a copy," I told him.

"Right," Adrian said, and smiled.

I watched them walk down the steps toward J.D.'s truck and they looked like a "junior" and "senior" if ever there was a picture of one. My heart was so filled with an undeserved happiness. I wanted one more date with a crying towel, but I shook my head and denied myself the indulgence.

In the first place, it was rather miraculous that neither J.D. nor Adrian had screamed his head off at me for keeping him in the dark about the other's existence . . . but maybe my day of reckoning was yet to come.

Move in with me? There were other looming monsters to be slain first. Louisa, for one. I couldn't wait to see the look on Louisa Langley's face when she saw Adrian. I knew Big Jim would adore him, but Louisa was another matter. Daddy would love Adrian, too. Perhaps Adrian was just what Daddy needed to take a new interest in life. And Joanie? Well, she was a crackpot. Who knew how she would react?

But J. D. Langley was not moving in with me. Period. Well, maybe comma. But I was determined to take any and all steps related to deciding my future slowly. Very slowly.

I wasn't prepared to decide my entire future on the turn of a tide. Too much had happened in too short a time, and each incident that had occurred and each decision needed careful consideration. And as far as I knew, I still had a job in New York and a home as well.

Yes, Adrian deserved a father and a family. But I was holding back until we all adjusted to the new realities.

I called Sela.

"You're my first call on my new phone," I said.

312 | Dorothea Benton Frank

"Girl? How? Are? You? Doing?"

"Oh, Sela, Sela! It's been one helluva twenty-four hours, hasn't it?"

"Ed said you're bringing the whole gene pool for dinner? I'm closing the door to the public. It's a private party tonight, but you're going to have to eat a lot of pigs in blankets, you know."

"Sela? Adrian's here."

"No. Way. For real?"

"I'm getting dressed and coming straight over. I'll help you set up."

"I'd better do inventory on the bar. Gonna be a big night. Sandi's here, by the way, with one of Ed's hunkier specimens. They're folding napkins. Her coat's shiny."

"Sela? You are so bad!"

It wasn't long before I arrived at O'Farrell's, Sela and I were caught up, and everyone began to drift into the restaurant.

J.D. took me aside before we all sat down and said, "Listen, Doug Traum called as soon as they landed at Teterboro. Carol Bruton feels very strongly that she wants Bulls Island to go forward, especially since it was Ben's last project. Traum is putting up two million in Ben's honor to build a park in his name and another million to dedicate the dock to Smitty. And here I thought the guy was a big blowhard . . ."

"See? You never know. That's wonderful!"

I kept Adrian by my side as each person was introduced to him.

Joanie said to me in a whisper, "I knew it, you know," referring to the existence of my son.

I said, "I know, Joanie. Remember?"

Then she turned to Adrian and blew my mind. "Well, you certainly are a handsome young man, Adrian. Welcome to the family! Daddy and I can't wait to get to know you!"

Wait a minute, I thought. Was that *Joanie*? Who kidnapped my sister and replaced her with a nice person? Then

I had an epiphany. Joanie was sleeping with Cam! Sex had caused a personality change!

Daddy was an angel to Adrian.

"Oh, my dear boy! Look at you! You are the spitting image of your father, but you have your grandmother's dimples! What a joy it is to know you! What a joy!"

"Now don't hog my grandson, Vaughn! Let's let your paternal grandfather look at you!" Big Jim held Adrian's chin up to the light. "Ah, yes, he's a Langley all right. Look at that patrician profile!"

Then came the aria of Sweet Louisa the Diva from the sidelines.

"I demand a DNA test before I will even consider changing my will," she said.

"Oh, come on, Mother!" J.D. said. "All's well that ends—"

"I'll be the judge of that," she sniffed.

I was so stunned by her rudeness that I wanted to slap her. But Adrian surprised us all by saying, "Suits me."

"It does?" I said.

"Heck, yeah. What do I care? Don't you think I'd like to be sure, too?"

Big Jim stepped forward and took Louisa by the arm, and for the first time in his entire existence and for everyone to hear, he said, "Louisa? Why don't you learn to shut your arrogant damn mouth? Step away from my grandson. You poison his air."

Everyone in the room took a collective gasp.

"Whew, Dad!" J.D. was flabbergasted . . . there were a lot of flabbergasting things afoot. "Son? This seems like the perfect moment for you to come meet your, uh, uncle Mickey!"

I thought we would have to call for oxygen when young Mickey stepped up and shook Adrian's hand.

"Uncle Mickey," Adrian said, towering over his uncle whose voice had only recently changed. "Do you happen to have an Xbox?"

"Nope. Do you?" Mickey said.

"Yep. The Three-sixty. And Rock Band."

"Oh, this is very cool news."

"Holy cow," Joanie said, recognizing another truth. "What's next?"

What followed was a lot of laughter as the flame of our ages-old family feud sputtered to a final fizzle. I watched them all as love bloomed and old wounds healed as though bathed in the waters of Lourdes. It was like nothing I would ever witness again. Or that any of us would ever witness again. Generations of ghosts roamed the room, whispering warnings of eternal unrest, please free them from all of it. I could hear Bruton's voice in my ear: *Don't be a fool, Betts. Life is short.* My mother's breath was all over my neck: *Love him, forgive them, bring my family back together, please do this for me, for all of us.* It was up to me, up to everyone. Most of us were game. Something larger was at play as, God help us all, Louisa herself had once said.

Okay, I thought. I'll be the fool for this generation. After all, the odds were finally on my side. I'd take the risk, the gamble, the bet. And you know me; I'm only Betts when I know I'm going to win. I like a sure thing.

EPILOGUE

2008

There are some things you need to know before we part. I am not an evil woman but I certainly committed a terrible crime. I paid for it with more cold sweats and heart-skipping nightmares than you could count. In some ways, I will probably continue to pay for it forever. Now, one year later, there are still residual eruptions of anger and resentment from J.D. and Adrian, though fortunately not at the same time.

After Bruton's funeral, I decided to stay in New York for an extended visit to be near Adrian in case he wanted to talk. Adrian did not want to talk to me or anyone.

He kept saying, "Look, Mom. This doesn't change the fact that I still have to study and make grades. . . . I have a job to do." His tone of voice was terse and I knew his quiet rage bordered on volcanic. I did not blame him.

"So do I, Adrian. I just keep thinking that there must be questions that you have. . . . I don't know, things you want to know?"

"I guess I want to know how you could do this to me, to all of us? How could you?"

These are the words I had dreaded, absolutely dreaded,

hearing for the past twenty years. There they were, naked and cold, spoken quietly and matter-of-factly by the one person I had ever loved so dearly. Not hurled at me like hot coals, not chucked in my direction on a tail of fire, but spoken by my beautiful son, of whom I was so proud, from a place of unimaginable pain. I wanted him and everyone— J.D., Daddy, Joanie, J.D.'s family, Sela, and Ed—to look in my face and down the tunnel of my years, to see my life through my eyes, what I had seen and lost, and the family celebrations for which I had yearned. Christmases. Birthdays. Graduations. I had celebrated them all alone, except for the company of Aunt Jennie and an occasional visit from Sela. If they could have seen with my eyes, father and son might not have been so judgmental in those early weeks, once the initial joy of knowing each other wore off and their questions became more hostile and begging for answers I could not provide.

I wanted them to know that my whole heart had been a lifelong investment in Adrian and that eventually I would've told them all the truth. I had planned to and I *would* have told them, I swear. I said so, didn't I? The horrors of reality had beaten me to the punch.

Sela says I have to quit torturing myself, and she's right. I could not undo what was done. Whether we want to ride the tides or not, life washes over us until the passage of time can dull the pain of our betrayals. Thankfully, eventually everyone began to come around. The thaw began to show itself at Christmas.

Adrian and I agreed to spend the holidays in Charleston, and we were actually looking forward to it. I figured the answer to happiness would be found in a higher incidence of exposure to J.D. and the family, giving us more chances to adjust and less time to consider our many regrets.

The Bulls Island construction was well under way; I still had the condo at Wild Dunes and was only too happy to spend Christmas Day morning watching the ocean rolling in. I had spent the last six months or so nursing a fantasy that time had done some healing and I could set things right. Adrian and I were walking on the beach in the morning and after many weeks of stilted conversations and without provocation I felt Adrian's arm loop around my shoulder. I had missed that arm and that assuring hug so much. Well, just ask any woman with a son how important her boy's love is and she will sigh with the force of a hurricane wind.

"It's okay, Mom," he said. "Merry Christmas."

"Oh, son." I stopped and put my arms around him. "I love you so! Merry Christmas."

"I love you too," he said. "I really do."

With that, I could feel my stress melting away and I began to cry.

"Hey, Mom?"

"Yeah?"

"No more tears. Everything's gonna be okay. Trust me."

And thus I began to recognize that the man inside my boy had decided that perhaps I had suffered enough. We drove over to the city to have our Christmas at Daddy's with Sela and Ed, J.D., Sandi, Cam, and Joanie and we enjoyed a traditional turkey dinner and jokingly fought over the wishbone amid many toasts. If we couldn't have peace on the whole earth, at least we could bow our heads and pray for peace among us.

Then we exchanged gifts. I bought J.D. a spotter lens to be used in the ongoing efforts to find Gatorzilla. We all had a good laugh about that, except that the poor fellow who had been a gator snack had passed away, so we sadly toasted his memory wishing him eternal rest. Then J.D., whose divorce papers had damp ink but would be final any moment, handed me a small velvet box from Crogan's Jewel Box. I held my breath as I opened it, thinking perhaps it was an engagement ring, but it was not. Inside was a stunning pair of diamond stud earrings with removable pearl drops. They sparkled and flashed and I didn't know what to say. Simply gorgeous!

"I planned to start with your ears," he said. "Like them?"

Start with my ears, indeed.

"You know I do! Oh, J.D.! They're beautiful!"

"A man who gives a woman a gift like that had better have honorable intentions," Daddy said.

"Yes, sir," J.D. said. "I think you know this is not the first time I have attempted to declare my intentions."

We swapped sweaters and books, bottles of perfume, DVDs, and all manner of remembrances until we had exhausted Santa's booty for 2008. There had been thoughtful gifts for everyone and it became clear that J.D. and I were not the only ones taking one step closer to a commitment. Joanie and Cam were looking very cozy, too.

A week or so later Daddy announced that he had taken an interest in the Bulls Island housing and was considering buying something spectacular for himself, saying that Joanie and I could have the house downtown if he relocated full-time. He thought he might open a grocery store on Bulls Island, nothing very complicated, a high-end greengrocer that also carried eco-friendly household goods.

"I can't see people taking a boat to go get milk, can you?" he would say.

"No, and no one understands the business as well as you do, Daddy."

"Maybe my grandson would like to have, I don't know, a summer job? Work his way up? You know, he would have to sweep the floors. Pay his dues like everyone else in the world. What do you think?"

"I think Adrian would be tickled to pieces, Daddy. I really do. But I'll have to ask him."

"I'll call him myself," he said. Then he smiled.

I thought it showed great optimism and tremendous love that Daddy wanted to be involved in something that might forge another link in our chain. After all, Bulls Island had brought us all together in one fashion or another.

What about J.D. and me? Well, J.D. divorced Valerie, and I'm sure that comes as no surprise to anyone. Louisa refused to discuss it, not that she spoke to me very often, which was the perfect arrangement in my opinion. I felt enormous pity

or sympathy or call it what you want for Valerie because
here was a woman who got dealt a lousy hand and went on
to make her life worse. She went back to her family in Georgia, who underwrote and guided her to one rehab facility after another until around Easter we heard that she finally met
a sympathetic psychiatrist and they fell head over heels in
love. Her most recent communiqué said that she was looking into becoming a counselor herself. I wished her all the
best.

But back to J.D. and me? Well, there's no rush. I resigned
from ARC, staying on with Triangle until our island paradise
would be completed. McGrath, Pinkham, and even Traum
understood and offered me return employment any time the
mood struck.

"I envy you, McGee," McGrath said. "All that free time?
But I understand."

"So do I," Pinkham said. "You're a young woman and
there are many roads to heaven."

"Thanks, y'all. I'll miss you like crazy!"

"That's some bull," McGrath said.

"He'll never stop with the bull jokes!" Pinkham said.

Somehow, I couldn't see myself in New York anymore. I
didn't have a lick of enthusiasm to return to the craziness
of private equity and all that that lifestyle demanded, so I
put my co-op on the market and went back to Charleston.
Just like that. No one was more surprised by my actions than
I was. And as everyone except me probably would have expected, the more I gave into my past, and the more I brought
Adrian along on the journey with me, the happier we all
were.

I had given the woman I had become so much thought
and there were some radical changes I wanted to make. I
didn't want to be cynical anymore, strapped to a sword, doing battle with currency markets, housing markets, or any
market at all. I wanted to wipe out the suspicious, calculat-
ing side of myself and see what it would be like to trust
somebody else's judgment for once. And that somebody was

J.D. It always was J.D. At some point you might receive an invitation in your mail. *The pleasure of your company is requested* ... and then you'll know what I have always known. Life's design is only drawn up to a point by your hand. The rest looms out there by the sea. All you have to do is face west at sunset or east at sunrise or walk out on a crisp night and look up at the sky. Especially on Bulls Island.

Author's Note

Bulls Island is a real place and is indeed and hopefully will always be part of the Cape Romain National Wildlife Refuge. There is great discussion over whether to call it Bull Island or Bulls Island. I have called it Bulls Island because that is what we called it when I was growing up on Sullivans Island, which used to have an apostrophe and now does not. Nonetheless, Bull Island and Bulls Island are one and the same and I ask my readers to kindly indulge this tiny reach in artistic license.

If you would like to visit, one way to do so is with the wonderful folks at Coastal Expeditions. Please stop by their website at www.coastalexpeditions.com or call them at 843-881-4582. They also offer family kayak tours and many other short trips to acquaint people from "over the causeway" to the exquisite and unique pleasures of Lowcountry living.

To learn more about conservation of the Lowcountry's incredible landscape, wetland protection efforts, water- and air-quality protection efforts, and what's on the agenda around the State of South Carolina in overall environmental concerns, please visit www.coastalconservationleague.org or e-mail info@scccl.org.

A+

AUTHOR INSIGHTS, EXTRAS & MORE...

FROM

DOROTHEA BENTON FRANK

AND

WM

WILLIAM MORROW

If you enjoyed *Bulls Island,*
read on for the next
delightfully heartwarming new novel
from *New York Times* bestselling author

Dorothea Benton Frank
FOLLY BEACH

Available now in hardcover from William Morrow

CHAPTER ONE

Folly Beach
A One-Woman Show with Images

By Cathryn Mahon Cooper

Setting: St. Philip's Cemetery in Charleston, South Carolina. Dorothy Kuhns Heyward rises from her grave and dusts herself off. She kisses her fingertips and touches the tombstone of DuBose Heyward, which is next to hers. She walks to center stage near the footlights and speaks.

Director's Note: Images to run on back wall scrim: photo of Folly Beach, the beach itself including the Morris Island Lighthouse, photo of Murray Boulevard with an enormous full moon, map of Ohio and Dorothy in evening dress, and DuBose in smoking jacket. Dorothy has a serious side but she's also very funny.

Act I
Scene I

Dorothy: I married an actual renaissance man. Yes, I really did! The story I have to tell you is about the deep and abiding love we shared. *Not* the carnal details, *please,* but some of its *other* aspects such as the sacrifices we were willing to make and the lengths to which we would go for each other. DuBose Heyward was the real and only true love of my life.

It was the summer of 1921 and when we met for the first time, we were both guests at the MacDowell Colony in New Hampshire. Mrs. MacDowell was a wonderful woman who had a very large estate but a very small family. But she *loved* the arts! So every summer she invited certain writers and artists of every genre and we packed our gear and took ourselves there to work. The minute I laid eyes on DuBose Heyward I knew he was going to be mine. We sized each other up and, without so much as a nod, we knew our feelings were mutual. When the summer had ended, he returned to Charleston and I returned to New York. We wrote to each other each week and sometimes more often and saw each other when we could. Finally, after our third summer together at MacDowell we were married on September 23, 1923, at the Little Church Around the Corner in New York City.

DuBose returned to Charleston without me because my play *Nancy Ann* was about to open in New York. *That* set the Lowcountry jungle drums thumping like mad! *Where was his wife? And who was she anyway? From Ohio? She writes plays? A lady in the theater?* Well, I had to do the work I was being paid to do! But I knew enough about Charleston to know I'd better watch my step, so early on I adopted the *zippered lip* posture and took my lead from DuBose. It was his reputation we had to protect and he was so much smarter about those things than I was.

Oh! There is so much I want you to know. This was a crazy time in the world. The economy was going down and hemlines were going up. Women were bobbing their hair, throwing away their corsets, and kicking up their heels, doing the Charleston, especially in Charleston! And in the arts? In Charleston? Well, DuBose and his friends decided that big nasty misunderstanding with the Yankees was behind them and they had to look to the future. I mean, please! Charleston was spared a visit from Sherman but sentiments still ran so strong sixty years after the war ended? Honey, the way people whined and carried on, you'd think old Sherman barged into every lady's house on the Peninsula, broke all her china, stole her daughters, and punched her husband in the nose! Just ridiculous. I mean, people moaned and moaned about how much better things were before . . . wait, do you know the story about Oscar Wilde? No? Well then, listen to this. Oscar Wilde came to Charleston sometime around 1885, the exact year is a little fuzzy to me, but anyway, there's Oscar standing on the High Battery with a Charleston gentleman admiring the full moon. Oscar says, *My word, would you look at that extraordinary moon!* The Charleston gentleman says, *Ah, you should have seen it before the war!* So now you see, Charleston was reluctant to embrace the future if it meant deemphasizing the past one tiny iota. DuBose and his cohorts wanted to hold on to all the glories of the past but have their work reflect their observances of their present day *and* their hopes for the future.

God, I loved that man. We're not talking about moonlight and magnolias here. This is about the magic of a spectacular marriage and how it fueled our creative life and shaped our worldview.

There have been so many stories about DuBose and me and all of them are wrong. Not diabolically wrong, but just skewed at an off angle, enough to make our lives seem like something other than what they were. In public we were both extremely quiet, especially DuBose. In private we laughed about everything and argued loudly over every issue of the day. Well, maybe I was the one who provided the volume. The point is, very few people *really* knew us.

Maybe my words will be kind of a memoir of the Charleston Renaissance. I don't know. But someone has to paint the mood of the time and set the record straight. I guess that will have to be me, the spitfire from Ohio who was never afraid of the truth. Or passion. Not that DuBose was afraid of passion or of the truth. He was never a coward. It's just that his heart pumped the holy blood of old Charleston. Let me tell you this, old Charlestonians would just as soon be caught in their birthday suit walking down Murray Boulevard as reveal their hearts to outsiders. But in Canton, Ohio, we ladies were perhaps more inclined to gently speak our minds.

DuBose and I may not ever have earned a lot of money at one time, but ah well, such is a writer's lot in life. After he published *Porgy* with Doubleday in 1925, we had a few more cookies in our cookie jar and were able to acquire a little house in the wilds on

Folly. We adored the island and every peculiarity about it. Yes, we did. In fact, the happiest days of my life all happened on Folly Beach. We were young then, our heads spinning with creativity, and we thought we had plenty, because we were rich in so many other ways. Who needed a telephone anyway?

And we had daily rituals that brought order and all the dignity of a Park Avenue parlor to our lives. For example, to celebrate civility, my darling DuBose and I enjoyed our own private happy hour every afternoon around dusk. Right before the sun turned deep red and began its slow descent into the horizon, we dressed for dinner. We both loved Hollywood glamour and sometimes referred to Folly Island as Follywood for the fun of it. And why not have a little glamour in our lives? No, I didn't put on a long satin frock and call for Jeeves to make highballs. Oh, no. Our life was substantially more modest! I simply reapplied my makeup and cologne, put on a fresh dress, and brushed my hair. DuBose slipped on his velvet smoking jacket and carefully slicked his hair back, so that in the rose-hued early evening he resembled a very dapper Fred Astaire, but younger and with more hair. And he always smelled like something delicious.

Fade to Darkness

CHAPTER TWO

At the Cemetery

Yea, though I walk through the valley of the shadow of death . . .

The minister's voice was a booming gothic drone. Pastor Edwin Anderson, our pastor with the movie-star looks, suffered from the unfortunate delusion that he was Richard Burton. He really did. Today of all days, it seemed he was brushing up to deliver the soliloquy from *Hamlet*. It was ridiculous. On any other occasion I would have been chewing on the insides of my cheeks until I tasted blood. I didn't dare look at my sister Patti or I'd surely blow my composure. What was the matter with that portion of my brain? Gallows humor? Wait! Did I really say *gallows humor*? Honey, that is the *last* term in the world I should use and that's for sure. But there it was. Some small twisted secret pocket of my mind, with no permission from me, plucked out the most insensitive detail of this somber and terrible event, made a joke of it, which would surely and extremely inappropriately reduce me to a snickering idiot if I didn't pay attention to myself. I cleared my throat, hoping it would send a signal to Pastor Anderson to bring it down a notch. He shot me a look and continued channeling Burton. God, he was unbelievably good-looking. Another inappropriate thought. It was true; I was verging on hysteria but who wouldn't?

The miserable weather just added icing to the unholy dramatic cake of a day. One minute, the skies above New Jersey were dumping snow and in the next, sleet fell like tiny ice picks. I was amazed that the governor had not closed the turnpike and the Garden State Parkway. Everything was a sheet of ice, the temperature around twenty. It was only by God's holy grace that we had all made it to the cemetery without flying off the highway and into a ditch. I was pretty sure the ditches were filled with mangled bodies.

There were probably only twenty of us huddled under the tent at the gravesite, standing, because the seats of the folding chairs were soaking-wet. We all attributed the sparse turnout to Mother Nature, but to tell you the truth I was in such a fog I barely knew what was going on around me. I could not have cared much less who showed up and who didn't. Over the last eighteen months, my life had become so isolated and my circle of friends had narrowed to almost no one. And now this.

We had skipped the traditional wake, deciding on a simple graveside service with the most accommodating pastor from our church. I didn't feel like talking to a lot of people, especially given the circumstances, and Addison was not particularly devout.

"Are you all right, Cate?"

Patti spoke in her normal tone for the hearing-impaired right over the minister, the sleet, the rain, and the wind. Considerations like when to say what and how loud did not occur to Patti. At all or ever. Sometimes that could be humorous, but other times it was unnerving. I was definitely startled by the pitch of her voice. Was I all right? Was I? No. I wasn't all right and we both knew it. Sisters can read each other's minds. I just looked at her. Answer this, Patti, I asked her telepathically, how could I *possibly* be all right? We were gathered in the most inclement conditions February in New Jersey could offer to bury Addison, my husband of way too many years.

"I'm okay," I lied, pushing aside my stupor and trying to gather my thoughts. I stepped forward and put my gloved hand on Addison's polished casket.

In the last two days, I had relived our entire twenty-six-year marriage, looking for clues for how Addison's zeal for life had deteriorated and how all the love we had shared over the years had completely and totally become unraveled. In the early days, we were *insane* over each other. I had never met a man like Addison. There I was, playing Cassie in a revival of *A Chorus Line,* when I caught his grin in the footlights. Sure, he was much older (twelve years) than I was, but he swept me right off my feet and then the stage forever, which, oddly enough, I never missed.

I was crazy about him. All I wanted to do was make him happy, and even now I believe that for a long time he had felt the same way. Our eyes were filled with each other and everything we did together seemed so perfect. A simple meal was a royal feast because we shared it. A country club waltz in a crowded room belonged only to us. He was ambitious, funny, charming, and so, so smart. The almost manic exuberance we felt was clear in every single photograph of us, and there were dozens of them from our early years all over our house. But as the children came along, demanding most of my time, he became consumed with business and slowly, slowly my diamond of a marriage began to lose its sparkle. I guess no honeymoon can last forever.

Oh Addison, I thought, how could you do it and *why* did you do it? Other men his age died from heart disease or cancer. But not my Addison. As he did most things, he leaped into projects full-strength and was a mad dog gnawing and growling until his battle was won. He leaped alright, but this time it was from the top of my piano with the extra-heavy-duty extension cord from our Christmas decorations tied around the rafters and his neck. I was the one who found him. I'd never get that vision of him out of my mind if I lived to be one hundred and ten years old.

I was white-hot furious with him for doing this to himself and to us. *Who's going to walk your daughter down the aisle, Addison?* I strummed my fingers on the top of the casket and began pulling flowers from the blanket of white roses until I had six or eight clenched in my fist. I just needed to pull something apart. I dropped them on the ground and began pounding the casket with my fist. That was when I felt the strong hand of Mark, Patti's husband, on my arm.

"Come on now, Cate. Come stand by me."

I backed away from the remains of my husband and let Mark put his arm around my shoulder. Mark was a great human being, even though he could be very cheap, which to my way of thinking was a really terrible and unattractive trait. Still, I considered myself lucky to have him as a brother-in-law, because he was the one who would step forward in a situation like this and take any potential problems in hand. Following his uncle's lead, my beautiful son Russ moved away from his contentious wife, Alice, and took my hand.

"It's gonna be okay, Mom. You'll see."

"I know," I said and thought I should be the one reassuring him.

But I *had* reassured him and Sara, my daughter. I had told them at least one hundred times in the last forty-eight hours that we would get through this together and everything would be all right. Talk about self-delusion? I didn't believe that any more than they did. Together was over. We would get through the *funeral* together. But then they would go back to their lives and resume them, maimed a bit, sad for a while, but they had lives and careers that waited for them. Well, to be honest, Russ had a satisfying job teaching and coaching high school basketball. But my daughter, Sara, did not. Sara was my soufflé, soft in the center but always in danger of falling if the temperature wasn't perfect. Even though we resembled each other—petite, dark-haired, blue-eyed—I was much stronger than she was. Still, she was on her own in California and reasonably solvent.

Anyway, at that moment, I had lost my rudder, because life without Addison wasn't a life I could simply pick up and navigate without missing a beat. You see, I lived in a world of *his* making, not mine. Everything, every single material thing we owned was a product of Addison's image of himself, how he thought he should live and how he wanted to be perceived by the outside world. The wine cellar, the cars, the art collection, the antiques—he had scoured auction houses and galleries, collecting and amassing that which was worthy of a financial czar. And the house? It was one of the largest homes in Alpine, located in the fourth most expensive zip code in America, roughly ten times the house that would have satisfied me but Addison wanted it all. He wanted just a mere glimpse of our home to make his investors, partners, and his enemies weak in the knees. And it did.

Every now and then I would moan a little with him in private, that I'd surely prefer a simpler life, one that (until I found Albertina, that is) was not so burdened with bickering staff who chipped your crystal, cleaned your silver with steel wool, and used *Shout!* on your vegetable-dyed antique rugs from Agra. Never mind the unending stream of workmen that came with the constant repairs and upkeep a large home required. Too often my days were defined by waiting for someone to show up to do something the right way, because Addison held me responsible for every last detail of our life outside of his business. Sometimes, no, a lot of the time, I felt more like a building superintendent than the beloved wife of a successful man. There were times—often, in fact—when I was merely the director and producer for the domestic theater of his life and I knew it with certainty when he would rate my performance after a holiday or a dinner party for clients.

"The centerpieces looked cheap, Cate," he might say. Or, "The meat was overcooked. Shoe leather." Or, "Your staff didn't show well tonight, Cate. Service stunk. I thought you knew how important this dinner was to me."

It was never, "Gosh, honey, you went to so much trouble! I'm a lucky man! Thanks so much!"

He was so self-absorbed and pressured with work that days would pass without him saying anything particularly personal or pleasant to me, or without even making eye contact. I knew he was preoccupied because he was extremely worried about his investments, but still, his freezing-cold attitude chipped away at whatever affection I felt for him and I felt more and more detached from him. But I was grateful to God to have my children and I gave them everything there was in my heart. I had Patti. And Mark.

It didn't pay to moan about life in the gilded cage. Not a single member of the human race would have felt sorry for me for one second. Especially Addison. His familiar bark went like this: "Look, Cate. I work like an eff-ing *animal,* putting in *crazy* hours, dealing with more stress than the GD eff-ing president himself. So? When I come home I want to look around and believe, somehow believe, even if it's just for five minutes, that it was all worth the sacrifice! Why is that so eff-ing hard for you to understand?"

Nice, right? My neck got hot even then, remembering how terrible he made me feel. How low. How insignificant. The belittling, the judging, and then the terrible silences that followed.

Addison became possessed by the decadent spirits of his own desire. If he wanted to get in his Lamborghini and run it, he did. If he wanted to open a five-hundred-dollar bottle of wine and drink it with microwave popcorn, he did. Many afternoons I would find him downing an old Bordeaux while he watched the Golf Channel ad nauseam on our home theater screen that rivaled an IMAX. Once he paid to play with Tiger Woods to raise money for some charitable cause he could not have cared less about just so he could tell that story over and over as though he was Tiger's best friend. He stored a set of custom Majestic golf clubs in ten different locations from St. Andrews to Pebble Beach so he didn't have to say, "Gee, I wish I'd brought my clubs." He kept his G550 at the ready, in case he wanted to fly to Vegas with a few of his partners or friends and hear Barry Manilow sing or watch Siegfried and Roy play with their big cats. Sick.

I hated all his toys because they represented just how horribly shallow he could be. We could've done so much good with all that money. If I wanted to support something like the library or the children's schools, he refused, saying he only wanted to give money to things that would thrill *him*. And he also never missed an opportunity to remind me that he earned the money, not me. He could and would do as he wanted.

He wanted, he wanted, he wanted . . . well, the wanting was at an end because the greedy, covetous, acquisitive son of a bitch was dead. Did he run around? Probably, but I never really knew for sure. That didn't mean I didn't have some very real suspicions.

In the last few years, it came to a point where Addison barely resembled the wonderful extraordinary man I had married. How, I wondered, had I managed all those years to keep my mountain of frustrations and deep disappointments out of the conversation with my children? It was either a miraculous accomplishment of mine or massive denial on their part that they merely viewed him as a well-meaning, very distracted man who was sometimes a difficult and demanding grump. I mean, they had their criticisms of him. When Russ was a teenager, he thought he worked way too much and would shrug his shoulders in disappointment when his father missed a basketball game. Russ was the captain of his team and had gone to the College of Charleston on a full ride, which was a point of pride for him to say he didn't owe that part of his education to his father. And Sara? She didn't fare as well. Sara suffered horribly from Addison's lack of attention and spent her high school years dating the wrong boys, getting her heart broken all the time. College had not been a lot better for her socially and so she turned to acting in theater, where she could express herself.

But when they heard the news about their father's death, they both swore that they adored him and they were honestly devastated to learn that he was dead.

The only person who knew the truth about how I really felt about my marriage was Patti, and she would never betray my confidence. Never in a million years. We both figured we may as well bury the old bastard on a high note.

In some bizarre way, I still cared about Addison and always would. He had given me two wonderful children, a luxurious life, and a long list of things for which I would always be in his debt. After all, we had traveled the world as a family, the children had been sent to good schools, and he gave them incredible opportunities to learn, see, go, and do. If I had ever really felt our lifestyle was that unacceptably vulgar or that his cruelty was too much, could I have left? Of course I could have but we were a family, with all the good and bad, and I wasn't tearing my family apart over something so stupid as Addison's conspicuous consumption or because he became more unsatisfied with his entire personal life when the markets declined. It would only have made a bad situation worse. And living with Addison was generally a tolerable situation. Not a joyous one, but tolerable. But let me tell you, markets may rebound but chasing great wealth is a delusional trap.

Two years ago, Patti and Mark began to notice a marked difference in Addison, too, as he slid even further into a new hell. Mark would offer to talk to him all the time but I knew that would probably complicate things so we just held our breath and hoped that whatever problems he was dealing with would be resolved and the old Addison would soon reappear. He never did. And besides, Addison held Mark at a polite arm's length, because in his mind, he had no peer. He had liked Mark well enough but he probably believed his issues with declining global markets, international currencies, and what other troubles a Jedi like him had to endure and solve were far too complicated for someone like Mark, a mere podiatrist, to comprehend.

It was after Russ married Alice and Sara moved to Los Angeles that the most dangerous aspects of Addison's transformation began to materialize. He stopped sleeping regular hours and his normal voracious appetite seemed to disappear. He lost a staggering amount of weight. And he was frequently out of the house until late at night. And the outbursts began. I heard him raging for hours on the telephone with his partners. Like a lot of men, Addison didn't hesitate to raise his voice if he felt like it, especially in business, but this rage was something different, frightening. It was as though he had developed some kind of an evil personality disorder. I began to suspect he was using cocaine or something like cocaine. He had to have been. Or some kind of pills? But when he left for the office and I searched his office at home, his bathroom, and his drawers, I could find nothing. I looked under the mattress, in the toes of his shoes, and behind the books in his study. I read the labels of everything in his medicine cabinet and looked them up on the Internet. Not a speck of anything untoward. If he was abusing drugs, I couldn't prove it.

So what then was the source? I had seen him pitch tirades before but they had always blown over pretty quickly. Not lately. This anger was smoldering, always right under the surface, ready to explode. Anger became his new way of dealing with his life. Sure the economy was terrible, but the recession couldn't last forever, could it? I worried deeply and constantly. Sure he had always had a quick temper but never like this. I was afraid he was going to have a stroke or a heart attack.

As fate would have it, about a year ago, he became fanatical about his health, complaining of every ailment in the Merck manual. Good, I thought, now he'll get some help. And he did. Not a week went by that he didn't visit a doctor of one sort or another to medicate everything from his ears (tinnitus) to his big toe on his right foot (gout). He swore he'd clean up his diet but Addison following any of these doctors' orders didn't last long. The gastrointestinal specialist told him to give up lunchtime martinis and hard liquor of every kind, that his liver and esophagus were turning on him. For a short period he was sober but then I heard him say to someone laughingly that he didn't give a rip—not exactly the language he used—that he would send someone over to a Chinese prison and just buy a liver from some coolie on death row if he needed it. He thought it was a riot to look upon the horrified faces of his politically correct listeners. He bellowed with laughter, recounting his outrageous conversation with his doctor. I was mortified over and over again by his behavior and even his partners' wives, some of the most calcified, impervious women on earth, even *they* began to regard me with sympathy. I was so glad our children were out of the house by then so they didn't have to witness their father's slide into madness.

It just went on and on. His pulmonary physician told him he had to give up cigars, that his blood pressure was dangerously high, and I wouldn't even want to tell you what he said about that. Addison's humidors were bulging with imported Cohibas that he fully intended to smoke. Needless to say, his cholesterol was out of control, too, just like every other aspect of his life. Addison continued to drink what he wanted, eat what he wanted, and to smoke whenever the mood struck. No one could make Addison listen. No one could tell him what to do. In the end, still in charge, he died on a day of his own choosing. Ironically, all of these terrible habits had not killed him. Addison had the final word. He always did. If he had listened to his doctors' advice, maybe he could have dealt with his stress in a healthy way and he'd still be alive.

I looked around at the small crowd of people, shivering from the cold. Suddenly, it seemed that their jaws were tight and their faces unsympathetic. Was I imagining this? No. If that's how they felt, why had they come?

Amen.

The service was abruptly over, Pastor Anderson stepped over and shook my hand, and everyone stared at me. I had my arm around Sara then. My poor daughter had wept an ocean of tears. *Look what you've done, Addison. Look what you've done.* I just wanted to scream. I invited Pastor Anderson back to the house but he begged off. The weather, he said. I knew he was rushing back to that hot young thing he had married recently. Judi was her name and there wasn't a woman in our church who didn't want to be her. I thanked him for everything and thought, Gosh, everyone has a purpose in their life except me.

As Pastor Anderson turned and walked away, Addison's blond twenty-two-year-old secretary was the first one to approach us.

"Lauren, thank you for coming," I said. "You've met our daughter, Sara?"

"Yeah. I can't believe he's dead, and what he did, you know? I mean, he was so great back when we were together . . ."

"When who was together?" I said.

"Uh, *you* know," Lauren said and then paused, her eyes growing wide. "You mean, you *didn't* know?"

"Know what?" I said, the sordid truth dawning.

"Jesus, Mrs. Cooper, don't look at me like that! I thought everybody in New Jersey knew it! It was all over Twitter last year! He hooked up with like every girl who ever worked in the office!"

"What?" I felt all the air rush out of my chest and I thought I was going to faint. Did she mean that Addison had sex with all of them? Little Lauren read my mind.

"Like we had a choice? If Addison Cooper wanted something, he got it and you know it! A bunch of us were gonna file suit for sexual harassment but now that he's gone . . ."

"Mom!" Sara said. "Do something!"

"Lauren?" I was at a loss for words. "I think it's time for you to leave. Now." It was all I knew to say. If I had been in possession of my mind, I might have given her the back of my hand right across her face. Who was this horrible young woman? The Lauren I had known over the phone was polite and kind. True or not, how mean and unforgivably rude to say such a thing at Addison's funeral.

I turned away from her and nearly knocked down Shirley Hackett, the wife of Addison's most senior partner.

"I just wanted to say that, well, I feel for you, Cate."

"Thanks, Shirley. This was such a terrible shock."

"I'm sure. Between you and me, there are probably more shocks to come."

"What do you mean? And where's Alan?"

"Humph. Cate? I mean this in the nicest possible way, but if Addison had not died, Alan would've killed him. I came out of respect for you and the children but believe me, there's no love lost with Alan."

"Why? What in the world are you talking about? We've been friends for years!"

Shirley stood there and stared at me for what seemed like an eternity until finally she spoke again.

"We're broke, Cate. Addison lost all our money and most of the firm's clients. It's going down the tubes. Chapter Eleven."

"You've got to be wrong. You're exaggerating."

"Oh, my God," Sara said.

"No, I'm not. Remember that gorgeous house we had in Upper Saddle River? Well, now instead of taking a Citation X to San Francisco for dinner I'm driving a used Kia. I'm shopping at the Path-mark and cooking ramen in a studio apartment in Tenafly."

"What on *earth* are you talking about? When did all this happen?"

"Am I to believe that you don't know *anything* about this?"

"Absolutely! I mean, I heard Addison wasn't himself for the last year or so, and I knew things weren't great at the firm but I had no idea!"

"Well, then, darling? You'd better brace yourself."

She couldn't have been more like the Oracle of Delphi if she'd shown up in robes and looked into a pool of water. As I turned to see who was tapping me on the shoulder, I got another slap in the face from my new reality.

"You're Ms. Cooper, right?"

"Yes. Did you know my husband?"

"I sure did but believe me, I didn't know he had a wife. Good thing I read the obituaries." She reached in her purse and pulled out a small album of photographs. "Have a look."

I flipped through them and there was Addison, with the woman before me and a baby boy of about two years old. The boy was the spitting image of Addison.

"Mom! What is this?" Sara said. "I'm gonna throw up!"

"Oh, my God," I said. My head began to spin. How could all of this be happening?

"So, what I'm wondering is who has the mortgage on my condo? And who has the lease on my BMW? I mean, I'm sure he provided for us in his will . . ."

Sara, who had stood by completely dumbfounded, doubled over and began gagging. That was the last thing I remembered before the ground came up to get me.

Debbie Zammit

New York Times bestseller **DOROTHEA BENTON FRANK** was born and raised on Sullivans Island, South Carolina. She resides in the New York area with her husband.

Books by
Dorothea Benton Frank

FULL OF GRACE
ISBN 978-0-06-137453-1 (paperback)

"Frank specializes in resilient characters who survive thanks to a saucy combination of grit and humor."
—*Booklist*

THE LAND OF MANGO SUNSETS
A Novel
ISBN 978-0-06-171570-9 (paperback)

"[A] warming female-empowerment tale with a side order of Southern magic."
—*Kirkus Reviews*

BULLS ISLAND
ISBN 978-0-06-207322-8 (paperback)

A satisfying tale of honor, chance, and star-crossed love infused with Southern wit, grace, and charm from the *New York Times* bestselling author Dorothea Benton Frank.

RETURN TO SULLIVANS ISLAND
A Novel
ISBN 978-0-06-198833-2 (paperback)

"Tight storytelling, winsomely oddball characters, and touches of Southern magic make this a winner."
—*Publishers Weekly*

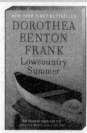

LOWCOUNTRY SUMMER
ISBN 978-0-06-202073-4 (paperback)

"Frank lovingly mixes a brew of personalities. . . . When Frank nails it, she really nails it, and she does so here."
—*Publishers Weekly* (starred review)

Visit www.DotFrank.com and find Dottie on Facebook!